MW00715400

None of it should have happened but all of it did and the mounting coincidences and innocent errors fatally confused the initial search for Mary Beth McBride. And by the time that search evolved into anything like a proper investigation it was too late.

Mary was already a victim.

Also by Harry Asher in Vista

THE PROFILER

HARRY ASHER

THE PREDATORS

VISTA

First published in Great Britain 1998
as a Vista paperback original

Vista is an imprint of the Cassell Group
Wellington House, 125 Strand, London WC2R 0BB

© Harry Asher 1998

The right of Harry Asher to be identified as author
of this work has been asserted by him in accordance with
the Copyright, Designs and Patents Act, 1988.

A catalogue record for this book is
available from the British Library.

ISBN 0 575 60164 7

Typeset by SetSystems Ltd, Saffron Walden, Essex
Printed and bound in Great Britain by
Cox & Wyman Ltd, Reading, Berks

All rights reserved. No part of this publication may be
reproduced or transmitted in any form or by any means,
electronic or mechanical including photocopying,
recording or any information storage or retrieval system,
without prior permission in writing from the publishers.

This book is sold subject to the condition that it shall not,
by way of trade or otherwise, be lent, resold, hired out, or
otherwise circulated without the publisher's prior consent in
any form of binding or cover other than that in which
it is published and without a similar condition including this
condition being imposed on the subsequent purchaser.

98 99   10 9 8 7 6 5 4 3 2 1

To Valerie and Andrew, with love

CHAPTER ONE

None of it should have happened but all of it did and the mounting coincidences and innocent errors fatally confused the initial search for Mary Beth McBride. And by the time that search evolved into anything like a proper investigation it was too late.

Mary was already a victim.

It began with something as ordinary as a puncture, which briefly caused a traffic jam on the rue du Chêne along which the embassy driver, a local Belgian named Claude Luc, was taking a short cut to the school. The US security officer, William Boles, agreed that it was a bastard even as he was strictly following the well-rehearsed routine. Before allowing Luc to change the wheel he telephoned the embassy from the car phone for a back-up vehicle to collect Mary. And then he called the school to warn of the delay.

The confusion arose when the embassy duplicated that warning call: misunderstanding the second contact, the school secretary thought that the relief vehicle had already arrived and it was no longer necessary to keep the child on the premises.

The last of the stragglers were just being collected or driven away when Mary Beth McBride emerged on to the rue du Canal and realized there was no car waiting for her. Mary's security briefing was as well rehearsed but far simpler than that of William Boles. She should have turned back into the building and asked someone to telephone the embassy to find out what had happened.

But Mary Beth McBride was a wilfully precocious, brace-toothed ten-year-old who welcomed the chance not only to prove she was quite capable of finding her own way, unescorted, around Brussels, but also to see her usual driver and escort, who she knew didn't like her, take the blame during the later telling-off. It was they who would be punished, not she. No one ever punished her.

To make sure she thoroughly worried everyone Mary decided to take the most roundabout route possible to get home. She would use the Métro, and let her mother find the ticket in her pocket. Mary was absolutely forbidden to use the system – had never in her life been on an underground train anywhere in the world – but was sure she could work it out from the map at the street entrance. They'd hardly be able to believe it in class tomorrow when she told them. She knew all the other girls admired her: she wasn't frightened of doing things, as they all were. That's why she was the leader, the person they all copied. It would cause one of those fights between mom and dad, too.

Mary never reached the Métro, although she could see a station at the next road junction. She frowned sideways at the car that suddenly drew up beside her, irritated at the disruption of her plans and by the shape of the Mercedes, different from the car that normally picked her up. Her escort wasn't normally a woman, either. Mary didn't recognize this one although she knew there were women among the embassy's security detachment. A car behind them began sounding its horn impatiently.

'Are you from my father?' Mary demanded imperiously. They'd already know they were in trouble for being late.

'Yes,' lied Félicité Galan, speaking in English because the child had. 'Get in.'

'Where's Bill and Claude?' asked Mary, demandingly offering her backpack for the woman to take before sliding into the rear beside Félicité. It was grown-up to address the men who normally came for her by their given names: would let these two know how they had to behave. The car behind hooted again.

'They had to do something else,' improvised Félicité. She was looking intently at the girl, smiling in anticipation. To Henri Cool, at the wheel, Félicité said in French: 'She's lovely. We've done well.'

Mary couldn't remember any of her escorts talking French, which she knew well enough to interpret the remark although not understand it. 'You're going to get into trouble for being late.'

'No we're not,' said Félicité. The driver laughed.

Mary knew Brussels sufficiently to identify the Cathédrale de St Michel. She said: 'This isn't the way to the embassy!'

Momentarily Félicité hesitated, off balance, aware of Cool's startled look in the rearview mirror. She said: 'We're not going to the embassy.'

'Where then?' demanded the child.

'You're going on an adventure,' promised the woman, prepared for the question.

The driver pressed the central locking system and the buttons on all the doors clicked down, even though the rear-door child-locks were already in place, disabling the handles.

'What sort of adventure?' demanded Mary. This woman wasn't as respectful to her as Bill was: she'd tell dad.

'Wait and see.'

'I don't want to.'

'You don't have a choice.'

At that moment the second security man in the back-up collection vehicle reported to the American embassy on the Boulevard du Régent that Mary had vanished. And the panic began in the office suite of the United States' ambassador to Belgium, James McBride.

CHAPTER TWO

They usually got frightened during a drive as long as this, crying, wetting themselves. Hysterical. But this one didn't. Rather, she was defiantly unafraid – arrogantly unafraid – and Félicité, a constant seeker for anything new, anything not tried before, was excited. Would the child fight, later? None of the others had ever tried, not seriously. Hysteria gave way to cowed, bewildered acceptance: submissive apathy. Boring. It really would be exciting if this one fought back. Defied them. She was small, maybe no older than eight, although that would have been very young to be walking by herself. The prime requirement, to be as young as possible: young but aware. Hair – good, lustrous hair – in plaits. Oscar Wilde's hair: *All her bright golden hair tarnished with rust, She that was young and fair fallen to dust.* Félicité mouthed the creed, part of her article of faith. This child's hair was golden, tarnished by a suggestion of redness. Pity about all that metal clamped in her mouth. Proof, if it were needed, that Mary Beth McBride was an American. Why did all American children have to have the output of a steel mill in their mouths? Never had an American child before. Have to get rid of the brace.

Félicité reached out, to stroke Mary's cheek, but the girl jerked away although still without fear: it was an impatient, irritated movement. 'Where are we going?'

'I told you, an adventure.'

'I want to go back to Brussels. Now!'

'If you're a naughty girl I'll slap you.' Part of the fun,

the control. The best part. She'd make her cry. Plead. But not now. Too soon now. When she chose to. Maybe just the slightest correction.

'No one slaps me!'

'I might. Be careful.' An idea was forming in Félicité's mind, a new fantasy. It would give her the sort of absolute, supreme control she'd never had before. Her very own marionette show: a jumping, contorting cast of dozens, if not hundreds, performing to her will as she pulled the strings.

'I have already told you my name is Mary Beth McBride and that my father is the American ambassador to Belgium!'

'I heard you.' So had Henri Cool. Félicité knew he wasn't excited, as she was, sufficiently aroused for her voice to be fragile. He was scared, very scared, driving erratically out of Brussels until she'd warned him. He was driving erratically again now. 'You're going too fast,' she said sharply. 'What the hell's wrong with you!'

He slowed, but only just to within the limit. 'We've made a mistake. We've got to get . . . to do something about it.'

'Shut up!' snapped Félicité, wondering how good the American girl's French was.

'Take me back to Brussels immediately!' demanded Mary again, in English, giving the woman no indication of her language comprehension.

Félicité managed to pat Mary's leg, before the child pulled away. 'Don't be a silly girl.'

'You'll get into dreadful trouble, both of you.'

Cool took the Beveren road, better to bypass Antwerp, but too abruptly. The tyres screeched, the rear of the car sliding slightly. Félicité said: 'Almost there now.' To the man at the wheel, whose eyes were more often in the rearview mirror than on the road in front, she said: 'I told you to slow down!'

11

'Do something! Get us out of this!' said Cool. His voice was cracked.

'I make the decisions. You do the driving. So drive.'

'What's your name?' Mary demanded of the woman at the opposite end of the seat.

Félicité laughed. 'I know yours but you can't know mine. It's my secret.'

'I know what you are! What you're going to do!' This *was* an adventure. Much better than riding the Métro.

'Do you?' smiled Félicité, aware of Henri's startled reflection.

'My father will pay. He's very rich.'

The woman's smile widened; the child's remark chimed with the idea that had already occurred to her. 'Of course he'll pay for someone as pretty as you.'

'So you understand?' demanded the child.

'Totally.'

'I meant what I said, about no one slapping me.'

'I'm sure you did.'

'So don't forget!' Abruptly, reading the signpost as they passed, she said: 'Antwerp. Is that where we're going?'

'To a big house on the river. You'll like it.'

'I won't.'

'We'll see.'

The child looked away, to stare out of the car. The rain had started almost as soon as they left Brussels and the clouds were thicker, heavier, nearer the coast, ushering in the night-time darkness. Félicité lounged back, as far away on the seat as she could get, studying the girl's mirrored image in the window glass. It *was* a good idea: would be an experience she hadn't enjoyed before but had to savour now she'd thought of it, as she had to taste every forbidden fruit. The others probably wouldn't like it – they'd be frightened, like Henri – but they'd do as they were told, as they always did. She'd have to rearrange things with the estate agent in Namur. And speak to Eindhoven and Lille to tell them everything was postponed. Simple reorganization. She was good at organization. That's why everyone had been so happy – relieved – for her to take over, after Marcel's death. Yes! Félicité decided. She'd definitely do it.

Cool was forced to slow by the volume of traffic on his back-street negotiation around Antwerp but it wasn't until he was almost clear of the city that he was brought to a positive halt at traffic lights. Félicité didn't move when Mary snatched for the door handle, exaggerating her laugh at the child's helpless yanking on the useless, unconnected lever. The woman did react, though, when Mary opened her mouth to scream. Sure of not being seen from the outside, rain-sodden gloom, she lashed out, hard, before the cry was formed, catching the unsuspecting girl fully in the face to strangle the sound into a whimpering gasp, as much of astonishment as of pain.

'I told you I'd slap you, didn't I?' said Félicité casually, as the flat grey ribbon of the sluggish Schelde river broke occasionally to their left through the vast skeletal forest of cranes and container rigs of the port. 'You've got lessons to learn. Rules to obey.'

Mary glared malevolently across at her, lips tight against any blood leaking from the split inside her lip and cheek.

'You're still not going to cry, are you?' demanded Félicité hopefully.

'No,' Mary allowed herself, tongue against the cut. The blood tasted nasty: metallic.

'I'm going to enjoy you,' said the woman. 'Enjoy you a lot.'

Mary didn't understand the remark and couldn't think of anything to say, although she wanted to, so she tightened her mouth again. She was very proud of not crying, despite the pain in her mouth where the brace had cut. She didn't have anything really to cry about: be frightened of. Dad *would* pay. And he'd punish them. He had men to do that: men with things like hearing aids in their ears and sometimes little knobs pinned to their jacket lapels that they talked into. She'd have to be careful not to miss anything out, when she got back to school. It really would be difficult for the rest of the class to believe.

The beach house wasn't really on a beach, although there was a shoreline and shingle and a bathing hut collapsing from neglect and the constant battering from North Sea winds. The main building was just short of the Dutch border where the river fanned out into the Westerschelde, isolated by at least two kilometres from its nearest neighbour, a major consideration for its use. Its basement encompassed and utilized, with specific modifications, the impregnable blockhouse constructed by the Nazis in the Second World War to protect such an essential waterway.

The North Sea gale was driving the rain horizontally by the time the Mercedes reached the three-storey, shutter-protected house in front of which three other cars, all Mercedes, already stood. Henri Cool had to stand against the rear door to hold it open to release Félicité and the child. As she got out, Mary was caught by the force of the wind and became entangled in the straps of her backpack; she would have fallen completely if the woman hadn't grabbed her. Wide-armed and protective, Cool propelled them towards the house.

In its lee the wind was only slightly less fierce, and still more than enough to defeat the sudden dash that Mary had intended. She didn't even try, allowing herself instead to be shepherded through the unlocked door into the vaulted, high-ceilinged entrance hall. The relief was abrupt and disorientating – Félicité and Mary staggered afresh without the need to brace themselves against the storm – although the wind continued to hammer at the closed shutters as if trying to get at them.

Félicité still clutched Mary, a hand on each of the child's shoulders. She hurried her across the hall, not giving her the chance to recover. Alongside, Cool had the basement door already open. Mary was gasping, finding it difficult to breathe, when they got to the bottom of the stairs.

She stood there, trembling from the cold wetness but still, she told herself, not from fear. She felt, instead, bewilderment and she did her best to hide that too, not wanting the woman who had hit her to misunderstand: not wanting to give her any satisfaction.

It was a huge room extending the length and width of the house, which was in effect a lid put over the entire original German bunker. Its metre-thick concrete, concealed now behind lighter wood panelling than that in the upstairs hall, totally silenced the outside tempest. More important, it contained any sound from what now regularly occurred inside, making its remoteness from neighbours unnecessary. The floor was thickly carpeted, too, except for the very centre where there was a cleared wooden circle, for dancing. The ceiling was entirely glassed. There were lounging divans around three walls. Dominating the fourth was a huge television or movie screen. On either side there were five separate doors. All were closed. Two were solid, their only break an eye-level sliding metal viewing strip. Both were shuttered. In the furthest corner was an array of music-playing equipment, incongruously surrounded by disco and strobe lights. It was very warm – almost too hot – and there was a cloying, perfumed smell.

Mary shivered, for the first time positively uncertain. Quickly she said: 'I'm cold. My clothes are wet.'

'It's too warm here for you to be cold. But take your clothes off if they're uncomfortable.' There was harshness in the woman's voice.

'No,' the child said quickly, more through instinct than understanding.

'We've got to talk to the others,' insisted Cool impatiently, at the doorway.

'We don't want her to catch cold, in wet clothes.'

'Come on!' protested the man.

Félicité hesitated before shrugging reluctantly. She grabbed Mary's arm again, holding too tightly, thrusting her towards the blank, peep-holed doors. 'This is the room where we play games . . .' she said as they scurried across it. She opened the door to the left, pushing the child through. '. . . and this is where you're going to live.'

There were five men waiting in the upstairs room they entered minutes later and the excited expectation was palpable.

'We saw you arrive,' said Jean Smet. 'She's pretty.'

'There's a problem,' blurted Cool.

The atmosphere was still palpable but very different from when they had entered. Félicité sprawled in the huge, encompassing chair she'd adopted as her own – her throne – when they used this house, not trying to hide her contempt at their instant response to what they had been told.

There were six men in the group that Marcel had brought together, a disparate gathering with only their sexual predilection in common. None, in fact, particularly liked each other. Jean Smet and Michel Blott were lawyers, Smet usefully in the Justice Ministry, Blott in richly rewarding private practice. August Dehane was a senior executive in Belgian state telecommunications, Belgacom, and Henri Cool, who had just identified Mary McBride as an ambassador's daughter, was a deputy headmaster. Gaston Mehre ran an antique gallery in Antwerp and provided a home – and protection – for his mentally retarded brother, Charles. It was Charles who maintained the beach house when they were using it, a willing slave to them all. He was also the most unpredictably dangerous.

'No. Definitely no,' said Smet, leading the opposition. He was a tall, thin, smooth-skinned man whose receding hair was greased straight back from a long-ago forehead.

'Yes,' insisted Félicité mildly. The side of the lounge to her left, overlooking the river, was glass and the shutters weren't closed. It was double glazed, keeping out most of the sound, but the waves churned and crashed to the boundary wall, throwing up spray against the outside pane. Idly, with no intention of provoking any of the men – with all of whom, except Charles Mehre, she'd had sex – Félicité unbuttoned her shirt. She was not wearing a bra and just as casually as she'd unfastened the shirt she began massaging her nipples.

'She's seen us, you and me,' protested Cool, a burly, disordered man whose clothes never fitted. 'She could identify us. And she was paying attention to how we got here, from Antwerp. I saw her in the mirror.'

'Who said anything about letting her go?' demanded the woman.

'Henri's right,' said Blott, a glandularly fat man whose eyes blinked in constant nervousness behind wire-framed glasses. 'It was a mistake, easily made. It's no one's fault. But now she should be killed.'

There was no shock from any of them at the easy insistence upon murdering a child, as there hadn't been when Cool and Dehane had made the same demand earlier. A year before a boy they'd snatched had died during a party in the house. Since then they had used child prostitutes, usually brought in from Amsterdam. Perhaps, she conceded, the idea upon which she was by

17

now quite determined stemmed from the excitement she'd got then, knowing she was being hunted but always able to evade suspicion or capture because of how cleverly Smet had inveigled himself. Which he could do again now.

'She knows we're near Antwerp?' asked Gaston Mehre.

'She read a sign out when we passed it,' confirmed Cool, taking off yet again thick-lensed, heavy-framed spectacles for another unnecessary polish.

'Then it's madness to keep her alive,' said Dehane. He was a slightly built, self-effacing man always eager to follow where others led.

'It's an unnecessary danger,' agreed Gaston Mehre. He and Charles had been born just nine months and seven days apart, both red-haired, their features practically matching, even to identically twisted teeth. It was Charles who had been with the rent boy when he'd died. He'd badly hurt another young male prostitute three months earlier.

'What danger?' said Félicité. 'She's in a cell, where she's going to stay. And we can't be traced to the house in which she's being held.' It had been Félicité's idea that the houses they used should be owned by others with the same interests who lived in conveniently close neighbouring countries. The Antwerp beach house was registered in the name of Pieter Lascelles, a sixty-year-old Eindhoven surgeon. Georges Lebron, a parish priest in Lille, owned the country cottage near Herentals where the Dutch met, and Félicité had a bigger house at Goirle for larger parties.

'James McBride is the American ambassador!' implored Smet. 'It's his daughter downstairs! You can't imagine what sort of outcry there's going to be.'

'Which is precisely why it's going to be so exciting!' said Félicité.

'Before, it was the son of a bankrupt Jewish shopkeeper

in Ghent and the investigation was handled by police who would have been overstrained by a bicycle theft!' argued Smet. 'This won't be anything like that. This will be enormous!'

'You're just going to have to be as clever as you were last time,' smiled Félicité, enjoying the man's terror. She wondered if she would ever weary of the weakness of these men; the ease of manipulating them. She knew Marcel was becoming increasingly bored just before his heart attack. She still missed Marcel, not only for the loss of the sexual avenues along which he'd led her. Marcel would have seen the thrill – the pleasure – in what she wanted to do: might have tolerated this dispute, as she was tolerating it, but wouldn't have allowed it to go on for so long.

'What's the point!' demanded Dehane.

'It's something we haven't done before,' said Félicité simply.

'The thought doesn't excite me,' said the lawyer.

'Nor me,' said Cool.

'But it does me,' insisted Félicité. 'I got her. I decide what we do with her. And I've decided that before the party at which our ambassador's little daughter will eventually be the star I'm going to organize the perfect crime, a kidnap.'

'It's an insane idea,' protested Smet. 'I won't have it.'

'*You* won't have it?' challenged Félicité, recognizing her moment.

'Please!' muttered the tall man, in immediate retreat.

'I want you to do what you did before . . .' She switched to Dehane. 'And you must make it impossible for them to trace us when we start making our demands. It's your chance, August, to show us all how clever you are . . .'

She let her voice trail, looking around the assembled

men, determined to end the dispute. 'Who's the link with Lille, taking the risks no one else does?'

No one spoke immediately. Then Smet said: 'You are.'

'And with Eindhoven?'

'You,' said the Justice Ministry lawyer.

'What would happen to all of you if I abandoned you?'

Gaston said: 'Please don't do that.'

'Jean?' she persisted.

Smet shrugged. 'It's a good group.'

'Which you don't want broken up?'

'No,' he conceded weakly.

'Good!' said Félicité briskly. 'So we're agreed about what I want to do?'

Their 'Yes' came as a muted chorus.

Pieter Lascelles said the postponement was unfortunate: his friends had been looking forward to it.

'It won't be for long,' Félicité promised. 'You'll love what I've found in Namur. An actual medieval castle, with turrets and towers. And dungeons!'

'How long?' asked the surgeon.

'A couple of weeks, that's all.'

She gave the same reply to Georges Lebron. The priest said: 'We'll wait before we choose someone then. We don't want to attract attention.'

'Yes,' agreed Félicité. 'Do that.'

Hans Doorn, the Namur estate agent with whom Félicité had agreed the rental of what was, in fact, a sixteenth-century château, said he hoped it was only a postponement. Félicité reminded him that he already had the deposit. Doorn, reassured, hoped to hear from her soon. Félicité promised he would.

CHAPTER THREE

The ambassador's study was overcrowded with people and wide-awake nightmares no one wanted or knew how to confront.

The very worst, obviously, was the every-parent horror of James and Hillary McBride. The ambassador was hunched at his enormous desk, all courtesy forgotten, his bird-like, sharp-featured, strident-voiced wife close beside him, her hand on his shoulder in what everyone mistook for reassurance. It was, in fact, to urge the man on. It was also the closest they had physically been to each other, publicly or privately, for years. And the first occasion for an equally long time that they'd come together with anything like an agreed purpose, apart from their consuming political ambitions.

Paul Harding, the portly, stray-haired resident FBI station chief, was moving jerkily about the room. He was engulfed by the scale of his own problem: just three years – three miserable fucking years! – from retirement from a damage-free Bureau career and his world was threatened with cosmic destruction. Just one misstep – the tiniest mistake – was all it would need.

William Boles accepted he had already been vaporized, despite having done everything strictly according to the book from the tyre-punctured car: being entirely blameless was no defence in an hysterical scapegoat hunt. That was in the book, too: just unwritten.

He'd explained this philosophy to Claude Luc on their nervous way back to the embassy, and the bewildered

Belgian had already warned his wife that the job of a lifetime was probably over.

Harry Becker, the security dispatcher who'd taken Boles's call, had four times lied unwaveringly that he had not made the confusing duplicate call to the school. He was ready to go on denying it, although he knew he wouldn't survive.

Lance Rampling, the crew-cut, normally energetic CIA officer, hadn't yet contributed to the discussion, for once not wanting to attract attention to himself. He wasn't sure what the pecking order was in this situation and until he got guidance from Washington he was going to keep his head well below the parapet.

'Let's go through it one more time: we could have missed something,' said McBride desperately.

'I don't think we have, sir,' said Elliot Smith. The legal attaché was a late arrival, behind all those actually involved whom McBride had assembled personally to cross-examine, to find culprits. The lawyer wasn't yet endangered but he still wasn't comfortable: when shit hit the fan it sprayed everywhere.

Burt Harrison, the chief of mission, was thinking the same thing, although not in such crude terms. As gently as possible, not wanting to cause Hillary McBride any further distress – although the woman actually wasn't showing any – the plump career diplomat said: 'I think it's time we accepted it's not a good situation.'

'Five hours,' agreed McBride dully, an unnecessary reminder. He was a large, beetle-browed, intimidating man who wore a thin moustache and an overly sweet cologne. Neither suited him. His bulk was exaggerated by the closeness of his wife. She was normally a neat, perfectly kept and preserved chatelaine of the embassy empire, colour-coordinated clothes never creased, scarlet nails impeccably polished, expertly tinted hair lacquered in wave-frozen ridges. Now the hair was disarrayed and her crumpled blouse had pulled free from her skirt on her left hip. She was chain-smoking the extra-long cigarettes she favoured.

'It could still be a game,' she said. 'You know what she's like. It's the sort of thing she'd do.'

McBride abruptly emerged into the reality he had been trying to avoid, swinging from one extreme to the other. 'No!' he insisted brutally. 'Someone's got her. Some bastard . . .' The self-absorption was unavoidable. 'It's to get at me.'

'Get her back!' said the woman, more an order than a plea.

'We will,' said Harding, unwilling to speak – to make any commitment he might not be able to keep – but knowing he had to because the ambassador's wife was looking expectantly at him. Knowing, too, from the expression on McBride's face that he hadn't said the right thing.

'Of course we'll get her back!' said the ambassador. 'I don't care what it costs or what it takes. Just do it! Now!'

'I understand. Immediately,' said Harrison, in too hurried agreement, wishing from the stare he got from McBride that he hadn't spoken, either.

McBride went to speak but apparently changed his mind. Straightening further – recovering further – instead he said: 'I've got to tell the President.'

It wasn't an exaggerated, shock-affected remark. Political commentators in Washington DC had speculated openly that the Belgian ambassadorial posting was the first supposedly comfortable stepping stone to higher and more glittering rewards – maybe even the secretaryship of state – for the largest single financial contribution to the President's successful first-term election. It certainly gave McBride personal access at the lift of a telephone.

Harding fervently thanked whatever guardian angel had prompted him to send an 'alert-but-don't-act' message to the Bureau in Washington when he'd excused himself earlier to fetch the legal attaché. He said: 'I need to send a full report to Washington as soon as possible.'

'What about the local authorities?' asked the lawyer. It was Elliot Smith's first embassy posting and he was uncomfortably aware that he looked too young for it, which was why he'd grown the moustache. Unfortunately, instead of giving the intended impression of maturity, it looked as if he'd glued it on for a costume party.

'What about them?' demanded McBride.

The young man steeled himself. 'Belgium is a foreign country, part of the European Union. Neither the Bureau . . .' he hesitated, indicating the silent Rampling '. . . nor the Agency has any operational jurisdiction here.'

Colour suffused McBride's face and he rose further at his desk, as if physically meeting a challenge. 'Are you telling me neither the Federal Bureau of Investigation nor the Central Intelligence Agency of the United States of America can do anything to find the missing daughter of one of its ambassadors?'

'Don't be damned ridiculous!' said Hillary, in rare agreement with her husband. Another embassy tenet was that she was even more politically ambitious than her husband, to the extent of seeing the White House as a future mailing address. It was the only reason each remained married to the other, she to be the President's wife, he to avoid the slightest electoral hindrance a divorce might create. Neither sought outside relationships. Totally focused political achievement was sex enough for both of them.

'Of course every Bureau facility will be available,' said Harding. 'But Elliot's right, sir: we've got no authority – no legal mandate – to work on the ground here. At best the Bureau is accepted as liaison . . .' Seeing McBride's colour deepen, he hurried on, speaking faster. 'There's only one requirement here: to get Mary Beth back. Safely. And quickly. So everything's got to be done correctly from the very beginning. Trying to mount an investigation any other way will just obstruct things.' He was pleased with the final, blurted reasoning: it would read well – sound well – at any later review.

Knowing he had to contribute, Rampling said: 'I need to talk to Langley, obviously. A task force will have to be assembled.'

'And pretty damned quick,' agreed Hillary. 'So far I'm not impressed with how you guys are treating this.'

McBride gave his wife an irritated side glance before switching his attention between the lawyer and the two intelligence officers. 'Now listen up . . .' he widened the audience to include Burt Harrison '. . . all of you. Listen good. If it's necessary, diplomatically or for any other half-assed reason, to involve the Belgian police then do it. Do whatever you've got to do to find Mary Beth. But I want American investigators – Feds who know what they're doing and know what'll happen if they screw up – in charge of finding my baby. We all clear on that?'

'Yes, sir,' said Harding and Rampling, in unison. Asshole, Harding thought.

The other two men nodded, not speaking.

It was mid-evening when the Brussels police commissioner, André Poncellet, reached Belgian Justice Minister Miet Ulieff at home. They met there within the hour.

'This is the tenth child to disappear without trace in eighteen months,' Ulieff said without preamble.

'I don't need reminding,' protested Poncellet.

'Then let me remind you of something else,' said the politician, a normally urbane, white-haired man who'd replaced the previous Justice Minister because of the ineffective investigations. 'Unless we get her back, safe and well, we won't have jobs.'

'I know that, too,' said the police chief, a fat, asthmatic man who perspired easily. He was sweating and wheezing now.

Even before the emergency cabinet meeting that followed they decided there were overwhelming reasons for an investigation into the disappearance of an ambassador's daughter to be headed by the European Union's FBI, chief among them the need to spare themselves as much responsibility as possible if it ended in tragedy, which these sorts of cases invariably did.

'But publicly we have to appear very much involved,' insisted Ulieff.

'We will be,' promised Poncellet. 'I'll initiate all the obvious things before they arrive.'

Mary accepted she was uncertain – but definitely not frightened – but thought she was hiding it well. Where the woman had put her and the men in scary masks had come to look at her was like a real cell, in a prison, as if they were going to lock her up for a long time. Its total quietness unsettled her most, the walls and door so thick she couldn't hear anyone outside until the flap snapped open and unknown eyes stared at her, as if she were a pet – like her rabbit, Billy Boy – in a cage. There was a bed, with blankets and sheets, and a toilet which she didn't want to use in case anyone looked in when she was going. And a table, in the middle of the room, with food on it that the strangely giggling man, also masked, had brought a long time ago. It was cold meat, sliced sausage, but she didn't want to eat it even though she was hungry because it might be drugged or poisoned. She'd read books about people – wicked uncles or mothers or witches – who drugged and poisoned children. She didn't believe them, of course. They were just made-up stories, but what was

26

happening to her wasn't made up. It was real. Happening. She'd been kidnapped, like in the made-up stories. Although it had stopped bleeding her mouth hurt where the woman had hit her and she wanted to go home to her mother. Be in her own bed. She wouldn't cry, though. She definitely wouldn't cry. And she wouldn't cheek the woman so much next time. She didn't want to be hit again. It really did hurt. She slipped the brace off, to lessen the discomfort. She wanted very badly to make pee pee and knew she was going to have to, soon. She hoped mom remembered to feed Billy Boy.

He'd do it, decided Henri Sanglier. He accepted they would be using him, for his name, but then he would be using them – and his name – for the same purpose. It meant he would initially continue to live as he'd always lived, in the shadow of his father, but politics would give him the opportunity to establish his own public recognition. Europol had served its purpose, as he'd always intended it should. This one last case would be the bridge from one career to the other. No mistakes and no misjudgements, like the ones in the past, he warned himself. That's all he had to be careful of.

CHAPTER FOUR

Coincidentally Claudine Carter approached the elevator to the executive floor at the same moment as Peter Blake. He smiled, slightly uncertain, and said: 'Sanglier?'

'Yes.' An assignment, not a review of a previous case!

'Any idea what it is?'

'No.' It didn't matter what it was, she thought, entering the lift ahead of the English detective with whom, presumably, she was going to be partnered. Whatever it was, it would be an investigation in which she could totally immerse herself to the exclusion of everything and anything else. She was blurring her self-imposed boundaries, she realized. She had been appointed to the FBI of the European Union because of her unquestionable brilliance as a criminal psychologist, an ability she guarded jealously. The most essentially observed protection was never to allow anything in her personal life to become a professional consideration. Now she was permitting it to happen. She was eager to submerge herself in her job, hoping to shed for as long as possible the frustration of being in love with a man whom religion and honour prevented from letting their relationship become anything more than platonic.

Claudine wedged herself into the corner of the elevator, facing the Englishman. Blake was a tall, heavy man with a lot of blond hair he still wore long, from the time he'd spent under cover on Special Branch secondment in Northern Ireland, for which he'd been promoted to

Detective Chief Superintendent. He'd been the lead witness at a trial the prosecution claimed had virtually destroyed the IRA's Army Council, and although he'd given his evidence anonymously and shielded behind screens he'd been transferred to Europol immediately afterwards for his own protection. It was understandable – although contrary to the homogeneous intention of a police organization empowered to operate anywhere in the European Union – that each of the fifteen nationalities formed its own social ghetto. Claudine was not antisocial, simply not a group person, but on the few occasions she'd been among the English crowd she'd twice heard Blake asked about infiltrating terrorist cells knowing just one mistake would be his death sentence. He'd avoided the questions, turning the conversation aside with an amusing anecdote against himself. As the lift started to ascend she wondered if he found The Hague – Holland itself – boring after the Irish experience. Certainly she couldn't professionally detect inherent signs of stress. But it was fatuous to attempt a psychological assessment from their few brief encounters, automatic though it always was for her to try.

'What's Sanglier like?'

Claudine was known to be the only criminal psychologist in Europol to have worked operationally with the French commissioner and guessed she had been asked that question as many times as Blake had been pressed about Northern Ireland. 'Likes to play by the rules. It's a useful name to have when dealing with national police forces that resent a federal organization like ours, which all of them do.'

'Any guidance, for a new boy?' Blake was examining Claudine as intently as she was studying him. Class, he decided. The simple jewellery – the single-strand gold choker and black-stoned gold ring – looked real and the black dress expensive. It was too loose for him to decide about her figure but she was obviously slim. Good legs, too.

'Proud of the legend attached to his name, obviously. He'll take advantage if he's shown too much deference, but he expects a certain amount.'

'You like him?'

'We worked together well enough.'

Blake seized on this at once. 'So you don't like him?' He stood back for her to leave the elevator ahead of him.

'Like or dislike doesn't come into it,' Claudine said evasively, unhappy at having been backed into a conversational corner. 'He keeps things strictly professional, as they should be kept.' She hurried along the corridor, hoping Blake recognized he'd been given a ground rule by which she intended to operate.

The difficulty of how a European FBI should operate had been tentatively resolved by forming a ruling commission of senior police representatives from each of the fifteen countries, with each commissioner acting as chairman on a monthly rotating basis and one of them acting as the task force commander for each fully fledged investigation. Claudine decided it had to be nothing more than coincidence that Sanglier was again to lead whatever assignment they were on their way to be given: just as it was a fluke that her father, at the time chief archivist at Interpol in Lyon, had twenty years earlier assembled the wartime material upon Sanglier's father for its entry into the National Archives in Paris.

It was, in any case, an intrusive reflection. To cloud her mind with unnecessary reexamination of their previous association would be not just ridiculous but totally unprofessional. And the basis of Claudine's 'know thyself' creed was at all times and in every circumstance to be absolutely professional. After the personal disaster of England and the confused mess of what little private life existed here in The Hague her unquestioned professionalism was the only thing of which she felt sure.

Sanglier's matronly personal assistant ushered them immediately into the man's presence. The French commissioner was in his preferred position at the far end of the room, confronting any visitor with the intimidating approach that Claudine had several times endured. From the beginning she'd mentally listed the long march – and the overly large desk – among several peculiarities hinting at an inferiority complex clinically possible in someone carrying the name of a French national hero. She wasn't overpowered by the charade and from the easy way he was walking beside her – strolling was the word that came to her mind – Claudine didn't think Blake was, either.

There was still some way to go when Sanglier rose politely to greet them, an extremely tall, outwardly courteous man with only the slightest suggestion of grey in the thick black hair. He was, as always, immaculately dressed, the suit a muted light grey check, the black handkerchief in his breast pocket matching the black, hand-knitted tie worn over a deep blue shirt.

Claudine had anticipated a larger meeting, but there were only two chairs set out in readiness.

Sanglier steepled his hands in front of him, elbows on the desk. 'The daughter of the American ambassador to Belgium has disappeared.'

'How old?' demanded Blake.

Sanglier consulted the single sheet of paper before him. 'Ten.'

'Any history of running away?' asked Claudine, impressed by the immediate, no-unnecessary-questions atttitude of the fair-haired man beside her.

'Not that we've been told.'

'Ransom demand?' asked Blake.

'Not yet. But the Belgians favour kidnap.'

'Why, if there hasn't been a demand?' persisted Blake.

31

Sanglier shrugged. 'There's no indication, from what we've been sent so far.'

'When was she last seen?'

'Leaving school yesterday. There was some mix-up over transportation. Some classmates saw her walking away by herself.'

'And there's been no contact from anyone?' pressed Claudine.

'Not according to what we've been told.'

'So the Belgian police are pushing a kidnap theory because that's what's been suggested to them by the Americans, who'll want to believe it because it's a lesser horror than what else could have happened to her,' predicted Claudine. Her job as a criminal psychologist was to examine clues left at crime scenes – invariably violent crime scenes – to create a physical and mental picture of the faceless perpetrator. She had never been involved in a kidnap and was unsure what value she had at this early stage.

'The embassy will have its in-house security,' said Blake. 'Intelligence personnel, as well. And probably there are a lot more in the air already on their way to Brussels.'

Sanglier had collapsed his steeple and lounged back in his encompassing chair, making his own assessments. If his transition from policeman to politician was to go as he intended it was essential that these two were the best available in Europol. He'd made a mistake with Claudine Carter on their first assignment, he now acknowledged: behaved stupidly in the belief that from her father she might know something damaging to the Sanglier legend, which he himself doubted. Nevertheless, she had performed brilliantly. It was important that Peter Blake was equally good. Their success would become his success.

Sanglier's initial impression was of a man verging on over-confidence, but he accepted that Blake would have had to be to have done half of what his personnel file listed in Northern Ireland. That file was specially designated, recommending that Blake be armed at all times. His responses so far showed an operational intelligence that had probably got him to Ireland in the first place, and in addition to whatever weapon he carried, kept him alive while he was there. And further, again listed in the file, was the degree in criminal law showing he was as strong on theory as he unquestionably was in practice. Physically bigger than Sanglier had imagined, although there were photographs and statistics on his record. It also said that Blake was a bachelor and Sanglier wondered if there would be any sexual attraction between the man and Claudine. The thought was an uneasy reminder of one of those stupid mistakes, introducing Claudine to his predatory wife. He said: 'It's going to be a minefield, diplomatically and operationally.'

The beginning of the walk-on-eggs lecture about in-country jurisdiction and diplomatic protocol, Claudine recognized. Only half listening, she went back to studying Blake, as determined as Sanglier against being burdened by someone of doubtful ability: so despised was Europol by national forces that it was all too frequently used as a graveyard for dying police elephants.

Blake was sitting attentively and slightly forward in his chair, but she suspected he'd heard it all before: it really was the standard, day one induction speech that came before directions to the cafeteria or the lavatories. If there were any psychological scars from what Blake had endured in Ireland she would have expected tell-tale signs, however slight, at the moment of being briefed to go back into the field.

When the commissioner had finished Blake looked briefly sideways at Claudine. 'Just the two of us?'

'We don't know what we are investigating at the moment,' Sanglier reminded him. 'Until we do we can't decide what manpower is needed. *When* we do every provision will be made.'

Claudine said: 'Kidnapping is more an American than a European crime. Over half end with the child being killed.'

'I've heard the statistics,' said Sanglier. 'I'm not underestimating how delicate any negotiations are going to be.'

The implication startled Claudine. 'I'm to be the negotiator, if it is a kidnap?'

'That was the specific request from Belgium,' disclosed Sanglier. 'They say they haven't got a qualified negotiator.' Which was a lie, he was sure: Europol was only ever asked to help when a national government wanted to escape the responsibility. One of the first things he intended to propose when he transferred to politics was that Europol should be empowered under federal legislation, like the American FBI, automatically to investigate major crimes. Kidnapping – as it was in the United States – would obviously be a federal offence. Quickly he finished: 'If it comes to negotiation, Europol will have the unquestionable authority and jurisdiction. If it's murder we will still be the responsible investigating force, in view of who it is. And there will be the same need for your involvement.'

'I haven't heard anything about it on a newscast,' said Blake.

'The Americans have asked for a publicity black-out.'

'Which means they want to negotiate – themselves – and possibly pay any demanded ransom,' said Claudine. 'And that's two different things. Negotiating we've talked about. Paying we haven't.'

'Ultimately I suppose that's the decision of the parents,' said Sanglier.

Claudine and Blake erupted in unison, stopping just as abruptly. Blake waved his hand invitingly to Claudine and said: 'After you.'

'Paying should be the last resort, not the first,' insisted Claudine. 'If they get the money there's no reason to keep the child alive. If she is still alive, that is.'

'I agree,' Blake confirmed.

'And I agree with both of you,' said Sanglier. 'We haven't established that it is a kidnap yet. So we can't answer any of these questions. We have to wait.'

Claudine hesitated, aware that Sanglier had avoided a commitment. 'We'll operate out of Brussels this time?' Their previous investigation had been into a Europe-wide series of horrific murders committed by a Triad group terrorizing young illegal immigrants into prostitution: without a central focus a co-ordinating incident room had been established at Europol's headquarters at The Hague.

'I would have thought that was obvious,' said Sanglier.

'We're going to need proper communications from the beginning,' declared Claudine.

Now it was Sanglier who hesitated, looking at her steadily. 'You want Kurt Volker?'

'He's brilliant.'

'He also operates unconventionally,' Sanglier reminded her, knowing the protest was a weak one: because it had been expedient, during the Triad investigation he'd unwillingly condoned the German expert's method of hacking his way through every computer system in Europe like some lost explorer cutting a path through jungle undergrowth.

'Our previous case was Europol's first. And established the need for its existence: *our* existence. We wouldn't have been able to do that without Kurt,' Claudine said simply, confident she had an unarguable case. She went on: 'If America's involved – the very FBI that we're modelled upon – we can't afford to fail, any more than we could have the first time. At *any* time.'

'I'll have to see if he's available.'

'He is,' said Claudine. 'I checked before coming here.' She stopped short of adding that the German was as anxious as she was for another assignment.

'That was extremely prescient of you,' said Sanglier testily.

It had to be the father, concluded Claudine: the fear – maybe even the knowledge – that the old man didn't fully deserve all the homage for his wartime exploits, and that Claudine knew it. Would she ever be able to find a way to tell this confusing, deeply uncertain man that his father's genuine bravery totally justified every accolade and honour?

Blake said: 'Will you work from Brussels with us?'

Sanglier shook his head, intending to be instantly available for any call from Paris. 'Not on a day-to-day basis. Brussels is easily reached. I'll come as and when I judge it necessary.'

As they rose to leave Sanglier said: 'This could be even bigger than the Triads. Don't forget that.'

Claudine doubted that they would be allowed to.

On their way back along the corridor Blake said: 'You two have any personal problems the last time?'

'Not really,' said Claudine. If she were right about Sanglier the bastard had virtually offered her to his lesbian wife, which was difficult to conceive, unless he was sexually perverse. It could explain their marriage, she supposed. 'Why?'

'Thought the atmosphere was a little chilly at times.'

'Just professional, as I told you on the way here.'

'He's right about its importance.'

'Unless she's found, safe and well, by the time we get to Brussels.'

He stood directly opposite her in the elevator, looking at her unblinkingly: his eyes had a strange blueness, seeming to vary from light to dark. He said: 'Well, how did I do?'

'You could have been a little more deferential,' replied Claudine honestly.

The easy smile came at once. 'What the hell! He can't put electrodes on my balls or shoot me, can he?'

Shit, thought Claudine, at once recognizing the psychological flaw. He'd survived Ireland and convinced himself he was invulnerable. So everything now had to be a test, pushed to the limit. Such people were dangerous.

Claudine did not return to her own office but went immediately to Kurt Volker's on the floor below. The plump, habitually dishevelled German beamed at the announcement but agreed there was no purpose in his travelling with her to Brussels until they learned what sort of investigation it was.

The man gestured to his terminals. 'I don't really need to be with you at all. These can take me anywhere I want to go without getting out of my chair.'

'I'd feel more comfortable with you closer,' said Claudine.

'I'll be there,' he assured her.

The late afternoon train connections gave her time to lunch with Hugo Rosetti, although in the cafeteria not in one of the better restaurants outside the Europol building. The forensic pathologist was already at a table when she arrived.

'A lot of supposition,' he said, after she outlined the assignment.

'That's what Kurt said. It's the familiar Europol shell game, everyone shuffling responsibility.'

'It might not even be a case at all.'

'Let's hope it isn't. She's just ten years old.' Claudine abruptly cut herself off, alert for any reaction from the

Italian. Sophia had only been three when she'd died, in a car crash with Rosetti at the wheel, so the circumstances were entirely different, apart from the loss of a daughter. But she always tried to avoid reminders. Rosetti gave no reaction.

'Kurt's part of the team?' questioned the Italian, as their meal arrived.

'We're going to need him, if it turns out to be a crime.'

'But not a pathologist?' They'd met when Rosetti was appointed to the Triad investigation.

'We don't have a body yet. Hopefully we won't get one.' She paused, momentarily uncertain. What the hell, she thought. 'And it might be a good idea for us to give each other a little space, don't you think?'

He sipped his wine, to give himself time. 'Do you?'

Now it was Claudine who didn't immediately reply. 'I believe you know how I think. And how I feel.'

'And you know how I feel.'

Claudine pushed her plate aside. 'Round and round we go in a circle.'

'I haven't misled you, ever.'

'I'm bloody glad I don't have any religion!' she said, with sudden bitterness.

'It isn't just my being Catholic. In fact that's the least of it. As you know.'

'Are you going to see her this weekend?' Claudine could not think why she'd asked. He went most weekends to the Rome clinic where Flavia, who'd suffered brain damage in the car crash, lay in the irreversible coma into which she'd lapsed after being told Sophia had been killed.

'Of course,' he said. 'What's this British detective like?'

Claudine was momentarily thrown by the obvious change of subject. 'Big. The rumour is that he did something special in Northern Ireland but no one's found out what it was.'

'Maybe you will.'

Claudine shrugged. 'Maybe.'

'Did you like him?'

Claudine began to concentrate, curious at the remark. 'I've not really met him before. Haven't now, really. I haven't formed an opinion.'

'If it becomes a proper case – kidnap, I mean, not anything professional as far as I'm concerned – maybe I could come down. Brussels isn't far.'

'Your choice,' said Claudine. Heavily she added: 'Like everything's your choice. I just want you to make it.'

Mary couldn't understand why it was taking so long. She'd been held for almost a whole day from the time she'd been tricked into the car and dad still hadn't got her out. Maybe the woman and the stupid men in masks had been caught. That could be it: caught while trying to collect the money and refusing to say where she was. Except that one man hadn't been caught. The one who giggled a lot, like some of the girls at school, Martha especially, when they were nervous or expecting a surprise.

She'd managed to make pee pee twice – and do the other thing – without him seeing her through the peep-hole. And she'd eaten all the bread he'd brought for breakfast and the roll at lunch. You couldn't poison bread, could you? But she hadn't drunk the soup. Or the milk that morning. Just in case. It wasn't difficult to cup her hands and drink water from the sink faucet, in the cell.

She wished dad would hurry up. She still wasn't properly frightened, not all the time anyway. It was just boring, in this silly room. Silly room and silly men. She was glad the woman hadn't come. She didn't like the woman. Gently she put her tongue against her cut cheek. It still hurt.

She jumped, startled at the sound of a key turning in the lock but had recovered by the time the heavy door swung open. The sniggering man blocked the opening.

'Am I going home?' Mary demanded at once.

'You've got to come into the big room, for exercise,' said Charles Mehre.

He scarcely moved aside, forcing her to brush against him to get by. She didn't like it. Mary looked cautiously around the huge underground chamber. It was empty, apart from the man, and not as hot as the previous day. There wasn't the sweet smell, either. 'Where are the others?'

'Not here.'

'Where?' Mary insisted.

'Don't know.'

'The police have probably got them,' she declared.

'I'd have known,' said the man, although uncertainly.

'How?' persisted Mary.

'I would,' insisted the man, with child-like logic. 'You're to shower, in there.' He pointed to a door, as if recalling a mislaid instruction.

He'd probably look at her with no clothes on, through a peephole she couldn't see. Mary said: 'I don't want to shower.'

'She said you must. She doesn't like smelly girls,' protested Mehre.

'Who said?'

'You know.'

'You tell me.'

'No,' said Mehre, looking away as if to avoid her direct stare. 'Don't shower if you don't want to.'

That had been easy, Mary decided. Easy and interesting.

'You're to walk around. Exercise,' ordered the man, although weakly.

Mary began at once, not to obey him but because she

40

wanted to think, to see how far she could take things. She was right not to be frightened of this man. There was nothing to be frightened about. She could bully him, the way she made girls at school do things when she wanted. He stood in front of the large screen, making small grunting sounds, and Mary was sure he hadn't realized she was gradually making her way towards the door leading up to the panelled hall. She was very close when she lunged at it, grabbing the handle and pulling at the same time. The door remained solid, unmoving, and behind her Mehre expanded his childish giggle into an open laugh. 'I knew you'd do that. I locked it. I'm clever. But you're a bad girl.'

Mary, who hated appearing foolish in anything, turned furiously back into the room. Momentarily not knowing what to do, how to recover, she pointed to the huge screen and said: 'I want to watch television.'

There was a snicker. 'We only watch special films.'

'I'll watch a film then.'

'Not until you're allowed. Until she says.'

'Why not?'

'She's got to say so.'

'Who?' Mary tried again.

'The others,' he generalized.

'Who are the others?'

'You're not allowed to know.'

'What are your names?'

'You're not allowed to know that either.'

'Do you know who my father is?'

'Yes.'

'He's a very important man.'

'It doesn't matter.'

'He'll be very angry.'

'It doesn't matter.'

'If you let me go I'll tell him you were kind to me. I'll

tell him not to be angry at you as he is going to be at the others. At her.'

'I think you should go back into your cell,' said Mehre. 'You've been bad. Naughty. Now you won't get any supper.' He held her wrist with one hand and put his other on her buttocks, but not to push her forward. Mary twisted away from the groping fingers before pulling her arm free to enter the cell by herself.

She hadn't liked the way the man had touched her bottom because it was rude but otherwise she felt very sure of herself. He was what mom called simple-minded: did what he was told. There was a gardener's help like that back home in Virginia. She'd make this man do what she wanted, like the gardener's boy. Trick him, so that she could get away, the way girls got away from bad people in the adventure books.

He caught her making pee pee but she didn't care. She had to let him look if he wanted: let him think there was nothing she could do. It wasn't as if he could see anything. She didn't want him to squeeze her bottom again, though.

She hunched on the bunk, watching the second hand on her watch bring the time round to six o'clock. The time she usually fed Billy Boy. She couldn't trick the silly man tonight. Maybe not even tomorrow. She hoped mom and dad weren't arguing about her, as they often did: didn't imagine that she'd run away on purpose. She couldn't understand why no one was doing anything to get her away.

A lot of people were preparing to.

At Brussels airport the US military aircraft touched down carrying twenty-five FBI and CIA personnel, under the overall command of the Bureau's deputy operational director and chief hostage negotiator John Norris.

Paul Harding was waiting at the bottom of the ramp

when Norris disembarked. Harding said: 'There's nothing new.'

'If there had been you'd have patched it through to the plane, wouldn't you?' Norris was impatient with empty words and gestures.

At her creeper-clad Brussels mansion off the Boulevard Anspach Félicité Galan personally poured the champagne for the two men with her and said: 'So there! It's all going to work perfectly.' When neither replied, she said to Jean Smet: 'There's nothing to worry about.' And to August Dehane: 'You've done very well: very well indeed.' Reluctantly they followed her lead, raising their glasses in a toast. 'To something we haven't done before,' the woman declared.

And Claudine Carter and Peter Blake reached the Metropole Hotel on the Place de Brouckère.

'This is the first time I've arrived on a case without knowing what it was,' said Claudine.

'I've done it far too often,' said Blake.

CHAPTER FIVE

John Norris, who tried hard to know everything, knew that more than once local FBI stations had been advised by Bureau headquarters of his impending arrival with the words The Iceman Cometh. And liked it, although there wasn't any similarity between him and the way he operated and any of the has-been characters in O'Neill's play, which he'd particularly gone to see when he discovered the intended in-house mockery. Norris didn't see it as a lampoon of his style and character. He was quite happy to accept it as an accurate description.

He was a sparse, bespectacled man who had learned totally to control what emotions he possessed, which were limited to begin with. He neither drank, smoked nor swore and his devotion to the Bureau was to the absolute exclusion of everything else: whenever he spoke of the Bureau's founder Norris called him *Mr* Hoover. His marriage to a college sweetheart, his one and only relationship, had ended in divorce and her accusation that he preferred to be at Pennsylvania Avenue than at home with her. Norris had agreed with her. What little physical need he had was met once a month – usually on a Friday – always in the missionary position and lasting no more than fifteen minutes, by a discreet but expensive professional who worked out of an apartment in the Watergate complex. She'd long ago decided he'd get as much satisfaction riding an exercise bike but she was a working girl and wasn't going to argue with how he spent his $500. He'd telephoned before leaving Washington, to tell her he was going out of town and couldn't make that Friday. She'd said she'd miss him and to hurry back. He'd cancelled the paper and magazine delivery, too.

His Masters degree was in psychology. As the Bureau's foremost expert on hostage, siege and kidnap negotiations Norris lectured on behavioural science at the FBI's National Centre for the Analysis of Violent Crime at their training academy at Quantico when his operational commitments allowed. He knew the Iceman tag was common knowledge there. It was useful, being preceded by a hard man reputation: saved time having to make people understand that when John Norris said jump they had to jump through fire, hoops, hell and high water. He didn't take prisoners. He got them released.

From the nervous way he was driving, both hands white-knuckled around the wheel, it was obvious Paul Harding had heard about the Iceman: idly Norris wondered if the term had even been used in the overnight advisory cable. He listened in disconcerting, unmoving silence while Harding obeyed his instruction to go verbally through everything that had happened since the first alarm at the embassy. People sometimes spoke more openly – more carelessly – trying to express themselves verbally than they did writing official reports. Listening without movement or interruption – letting echoing silences into conversations – hurried people into unthought revelations.

'I don't like it that there hasn't been any contact by now. That doesn't fit,' said Norris. He had a nasal, New England accent.

'You think she's dead?'

'I will do if there's nothing in the next twenty-four hours.'

'I hit the button the moment it became a crisis,' Harding reminded him quickly.

Back-covering time, recognized Norris. 'What about

the others? Our man, Boles? And the local driver, Luc? They clean?'

'Absolutely. It was a puncture, pure and simple.'

'How?'

Harding snatched a frowning glance across the car. 'How?'

Norris sighed impatiently. 'You've got to understand something about me, Paul. I don't believe in God. I don't believe in coincidences. I don't believe in accidents. I don't believe there are good people, only bad people. I work on the principle – so you'll work on that principle too – that everyone's guilty until I – me, no one else – decide otherwise. And it takes a lot for me to decide otherwise. You got all that neatly memorized, so there won't be any misunderstandings between us?'

Two positive indications that he was going to remain part of the investigation, realized Harding, relieved. 'I got it.'

'So. How?'

'Single nail.'

'Wall or tread of the tyre?'

'Tread.'

'Just the nail? No base to keep it upright in the path of the car?'

'Just the nail.'

'You've kept it, of course, as evidence? Haven't had the wheel fixed?'

Harding swallowed with fresh relief. 'All kept.'

'Good. Very good. What about the school? Anything wrong there?'

Harding hesitated, knowing there was no way of avoiding the answer but wishing he could. 'Vetted the place myself, before the kid was enrolled. Quite a few embassies use it so the principal and the governors are as careful as hell, knowing what there is to lose. They're shitting themselves over what's happened.'

46

Norris winced at the profanity. 'So they should. Who made the mistake with the duplicate call?'

Survival time, thought Harding: sorry, Harry. 'Becker says he didn't but he was on security dispatch duty. Boles says it was Harry he spoke to from the car.'

'You checked Becker's background?'

'I've gone through everything we've got locally, at the embassy. He's been here for two years. There's never been any trouble.'

'He drink?'

'No more than anyone else.'

There was the impatient sigh again. 'So he drinks?'

'Yes.'

'Gamble?'

'Not that I know of.'

'Local friends?'

'None that I know.'

'The ambassador's been told I want to see him immediately?'

'He's waiting.'

'I want you to sit in on that. As soon as it's over, I want you to check Becker again but better than you already have. I want everything Washington's got on him, for starters. Take as many people as you want, from those I brought in. I want to know if he's in debt or has got a drink problem or is involved with a local woman – or man if he's gay. I want to know anything that could have compromised Becker: exposed him to blackmail. Any problem with that?'

'None at all,' lied Harding, glad they would soon be at the embassy. It was difficult to conceive the problems he was going to have with this dead-faced, rigor-mortised sonofabitch. It was chilling just being close to. Determined not to be caught between a rock and a hard place, Harding said: 'The CIA station here – Lance Rampling's

47

the resident-in-charge – are pissed off not being included in the meeting with the ambassador.'

'Langley's been told who's running the show. Rampling should have been messaged by now, making it clear they're subsidiary. I'll see him after the ambassador: straighten him out.'

'He asked for a meeting.'

Dismissive of any CIA distraction, Norris said: 'What about the kid herself?'

'Awkward little brat. Knows she's the daughter of an ambassador and doesn't let anyone forget it. Makes a lot of people's lives a misery . . .' Anticipating the question seconds before Norris asked it, Harding added hurriedly: 'But definitely not enough to make anyone snatch her: do her any real harm. She just needs her ass slapped.'

'Is she wilful enough to have run away: staged the whole business?'

'That was my first thought. Like I said, I didn't wait to hit the button, but I expected her to show up with some fancy story. But she wouldn't have stayed away this long.'

Norris remained silent for several minutes. 'So what's the local situation?'

'We've been given total Belgian cooperation, guaranteed at Justice Minister level. The police commissioner, André Poncellet, is personally involving himself. And they've called in Europol, which is—'

'I know what Europol is,' snapped the other man. 'We advised, when they were set up. Same rules as with the local force. We'll take everything they've got to offer but I don't want them getting in the way of our investigating.' He shifted in his seat for the first time. 'That means maintaining the closest, day-to-day contact: officially we accept they're in charge, running the operation. You know how big a force Europol are committing?'

'No. I haven't got any names, either. Just know they're

coming in tonight. I've scheduled a leaders' conference at the embassy tomorrow. Included Poncellet.'

'Good deal,' said the thin man. 'Anything else that needs saying?'

'Not that I can think of.' At last they reached the Boulevard du Régent. Harding gestured ahead and said: 'There's the embassy.'

'We've filled in the journey very well,' said Norris. 'Got to know each other. That's good.'

Paul Harding couldn't remember a man who'd made him feel so unsettled, ever in his career. And that included three proven killers, one with a .375 magnum in his hand. Ever conscious of retirement just three years away, he said: 'It has been good. I've enjoyed it.'

Liar, thought Norris.

James McBride was waiting in his study, jacket off, tie loosened around an unbuttoned collar. Hillary sat some way away, the customary distance re-established, in contrast perfectly composed, perfectly dressed, every hair starchily in place. The ambassador already had a large Jack Daniel's on the desk in front of him and gestured them towards the open cabinet while the introductions were made. Harding was already going towards it before he realized Norris had refused and thought, fuck it! With no alternative he carried on, desperately seeking a soda. Then again he thought fuck it, defiant this time, and took at least three fingers of Jack Daniel's, too. It looked even larger from the amount of ice he added. It had been one hell of a drive. The following days were going to be hell as well. Maybe worse.

'I heard through State that you're the Bureau's chief negotiator,' said McBride. 'That's good. That's how it's got to be.' His hand was visibly shaking when he lifted the whisky glass.

'Everyone with me is an expert in his field,' assured

Norris. He sat primly and very upright, his concentration absolute on the politically appointed diplomat with more back-door clout than anyone in the new administration.

'We want our daughter back, Mr Norris,' said Hillary. There was a note of impatience in her voice.

'I'll get her back for you, ma'am. All I need is the contact.' There was no doubt in the man's voice.

The head-on ego clash was deafening, thought Harding.

'I've made arrangements with my bank about money. I've guessed at three million,' said McBride.

'They were in touch before I left Pennsylvania Avenue. The Director dealt with it himself. The numbers are already being computer logged. And it'll be marked before coming here in the diplomatic bag.'

'Will three million be enough?' demanded the woman.

'It's enough to negotiate with.'

'What else can we do?' asked McBride.

'Let me talk a few things through with you,' said Norris.

McBride appeared to become aware of the hand tremor and put the glass down on his desk. 'Anything. What?'

For the first time Norris indicated the other FBI officer. 'The day your daughter vanished you told Paul that they – the people who've got her – had done it to get at you. I don't understand that, sir.'

McBride looked blankly at the strangely still man, wishing his hands weren't shaking so obviously, trying to reassure himself Norris would imagine it was solely concern for Mary. To gain even more time he turned to Harding. 'I don't remember saying that.'

'You did, sir,' insisted the resident officer.

'I was very upset. If I said it I probably meant directed at me as the official representative of the United States of America, not that it was personal.'

'Have there been threats against the embassy? Any reason for thinking that?' persisted Norris.

'Not directly. But there's a great resurgence of fascism – neo-Nazism – throughout Europe. Quite a lot of anti-American feeling.' He didn't want to go on down this road: it wasn't sounding convincing enough.

'Let's look at it from a personal viewpoint. What about your business before your appointment?'

McBride felt the first twitch of uncertainty, deep in his stomach: he wanted even less to go in this direction. 'I founded and headed a legitimate armaments corporation that always conducted business at official government levels.' He pushed what he hoped would sound like outrage into his voice. 'I'm not aware of offending anyone, which is what I guess you're implying.' It was too long ago. If the motherfucker had wanted to hurt him he'd have done it years ago.

'I wasn't implying anything specific,' said Norris easily. 'Just trying to cover all the bases. Arms dealing can have its uncertain aspects, can't it?'

The opening for further outrage. 'I was not operating in dark alleys with people whose names I didn't know. Mine was the corporation governments came to.' With a few exceptions. One in particular: the ghost always there to climb out of the closet. But he hadn't known: genuinely, honestly, hadn't known. They had to understand that, if it ever leaked.

Luigi della Sialvo *had* been a government procurer. Credentials a mile high. Sold a lot of stuff to Italy, every deal one hundred per cent kosher, every End User certificate stamped, sealed and countersigned. Except for that one occasion. Luigi fucking Sialvo working on the side, building up his own special pension with a bullshit line about having known the smiling Mr Lee for years, personally vouching for him, an introduction between trusted friends. And there had been an End

51

User guarantee. Singapore, a toe-hold in the Asian market, a new business opportunity. Thanks, Luigi, you're a buddy: sure the commission can go into the Zürich bank. Not unusual. Accepted practice. Good deal too. Twenty million to open, all up front, thirty-five to follow, same payment arrangements. And it did arrive, timed to the second. And a Singapore address, a bona fide company, to go with the End User requirement.

But the Sidewinders and the Cruise and the anti-personnel stuff hadn't ended up in Singapore. Just passed through, the arms dealers' law of perpetual motion. New company in Korea, shuffle-shuffle to Indonesia where the transport planes were waiting for the direct flight to Baghdad, all greased and ready for the start of the Gulf War.

He hadn't given in to the blackmail when it came. Not James Kilbright McBride's style. Faced down the no longer smiling Mr Lee when he'd set it all out, embarrassment after embarrassment, to force the order so urgent there wasn't time to ship through all the cut-outs. If I drop you'll drop, you bastard: you'll be the pariah in the arms business, never operate again, so go fuck yourself.

There was much further to drop now though, if it ever came out. And it wouldn't be a Chinese entrepreneur falling with him. US President funded by Saddam gold. A no defence catastrophe.

McBride made a conscious, determined effort to curb the panic, pressing one shaking hand down upon the other. All in the past: too long ago in the past. Before the appointment he'd been Bureau vetted, as a matter of course. Come through squeaky clean. Like he would again. Ridiculous to think there was any danger.

'What about you, Mrs McBride?'

Hillary gave no outward, surprised reaction to the question. She said: 'I may have offended a few people in the past but none that would have done a thing as unspeakable as this.'

'You sure about that?' demanded the emotionless man.

'I'm talking secretaries or staff I've had to let go, for inefficiency. I don't like inefficiency.'

'Secretaries and staff have kidnapped in the past. You got names?'

Hillary frowned. 'I suppose there'll be records somewhere: not here, home in Virginia.'

'Can you arrange for them to be made available to the Bureau there?' said Norris.

'I suppose so, if you consider it important.'

'Everything's important to get your daughter back.'

'I don't need to be told that!' snapped the woman. 'I'll arrange it.'

McBride discovered his glass was empty and offered it sideways to Harding, who hesitated and then took it. Yes'm boss, thought the FBI man. Fuck it, he thought again, filling his own glass while he was about it. He didn't bother with as much ice this time: the last one had become very watered down at the end.

'We'll need to filter everything coming into the embassy, certainly to you or Mrs McBride personally,' said Norris. 'That includes everything in the diplomatic bag, in the event that this might be a conspiracy starting out in Washington. The Director's arranging for State to confirm my level of security clearance. Some of the people with me are communication experts. There'll be a tap on every landline in and out of the embassy. Scanners will monitor mobiles. We'll get a daily telephone print-out from Belgacom. Those precautions will, of course, cover the ambassadorial residence and extend to the homes of every senior official in the embassy. I'll need a list. I accept it's an invasion of individual privacy but I want it made clear that has to be secondary to recovering your daughter. My sole interest – the sole interest of everyone with me – is the whereabouts of Mary Beth . . .' He paused to emphasize the importance of what he was going to say. 'Everything that comes to our attention during the investigation will be considered with the utmost discretion: nothing that isn't part of this case is of any interest to us whatsoever. I'd like that assurance circulated throughout the embassy, along with my request for absolute cooperation from everyone.'

'Give me an honest answer, Mr Norris,' demanded Hillary. 'How bad does it look?'

'Bad.'

'You think she'd dead?' The woman's voice was quite firm.

'I think we need to hear something very soon.'

'How long?' said the ambassador.

'Twenty-four hours.'

McBride closed his eyes, the despair genuine. 'I keep thinking, trying to imagine, what she's going through.'

'Don't,' urged Norris. 'It doesn't help. Doesn't achieve anything.'

'What does?' asked Hillary.

'Nothing, in the position we're in at the moment.'

As they walked towards the Bureau offices Norris checked, turning fully behind him to ensure no one was within hearing, before saying: 'Shaking a lot at the beginning, wasn't he?'

'He's lost a daughter, for Christ's sake!' said Harding, emboldened by the whisky.

'So's Mrs McBride. She was holding herself OK.'

'What did you expect from McBride?' asked Harding.

'More outrage: exaggerated threats about what he'd like to do to whoever's got her.'

'That happen always?'

'It's a common reaction.'

'You're the psychologist.'

'Add a request to what you're going to ask Washington

for, on Harry Becker. I want everything that came out of the vetting procedure on McBride before his ambassadorial appointment was confirmed. And get that stuff on Mrs McBride picked up. I'll message the Bureau myself, authorizing every single person she's ever fired to be traced and interviewed.'

'Did you mean it, about not being interested in anything other than what might apply to this specific investigation?' queried Harding.

'I told you how I operate on the way in from the airport,' Norris reminded him. 'There's no such thing as a half-right or a half-wrong. We wouldn't be doing our duty if we looked the other way when we discovered a wrongdoing, would we?'

'No,' Harding managed. Holy shit, he thought.

Claudine liked the vaguely faded, turn-of-the-century ambience of the Metropole, complete with its overfurnished art deco lobby, exuberantly potted foliage and rattling, open-grilled elevator. Peter Blake was already waiting, wedged into the corner of the inappropriately small bar for a complete view of the lounge, the lobby beyond and the hotel entrance to the sidewalk café. His beer glass was half empty. She chose white wine. They touched glasses.

'More guidance for a new boy,' demanded Blake. 'What's Europol like for expenses?'

Claudine frowned. 'OK, I guess. I never got a query the last time. But they like receipts. Why?'

'The concierge recommends La Maison du Cygne, which is just around the corner on the Grande Place,' said the man. 'But says it's expensive. Chez François is good for fish and is slightly cheaper but it's not so close, on the Quai au Brigues. Your choice.'

Getting-to-know-each-other time, realized Claudine. That slightly surprised her, too: on the train from

Holland Blake hadn't made much of an effort, engrossed for most of the journey in a book by Elmore Leonard, whom he'd called the best detective writer in the world. The name of the fish restaurant was an unfortunate reminder of Sanglier's marauding wife, Françoise. 'Let's walk around to the Grande Place.'

La Maison du Cygne was old, with a lot of dark wood and an air of being sure of itself without conceit. It reminded her of the Michelin-starred restaurant her mother had run in Lyon until her death, eight months earlier. Claudine had the lobster, which was superb. Blake had moules and chose the wine without consulting her, which is what Hugo Rosetti had done during their first outings.

Claudine was curious, although not apprehensive, about this initial encounter. It hadn't taken her long to realize that sex and the pursuit of it was the only way Europol's ghetto barriers were breached, the majority of the polyglot male detectives and crime staff appearing automatically to consider the majority of the polyglot female contingent available prey to be hunted, with no closed season. There was an irony, she recognized, in the fact that after becoming so adept at rejection it was Hugo Rosetti, the one man she wouldn't have rebuffed, whose principles prevented his attempting what most other men in the organization tried all the time.

Careful not to be obvious – determined against any irritating misunderstanding – she studied the man, as intent upon any signs she might professionally isolate as she was upon his physical appearance. He didn't have the awkwardness of a lot of big men and on balance she decided the always direct look from those oddly blue eyes was polite, unstraying attention, not appraisal. She liked, too, the fact that he hadn't invaded her space escorting her from the hotel: there had been no physical contact, cupping her elbow or putting his hand at her back to guide her. Extremely confident, she thought again, without the need for gap-filling gestures or movement. She guessed the barely discernible Irish accent had been exaggerated on the assignment that preceded Europol.

'Who's going to go first?' he demanded openly.

'I didn't think you liked talking about yourself?'

'The observant psychologist!'

'You made it pretty obvious whenever anyone tried to make you.'

'I can't be bothered to help people get off listening to imagined James Bond exploits.'

'Weren't they James Bond exploits?'

He held his wine glass in both hands, staring at her over its rim. She was too strongly featured to be a beautiful woman but there was a very positive attractiveness he found intriguing. He liked the way she wore her black hair short, cut into her neck, and how the grey eyes met him, in neither challenge nor flirtation: if there was a message it was that they were equals. Strictly professional, he thought, remembering her remark at their first meeting. 'I didn't drink vodka martini, get seduced by any big-breasted virgins or drive a car that fired rockets.'

Claudine recognized the self-parody avoidance. She went only partially along with it. 'But it was one bloody great gamble?'

Blake had been half smiling, inviting her to join in the mockery. Abruptly he became serious. 'There was an attempt on you, during the serial killing investigation? An attack? I read the archives, after Sanglier's briefing.'

'I got trapped into some publicity: French police wanting their pictures on television. Mine was there too . . .' Claudine slightly lifted her left arm, along which the knife scar ran from shoulder to wrist. 'That's why I have to wear long sleeves.' The advice was to wait another year before considering cosmetic surgery. She looked steadily at him. 'We were talking about you, in Ireland?'

'No we're not.'

There were mental scars and she guessed they were deep. 'You're not showing any signs.'

'It took a while to get rid of them: to get rid of a lot.'

'Inpatient?'

'For three months.'

'What about medication now?'

'I carry it, as a precaution.'

'Worried about the pressure of this?'

'I don't think so. It'll be a lot different from what I did before.'

'Sure you don't want to talk about it?'

'Positive. It's locked away.'

Was there guilt, as well as stress: the sort of eroding remorse that a mentally well balanced person would suffer if he'd had to go as far as killing someone? Angrily she stopped the reflection: she was behaving – thinking at least – like his cocktail party interrogators. 'If anything starts to become unlocked and you think I can help, professionally, while we're here . . .'

'It won't,' he insisted. 'I've thrown away the key. But thanks.'

Claudine knew she should move on but she didn't want to. It was impossible for her to make any proper judgement without knowing what he'd gone through, but in her professional opinion traumas weren't adjusted to by sealing up the experience and pretending it never happened. She'd lost a husband who'd thought he could handle a mental problem like that. 'How was it for your family?'

'There isn't one. No wife, current or prior. Only child. Both parents dead. I was well selected.'

There *was* bitterness, so the door wasn't as securely

bolted as he would have liked to imagine. 'Selected?' she challenged. 'You would have had to have volunteered, surely?'

'I did,' he admitted.

'So you got yourself into whatever it was. You weren't pushed into it unwillingly.'

Blake nodded ruefully. 'Thank you, doctor.' There was a grin, to show there was no offence. 'So far this has all been a bit one-sided, hasn't it?'

Claudine didn't mention it was through being an English representative at the Lyon-based Interpol that her father had met her mother. Nor did she mention that her father's archival investigation into Sanglier's father's wartime heroism had created the fluke she was now convinced formed the basis of the man's uneven and at times bewildering attitude towards her. She talked of her husband's death but not that it had been suicide from work-stressed depression she'd been too professionally preoccupied even to notice. And she didn't say anything about Hugo Rosetti.

'And what about Kurt Volker?' he demanded. 'You seemed very keen to get him aboard?'

'Kurt you've got to see for yourself!'

Blake regarded her with raised eyebrows. 'Sorry if I'm venturing on a personal situation!'

'You're not. Not that way. Just wait, if this comes to anything. How do you want to handle tomorrow's meeting?' she asked, in a suddenly decided test. There'd been some distracting, who's-in-charge problem with the French detective with whom she'd worked during the serial killing investigation.

He shrugged. 'According to all the warnings about how Europol is viewed it looks as if it's going to be you and me against the world. I think it should be a double act, don't you?'

It wasn't the reply Claudine had expected but she liked

it. She thought she was going to enjoy working with this man. Only, of course, professionally.

'Your fault!' screamed Hillary.

'You agreed Mary Beth should go to a local school,' McBride yelled back.

'I didn't want it.'

'It's too late to talk like that now.'

'If she's dead – if anything happens to her – it'll be *your* fault. On *your* conscience.'

CHAPTER SIX

John Norris and his squad swept through the American embassy with the Washington-backed force and disruption of a Force Nine hurricane. By 8 a.m. the following morning – less than twelve hours after their arrival in Brussels – the Boulevard du Régent legation as well as the official residence of James McBride was totally isolated, electronically as well as physically.

No telephone, fax or e-mail communication could be received or sent without passing through the specially installed, twenty-four-hour-manned communications centre complete with its own roof-mounted satellite dish.

All incoming letter mail, including the contents of the diplomatic bag, had first to be opened and examined in an adjoining room, transformed into a sorting office: Norris's only concession was to agree to the demand from Burt Harrison, the chief of mission, for a member of his staff to be present when the supposedly inviolate diplomatic exchange was sifted.

Some of the thirty embassy staff whom Norris considered sufficiently senior to be blanket-monitored had been awakened overnight at their homes to agree to listening and recording devices being installed on their telephones and to their incoming personal packages and letters going through the embassy sorting procedure.

The assessment in the FBI's much more comprehensive personal file upon Harry Becker, which was faxed in its entirety from Washington, was of a completely responsible and absolutely competent operative, but after only fifteen minutes' interrogation by Norris the man broke down and confessed to lying about duplicating the call to Mary Beth McBride's school. Upon Norris's authority Becker was immediately suspended from duty but not as quickly repatriated, kept in Belgium – although virtually under embassy house arrest – to enable further investigation into his local associations and habits during his posting in the country. Norris personally briefed five of the agents who had arrived with him before assigning them to the task with the warning to forget Becker was – or had been – a colleague. 'Whatever happens he's finished. He isn't any longer one of us: he doesn't qualify.'

The full FBI evaluation of James Kilbright McBride was of a man fulfilling every requirement to be a United States' ambassador, with nothing questionable in his prior personal or professional background. Norris responded with an 'Action This Day' priority demand for the armament-dealing background to be gone into again in greater depth.

Norris's encounter with Lance Rampling, which the CIA station chief had entered believing it to be a meeting of equals, lasted precisely ten minutes. Rampling emerged, white-faced from a combination of fury and shocked bewilderment, to demand from Harding whether the sonofabitch was fucking real or not. Harding said he thought John Norris was a mutant alien from another planet, although he'd prefer not to be quoted.

The scene-of-crime forensic expert thought there was nothing whatsoever suspicious about how the nail was embedded in the tyre of the original collection car but Norris had wheel, tyre and nail shipped back in the returning military aircraft for detailed scientific examination in Washington DC.

Claudine and Blake were early for the coordinating meeting but Norris, flanked by Harding and Rampling, was already waiting in a hastily contrived incident room created from the largest unit of the normal FBI accommodation. André Poncellet was early, too, but from the way he hurried the introductions Norris managed to convey the impression that the perspiring, tightly uniformed Brussels police commissioner had kept them waiting. Neither Harding nor Rampling wore jackets and the CIA resident had his tie pulled loose. Norris sat with both buttons of his jacket fastened: he was facing the window and the light flared off his rimless glasses, making him appear sightless. It was Rampling, a fresh-faced man with an extremely short crewcut, who gestured to the Cona percolator steaming on its hotplate: when Claudine nodded acceptance he poured a cup for her.

A technician with recording apparatus sat by the door. Seeing Blake's look Norris said: 'I like keeping tight records. About everything. Anyone got any objection?'

Blake shook his head. Claudine didn't make any response, intently studying the newly arrived American. Poncellet said: 'No. Of course not. Very wise.' He spoke too quickly, too nervously.

'In answer to your obvious question,' Norris began, 'the embassy has heard nothing of or from Mary Beth since she was last seen by two of her classmates walking off, alone, up the rue du Canal. So she's now been missing for thirty-six hours . . .' He paused, looking towards the recording technician, who nodded at the adequate sound level. 'I've satisfied myself that she has not run away of her own accord. The most obvious conclusion is that she has been grabbed and is being held against her will. I fully accept and recognize under whose authority this investigation has to be conducted . . .' He stopped again, looking directly at Blake. 'We greatly appreciate your involvement and want to work extremely closely with you. My government is committing whatever additional support might be necessary. I brought twenty-five men with me from Washington last night, to be part of whatever force you are assembling. Today we need to evolve a strategy—'

'Won't that be difficult until we know what we're investigating?' Claudine broke in. It could be worse than she'd feared: far worse.

Norris frowned, both at the interruption and because it came from a woman. He needed to know what her function was. 'I think we should proceed on the assumption that she has been kidnapped.'

'Why?' demanded Claudine. 'Thirty-six hours is a long time without a demand, isn't it?'

'Not necessarily, in my experience.'

Harding managed not to show any reaction, although Norris's reply directly contradicted what he had said on the way in from the airport the previous night.

So Norris was the negotiator, Claudine thought. And clearly the man in charge of the FBI and CIA contingent. 'She could have been attacked. Be lying injured somewhere. Had an accident and be – or need to be – in a hospital. I don't see the point of maintaining the silence about her disappearance that I understand has been asked for.'

'I don't want to panic whoever's got her,' said Norris flatly.

'We don't know that anyone *has* got her,' protested Claudine. 'How long do you think we should sit around doing nothing?'

Norris's face became tinged with pink at the unfamiliarity of being confronted so openly. Before he could speak Poncellet declared with triumphant eagerness: 'The Brussels police force hasn't sat around doing nothing. I have assigned squads to the rue du Canal at the precise time she walked along it. Everyone – and I mean everyone – will be stopped and questioned and shown a photograph of the child, in the hope they regularly use the road at that time and might have seen her. In addition there will be road blocks stopping all vehicles for their drivers to be questioned. Checks were started, within an hour of our being told of her disappearance, on every shop, business and private house along the entire length of the road, not just in the direction in which she was seen to walk but also the opposite way.' He looked proudly around those assembled in the room, saddened at the lack of approval.

'What's come out of the premises check?' demanded Blake.

In his disappointment Poncellet tried condescension. 'If there had been anything I would have obviously told you.'

Unperturbed, Blake said: 'How long's it been going on?'

'Since the opening of commercial business this morning,' said Poncellet tightly.

Blake nodded, as if the reply confirmed something. 'And this afternoon one of the city's busiest thoroughfares is going to be virtually closed off. By this evening it will have leaked that the daughter of the American ambassador has vanished. It would be better to have a media release, with a photograph, than run the risk of speculation's getting out of hand and having to be corrected.'

'I do not consider that's the right way to operate at this time,' said Norris.

'I thought our understanding – the only possible jurisdictional understanding – was that it was how *we* considered it right to operate,' said Claudine. So much for diplomatic niceties. They were always bullshit anyway. She'd expected antagonism – come prepared to confront it, which she was doing – but not to be as worried as she was becoming.

Norris grew redder. 'Kidnappers are frightened once they've got a victim. Premature publicity can panic them, as I've already tried to make clear. I don't want . . .' He stopped, in apparent awareness of the implications of talking in the first person. 'It would be a mistake for anyone to be panicked. It's better for negotiations to be conducted as quietly and as calmly as possible.'

'Quantico text book,' identified Claudine.

'With which I am extremely familiar,' said Norris, who'd contributed two of the manuals from which it had been created.

'So am I. I've read it,' said Claudine, who had, as part of her hostage negotiation lectures. Throwing the man's condescension back at him she said: 'We don't yet know we're investigating a kidnap. We're looking for a missing child. Missing children are best and most often found through public appeal. And as Europol is the jurisdictional investigatory body into the disappearance of Mary Beth McBride this is the way we consider this investigation should begin. A lot of time has already been wasted: I hope not too much.'

Norris was astonished at the effrontery, and then furious. 'Have you forgotten who the victim is?'

'It's because of who the victim is that we are here,' Blake reminded him. 'Lack of contact for thirty-six hours hardly indicates panic. It indicates the very opposite, if she has been snatched.'

Inwardly Harding and Rampling wished they could wave flags or punch the air. Poncellet could hardly believe either the dispute or his good fortune in being safely on the periphery.

Norris was momentarily dumbstruck. Struggling desperately, he said: 'It's an official diplomatic request that this situation is not made public for at least another twenty-four hours.'

'What's diplomacy got to do with it?' challenged Claudine. 'If it is a consideration – and I cannot imagine how it can be – then perhaps it would be better if my colleague and I discussed it personally with the ambassador. We're not achieving a lot here.'

'This is ridiculous!' Norris was floundering.

'I agree. Totally ridiculous,' said Blake. 'We came here today to arrange cooperation: a strategy, to use your word. This discussion so far isn't doing that. If the child is in danger all we're doing is furthering it.'

Norris looked sideways, suddenly reminded of the tape. He couldn't retreat. It wasn't his style. And certainly not on record. Compromising wasn't retreating: compromising was an essential part of negotiation, give a little here to gain much more there. And what was the point of confrontation anyway? These two weren't going to be actively involved: just given the impression that they were running things. And on the way in from the airport he'd put a time limit on what he considered might be the worst scenario and thought there was a way he could avoid losing face. Looking from the recording apparatus to the plump Belgian, Norris said: 'The road block and street checks do create a risk of ill-informed speculation.'

'Which should be avoided,' reiterated Claudine. The man had to be given a way out in front of his own people. 'The release could be timed for this evening: that would catch television and radio and ensure fuller cover in tomorrow morning's newspapers. That, effectively, fits with the time scale you were thinking about, doesn't it?'

'I think so. Yes,' said Norris. The bitch was patronizing him.

Claudine was conscious of Blake's attention. She didn't respond to it. Instead she said: 'As we're devising strategy, the Quantico guidelines favour paying ransom, don't they?'

'The prime consideration is a safe release,' said Norris, seizing his escape. 'The perpetrators can be pursued afterwards.'

'What about the victim's becoming disposable if a ransom is paid?' asked Blake. 'Once the kidnappers have got the money the consideration is minimizing their risk of being identified.'

'It's better to pay,' insisted Norris.

'You're a negotiator?' challenged Claudine.

'The Bureau's *chief* negotiator.'

'You've always paid?'

'Yes.' Norris's colour had been subsiding. It began to return at the obvious direction of the questioning. He looked again at the recording equipment.

'How many victims have you lost?'

'I've got six released, unharmed,' declared the American. 'All the kidnappers were arrested, in every case.'

'That wasn't the question,' Claudine reminded him. Why did the silly bastard run head-on into every argument contrary to his own? Because, she reasoned, he was unaccustomed to having to argue in the first place. But this wasn't negotiation! This was confrontation. Her unease deepened as her professional assessment of the man hardened.

'Two died,' admitted Norris.

'What about the kidnappers?'

'They weren't caught.' Norris looked between Claudine and Blake, positively settling on Claudine. 'You're Europol's negotiator.'

'I will be, if it comes to that.' He should at least be allowed the appearance of revenge, she supposed. But only the appearance. He was the creator of his own problems. She didn't want him to be the creator of hers. Or those of a missing child.

'How many kidnap victims have you successfully freed?' Norris pounced.

'None,' admitted Claudine at once. 'I haven't yet been called upon to do so.'

Norris stretched the silence, exaggerating his astonishment in his determination not just to recover but to crush this arrogant woman in the process. Spacing the words as he uttered them he said: 'You haven't operated in a kidnap situation until now?'

'No,' said Claudine easily. 'But before joining Europol I freed a hundred and twenty people from an airliner hijacked by Islamic fundamentalists. And ended four separate sieges, one by a convicted murderer who took a hostage to avoid capture.' She paused. 'No one died.' Touché, she thought. Mixing the metaphor, she added: Game, set and match.

Blake appeared to think so, too. Smiling, he said: 'I think that covers the relevant CVs, don't you?'

Rampling couldn't avoid the brief smirk, although not at Claudine, and was glad they were sitting in a way that prevented Norris from seeing it. Claudine was unconcerned that the thin American could see her brief sideways smile, which wasn't in any case an intended sneer at the man.

Norris took it as such, but more than matched it when Blake disclosed that the Europol force at the moment consisted of just himself and the woman. 'I can't believe what you're telling me. Europol isn't taking this seriously! This isn't an investigation on Europol's part: it's a joke.'

'It'll be an investigation within an hour of its becoming clear what there is to investigate,' promised Blake, unimpressed by the other man's obviously overstrained amazement.

Norris shook his head. The woman had irritated him into pointless argument, but it didn't matter any more. His only annoyance now was at himself, for allowing it to happen. These two – their entire cockamamy organization – were of no importance. They had just made themselves irrelevant by admitting – casually admitting! – they considered that the disappearance of an American ambassador's child could be handled by just two people, with the further incredible admission that the appointed negotiator had never conducted a kidnap release in her life! McBride – probably the President himself – would hit the roof when they were told: not just hit it, go right through it!

It all came down to giving him a clear, unimpeded run. All he needed to do was go through the barest of motions – which, he reflected, was all he'd intended from the start – and get them out of the way. Out of his way.

It took them thirty minutes to agree the wording of the proposed media release and that the greatest impact would come from the ambassador's personal appearance at any requested press conference. Norris promised to put the idea to McBride, and Poncellet brightened visibly at Blake's suggestion that the Belgian police commissioner should also appear. Commissioner Henri Sanglier would be Europol's representative, added Blake, to Claudine's well-disguised surprise. Norris's contempt grew as he inferred that neither Blake nor Claudine was permitted to represent their organization. It perfectly summed up their inadequacy.

It was as they decided upon daily morning and afternoon conferences that Norris apologized that there was not enough space at the embassy's FBI facility for Blake and Claudine to work from there. André Poncellet at once offered whatever facility and accommodation Europol might need at Brussels' central police headquarters.

The entire charade lasted five minutes short of an hour and ended with an exchange of emergency contact numbers and smiling assurances that they had made a good beginning for whatever they were going to face in the immediate future.

Claudine held back until she was safely halfway across the open embassy forecourt before exploding: 'What a fucking pantomime!'

Blake showed no surprise at the outburst. 'I've seen better,' he agreed mildly.

'It was frightening,' insisted Claudine. She turned, looking directly at the man. 'And I really mean that. Frightening.'

Although the road checks hadn't started the rue du Canal was already congested. They were still early for their meeting so they abandoned the taxi and found a pavement café some way from the school, in the direction in which Mary was known to have walked. As they sat there two detectives, one a woman visibly carrying a photograph of Mary Beth McBride, were escorted from inside by a shoulder-shrugging manager. Blake shook his head against making contact and Claudine held back as well.

'So what's so frightening?' demanded Blake.

'In my professional opinion, Norris is very close to being mentally ill,' declared Claudine starkly. 'I believe he's severely obsessional, which is a clinical condition that needs treatment.'

Blake stared at her, coffee cup half raised. 'Yes,' he agreed. 'That would be something to be very frightened about. You sure?'

'He's beyond challenge: won't consider any argument contrary to his own. Because he doesn't believe there is any opinion other than his own. You saw it yourself, if you examine it hard enough. He won't countenance any possibility beyond kidnap. That's not the rationale of a psychological investigator: it's the very antithesis of it. Everything is possible at this moment: at the beginning. I don't think he's capable of being either objective or subjective . . .' She paused. 'Most worrying of all, I think John Norris is on the edge of losing control. And if he loses control during any negotiation for Mary's freedom, then she'll die, if she hasn't already been killed.'

Blake held up a halting hand. 'We went in there today

71

knowing that the Bureau were going to give us a load of runaround bullshit and empty promises and try to handle the entire show themselves. OK, so Norris is a supremely arrogant asshole who made it more obvious than we expected. But we're equals: people to whom he didn't have to prove any professional ability. He might be entirely different when he's negotiating.'

'Norris doesn't for a moment consider us equals. He thinks we're grossly inferior. He thinks everyone is inferior to him. John Norris is God in his own heaven. I'm frightened he could make Mary Beth McBride one of his angels.'

Blake regarded her doubtfully. 'Can you be that positive, from just one meeting?'

'Until he realized I'd picked up on it, virtually every sentence or opinion began with *I*. He's got more victims back than he's lost and probably been able to manoeuvre the failures into being someone else's fault, never his. He's become the Great Untouchable, the Great Unquestionable. It's affected him.'

'You're the expert. But all I've heard since I've joined Europol is that it's not just us against the villains but us against every national force and their dog as well.'

Claudine shook her head. 'The attitude of national forces is resentment, pure and simple: no one wanting their territory encroached upon. That's not what we're talking about here. I think Norris is operationally dangerous. To the child, I mean – who's probably in enough danger as it is.'

'So what can we do about it?'

'Nothing,' conceded Claudine. 'That's what upsets me most.'

'Recovering the child – if she can be recovered – is all that matters?'

Claudine frowned. 'Yes?'

'Why not feed the obsession: use it to our advantage?

Say you need his help: can't do it without him and let him believe he is in charge. Couldn't you control him if you got in on the negotiations?'

'Don't give up the day job,' said Claudine, smiling at the amateur psychology. 'He doesn't need to *believe* he's in charge. He's sure he *is*. He'd see that approach as *me* patronizing *him*.'

'What about getting Sanglier to intervene?'

'In what? About what? There's no way we could make any official protest, based upon my impression.' She hesitated again. 'Incidentally, you took a lot upon yourself naming Sanglier as our representative before knowing he'd agree to a press conference.'

'Appearing with ambassadors and commissioners is Sanglier's level. He more or less said that, at the briefing.'

'I think he might have liked prior consultation.'

Blake shrugged. 'If he doesn't want to do it he can refuse.'

More kamikaze disregard, thought Claudine. To go with a mentally disarranged man and a lost ten-year-old child and a controlling commissioner whom she didn't trust. Her cup was being filled to overflowing, and they hadn't even started yet. 'We were right to argue for a press conference. It would have been a miracle if something hadn't broken before tomorrow.'

'Norris conceded on that,' suggested Blake.

'We gave him the time he wanted.'

'I'm not arguing against you,' said Blake, before making his point. 'But wouldn't it be great if in that time there was an approach and Norris managed to get her back?'

Claudine looked quizzically at the man, disappointed for the first time. 'Great,' she agreed. 'But it won't happen, even if there is an approach. Norris might have been able to do it once but I don't think he's capable of doing it any longer.'

73

Which was suffering the greater delusion of grandeur? wondered Blake. He checked his watch. 'Time to go.'

Henriette Flahaur, the school principal, was an autocratic, grey-haired, stiffly upright woman trying hard to conceal a disaster behind aggression. The severe black suit reminded Claudine of how her mother customarily dressed to greet customers at the Lyon restaurant. She'd been autocratic, too.

The meeting was more for Claudine's benefit than Blake's but the detective led at the beginning, confronting the woman's insistence that she had already told as much as she knew to both American and Belgian investigators with smiling, sympathetic politeness that impressed Claudine and coaxed a third account from the woman within minutes. It was a terrible, inexplicable misunderstanding, the first time anything like it had ever occurred at the school. A new system had already been introduced, with security guards individually checking pupils in and out of the school. The world seemed to have become a dreadful place. The whole school was praying for Mary Beth's safe return. Blake said he was sorry but he didn't think the school's name could be withheld from the publicity.

'Have you – or any teacher or official – ever thought your school was being particularly watched?' he asked.

'By someone intending to snatch a pupil, you mean?'

'Yes.'

Madame Flahaur vigorously shook her head. 'Anyone would have seen how careful . . .' she began, trailing off in mid-sentence. 'That doesn't sound right now, does it?'

'It wasn't the answer to my question anyway,' Blake said gently. 'I'm talking about recent weeks or days: a car or a person hanging around that made you curious.'

She shook her head again, although less forcefully. 'There's a specific rule. If any member of staff notices anything like that, they have to tell me immediately. And I would have informed the police. There's been nothing.'

'That sounds as if such a situation has arisen in the past?'

'Never,' the principal insisted. 'That's the tragedy: I thought we'd anticipated everything to prevent something like this happening.'

'Mary Beth would have known she should not have walked off, as she apparently did?' suggested Claudine, choosing her moment. She needed to decide how well Mary Beth could face the terror of being seized. Upon the child's behaviour – her strengths or weaknesses – depended the way she would be treated. Literally, perhaps, her survival.

'Before she became a pupil someone from the embassy visited the school. Talked to me about security. He told me Mary had strict instructions never to leave the premises unless her transport was waiting. That's our rule, too, with every child. I made sure Mary understood that when she arrived . . .' Briefly the woman's composure wavered, her lip trembling. 'I know and accept she should not have been released in the first place but having found there was no car waiting she should have immediately returned inside.'

'Why then do you think she didn't?' asked Claudine.

'I don't know.'

'Is she a disobedient child?'

The other woman hesitated. 'She's extremely self-confident.'

'Walking away as she did, knowing it was forbidden, indicates wilfulness, doesn't it?'

Madame Flahaur nodded reluctantly. 'She liked being the centre of attention.'

'To shock?'

'To be the centre of attention,' insisted the woman.

'Was she a loud child? Exuberant?'

The woman frowned. 'Loud? I don't understand.'

Claudine gestured through the window to the road

outside. 'It's a very busy street. It would have been crowded at the time she disappeared. If she was snatched – actually grabbed into a passing car – would she have tried to fight? Shouted? Or would she have been too terrified to resist?'

'I think she would have resisted.'

'So she's not a nervous child? Sometimes wilful disobedience hides nervousness.'

'No. She's definitely not nervous.'

'The photographs I have seen are facial portraits. Is she a well-developed girl?'

Madame Flahaur looked quickly at Blake. 'She is beginning to form.'

'Has she reached puberty yet?'

The woman flushed, very slightly. 'Is this important?'

'Everything I'm asking you is important, Madame Flahaur. The shock of what's happened to her could cause her to menstruate. If she isn't familiar with it, even if her mother or a teacher here has told her about it, it would add to whatever difficulties she's suffering. She'd most probably have to tell a man.'

'I'm sorry. Of course. No, she is not yet menstruating but it is something about which we instruct our pupils very thoroughly, to take away any fear when it happens.'

'Does she look her age?'

The principal considered the question. 'No, I don't think she does. She is developing, as I said, but only just. And she's quite a small child, below average height for her age.'

'Has she had any sex education?'

'It began this semester.'

'You know her, Madame Flahaur. And can answer my next question more objectively than perhaps her parents could. Would you say Mary Beth McBride was a well-balanced child?'

Again the woman hesitated before replying. 'Yes, I think I would.'

'There is no proof of it yet, but the Americans believe she has been kidnapped: is being held somewhere. If that is the case, how do you think she would respond? Behave?'

'It would be terrifying for any child.'

'I'm not asking about any child. I'm asking about Mary. But let's make it general, if you like. Considering the terror of being held by total strangers and not knowing what was going to happen to her, would Mary stand up to it better or worse than most children of her age?'

There was yet another pause for consideration. 'Better, I think.'

'Sport activities are part of the curriculum?'

'Yes.'

'Is she enthusiastic? Or doesn't she like it?'

'She's a very active participant in everything.'

'Competitive?'

Madame Flahaur looked steadily back at Claudine, understanding the point. 'Yes, she's competitive.'

'Someone who likes to win, in everything?'

'Yes. Mary Beth likes very much to win.'

'Well?' demanded Blake, as they walked out on to the rue du Canal.

'Good news and bad news,' analysed Claudine. 'She's a wilfully disobedient child who doesn't frighten easily. That's good, if she's being held. She'll be able to stand up to the trauma. The bad news is that if she confronts too hard, too forcefully, anyone holding her will probably hurt her.'

'Kill her?'

'It would make it more likely.'

'You're supposed to make the forecasts,' he reminded her.

'She'll try to do something,' predicted Claudine.

'There's something we haven't talked about yet,' Blake pointed out. 'What about her having been snatched for sex?'

'It's something we're overdue considering,' agreed Claudine. 'I think it's a far stronger possibility than a straight kidnap. Mary should have been taken home by a car waiting to collect her at the door. But it had a puncture. It was pure chance that she was walking up this road, which she shouldn't have been doing. No one snatching her could have known who she was until *after* they got her. This isn't a well-planned abduction of the daughter of a millionaire ambassador.'

'I'd say that makes it even more likely they'll kill her, if they haven't already,' said Blake.

'I'd say the same,' said Claudine.

James McBride was furious, red-faced, temple veins throbbing. Hillary, who insisted upon being part of every discussion about Mary in which her husband was involved, had actually leapt up from her seat, incensed.

'Just two?' demanded McBride.

'And the woman's never been involved in a kidnap before. She admitted it, openly,' confirmed Norris. He sat primly on the chair, facing the ambassador across the desk, but inwardly he felt very relaxed, very satisfied. Everything was going precisely as he wanted, at the speed he wanted. He'd cleared his decks: got everything in place.

'When I've finished kicking ass this fucking country – this fucking continent – is going to regret the day they didn't take this seriously!'

'Sir!' said Norris quickly. 'You made it quite clear in your first message to Washington how you wanted this handled. By the FBI. Which the Bureau and the President completely understood. That's where we are now.

I've made all the necessary gestures – at this morning's meeting I even allowed them to think they'd out-argued me into having the media release, but they're behind us now. Unimportant. I'm asking you, for the sake of Mary Beth, to let it be. Let's wait for the approach, which I'll personally deal with to get Mary Beth back. And we've got the perfect rejection when they complain about being kept out: they didn't behave professionally enough to be included.'

'I don't need a perfect rejection!' insisted Hillary.

'But I need a clear field in which to operate, which I've got at the moment,' said Norris. 'And that's exactly what I need to save your daughter.'

McBride was about to speak when the study door burst open. Paul Harding remained at the threshold, formality forgotten in his excitement. 'Come! Quickly!'

He ran and automatically McBride, Hillary and Norris ran after him, not knowing where they were going. Six additional computers had been installed to supplement the embassy's regular four in the emergency communications centre and they reached it in time to see every screen filled by the same message.

MARY, MARY
QUITE CONTRARY
WHERE DO THEY THINK YOU HIDE?
NOT IN SILVER BELLS OR COCKLE SHELLS
BE PATIENT, MR MCBRIDE.

Even as Norris yelled: 'Who's it from? What's the sender address?' the message flickered, just once, and disappeared from the screens.

The FBI man turned triumphantly to the ambassador. 'Mary's alive. And I was right. It's a kidnap. We're going to get her back, safe and well.'

*

79

As usual Mary was alerted by the sound of the key in the lock, but wasn't prepared for it to be the woman standing outside when the door swung open. There was a jump, in her stomach, but she didn't think anything showed on her face. She hoped not.

'Come on out!' said Félicité, hard-voiced, beckoning the child into the outer room.

Mary obeyed because to have held back might have indicated she was frightened: she didn't want the woman to think that because she wasn't. But she didn't want to get slapped again. Behind the woman was the man who always seemed to be there, not giggling now, and another man. The woman's face, thin and sharp and deeply tanned with brownish blond hair tightly pinned to her head, was uncovered. The two men were masked.

'Are you taking me back?'

Instead of answering Félicité raised her head, animal-like, and sniffed the air. 'Smelly child. Nasty, smelly child.'

There was nothing to say. Mary stood legs slightly apart, showing no uncertainty, looking back at the woman.

'If you won't wash yourself you'll have to be washed,' announced Félicité.

'I'll shower myself,' said Mary hurriedly. 'Then are you taking me home?'

'Your father knows that we've got you: that you're safe.'

'What did he say?'

'He hasn't been able to say anything yet.'

'I don't understand. Hasn't he given you any money?'

'Not yet. We haven't asked for any.'

'Isn't that what you want?'

Félicité laughed. 'We want lots of things.'

'Why's it taking so long?'

'Because I want it to.'

'I don't understand,' Mary repeated.

'You don't have to understand. You just have to do as you're told. I keep telling you that. You'll be punished if you don't listen.'

Unthinkingly Mary's tongue strayed to her healing lip. She stopped the gesture, hoping her mouth hadn't bulged to show the woman what she'd done. 'I'll shower myself,' she said again.

'And I'll watch to make sure you do it properly,' said Félicité. 'We all will.'

'I don't want you to.'

'Are you asking me to slap you again? Harder than I did before?'

It wasn't right for the men to see her with no clothes on. Not even dad saw her like that. She didn't want the woman to see, either. But she didn't want to be slapped. 'I'll do it by myself.'

Mary flinched back when Félicité started towards her, unable to stop herself, and backed towards the door the giggling man had pointed to the previous day. She moved abruptly, suddenly quick, trying to get inside and close the door behind her, but Félicité caught its edge and jerked it back open. She hit out with her other hand, catching the unsuspecting child fully in the chest, thrusting her further into the bathroom, which was much bigger than Mary had imagined. There was a bath, against one wall, and three glass-fronted shower stalls arranged along the far wall. There were three separate handbasins and a toilet open to the room, not enclosed by a cubicle, and two stools, side by side.

Mary stood in the middle of the bathroom, staring back at the open door. The woman was in the middle, with the two men close behind her. For the first time there was a snigger from the man who normally guarded her.

'Do you want me to undress you?'

81

'No.'

'Undress yourself then.'

Mary turned her back. She dropped her skirt and her shirt on the floor, as she usually did, and behind her Félicité said: 'Fold your things up, neatly!'

Mary stooped, doing what she was told. It wasn't going to be as bad as she'd thought. With her back to them all they'd see was her bottom, nothing else. That wasn't so bad, although she wished they weren't able to. She'd tell dad. He'd be very angry. Angrier than he got sometimes with mom when they were fighting. As she half ran to the shower stalls she heard them laughing behind her. She stood with her back to them inside the stall, aware they'd be able at least to see her outline through the glass door. There was shampoo as well as soap so she washed her hair, even though she hadn't seen a dryer outside. She could use a towel to get most of the wet out and leave it to dry by itself. She hadn't seen a towel, either! And when she got out of the shower she'd have to face them. She stopped soaping herself, arms limply to her sides as the water poured over her, not knowing what to do. She wanted to cry, tears burning into her eyes.

Why hadn't dad paid: shouted at them and told them to let her go and given them the money and got her back! Why? It wasn't fair. Would mom and dad be shouting at each other? This shouldn't be happening. It was rude. Nasty. They were nasty. Nasty rude people in scary masks. She wanted to make pee pee. She did, knowing they wouldn't be able to see what she was doing with the shower gushing over her. The woman would probably hit her, if she knew. But she didn't. It was good, doing something they didn't know about. Defying them. That's what she had to do, defy them but not let them know, so the woman didn't hit her any more. She didn't feel like crying now. But she still had to get out, so they'd see her. Maybe there would be a towel, just outside. That's where towels were, just outside a shower stall. She wished she could remember.

Determinedly Mary switched off the water, turning to the door: she could vaguely make out the grown-ups through the clouded glass. She hesitated, pushing her wet hair back off her face, and then reached out with her left hand to slide the door open. She put the other hand in front of her penny box. She kept it there as she stepped out, immediately bringing her left hand and arm up across herself, although it didn't cover everything.

The woman was standing in the middle of the bathroom, holding the towel out. 'Poor little bedraggled Mary. Come and get your towel!'

It meant uncovering herself to reach out but if she got the towel they wouldn't be able to see anything. She put out her left hand but at the last minute the woman snatched the towel away and unthinkingly Mary tried to grab with her other hand and they all laughed at her when she realized her penny box was uncovered and jerked her hand back to hide it.

Mary and Félicité were dancing awkwardly round the bathroom now, the woman always lifting the towel just out of Mary's reach. The woman said: 'Dance, Mary. Dance for us,' and the masked men laughed and one said: 'This is good.' Suddenly the woman flicked the towel to the left but lowered it, so that Mary had to twist to get it. As she did so the woman released it, making her stumble further, and then Mary felt herself grabbed from the side and bent over, as the woman slumped down on the bathroom stool to bring her across her lap, with her bottom exposed. And then the woman began to hit her, chanting with each slap. They were very hard, and stung.

'This is for being a naughty girl and not washing. And this is for trying to run up into the hall when you were allowed out yesterday. And this is for thinking you could trick the nice man who is looking after you into letting you go. And this is for thinking you can get away from us. And this is to show you what will happen if you try to do it again . . .' Félicité stopped, breathless. She brought her hand down hard, once more, and said: 'And that's for taking your brace out, although I like you much better without it.'

It hurt worse than when she was slapped in the face and the men were looking at her and still laughing but Mary didn't cry. She hoped the pee pee hadn't all washed away and the woman got some on her hand.

The message from Kurt Volker was waiting when Claudine and Blake returned to the Metropole.

'It's started, then!' said the German enthusiastically, when Claudine returned the call.

'What?'

There was a brief silence from the other end. 'Didn't you know? The people who've got the girl have made contact with the embassy.'

'No,' admitted Claudine. 'How did you find out?'

'I hacked into the embassy home pages as soon as you told me I was involved. It was the obvious thing to do, wasn't it?'

'Oh yes,' said Claudine, feeling a sweep of euphoria. 'That's how the approach was made, by computer?'

'Anonymous e-mail,' confirmed Volker. 'A kidnap first, as far as I'm aware. Isn't that fantastic?'

'Fantastic,' she agreed.

'You want me to come down?'

'Yes,' said Claudine. 'And transfer me to Sanglier. He needs to come, too.'

It was Marcel who had taught Félicité his own definition of hedonism, the pursuit of ultimate pleasure in all things, without bounds. And Félicité accepted she'd been an eager pupil. There'd been a sexual excitement – still was

– in working the stock markets of Europe, which he'd been so adept at plundering, rarely losing as she rarely lost. But most of all in laughing at other people's naivety, even those in their special sex group who imagined they were bound by a common bond, when all the time she and Marcel had laughed at their inadequacies, mocking them.

Laughing at everyone else, too. It was still amusing to serve on the charities, two of which Marcel had actually founded for tax reasons, and hearing herself described as a good person.

She had deeply and genuinely loved Marcel. She knew she could never love anyone else.

CHAPTER SEVEN

Henri Sanglier was furious. It was procedurally correct that he should publicly represent Europol at the ambassador's side the following day, but Blake should have consulted him first. There was nothing he could do: no protest or rebuke he could make. But by appearing at a press conference he would be identifying himself as a controlling Europol executive – *the* controlling Europol executive, shortly to ascend even greater heights – while knowingly involved in an act not just flagrantly illegal but of incalculable diplomatic implications if it ever became known.

He would also be appearing beside a US ambassador aware – but again helpless to protest – that the Americans despised both him and his organization. It was like being cuckolded, which in fact he had been for years by countless women in the marriage of convenience that had provided Françoise with a husband of legendary name and him with the adornment of one of France's most beautiful and legendary models. Who, by her outrageous lesbian promiscuity, was increasingly becoming a career risk.

And finally there was Claudine Carter. Sanglier found it difficult to believe how many mistakes he'd made about her, in his inability to believe that her appointment to Europol had been a coincidence. Yet that was surely all it could have been. Had she known the truth about his father's wartime exploits – the truth he himself only suspected – she would have given some indication by now. All he'd done in his determination to protect the family name and reputation was probably to make himself look ridiculous. He would be adding to that stupidity if he tried to make amends. And he would, anyway, soon be away from her and Europol: how much he wished he could free himself from Françoise too. He'd make a superb Justice Minister. All he had to do was avoid any scandal or embarrassment – like being involved in hacking into a US embassy computer system – until the conclusion of the final negotiations, now interrupted by having to be here in Brussels, instead of in Paris.

The value of visiting the Belgian police headquarters went far beyond accepting the offered working accommodation: André Poncellet's obvious ignorance of the computer contact confirmed the contempt with which the Americans were treating the Belgian police as well as Europol. The local police commissioner was effusively attentive, personally escorting them round the first-floor, five-roomed corner suite and then insisting upon dispensing drinks in his own lavish quarters to discuss the following day's public appearance and an intended meeting afterwards at the Justice Ministry.

It was, therefore, two hours after taking up their accommodation before Sanglier was finally alone with Claudine, Blake and Kurt Volker. Even then it took another thirty minutes for Volker to access his on-line computers at Europol to check for any further messages before closing that tracer down to log on to the embassy circuits from the newly provided Belgian machines.

By the time any worthwhile discussion was possible Sanglier had become tight with frustration, stumping aimlessly around their allocated space and for a lot of the time gazing unseeingly through the panoramic window in the direction of the EU's Palais d'Berlaymont building, trying to rearrange the mental disorder into some comfortable, logical sequence. He failed. He turned at the German's entry and said: 'Well?'

'Nothing,' said Volker.

'You sure you would have picked it up, had there been anything?' demanded Blake.

Volker's customary amiability briefly faded at the question. 'There are two obvious pathname words: Mary and McBride. Before I left Europol I created programs to record both, either separately or together, in any communication into or out of the embassy. There's been nothing. I've downloaded everything on to my system here now.'

Claudine sat back easily in her chair, for the moment content for Sanglier and Blake to go through the preliminaries, even able mildly to amuse herself at Blake's lingering surprise at meeting Kurt Volker for the first time. As always the German looked like a scarecrow that had been left out in the rain, the blond hair a disarrayed thatch over the owlishly bespectacled face, the shapeless suit crumpled and strained around an indulged figure unaccustomed to weighing scales or tape measures. Blake wasn't allowing any time-wasting reactions, but he was still regarding Volker like a rare species in a natural history museum.

'I want to understand how it was done,' persisted Sanglier.

'Simple,' said Volker patiently. 'And like most simple things, it's brilliant. Whoever's got Mary knows about computers and how to hack in and out of them. The embassy's e-mail address is available on the Internet through the US Information web site server. All they had to do was access it and send their message.'

'That doesn't help us,' protested Blake. 'Surely the sources of e-mail messages are recorded? So we must know where it came from.'

Volker nodded, his chubby cheeks wobbling. 'In the

majority of correspondence, yes. Otherwise the receiver wouldn't know who to reply to. But whoever sent the message didn't want a reply . . .' the man hesitated, looking apologetically at Claudine '. . . and they beat me. I didn't time it – I will the next one, obviously – but I calculate that the message was displayed for precisely sixty seconds, not long enough for me to get a print-out. But I do know there wasn't a respond address. It was the logical thing to look for. The embassy uses the UNIX Internet server. I went straight into it when the message closed down. There was no trace.'

Claudine said: 'So how did the sender remain anonymous?'

'I've introduced my own entry code as a bug to their main terminal,' said Volker. 'Only I know what it is so the Americans aren't aware I'm there: and there's no way they can discover me. I can go in and out whenever I want.' He gestured to the three newly installed blank screens glowing in the adjoining room. 'I'm permanently linked, waiting for the next communication using the names Mary or McBride.' He paused, frowning at the lack of comprehension from the two other men, then explained. 'I believe that's how whoever's holding Mary is operating, with a slight variation. They certainly won't be working from their own traceable terminal. They will have hacked into somebody else's system – that's their initial concealment, quite apart from avoiding any user costs – and installed their own entry code in what's usually referred to as a Trojan Horse. That's a program in which automatic commands can be stored. In this case I'm guessing they didn't want their Trojan Horse to be permanent, as I want mine to be. I imagine they'll have added to their bug a program that self-destructs to a certain trigger: a timed suicide, in fact. I believe they got into somebody's system, like a cuckoo in the nest, and sent their message, and after sixty seconds the Trojan

Horse destroyed itself instead of the host system, which is the normal way such viruses work.'

Claudine said: 'They wanted McBride to know they've got his daughter but didn't give the man any way of responding. That doesn't fit a usual kidnap pattern.'

'What are they doing then?' demanded Sanglier, needing to catch up. At the same time, like a mantra in his head, he was thinking: What am I doing, sitting here, calmly discussing breaking the law, condoning it, agreeing to it, learning how it's done?

'Amusing themselves, taunting McBride,' said Claudine. She looked briefly at Blake. 'And it fits how Mary was grabbed in the first place. I think she's being held by paedophiles.'

'What!' demanded Sanglier, incredulous, just ahead of Blake, who said: 'How the hell do you reach that conclusion?'

Speaking more to the detective than the commissioner, Claudine said: 'We've already decided it didn't start as a planned abduction. She was snatched by chance, a child looking younger than her age. The message is derived from a child's nursery rhyme: that's paedophile thinking, maybe more subconscious than a positive choice. It's a taunt—'

'Aren't you literally reading a lot from very little?' broke in Blake.

'That's what I'm supposed to do,' Claudine said, unoffended. 'And I haven't finished. There are variations of Mary, Mary Quite Contrary recited in continental Europe but it's really an English nursery song . . .' She paused again, looking at Volker. 'And the message sent to the embassy was in English?'

'Yes,' he confirmed.

'And although it's a pretty rotten poem the English was good,' continued Claudine. 'One or more of the people holding the child could be English by birth, although I doubt it. I think it's more likely that they were educated at an expensive private school where English was well taught as a second language: it might be, even, that the person who wrote the message had an English governess or nanny.'

'So they'll be rich?' suggested Blake, prepared for the moment to go along with Claudine's reasoning.

'Possibly,' she agreed. 'Or were, once.'

'How does that square with the computer use?' demanded Blake. He looked at Volker. 'The contact method might seem simple to you but it's not to me. To me it's complicated and technically obscure. Only someone who uses computers all the time would have that level of expertise. How many rich people need to reach that level of computer literacy?'

'Mary is being held by more than one person,' said Claudine. 'Paedophiles usually hunt in packs and take their pleasure in packs. It doesn't follow that the person who wrote the message was the one who physically sent it.'

Blake switched his attention fully to the German. 'Now you think you know how they're going to communicate, will it be possible to trace a source before the thing self-destructs next time?'

'Maybe,' said Volker cautiously. 'I'm ready to go into UNIX the moment another message appears. But don't forget it literally is the World Wide Web. The next message could originate from somewhere in Belgium – right next door to this building if you like – and ride piggy-back through two or more totally unsuspecting host systems in two or more countries anywhere around the globe before appearing on the embassy screens back here.'

Momentarily there was complete silence as the awareness settled in the room. Blake said: 'Are you saying we can't stop them? Or find them?'

Volker said: 'It's not going to be easy. They can come from anywhere and close down before we've alerted any local police force. And I really mean *anywhere* in the world.'

'But at some time there'll have to be proper contact if they want a physical hand-over of a ransom,' said Blake.

'*If* they make it a proper kidnap,' Claudine pointed out. 'The messages might just be an additional amusement that they'll tire of . . .' She hesitated. 'And even if they do try to get money they'll still use Mary in the way they originally snatched her for.'

Volker, who doted on his five children, said: 'Are you absolutely sure she was originally taken for sex?'

'That's my professional opinion,' said Claudine bluntly.

The German shuddered, very slightly. 'Would they let her go, afterwards? Exchange her for a ransom, I mean?'

'There are too many variables for me to give a definite opinion,' Claudine replied. 'The most difficult to assess is the Americans and their negotiator, Norris. We're not on the inside by invitation, remember.'

'No. We're inside illegally,' protested Sanglier. 'We can't officially do anything about what we know. We can't even tell the Belgian police, with whom we're supposed to be working. Can you imagine how it could affect us: affect Europol?'

Looking directly at the Frenchman, Claudine said pointedly: 'I can certainly imagine how it could affect a ten-year-old child.'

Sanglier flushed. 'Don't misunderstand me.'

No one spoke because no one had to.

Hurriedly, Sanglier said: 'There can't be any question of the Americans' keeping us out?'

Claudine hesitated momentarily, undecided if it was the right time to introduce her concern. Then she said: 'Whether they do or not, it's my professional judgement that John Norris is incapable of conducting a proper negotiation even if the opportunity arises.'

'What are you talking about?' said Sanglier, knowing how the other three had interpreted his concern at legality and hot with self-anger because of it.

In clinical detail – itemizing her indicators against Norris's attitude and remarks – Claudine recounted that morning's meeting with the FBI negotiator. 'People like Norris, on the verge of losing personal control, invariably overcompensate by imposing as much external command as possible on those over whom they believe they have authority,' she concluded. 'The operational danger is in their thinking they have authority over those with whom they're negotiating. That's the road to disaster for a victim caught between opposing sides each believing they can manipulate the other: quite literally it's the rock and a hard place syndrome.'

Sanglier, who hated betraying any weakness, felt totally helpless at his inability to think of anything. The other three were actually looking at him expectantly! 'I think I should meet the ambassador before the conference.' It sounded positive, but only just.

'McBride will be guided entirely by Norris,' Claudine warned him.

Sanglier said: 'And I can use your opinion as a counter-argument. You're clearly right about a planned kidnap's being the wrong assumption from which to begin the investigation. If I can make McBride see that – realize Norris's fallibility – his attitude might change.'

'I'm sure I'll get any more e-mail correspondence,' said Volker. 'If there's something as positive as a sug-gested meeting are we going to hold back from acting upon it?'

Claudine saved Sanglier from having to admit that he didn't know. She said: 'Nothing is going to be as positive as an arranged meeting. We're watching a game that's only just begun.'

The relief was incomplete and short-lived and ended in bitter ill temper. The combined, disbelieving fury of James and Hillary McBride was the greatest and most easily understandable. When the amateur poem had faded from the computer screens, Hillary had swept in to join the inquest in her husband's study, shouting for answers that no one had.

'What the fuck's going on? I hear from someone who's got my daughter but doesn't tell me how to get back to him!' McBride said.

'It doesn't make any sense!' Hillary added. 'How can we pay without knowing who or how or when or where?'

'I don't know,' admitted Norris uncomfortably.

'You!' demanded the ambassador, jerking a wavering finger at the computer programmer in Norris's team. 'What the hell happened? Why wasn't there an address to get back to?'

'It's not always automatic,' said Howard Williams. He was a thin-haired, facially twitched young man whose elbow-scaled psoriasis was on fire from the nerve-racked tension of being in charge of a communications team that appeared to have failed its first test. Williams was an excellent technician who could dismantle and reassemble any known make of computer, but a virginal stranger to the shadowed side roads of cyberspace along which Kurt Volker prowled with the sure-footedness of an alley cat.

'You didn't even record the fucking message!'

'It closed down before there was time,' said Williams miserably. 'We didn't expect it to come like it did.'

'Then why the hell were four supposed computer experts included in the Task Force? You told us you'd set up a foolproof system!' Hillary directed the question to Norris, not the dejected specialist.

Norris, who never allowed himself a single mistake, inwardly squirmed at having to accept the ultimate responsibility. 'Telephone links go down all the time,' he tried, desperately.

'Is this what happened here, something stupid like a bad connection?' McBride asked Williams, who shuffled uncomfortably, refusing to meet the ambassador's bulging-eyed stare.

'I don't think it was an actual line collapse, sir. I think it was intentionally wiped at source.'

McBride went back to the FBI commander, purple-faced but speaking once more with ominous quietness. 'Mr Norris, we were connected to the bastards who've got my little girl. And they got away. You want to explain that to me in a way I'll understand so that I won't think you and your team are a bunch of losing, fucking incompetents? Because that's what I'd like you to do, starting now!'

There was a sweep of mind-blanking dizziness and Norris thought he might have stumbled – fallen even – if he hadn't fortunately been sitting in one of the few chairs fronting the ambassador's football-pitch desk.

Although he despised his superior – thought him a total, off-the-wall jerk – Paul Harding momentarily felt sorry for the man. Lance Rampling was trying mentally to compose the message to Langley that would convey the full extent of the FBI fuck-up without letting the intercepting Bureau realize every error, no matter how small, would go into the CIA's infighting armoury, to be broken out and fired at the first skirmish of a political battle between the two agencies.

'I'm waiting,' threatened McBride.

'It wasn't a demand,' Norris said desperately. 'It was to tell us they've got Mary. For us to be ready. They're softening us up: proving they've got all the winning cards.' The last part, admitting that he wasn't orchestrating everything, hurt almost with a physical pain. Whoever had the child would pay, for making him do that. He'd teach them who was the boss, the moment they began proper negotiations. And then really teach them, once Mary was safely recovered. They'd know what it was like to be hunted by the time he'd finished with them.

'You saying we've got to wait until they feel like getting back to us?' asked Hillary.

Norris fervently sought an alternative but couldn't think of one. 'It's a negotiating ploy.'

'I don't give a shit what it is,' said McBride. 'I'm not waiting. We *are* ready. The money's here. I want to get back to them. How are we going to do that?'

Norris felt a sink of helplessness, unthinkingly half turning towards Williams. Anxiously the technician blurted: 'We could log a message on the browsers.'

'What the hell's that?' said McBride sharply.

'A browser is like a subject directory or index, in a classified telephone book. People surf the Net through browsers, searching for information logged there. We're doing the press release tonight so there's no need for secrecy any more. Why don't we make an entry – it's called starting a thread – naming Mary through News-cape and Microsoft Explorer? It would be inviting them to come back to us.'

It sounded good, some positive action, conceded Norris. Eager to contribute – and to illustrate his psychological ability – he said: 'To let them know it's aimed at them and that we want to deal, our response should be along the lines of their message to us.'

'Whatever it takes,' insisted McBride. 'Get it done! Get Mary back.'

They were very late returning from Antwerp – they hadn't driven down until after Jean Smet had left his office – but he still invited Félicité Galan into his house off the rue de Flandres to watch his latest movie from Amsterdam. Afterwards Félicité said: 'One of the boys was at least sixteen. And a professional.'

'It was still good,' defended Smet. 'The others will like it.'

'I wonder what Mary will think of it.'

'You said she wasn't going to be touched,' said Smet.

'I said no one else was to touch her. And it was only a little slap on her ass.'

'It was a hiding. You hit her too hard.'

She knew the man was right. 'A necessary lesson. She'll do as she's told in future, so I won't have to do it again.'

'Dehane did very well with the message, didn't he?'

'I knew it was technically possible. And I told you it would be completely undetectable.'

'I still don't like it,' said the man weakly.

'Why hasn't the Justice Ministry created a supervisory committee the way they did when the boy died?' she asked, ignoring the man's protest.

Smet smiled. 'It was proposed before I left the ministry this afternoon.'

'And?' asked Félicité, smiling too.

'I'm responsible for establishing it, just like before. And I head the legal advisory team that will sit with it.'

Félicité's expression broadened in satisfaction. 'So everything will be as foolproof as last time.'

'The Americans have brought in a huge team of people, apparently. And Europol's involved.'

'We anticipated it would be more high-powered than before,' Félicité said dismissively.

'Would you have done it? Broken up the group if we hadn't agreed about Mary?' asked the ministry lawyer, no longer smiling.

'I want things my way,' said the thin-faced woman. 'I get tired of telling you that.'

*

The military aircraft repatriating Harry Becker and his family was delayed for two hours that night to enable the even more distressed Howard Williams to travel back to Washington on Norris's personal authority.

From the US embassy Norris sent a 'Respond This Day' reminder to Washington for the requested in-depth reinvestigation into McBride's business affairs. That request as well as the browser message to the unknown holders of Mary Beth McBride, were both instantly picked up by Kurt Volker's ever attentive Trojan Horse.

CHAPTER EIGHT

The Americans' Internet message read WHERE IS MARY, MARY QUITE CONTRARY? and was signed off with the embassy's e-mail address.

It appeared a light-hearted, joking invitation except to those aware of the desperation of the plea. Claudine acknowledged the need for the nursery rhyme connotation but at the 1 a.m. conference for which she, Blake and Sanglier had to be awakened Volker, alerted by his computer-linked pager, warned the result would be chaotic on a never sleeping World Wide Web as user-crowded as Oxford Street or Fifth Avenue on Christmas Eve.

Volker had been proved right by 8 a.m. when they assembled again in Sanglier's Metropole suite to discuss their pre-conference encounter with the ambassador. By then there were two hundred and twenty responses – with more arriving on average every five minutes – the majority mostly eager to participate in an imagined Internet mystery game predicated on children's doggerel. Five were analysed – correctly as it subsequently turned out – by Claudine to be disguised paedophile approaches, although she decided none came from Mary's captors, which also proved correct. Not one reply emanated from Brussels: the only Belgian response, from Charleroi, proved to be from a wheelchair-bound crippled twelve-year-old boy only able freely to wander the world from his bedroom computer.

To Blake's unasked question at the breakfast strategy

meeting Sanglier announced at once: 'All right. They're excluding us and now we've got proof we can confront them with. They've identified themselves with their e-mail address. So how do we do it?' He was inwardly ecstatic at his escape from the problem of illegally entering the embassy system.

'Hard,' declared Claudine at once, knowing the question was directed at her. 'We've got to establish our control officially.'

'You really serious about Norris?' asked Blake.

'Absolutely.'

'What do we do about him?' said Sanglier, as Volker moved the coffee pot around the breakfast table.

'The same. He's guiding everyone at the moment. We've got to show he's wrong.'

'Then it's got to be you, psychologist against psychologist,' insisted Sanglier. He was supremely confident, knowing he couldn't lose the forthcoming encounter. He hoped the woman realized his acceptance of her ability. Not an attempt at amends, he reminded himself: the proper establishment of a proper team arrangement. After personally challenging the ambassador he'd insist Europol officially protest direct to Washington, too. A disaster – which was the most likely outcome if the woman's assessment was even half correct – could now be proved the result of unwarranted, technically illegal American interference, while a successful recovery could be manipulated into a brilliant example of Europol police work, personally headed by Commissioner Henri Sanglier. Either way, any condoned illegality on Kurt Volker's part would be smothered.

Henri Sanglier was an extremely contented man.

James McBride clearly wasn't. The American ambassador made the pretence of politeness when they entered his study, his attitude a mixture of his usual aggression

100

tempered by a growing acceptance of defeat. His eyes were red-rimmed and bagged and he coughed frequently, to clear a throat that didn't need clearing. Hillary McBride appeared far more controlled than her husband. She was smoking unusually long cigarettes. John Norris sat looking out into the room on the left of the desk, with Paul Harding and Lance Rampling alongside. Elliot Smith, the young legal adviser, was beside Burt Harrison, the chief of mission, to the ambassador's right.

'I want to say at once how much I appreciate the involvement of Europol. And your coming personally,' said McBride, anxious to get the diplomatic niceties out of the way and conclude the meeting as soon as possible to get back to where Norris's team were assessing the incoming Internet messages. 'I hope, Commissioner, that when you and I appear publicly, later, we'll be able to build upon what's in this morning's papers.' The over-night press release dominated the front page of every newspaper, with the issued photograph of Mary Beth McBride. 'I'm afraid—'

'Mr Ambassador,' Sanglier said quickly, discerning the imminent dismissal. 'I think there is something extremely important for us to discuss before talking about today's press conference.'

Immediate hope overrode McBride's irritation at being interrupted, but before he could speak Hillary blurted: 'You've found her!'

'No,' said Sanglier bluntly. Addressing Norris more than the parents, he went on: 'And our chances of doing so are seriously endangered by the interference of your own law enforcement agencies, acting without any juris-diction. I'm giving you notice, as the senior Europol representative in charge of this investigation, that as well as my protest here this morning there will be an official Europol complaint to both your State Department and the Federal Bureau of Investigation, in Washington.'

Claudine was astonished. This was a Sanglier she'd never seen before, although the persona fitted her impression of a man with a deeply rooted but well-concealed inferiority complex. She'd never intended Sanglier to be as direct, or indeed as undiplomatic. Totally confident of their strength, Sanglier was emerging a bully. And was, she decided, actually enjoying it, in fact, dropping all his pretension and for once actually being himself. It was oddly like curing a patient whose mental illness prevented his being the person he actually was, only in reverse.

McBride was also visibly astonished. He flushed and said: 'I think, sir, that you need to remember who I am as well as giving me an explanation.'

The legal attaché leaned sideways, whispering to Harrison. Claudine wondered if Blake was as surprised as she was.

'I think we should both give each other explanations,' said Sanglier. 'Before Europol was given its operational convention it was a computerized centre collating criminal intelligence between member countries. As such its operators learned the Internet was extensively used by pornographers—'

'Pornographers!' exclaimed Hillary, her composure going. The two FBI men exchanged looks. Norris shook his head.

'Dr Carter will explain that,' Sanglier said. 'Hear me out. As part of our investigation – an investigation we believed your government, your Central Intelligence Agency and your Federal Bureau of Investigation fully accepted to be under Europol's operational jurisdiction – our experts accessed various Internet web sites . . .'

Claudine was intently watching the interaction among the Americans facing her. McBride's face was beginning to burn. Hillary was expressionless but looking fixedly at Norris. The chief of mission, a professional diplomat, remained impassive, too, despite the legal attaché's frantic whispering. Norris was blinking rapidly and as she looked the man straightened in his chair and pulled his tightly buttoned jacket down, as if wanting to remove some creases. Harding was staring down at the floor and Rampling was suddenly engrossed in a manicure problem affecting his left hand. A gamut of guilt, Claudine thought.

'Late last night we read what appears to be a message sent generally through a large number of browsers, from the e-mail address of this embassy,' Sanglier bulldozed on. 'It obviously referred to your missing daughter. There'd been no prior consultation with any of my officers about that, which contravenes our understanding. It was also curiously worded, almost in code, suggesting some earlier correspondence of which my officers were also unaware . . .' He paused again, as if inviting an interruption, before finishing: 'That's my explanation, ambassador. I'd welcome hearing yours.'

Claudine calculated that Sanglier, the high priest of diplomatic correctness, was on the very edge of going too far. It was unlikely, with the fate of his daughter involved, but if McBride became offended enough to order them from the embassy the situation they were trying to correct would, in fact, become even more difficult.

But McBride wasn't sufficiently offended. He said, lamely: 'I'm trying to get my daughter back.'

Seemingly anxious to curb Sanglier, Blake said: 'And this isn't the way to do it. This is the way to lose her, permanently.'

'Say something!' Hillary demanded of Norris.

'They're wrong,' he replied dogmatically. 'I've promised I'll get your daughter back and I will.'

The first person delivery again, Claudine thought. She *was* right about the man. And he was inviting his own confrontation.

103

'For Christ's sake, let's sort this out!' implored McBride. 'A child – my child – is at stake here!'

'Dr Carter?' Sanglier said.

Claudine's concentration was absolute upon John Norris. The only controlling authority to which the man would defer would be McBride here in Brussels or recognizably titled officials in Washington. She had to face the man down now, in front of the ambassador. It would destroy any possibility of a proper working relationship between them but the alternative was the destruction of Mary Beth McBride. And Claudine was unafraid – eager even – to make one enemy she didn't doubt she could defeat to get to the far more threatening adversary she didn't, at the moment, know how to challenge.

Norris was equally intent upon Claudine, isolating her as his opponent. He was smiling faintly. Claudine attacked. 'The puncture was entirely accidental?'

'There are still some tests to be carried out.' Norris settled back comfortably, considering the encounter a further establishment of his position.

Claudine saw Harding's eyes flicker sideways, towards his superior. Rampling was frowning at the man, too. 'At this moment is there any evidence to suggest that the puncture was anything but accidental?'

'I'm awaiting the results of the test.'

It wasn't going to be difficult, thought Claudine. 'Could the misunderstanding at the school have been anticipated?'

'No. It should not have happened. The culprit has already been disciplined.'

'Mary should not have been permitted to leave the school?'

'No.'

'Nor should she have walked off, alone? She should have returned to the building?'

There was a vague wariness. 'Yes.'

'Could it have been anticipated that she wouldn't?'

Beside the FBI chief Harding was looking down hard at the floor again. McBride and his wife were moving their heads back and forth with each question and answer.

Norris said: 'No.'

Claudine prolonged the silence until McBride shifted impatiently. She said: 'You've just admitted totally mis-understanding the crime we are investigating. And by your refusal to listen to anyone's voice or opinion other than your own you're putting yourself – your reputation – before saving a child . . .'

There was an audible intake of breath from the legal attaché. McBride swivelled to the FBI man but before the ambassador could speak Norris shook his head, the smile broadening, and said: 'This is quite ridiculous. We're wasting time here, sir—'

'How could Mary have been targeted as a kidnap victim without its being known in advance that the car would have a puncture, the school would misunderstand a telephone message and she'd walk off up the rue du Canal when there was no one waiting to collect her?' demanded Claudine.

The room was frozen by silence. She had little right to condemn Sanglier for bullying, Claudine accepted. But there was a very important difference. She was knowingly doing it to achieve an essential end result.

'I really don't think this should—' Norris started, but McBride stretched sideways, stopping the man with a warding-off gesture. He leaned forward over his desk towards Claudine and said: 'You've got an audience, doctor. I'm going to listen to everything you say but by Christ you'd better be right.'

Claudine's attention hadn't wavered from Norris. His mouth was moving, the words barely held back, and she

105

decided that in his outrage the man was only just acknowledging the ambassador's authority. Remembering their supposed ignorance of the incoming Mary, Mary message Claudine demanded: 'Tell me what their approach was.'

For a moment the FBI chief remained motionless, until McBride made another gesture, a beckoning motion this time. Norris reached into the file propped against his chair, extracting a single sheet of paper.

'Read it to us,' Claudine insisted, forcing the imperious tone. It was a thin tightrope, trying to impose her will upon Norris at the same time as impressing the ambassador and his wife with her assessment to convince them that she should conduct any negotiation.

Norris did, his voice cracking in impotent fury.

'That an original print-out?' persisted Claudine, following the courtroom cross-examination principle of never asking a question to which the answer wasn't known.

'A copy. The screen cleared before we had time to get a print-out.'

'Analyse it for us,' insisted Claudine remorselessly. This was appalling, she knew. She didn't have the slightest doubt that Norris was suffering the clinical mental impairment she'd earlier suspected. And by doing everything she could – as relentlessly as she could – to expose the professional inadequacy she was actually treating the man in a way diametrically opposed to the path she should have taken. Know thyself, she thought. Was her behaviour justified by the excuse of trying to rescue a child in every sort of physical and mortal danger? Or was it worse even than bullying? Wasn't she guilty of her own impairment, the need always to show that Claudine Carter was the best and prepared to trample any opposition underfoot to prove it? More than that, even? Wasn't she really performing, after all, to impress Peter Blake?

'It's the initial contact from people who have kidnapped Mary Beth McBride,' said Norris formally, his confidence recovering.

'From whom?' she jabbed, refusing to let go.

Norris hesitated. 'The people who've got her.' Doggedly: 'Her kidnappers.'

'Tell us about them.'

Norris looked uncertain. 'More than one. It would have had to be a car, to grab her off the street. At least one to drive, the other to subdue her when she realized what had happened. Enough money to own or gain access to a vehicle. Computer literate, with access to a modem. Money again—'

'I meant from the message,' Claudine interrupted. 'That's police reasoning, not psychological profiling. Tell me what you learn from the message itself. What it tells you about Mary, too.'

Norris broke his direct gaze, looking down to the paper as if he expected more than the message to be there. He became aware of McBride's attention and briefly looked back before saying: 'Beginning of a familiar kidnap pattern: abductors knowing they are in charge. The absence of any initial demand or how to respond is to impose pressure . . .'

Poor bastard, Claudine thought. Poor mentally confused, mentally blocked bastard. 'You're not properly interpreting a single indicator. Mary was abducted by chance, not design. The only intention of those who're holding her was to get a child. They're paedophiles.'

'Oh dear God, no,' moaned Hillary softly. 'Not that.' Her composure left her completely, her face crumpling.

'I don't think using a child's nursery rhyme was necessarily intended to identify their sexual predilection, although in my opinion it does,' Claudine pressed on,

107

her sympathy switching to parents who from the beginning would have feared what she'd just openly declared. 'But the choice of that particular rhyme was most definitely intentional, far beyond the coincidence of the name. Mary's disobedient – a contrary child. She might have got willingly into a car but she's resisted – defied them – since.'

'Is she alive?' demanded Hillary. 'What will they have done to her?'

Claudine didn't want to create any false hope – it was difficult at that moment to imagine any other sort – but she believed there was a fragile straw at which the couple could clutch. 'She has to be alive for them to know how contrary she is, doesn't she?'

'What about . . .?' groped McBride, unable to say the words. 'Would they have . . .?'

'I don't know,' admitted Claudine. 'The message does mean they've turned it into an abduction. As long as it remains that, there's a possibility she'll be safe . . . safe in every way.' It wasn't the absolute truth but it wasn't an absolute lie, either. But there was no purpose in reducing to total despair people who had already lost their child, perhaps for ever. Destroying one man, as she feared she was destroying John Norris, was more than enough. The thin American had brought his head up to look at her again, his face fixed. Several times, as she talked, Harding and Rampling had nodded, as if in acceptance. So had the legal attaché. She assessed Burt Harrison's face-twisted frown to be both an acknowledgement of her judgement and disgust at what it meant. The ambassador was as crumpled as his wife, his whole body seeming to wither, a man – a father – brought face to face with the most unthinkable horror.

Desperately McBride said: 'You could be wrong! You could be the one misunderstanding!'

'It's my job not to be,' replied Claudine. 'And I don't think I am.'

'We've got a kidnap situation, which has always been my opinion,' persisted Norris. His voice was still cracked.

'There are young sexual deviants – juveniles even – but the people holding Mary are adult,' predicted Claudine, ignoring the other profiler. 'There's an intellectualism – almost a sophistication – in their message that young people wouldn't have. And there *is* access to money, going beyond the obvious of a car's being involved. There's access to a house or somewhere where Mary can be held prisoner, without fear of discovery. And there's a high degree of computer literacy . . .' She hesitated, her throat jagged, the strain of what had become a virtual lecture beginning to pull at her. 'The one message that's been received isn't an initial kidnap approach. It's a challenge. How we balance that challenge – and I really do mean balance – entirely determines our chances of saving Mary.'

Claudine paused again, looking at Norris. She'd had to be brutal, she convinced herself. It was nothing personal: certainly nothing done to impress anyone. And definitely not Peter Blake. From the ambassador's very obvious anguish Claudine was sure, quite apart from whatever censure might officially come from Washington, that it was time to attempt whatever flimsy bridge was possible with Norris. She said: 'That's why there can only be one finely focused negotiating stance. And one set of negotiators. Work independently and you'll never get Mary back intact.' She began looking among the Americans arrayed before her but abruptly stopped: that *was* performing! Uncomfortable with the realization, but sticking with her point, Claudine said: 'Your decision, ambassador. I believe you've only got one, which is the one we're asking you to make. Do you want to get Mary back, alive at least, horrifying as the implications of that question are? Or do you want your law enforcement agencies to go on working independently?' She allowed a gap. 'Our way, there's a chance. Your way there isn't.'

There was, momentarily, another chilled silence. Then Norris began to speak, but once again McBride quietened the man with an impatient gesture. It was Hillary who said: 'For God's sake, shut up!'

McBride said: 'There's been a bad misunderstanding. For which I apologize. Now it's been corrected: nothing will again be attempted independently. You have my word. But I want yours. Can you get our daughter back, alive at least?'

'Yes,' blurted Norris at once.

'I don't know,' admitted Claudine.

'I want you to lead the negotiations,' McBride told Claudine. He turned to the FBI man beside him. 'Do you understand?'

Norris was unable to reply for several moments. 'Yes,' he managed at last.

As Claudine had anticipated, the press conference was frenetic. She had also anticipated, correctly, that by the time it began the e-mail appeal would have been discovered by the already alerted media, and advised McBride and Sanglier to respond to every question in the apparent belief that Mary's disappearance was a ransom-motivated kidnap, with no sexual implication. There was fractionally more time for her to prepare them than André Poncellet, who ascended the light-whitened platform more relieved than confused by her urging, which he accepted without argument, that he should let the other two men take the majority of the questions, restricting himself to agreeing with whatever undertaking they gave.

He wanted to hear from those who held his daughter, declared a choke-voiced McBride, his wife rigid-faced beside him. He was prepared to negotiate. He pleaded for Mary not to be harmed in any way. Towards the end he cried, openly and unashamedly, accepting Hillary's offered hand. Claudine was delighted because the helplessness was so genuine and conveyed exactly the impression she wanted: that whoever held Mary was in total control, able at a finger snap – or rather a keyboard tap – to manipulate not just the nations of the European Union but America as well.

John Norris understood everything. He'd underestimated the woman, who was activated entirely by jealousy – envy of his reputation and ability – and had managed to mislead everybody. Only a temporary setback: a mistake of stupid people traumatized by the loss of a daughter. Have to put it right, of course. He had a child to save. The woman could even be part of it. The idea settled in his mind. That was brilliant, her being part of it. Deceiving everyone. Everyone except him. Because he was cleverer than any of them. Cleverer than her, certainly. This could be his best case, proving that she was involved. Wouldn't be easy. Have to put a squad on her; strip her down to the bone. That was the way. Always was. Discover their secrets. Everyone broke down, confessed, when they were confronted with their secrets. Play it cleverly, though. Don't let her know that he knew. Go along with everything while he had her checked out: got to the secrets. Then save Mary. He'd get her back. He knew all about kidnapping. Knew the way their minds worked. Knew the way everybody's mind worked. That's what he was. A mind-reader. Don't worry, Mary. I'm coming. I'll save you. No one else but me.

Norris sensed Claudine's attention, switching from the closed circuit television upon which they'd watched the conference.

'I thought that went very well, didn't you?' she said, attempting some rapport.

'Let's see what the next message is.'

Claudine turned to face him. 'Let's talk about what we're going to do,' she said urgently. 'Talk to me about how you're thinking: what you're thinking. We both know she'll die if we don't. Let's try to save her, together.'

'You're right,' said Norris. 'We've got to save her together.' If he told her what he was thinking she'd know and then she could tell the others who had Mary. She might be able to fool everybody else but she couldn't fool him.

The Justice Minister himself, Miet Ulieff, greeted the delegation. By unspoken agreement it was Peter Blake, not the weary Claudine, who for the benefit of the ten assembled Belgian officials repeated what they believed to have happened to Mary Beth McBride. He said nothing about the FBI dispute, which had also been kept from André Poncellet. The impression was that everything had come from the closest liaison between Europol and the Americans.

'I want to be kept in the closest touch with every aspect of this investigation,' announced Ulieff when Blake finished. 'I'm therefore appointing a member of my legal staff to work permanently alongside Commissioner Poncellet until this poor child is recovered.' He turned, gesturing a man forward. 'Allow me to introduce Jean Smet.'

Thanks to the communication system he had introduced John Norris was able to read the messages the ambassador sent to both the State Department and Bureau headquarters, and from the cables that came in personally directed to him later that day he realized the Europol commissioner hadn't been bluffing about making a direct complaint to Washington, either. He responded, as was required, with the assurance of total future cooperation with Europol, but with the reminder that by initially

112

working independently he had been following not just his instructions before leaving Washington but the ambassador's clearly expressed wishes, too.

It was late in the day when he detached Duncan McCulloch and Robert Ritchie, two of his best men, from the squad now sifting the responses to their Internet message and briefed them in detail on the investigation of Claudine Carter.

'Keep it tight,' he ordered. 'Report back to me, no one else. This case is being allowed to go wrong. We've got to get it back on track.'

CHAPTER NINE

Mary cried, finally. Although not for herself. For her mother and father: for her father mostly. Mom had just sat there, saying nothing, her face not moving, like when they played statues at school with the person who moved first losing the game. Dad had looked so helpless, weeping as he had, not being able to talk properly when he'd asked whoever was holding her to tell him what they wanted so that he could do it and she could go home. She'd never known him like that. Not crying. Not knowing what to do. That wasn't like dad. Grown-up men didn't cry. Not dad, anyway. He always knew what to do. That's why he was an ambassador, an important person. She didn't like it, dad not knowing what to do. It wasn't right. Made her feel funny, unsure of what was going to happen to her. She did know, of course. Dad would get her out: get her home. With lots of things to tell everyone at school.

It was the woman who made dad cry. Her and the stupid men in their stupid masks. But the woman's fault most of all. They all did what she told them to do. So she hated the woman, for making dad cry. Couldn't let her know, though. She might hit her again. Her bottom still hurt from the slapping in the bathroom. She hated the woman for slapping her, too. She ran her teeth over her brace, particularly the sharp bits. She wouldn't take it out again. Not because the woman had slapped her for doing so: because she'd said she'd liked her without it.

She wouldn't do anything the woman liked, anything to please her.

Mary realized she didn't have a handkerchief. She scrubbed her eyes and her nose with her fingers and tried to dry them on her skirt, only just preventing herself from jumping when the woman shouted.

'Don't be dirty! Get a tissue from the bathroom!' Félicité was glad she'd come out to the house by the river to let the child watch the televised conference. It made her feel good, being able to reduce the man to tears. She hadn't expected that. It was a bonus. Power. Much better than the satisfaction she got from making her group do what she wanted. Pity the wife hadn't cried, too. That would have been wonderful, making them both dance when she pulled their strings. One was enough, though: enough for now.

She hoped Jean wouldn't be too much longer. She wanted to hear what happened at the Justice Ministry. The rush hour in Antwerp might delay him. He'd sounded frightened on the telephone, but it only needed the smallest thing he didn't expect to frighten Jean Smet.

Mary came back into the huge room with her face and nose dry, but uncertain what to do. Dad and mom weren't on television any more, but there was a group of men talking about how kidnap victims were freed, and the strange giggling man who had felt her bottom had joined the woman to watch. The French being spoken on screen was very fast and Mary had difficulty following it. She thought she heard something about Belgium's having a bad record for child crime – she wasn't sure what *rapports sexuels* actually meant but it sounded like what they'd been told about in biology at school, how babies were made – and a succession of children's photographs suddenly appeared on the screen.

'Can you understand what they're saying?' demanded Félicité. By telephoning the school – another pleasure, speaking to the establishment whose pupil was hers now, to do with what she chose – pretending to be the parent of a potential student, she'd discovered the curriculum languages were German and English in addition to French.

'I'm not very good. Something about children being taken away from their parents.'

To Mehre, in English, Félicité said: 'The men on the television were talking about children getting punished if they're bad, weren't they?'

Mehre sniggered so hard it sounded like a cough. He said: 'Yes! Are we going to do it!'

Mary was sure they hadn't been speaking about punishment. 'I haven't done anything bad.'

'You're not going to, are you?'

'Let me, please!' said the man urgently.

'Dad said he wanted to talk to you.'

'Are you going to be naughty?'

'No,' Mary made herself say. The woman wanted to hurt her again. Why was the man snuffling?

'I really want to be nice to you. We all do,' said Félicité.

Mary couldn't think what to say. She lowered herself very gently on to one of the big chairs, like a movie seat, in front of the giant screen. Her bottom still hurt. The men weren't talking on television any more. *Sesame Street* was on, although it was in French. She could understand that easily enough. She tried to watch it but not so the woman would see and get angry.

'I want to love you. Be kind to you.'

'Take me home, then.'

'I will.'

'When?'

'Not yet.'

'When?'

'Soon. Would you like me to be nice to you?'

116

'I don't know.'

'You don't want me to slap you again, do you?'

'No!'

'So you've got to be a good girl. Do what I tell you to do.'

'All right.' Mary wanted to go back to her room: not to be with this woman and the man who was grunting more than laughing now.

'Did you like seeing your mama and papa?'

'Yes.' They were trying to make her cry again but she wouldn't. 'Are you going to talk to him, like he asked?'

'He knows you're safe.'

Mary swallowed. 'When can I go?' She wished she hadn't walked away from school. She wouldn't do it again. Ever.

The man gave a grunting laugh.

'Not yet,' said Félicité.

'When?'

'When I say so.'

'You're bad, for taking me.'

'Don't be rude. If you're rude I'll slap you again.' She smiled. 'And you know I don't want to do that.'

The woman's voice was thick again and Mary didn't like it. She didn't believe the woman wanted to be nice to her. If she wanted to be nice why had they taken her and locked her up and hit her? It didn't make sense. She didn't like not understanding what was going on. 'I'm not rude. And I don't want to stay here. I want to go home.'

That was better. Mary was being contrary again. 'Would you like someone to play with?'

Mary frowned. 'A pet, you mean?'

Félicité hadn't but they were going to need another identification. 'Do you have a pet?'

'A rabbit.'

'What's its name?'

117

'Billy Boy.'

'What colour is he?'

'White, with black ears. And a black leg.'

'Who'll be looking after him?'

'Mom, I suppose.'

'I didn't mean a pet to play with. I meant another boy or girl.'

'Does one live here, in this house?'

'Maybe.'

'Yes, I would.' Nothing bad could happen if there was another boy or girl in the house. Mary felt better. Safer. Perhaps they could become friends and whoever it was might help her get away, like in the books. 'Is there someone?'

'We'll have to see, won't we?'

Did she mean it? Or was she playing another silly game? She kept talking about games. This might be one of them, making Mary think she could be with someone and then saying she couldn't. Cheating her. She wanted so much to be home. Home with mom. Cuddling with mom, like mom wanted to do a lot but she didn't, saying it was silly. She didn't think it was silly now. She wanted to be with someone who cuddled her. 'Please let me go home.'

'Don't whimper!' said Félicité sharply.

'I hate you!'

'You'll love me in the end. Properly.'

'I won't.'

'I'll make you.'

Without warning the door leading upstairs opened. Without entering Gaston Mehre said: 'The others are here. They want you to come.'

'What . . .?' demanded Félicité, surprised.

'Please come.'

He wasn't wearing a mask and Mary saw a balding man with a red face. What hair he had was red, too.

118

She'd be able to tell people what he looked like when she got home. She wanted them punished for what they were doing to her, the woman most of all. But after she got home.

'They know!' declared Jean Smet. He strode round the room with its panoramic view of the now placid river, nervously smoking the cigarette he'd lit from the stub of the previous one.

'Know what?' demanded Félicité, lounged in her throne-like chair. 'And for Christ's sake stop running around.' She was angry at the man's panic, which was making the rest nervous. And at his summoning them all like this, without asking her permission.

The lawyer did stop but it seemed difficult for him to remain still. 'That we took her for sex, in the beginning. They're going back through police records not just in Brussels but throughout the country: Europol records, too.' He looked fleetingly at Dehane. 'They know computers are being used cleverly. They're sure there's no shortage of money.' He concentrated upon Félicité. 'Did you go to school in England?'

She laughed at the totally unexpected question. 'For three years. My father was at the London embassy. What the hell's that got to do with anything?'

'She thought the person who wrote the message learned the language properly.'

'So what?' Félicité said dismissively.

'They're clever. It's not confused, like last time.'

Only Félicité was relaxed, unworried. The Mehre brothers were side by side with their backs to the water, Gaston holding Charles's hand comfortingly. The obese Michel Blott was frowning at the apparent knowledge of those hunting them and August Dehane had started nibbling at a thumb nail, a nerve beginning to pull at the corner of his mouth. Smet lit another cigarette from his preceding stub and set off once more, moving up and down in front of the window. The heavily bespectacled Henri Cool sat with his arms awkwardly folded, as if he were holding himself for reassurance.

'We can't go on,' insisted Smet. 'We've got to get rid of her. We should have done it the first day. Not started all this.'

'That's what I said,' Cool reminded them.

'So they're cleverer than the last time,' mused Félicité, more to herself than the others. 'That's good. It makes it much more interesting.'

'They think that, too: that we're doing it more as a challenge than for the money,' blurted the government lawyer.

'They *have* worked a lot out, haven't they?' conceded Félicité. 'Who, exactly, is the clever one?'

'I don't know,' said Smet. 'An English superintendent, Blake, did most of the talking at the ministry, but there were two psychologists, a woman and an American. The Americans have brought in a lot of people and their man from the embassy, Harrison, said that as many more could be brought in as are wanted. Poncellet can second as many officers as they want from any force in the country. And the Europol commissioner, Sanglier, said there are unlimited resources once the investigation is focused. The entire Cabinet is determined to find her: find who's got her. Ulieff's job is on the line . . .'

'All of which I anticipated, and we expected,' said Félicité mildly.

'I'm not sure that we did, not properly,' said Blott, the other lawyer. There was the faintest sheen of perspiration on his forehead.

'Once the investigation is focused,' echoed Félicité.

The six men looked blankly at her, none of them understanding.

Félicité stared contemptuously back at them, one by one, finishing upon Smet. 'That's what you said, isn't it?'

'What Sanglier said.'

'So what we've got is nothing more than intelligent police guesswork,' sighed the woman. 'They don't *know* anything. And if they do, you'll know, won't you?'

'You're asking me to do too much,' complained Smet. 'I'm taking all the risk. You've no idea what it's like, sitting there listening to it!'

'You aren't in any danger and you know it,' said Félicité impatiently. 'It's all going exactly as I knew it would. Even better, with your attachment to Poncellet. That was my idea too, remember? But you did very well, making it work.'

Smet smiled gratefully, stubbing out his cigarette without lighting another. 'It was the only positive idea anyone had before we met them all. Ulieff almost cried with gratitude.'

'You've got full access?'

'Ulieff's told Poncellet he wants daily briefings.'

'Which means we'll have daily briefings, too. So where's the danger?'

'I think they're clever,' insisted Smet inadequately, his mind locked on a single thought.

Félicité looked at Dehane. 'And we're cleverer, aren't we, August?'

The deputy head of Belgacom's research and development smiled uncertainly. 'I suppose so.'

'You know so, all of you. Have I ever failed you?' They were like children themselves, always needing to be reassured.

'No,' mumbled Cool, for all of them.

'Did Marcel ever fail you, before me?'

'No,' said Cool again.

'So we're going to stop panicking, aren't we? Stop panicking and listen to me and everything will work out just as I want it to.' To Dehane she said: 'What happened after the Americans posted their message?'

'There've been almost five hundred responses, with an upsurge after the press conference,' replied Dehane, a greying, bearded man.

Félicité smiled. 'But not one from us. And every single one of those five hundred has to be eliminated, right?' The American response had been another bonus she hadn't expected but she wanted them to think that she had, because she'd already decided how protective it was.

Smet said: 'That's the only positive line of enquiry, according to today's meeting.'

'Which we already know is absolutely pointless,' said Félicité. 'People running round in circles like chickens with their heads cut off.' She looked pointedly at Smet, deciding the comparison fitted: a squawking, long-legged human chicken shitting himself at the first sight of the farmer's axe.

Aware of her concentration Smet finally abandoned his aimless wandering and sat down in an opposite chair.

'We've opened new lines into the embassy, at the Americans' request,' said Dehane. 'We've actually been officially asked to impose a monitor on the embassy's e-mail address. And we've sent some of our operators there to help with the backlog that's built up.'

'So we'll know all about that from you, just as we'll know all about the official investigation from Jean, won't we?'

'Yes,' confirmed Dehane. 'We are safe, aren't we?'

Félicité let the question settle in everyone's mind, conscious of the discernible recovery among the men. 'We're going to know what the people looking for us are doing and thinking, every minute of every day. And watch them, every minute of every day, buried under an avalanche of stupid messages.'

Gaston Mehre patted his brother's hand reassuringly.

Charles covered the comforting fingers with his own. Blott and Dehane looked at each other and nodded, smiling, as if Félicité had said something they already knew. Looking at Charles Mehre, Blott said: 'What about criminal records?'

'Restricted to children?' Félicité asked Smet.

'That's the remit,' confirmed the lawyer.

'It was indecency in a public place, twelve years ago,' reminded Gaston, patting his brother's hand again. 'The girl was sixteen. Charles was eighteen.'

'It won't show up,' said Félicité positively. She held out a wavering finger, as if she was holding a gun, stopping at Blott. 'You can compose the next message. I've got an identification. She's got a pet rabbit named Billy.'

The fat man shifted uncomfortably. 'What shall I say?'

'This one doesn't have to have any input from me,' said Félicité, impatient again. 'I don't want to know what it says. Just compose it and give it to August to send.'

'Should I make a demand? Get it over with quickly?' asked Blott hopefully.

'I think you should,' said Smet. 'I want to get it finished. I'm the one under all the pressure.'

'There's no hurry,' said Félicité. 'They're the ones under pressure. I want to increase it before the negotiations start.'

Cool said: 'We should kill her. We're going to anyway. Let's have a party, now, and get it over with.'

'You know the party we're going to have,' Félicité reminded him. 'The others haven't found their new friends yet.'

Before she left, Félicité beckoned Gaston away from his brother. She said: 'Charles was getting too excited this afternoon. I don't want him doing anything to Mary.'

'I know how to quieten him,' said the man. 'Don't worry.'

★

Before Sanglier caught a late afternoon train back to The Hague it was agreed to post an appeal on every Internet provider for users to leave the embassy's home page clear for whoever held Mary to make unimpeded contact, despite Kurt Volker's doubt that it would have any effect.

'It's a user's dream,' warned the German. 'Every surfer is a voyeur at heart. Think of the opportunity! The chance to become involved in a sensational investigation from the uninvolved comfort and danger-free safety of their own armchair! Certainly every journalist from every media outlet will be permanently connected.'

Claudine was depressed by the enormous traffic flow into the greatly enlarged computer centre, unable to believe it possible for a genuine kidnap message to be identified from the mass of material being sorted in front of her. Volker wanted to attempt a fast-track selection program and refused Claudine's dinner suggestion, so because it had been a hard day and La Maison du Cygne was conveniently close she and Blake ate there again. Exhausted, Claudine sat back, very content to let Blake order.

'A lot of battles won?' he suggested.

'But not the war,' cautioned Claudine. She supposed she should have felt satisfied by the events of the day but she didn't. She felt curiously flat, unsettled that there wasn't a positive direction in which to go. It wasn't, she knew, a properly dispassionate reflection but always in the forefront of her mind was the thought of an imprisoned child she had somehow to find.

'You think the Americans will still try to go it alone?'

'Norris will, if he gets the chance,' predicted Claudine.

'I can't see that happening now,' said Blake, looking casually round the room.

'I did a terrible thing to him today.' She supposed her guilt contributed to her despondency.

'It was justified, in the circumstances.'

'It's never justified for a doctor, which I am, to make an illness worse!'

'You think you did that?'

'Very possibly.'

'But you can't be sure?'

'I think I did. That's enough.'

'It will be, if you get Mary back,' said Blake, turning Claudine's words back upon her.

'It's supposed to be a combined effort,' she reminded him. The sole was excellent but she was having difficulty eating. Perhaps she should have stayed at the hotel.

'You were very impressive today,' Blake congratulated her.

Claudine's spirits lifted slightly. 'You were pretty impressive yourself.'

'Largely repeating your theories.'

'I'd say the input was fifty-fifty.'

'You think there could be something from the people who've got her among all the stuff that's come in?'

Claudine shrugged: 'If there is it's going to be a hell of a job finding it.'

'I don't like the helplessness of having to wait for them to make a move. They're orchestrating the entire thing.'

'That's the whole point,' insisted Claudine. 'They're getting their satisfaction from control: making us follow their lead.'

'Similar to Norris?'

'Marginally.'

'Let's hope it's the only way they're getting their satisfaction,' said Blake heavily.

'I wish to God I could be more certain about that,' admitted Claudine. 'If she is still alive and they've started abusing her she'll break – become subservient, and totally confused by adults doing things to her she won't fully understand. Why it's happening, I mean.'

125

'She's been gone more than three days,' the man reminded her.

'They might still not have touched her, physically. Don't forget the usual way is to try to convince the child that sex with an adult is quite normal: talk about it first and show them photographs and films of it happening to other children.'

'That sounds bad enough to me,' said Blake.

'I'm hoping for arrogance,' said Claudine. 'And that's how I'm connecting the daytime abduction with their first contact. Both are arrogant – the daylight snatch, on a crowded street – even reckless. That's in Mary's favour.'

'How long will it go on like that?'

'I wish I knew,' admitted Claudine honestly. 'Just as I wish I could guess how much longer Mary can hold on, whether she's being sexually molested or not.'

'We've established that she's strong-willed.'

'That will have helped at first. Made it easier for her to convince herself she isn't frightened. Which she will be, of course. Terrified. Gradually – there's no way of predicting how gradually – the terror will replace the resistance. When that happens she'll start wanting to ingratiate herself. Think that if she does what they want they'll treat her kindly. Let her go, even.'

'Making it easier to convince her about the sex?'

Claudine nodded, abandoning the rest of her meal.

'You haven't eaten much.'

'I'm not hungry.'

'That all?'

'It's been a long day. I'm tired.'

'It doesn't show.'

It would have done, if she hadn't concentrated upon her make-up, more than once rearranged her hair after showering and taken the time to choose between three dresses before coming out. She was glad she had. He'd changed too, she realized. 'I'd like to believe it.'

126

'After the knife attack on the last case you were authorized to carry a weapon?'

Claudine was startled by the abrupt change of direction. 'Yes?'

'You carrying it now?'

She was still bewildered. 'No. I'm embarrassed about it: it was an over-reaction.'

'Where is it?'

'Back in The Hague, in my safe.'

'Not a lot of use there, is it?'

'What about you, after Ireland?'

'Yes.'

'Are you carrying?'

He smiled sheepishly. 'I left it at the hotel. Which is not just stupid but a very good reason for me to be disciplined.'

'Touché!' What the hell was this all about?

'You enjoy Europol?'

Now which way were they going! They'd had this conversation, surely? 'I didn't want to stay in England after my husband died. I wish there was more to do.'

'Lots of opportunity to meet people.'

'If you want to meet people,' she agreed.

'Which I hear you don't.'

'From whom?' At least he'd held off for the first few days. She supposed she should have been irritated now but she wasn't. Oddly the tiredness was easing, too.

'Just talk.'

'I'm not interested in one-night stands. Any sort of stand, for that matter.'

Blake pushed his own plate aside. 'Is there anyone?'

Claudine realized, surprised, that she hadn't thought of Hugo Rosetti since the Brussels case began. 'There's a friend. Nothing serious.' Why had she said that, dismissing the situation with Hugo? She loved him and knew he loved her: was prepared – anxious even – for the affair

127

that his rigid, self-imposed rules prevented his entering into. So maybe the dismissal had been justified after all, although not describing it as 'nothing serious'. Bizarre was more accurate. How long was she prepared to go on with it? Until Flavia really died, instead of remaining suspended in a living death? The question was as repugnant as the actual prospect. No matter what she felt for Hugo, she couldn't tell him that. It would sound like an ultimatum: which it would be, she supposed. The way to end it, even. She didn't want to end it, unsatisfactory though it was, nor did she want it to drift on indefinitely. Impasse. What was the clinical word to describe someone supremely confident of their professional ability whose private life was an insoluble mess? Idiot came easily to mind.

'I think I've overstepped the boundaries,' said Blake.

'Perhaps you have.'

'Are you offended?'

'No.'

'I'm still sorry. Embarrassed, too.'

Claudine didn't think he was. 'We should be getting back.'

'Kurt's got this number, if anything comes up.'

'I'd still like to get back.'

'So you are offended.'

'Tired.'

Claudine thought Blake was going to protest at her paying her share of the bill – shifting the colleague-to-colleague understanding – but he didn't and she was glad. On their way back across the square he kept even further away from her than he'd previously done. There were two telephone calls from Rosetti logged at the reception desk.

'Anything?'

'Personal.' She didn't feel like returning them tonight.

'Goodnight, then.'

'Goodnight.'

He nodded towards the corridor bar, holding her eyes. 'I thought I'd have one last drink.'

Claudine answered the gaze. 'I'll see you in the morning.' She wasn't offended, she decided, as the open-sided elevator took her upwards. There wasn't any possibility of a personal situation developing between them, but the suggestion she might have responded to one was flattering. He was, in fact, a very attractive man.

'You looked very grand on television. Autocratic, like de Gaulle.' Françoise was totally naked, examining herself in the full length mirror. She did it most nights when she slept there, which wasn't a lot. It went beyond narcissism to become a permanent taunt directed at him.

Sanglier had collected the Europol masterfile on the McBride disappearance on his way from the railway station. He didn't bother to look up from it until he became aware of the woman, close to his bed.

She turned with a model's grace, jutting out her left hip. 'What do you think?'

There was still some distorting soreness around the small tattoo of a yellow and blue bird, high on her thigh. 'What is it?'

'A love bird. Maria's got one to match.'

'Who's Maria?'

'She makes films: sometimes very special films. I love her very much.' Gauging his sudden interest, she said: 'But not enough to leave home. It suits me to be married to you, just as it suits you to be married to me. We adorn each other.'

Once but not any more, thought Sanglier. How – and when – was he going to tell her about returning to Paris? Not yet. She'd probably be glad to be going back. She hated The Hague. 'I was with Claudine Carter in Brussels.'

'One of the few to get away,' pouted Françoise, in mock regret. 'Why did you bring us together?'

'Another mistake,' conceded Sanglier.

'You'd never think of involving me in a situation to get rid of me, would you?' demanded Françoise.

'With a member of my own staff? Hardly!'

'Don't even think about it,' she warned.

She would embarrass him one day, Sanglier knew. And he did want to get rid of her, so very desperately.

CHAPTER TEN

The message said MARY, MARY QUITE CON-TRARY IS MISSING BILLY and at the first combined gathering of the day Claudine stressed that she might have missed the identification without Norris's complete background on the McBride family. Initially she actually held back, hoping the American himself would isolate what was so glaringly obvious from the ten other possibilities thrown up by Kurt Volker's fast-track word-recognition selection, but Norris didn't. He didn't respond to her praise, either.

The success anyway was more Kurt Volker's than hers. He'd filleted Norris's background information of trigger words for his tracer program, which had instantly flagged the only reference to Mary's pet in any of the incoming e-mail. It also activated a print-out, and timed the duration of the message precisely at sixty seconds – confirming Volker's earlier estimate – before clearing.

'What about a trace on the source?' demanded Norris, hiding any approval he might have felt, which Claudine didn't think was much.

Volker shook his head. 'There's still too much incoming, slowing down any possible response. All the key words – in this case "contrary" "Mary" and "Billy" – spelled with an "ie" as well as with a "y" just in case – had to be matched by my comparison program. It's like trying to swim against a tide.'

'Could you get a location if the traffic eases?' asked Poncellet, responding to Jean Smet's obvious prompting.

'Yes,' said Volker, immediately and confidently.

Poncellet went sideways, to a fresh nudge from the ministry lawyer, before asking in apparent disbelief: 'In as little as sixty seconds?'

'I think so.'

Looking invitingly at Norris, Claudine said: 'They've maintained contact!' Come on, she thought, hopefully: analyse it as you should be able to and show me I haven't done as much harm as I think I have. Harding, Rampling and Harrison were all looking expectantly at the FBI supervisor.

'Not properly,' complained Norris. 'There should have been a negotiating link established by now. They've been frightened off by the publicity.'

'Don't you think we might still be in the power stage, their showing us they're calling the shots?' she suggested. How could she hope to help this man – treat this man – when saving the child took precedence over everything?

'They already know that.'

'But psychologically they need to prove it, to themselves more than to us at the moment. It's the predictably established formula: your formula,' said Claudine. By trying too hard to be kind she was coming close to exposing the man's mental limitation!

'The longer it goes on, the more dangerous it gets for Mary,' insisted Norris.

'I agree,' said Claudine at once. 'Today's message was important.'

'How?' demanded Blake. He was the only one in the room aware of how much reconciliation Claudine was attempting with Norris and he was professionally impatient with it. Having operated alone for so long in Ireland Blake was unused to working with or considering the feelings of over-sensitive committees. It was diplomatic bureaucracy and that wasn't the way to solve crime. He was anxious to start an investigation he wasn't yet prepared to discuss with anyone, not even Claudine, and he was personally unsettled by the previous evening. He certainly wasn't prepared to discuss that with her, either. He'd hoped, perhaps stupidly, that the days of having to carry the Beretta in his belt-line, where it was chafing him now, were past, too.

'It wasn't composed by the same person who wrote the first Mary, Mary rhyme,' declared Claudine, grateful for the opportunity Blake created. 'The first approach was considered, measured: a look-at-me, aren't-I-clever message. Today's wasn't. It was hurried: impatient or nervous. But that's important. The immediate significance of their knowing the name of Mary's pet is that they've begun mentally to work on her: to confuse her by how they treat her, so that she won't know what's going to happen next: what's right or wrong, real or unreal. They're talking about her pet: might even have told her the sort of message they were going to send—'

'And having started to build up a trust, they'll break it,' interrupted Norris.

'That's the pattern,' agreed Claudine, pleased. It hadn't all gone!

'So what do we do?' asked the American chief of mission. 'We're pretty strong on psychological theory but I don't see anything practical coming from it, like getting Mary back.'

'We wait for the next message,' declared Norris. 'That'll take us forward: they'll give us the link the next time.'

Claudine sighed, sadly disappointed. 'I don't think we should wait. I think we need to bring them forward. The ambassador publicly cried yesterday—'

'And is as embarrassed as hell about it,' disclosed Harrison.

'He shouldn't be,' insisted Claudine. 'He did a lot to help Mary, breaking down like that. They reduced an ambassador of the United States of America, the most powerful nation on earth, to helpless tears. The power – their ability – to do that makes Mary very valuable to them. Protects her.'

'So what should we do?' persisted Harrison.

'I think the ambassador should meet the media again: television particularly, to enable Mary's abductors to see the effect her disappearance is having. With Mrs McBride, too—'

'I'm not sure either will be prepared to,' intruded Harrison again.

Claudine decided it wouldn't be difficult to become thoroughly pissed off by the overbearing, opinionated diplomat. Restraining the temptation verbally to push the man back into his box, she said: 'Why don't we explain the purpose – which is to prove just how helpless we are and how much in command they are – and give them the chance to make up their own minds? If Mrs McBride cries, even better.'

'Mrs McBride doesn't cry,' said Harrison simply.

'Any emotion the McBrides publicly display will help,' insisted Claudine. 'We've got to establish a two-way dialogue as quickly and as effectively as possible. And the way to do that is for the ambassador to announce verbally, in public, that there has been another message . . .' she stopped, not wanting any misunderstanding '. . . but not, in any circumstances, saying what that message was. Not, even, that it arrived by e-mail. That goes way beyond keeping the computer route into the embassy as free as possible. *We're* inviting *them* – conceding that they rule our world – to take that one step forward and begin a dialogue.'

'From a position of weakness,' challenged Norris at once.

Momentarily Claudine didn't reply, looking away from all of them but focusing on nothing. Like so many doctors able to adjust the Hippocratic oath she'd favoured euthanasia long before helplessly watching the mother she'd adored physically eroded by cancer, just a few months earlier. But, incredibly she now realized, she'd never extended that image of physical erosion and that necessary release to include a mental illness. At that moment she did. Strictly obeying her know thyself creed Claudine fully recognized that her overweening professional confidence – the central core around which her life revolved – was what motivated her entire existence. As horrifying and as humiliating and as agonizing as her mother's physical decline had been, Claudine decided that for her personally to lose her analytical psychological competence – to lose her mind, in fact, as John Norris appeared to have lost his – equally justified the quick release of self-destruction. In her case perhaps more so than an irreversible physical condition. At once there came an unsettling unanswerable question. Did she really feel so strongly about euthanasia because of her mother's death? Or did her conviction come from what she couldn't fulfil with Hugo Rosetti because of the permanent, irreversible coma in which his wife existed? Claudine forced herself on, refusing even to attempt an answer, frightened of what it might be.

'John,' she said gently. 'That's exactly what it is, a position of weakness. We know it. They know it. They've got a public forum in which they want everyone else to know it too. We can't change that position until we get into a negotiating stance. You wrote that, in the text books: lectured on it at Quantico.'

Norris frowned, seemingly unable to remember. He didn't argue. Harding, alongside, frowned too towards Rampling but it was an entirely different expression for entirely different reasons. There was a long, unfilled silence.

'John?' prompted Harrison.

'It means exposing the ambassador.' The man tried to recover.

'Which is better than exposing his daughter,' said Blake shortly, and Claudine wished he hadn't.

Harrison said: 'I could suggest it. I understand the reasoning.'

Smet leaned sideways, whispering to the commissioner. At once the portly, uniform-encased man said: 'We have some positive sightings of Mary minutes before she disappeared.'

'Walking? Or getting into a vehicle?' demanded Blake.

'Both,' said Poncellet.

'Walking first,' dictated Blake, eager to establish the sequence. 'How many positive identifications?'

Poncellet hesitated at the intensity of the Englishman's demands. Claudine withdrew, giving way to a different expertise, interested in watching Blake operate.

Poncellet consulted a folder already set out in front of him. 'Three.'

'Absolutely no doubt it was Mary?'

'A positive identification, every time.'

'Was she by herself? Or with someone?'

'By herself.'

'Anyone close?'

Poncellet hesitated again. 'I don't think so.'

'The question wasn't asked,' decided Blake briskly. 'I'll need to go back to each witness myself, today. Can we get them in here now?'

'We could try.' Poncellet turned at once to the three-clerk secretariat that had arrived with him and Smet. One immediately left the office.

'How was she behaving?' came in Paul Harding. 'Walking normally? Slow? Fast? Agitated? Calm?'

Claudine was alert for any reaction from Norris to the local FBI man's intrusion and suspected that Harding was, too. There was a faint smile on Norris's face, the expression of a master watching inexpert pupils attempting to prove themselves. But nothing else.

'You'll have to ask them that,' said Poncellet. He was beginning to colour and his breathing was becoming difficult.

'How close to the school was the first sighting?' persisted Harding.

'Quite close, I think.'

'Any evidence of a car near her?' asked Blake.

'Not that I've been told.'

'Was she seen talking to anyone?'

'I haven't any reports of her doing so.'

'How reliable are these witnesses?' demanded Harding. 'Believable or questionable?'

'I think you should decide that yourselves.'

'I think we should,' said Harding, pointedly dismissive. He looked without needing to ask the question to Blake, who nodded.

'What about the car sightings?' said Blake.

'Two, of her getting into a vehicle.'

'What sort of vehicle?'

'A Mercedes.'

'No doubt about that?' pressed Harding.

Poncellet shook his head. 'Both are Mercedes drivers themselves.'

'Registration?' asked Harding.

'No.'

'Belgian or foreign designation?'

'I've no record of that.'

'Model?' demanded the American.

'I don't have the complete report.'

'Colour?' said Blake.

'Black, according to one,' said Poncellet, relieved at last to be able to reply positively. 'Blue, according to the other.'

'What about occupants?' said Harding.

'You really do need to speak to them yourselves,' Poncellet finally capitulated.

'We most certainly do,' said Harding. He needed to discover what the fuck was wrong with the FBI superstar sitting silently beside him, too. The Iceman seemed to be frozen into unresponsive inactivity, unaware of or uninterested in what was going on around him.

The questioning of witnesses was very much a police function but Claudine included herself, without seeking the approval of Peter Blake or anyone else, just as she visited whenever possible the actual scene of a violent crime and the post-mortem examination of its victim. She didn't consider it an arrogant refusal to trust the ability of others, which she knew to have been a London criticism before her transfer to Europol. Unless she had reason to doubt their competence, as she now definitely had with John Norris, Claudine never intruded into the assigned roles of those with whom she worked. What she didn't expect and most certainly didn't want was for those others to think they could do her job for her. One missed question vital to her from someone not examining a situation from her perspective was the difference between success and failure. Professionally it was better to offend than to fail.

She made a particular point of announcing her intention to re-interview the eye-witnesses, fully expecting Norris to stay as well. He didn't, saying it was more important he return to the embassy with Burt Harrison to prepare the ambassador for the second press conference. Poncellet and Smet did stay, which she had not anticipated. From the fleeting expressions she intercepted between them it seemed to surprise Blake and Harding, too. When Claudine pointedly remarked it would intimidate witnesses to be confronted by so many people

Poncellet dismissed the clerks, despite what she was sure were Smet's whispered objections.

The first person positively to identify Mary walking away from the school was a 28-year-old mother who took her four-year-old daughter along the rue du Canal at the same time every day to feed whatever birds might be on the nearby waterway: that day there hadn't been any. She definitely recognized Mary from the published photographs and correctly identified the colour – blue, trimmed with red – of the backpack, a detail that had intentionally been withheld from the media release. Because she was such a regular user of the road at such a regular time she was accustomed to seeing children collected from the school, mostly by car, and was mildly curious at a child walking away unaccompanied. There was no one close or in conversation with Mary, who'd been walking quite normally and not in any obvious hurry and had ignored her and the little girl when she passed.

The accounts of the two other pedestrians – a book-keeper the end of whose working day coincided with the school dismissal and a hotel waiter who always walked to his evening shift for the exercise – tallied in every respect, even to identifying the rucksack. The book-keeper thought Mary was walking fast, not as if she was trying to get away from someone but as if she was anxious to reach a destination.

All three were quite adamant that the child was showing no signs of distress or uncertainty. The waiter, in fact, had been struck by the confidence with which Mary had been walking, as if it was a regular route she knew well. It was that streetwise assurance that had attracted his attention: it was his regular route to work and he couldn't remember seeing her before.

Each of the three had been walking in the opposite direction to Mary and had no reason to look round once she had passed, so none had seen a car or the child being accosted.

The breakthrough came with the first car driver. His name was Johan Rompuy and he was a technical translator in English and Italian in the agricultural division of the European Commission. He was a 57-year-old grey-haired, grey-suited bureaucrat who had worked in the governing body of the European Union for eighteen years and thought and talked with the pedantry of a man whose life was governed by detail, order and regularity.

That was why he remembered the incident with Mary so well. He'd been summoned late to a Commission meeting of agricultural ministers and was in a hurry, although obeying the speed limit, which he always did. He'd been following on the inside lane directly behind the black Mercedes when it had suddenly stopped, making him halt just as sharply. The volume of traffic in the outer lane prevented his pulling out to overtake. He'd seen everything because it had happened directly in front of him.

Claudine had positioned herself to the side of the room, giving the encounters over to Blake and Harding, and had the impression of two tensed cats undecided which was to be the first to jump on an unsuspecting mouse: even the timid, grey-featured civil servant fitted the cat and mouse analogy. The local FBI man gave the slightest body movement, conceding to the Englishman.

For the briefest of moments Blake hesitated, preparing himself. 'You're very important to us and to this investigation,' he began, and Claudine at once acknowledged the basic psychology of the approach.

Rompuy smiled, a man rarely praised or flattered by superiors. 'I'm glad to be of help.'

'And I want you to be as helpful as possible. There are a great many questions we want answering. You're going to have to be very patient: what might not seem important to you could be of very great importance to us.'

The smile remained. 'I understand.'

'You're sure the car was black?'

'Yes.'

'What model?' asked Harding.

'A 230, I think.'

'Was the registration Belgian or foreign?' said Blake.

'I didn't make a note of it, obviously. But I'm sure it was Belgian. If it hadn't been I might have looked more closely. And I'm sure the country designation was Belgium, too. Again I would have looked more closely if it had been foreign. My job is identifying different nationalities.'

'Was it a Brussels registration?' pressed Harding, taking up the questioning.

'I don't know.'

'Was there anything unusual about the car: a badge or a sign in the rear window?' coaxed the American. 'Anything inside that you could see – about the car, I mean, we'll get to the passengers in a minute – like a sticker or a religious medallion or a permanent parking authority or even the sort of decoration people sometimes hang in their vehicles.'

The man made a visible effort to remember. 'I don't think so.'

'Was there a radio aerial?' asked Blake.

'Yes.'

'Positioned where?'

'At the rear.'

'Was it raised, for the radio to be playing? Or retracted?'

'Retracted.'

'What about a telephone aerial?'

'Yes,' said the man at once. 'In the middle of the rear window, at the top by the roof.'

'A straight aerial or a spiral one?' persisted the American and Claudine was aware of the quick approving look from Blake. Poncellet and Smet were sitting motionless, an audience to a special performance of experts.

'Straight, I think,' said Rompuy doubtfully.

'Now let's talk about the people inside,' encouraged Blake. 'How many were there?'

'Two. A man and a woman.'

There was a stir, from the two Belgians, which Claudine at once regretted because Rompuy looked at them and said: 'There were. I'm sure there were.'

'We believe you,' said Harding quickly. 'How were they sitting?'

'The man was in the front. The woman in the back.'

'So you could see the woman better?'

'Yes.'

Claudine hadn't moved, not wanting to risk distracting the man again, but there were questions she needed to ask. But the detectives had to finish first.

'Whereabouts in the back seat was she: to the right or to the left or in the middle?'

'More to the left, to give the child room to get in.'

'Was she like that when the car stopped? Or did she move over?'

'I don't remember her moving over. I think she was there when the car stopped.'

'How did the rear door open, then, for Mary to get in?'

Rompuy frowned. 'I'm not sure. I think the man turned and opened it but I can't really remember.'

'Let's go back to the woman,' said Blake, wanting to maintain a sequence. 'What colour hair did she have?'

'Blond.'

'Light, yellowy blond or dark blond?'

'Dark.'

'You could see her shoulders: part of her back?'

'Yes.' The man frowned.

'How much? Show us on your own body,' said the American.

Self-consciously Rompuy stretched over his shoulder, with difficulty pushing his hand down roughly to the bottom of his shoulder blade.

'So you could see what she was wearing?'

Rompuy's frown remained. 'It was a jacket, I think. Fawn or maybe a light brown.'

'Can you describe it?' demanded Blake.

'It was just a jacket.'

'What was the cloth like, rough, smooth? Could it have been suede? Leather?'

'It was cloth, of some sort. Smooth, I think.'

The questions were building up in Claudine's mind but still she held back. Momentarily Blake turned his eyes to her and she gave an almost imperceptible nod to show that she wanted to take up when they were satisfied.

'What about the style of her hair?' said Harding. 'Did she wear it loose or tied?'

'It wasn't tied, exactly,' said the man awkwardly. 'But it was tight against her head, one side sort of folded over the other . . .'

Blake looked hopefully at Claudine, who in turn looked round the room and then picked up some paper and quickly sketched. 'Like that?' Claudine asked.

'Yes,' agreed Rompuy at once, pleased at making himself understood.

'It's a pleat,' said Claudine. 'That's it, isn't it? Her hair was pinned into a pleat, so that it made a line down the back of her head?'

'Exactly,' said the man, smiling again.

Both men moved to speak at the same time and again Harding deferred to the English detective. Blake said: 'You're doing very well. You're telling us a great deal we need to know. Now you saw the back of the woman's head, looking from your car into hers. But they'd stopped for Mary, hadn't they?'

'As I now know, yes.'

'Did Mary get in immediately?'

'No.'

'What happened?'

'They talked.'

'How long for?'

The man shrugged. 'I don't know. A few moments.'

'Fine,' said Blake. 'They'd stopped and the rear door had opened, for Mary to get in. But she didn't, not at once. Who was she talking to, the man or the woman?'

'The woman.'

'So the woman must have looked towards Mary?'

'Oh yes,' said the man, as if he was again surprised at the question. 'That was when she kind of leaned across.'

Neither man showed any impatience at not having already been told that. The tension was palpable to Claudine. Blake said: 'If she was looking towards Mary, leaning across the car, you must have seen her in profile?'

'I did.'

There was a brief hesitation from both detectives. The noise of Smet moving in his chair sounded loud. Blake said: 'Was she full-faced or thin in the face?'

'Thin, I think. That was the impression I got.'

'Tanned or light-skinned?'

'Definitely tanned.'

'A lot of make-up? Or not very much?'

'I don't remember there being a lot of make-up.'

'You're looking at her in profile,' said Blake. 'Was her nose large or small? Straight or crooked? Describe it to us, in your own words.'

'Straight,' said the man, trying hard. 'And sharp. That's how I remember her, as a sharp-featured woman.'

At Blake's pause Harding took up the questioning.

'You could see part of her front now. What was she wearing under the jacket? A blouse or a sweater?'

'I don't remember seeing anything under the jacket.'

'You say she was thin-faced. What about that much of her body that you could see? Was she big-busted or small?'

The man looked embarrassedly towards Claudine. 'I don't think she was very big.'

Claudine smiled at the man and said: 'Don't feel awkward. There's no reason to be. All this is vital to us, so try to help as much as you can.'

'Quite small-busted. Not noticeable at all, really.'

'Was she wearing earrings?' asked Blake, returning to the questioning.

'Yes. Hoops. I think there were jewels in them.'

'What colour?'

'Clear. Like diamonds.'

'What about her ears? Large? Small? Close to her head?'

'Quite small. And close to her head.' The man sat back in his chair and said: 'Could I have something to drink?'

'Of course,' said Blake, looking to the police commissioner.

Poncellet quickly gestured to Smet. The lawyer hesitated, actually turning to where the clerks had sat before realizing they weren't there any more. He hurried irritably out of the room, a man demeaned by a chore that was beneath his dignity.

Rompuy said: 'I hope everything is all right.'

'You're doing remarkably well,' replied Blake. 'I wish every witness could be as helpful.'

'I want to help,' said the translator. 'She must be suffering a lot.'

'That's why we want to get her back as quickly as we can,' said Harding.

'*Will* you get her back?'

145

The media might discover the man, Claudine thought. As Smet came back into the room, carrying a carafe and glasses, she said: 'I'm quite sure we will. What you're telling us adds a lot to what we already know.'

The man drank the water gratefully. Smet leaned close to the police commissioner, who shook his head to whatever the lawyer said.

'Can you go on now?' Harding asked the translator.

'Of course.'

'You've given us a very good description of the woman,' said Harding. 'What about the man?'

'I couldn't see him so well, in the front.'

'Did he turn at all, for you to see him in profile?' asked Blake.

They'd started to hurry, overlooking questions that should have been asked, decided Claudine. The interview had been going on for over an hour, so it was understandable, but she had a vague feeling of disappointment in Peter Blake. It was fortunate she'd held back to allow the two men to finish.

'I don't remember him turning, although I suppose I must have done if he opened the rear door.'

'Was he wearing a jacket?' asked Blake.

'Yes. Black.'

'Like a chauffeur?'

'I suppose so. My impression was that he stayed looking to the front, as a chauffeur would have done.'

'Could you see more of his back than you could of the woman's?'

'Yes. And I remember he kept his seat belt buckled.'

'What about his hair?' asked Harding.

'Black.'

'Long? Short?'

'Short. And he was going bald, at the top . . .' Rompuy frowned, putting his hand vaguely to the back of his head. 'Here, like the way monks have their hair?'

'At the crown of his head,' said Blake. 'A tonsure.'

'That's it!' said the translator. He poured himself more water.

'What about his ears? Were they flat against his head, like most people's? Or did they stick out?'

'I don't remember anything about his ears.'

'Could you see his hands, sitting as he was? Was he holding the wheel?' asked Harding.

'I think so.'

'Could you see if he was wearing a ring?'

'I couldn't see.'

'Did he turn the engine off or keep it running?' asked Blake.

'He kept it running. And the brake lights were on all the time, so I suppose he was sitting with his foot on the brake.'

'What about indicators?' said Harding. 'Was there any signal that the car was going to turn in to the side and stop before it did so?'

'No. That's how I got stuck behind. It was too quick for me to get round him.'

'Didn't that inconvenience you?' asked Blake.

'It delayed me a few minutes. And I was in a hurry.'

'Did you sound your horn?'

'No.'

'Did the car move off immediately Mary got into it?'

Take your time, take your time, Claudine thought.

'Yes,' said the man.

'Fast?' asked Harding.

'There was too much traffic to drive really fast.'

'Was it as fast as the traffic would allow?' insisted Blake. 'As if he was anxious to get away?'

'I suppose it was as fast as he could go. I wasn't really ready and in the gap that opened up someone else overtook and got in front of me.'

'With another car in the way, were you able to see what

was going on inside the car after Mary got in?' said Harding.

'Not really.'

'Which way did it go?'

'I don't know,' said the man lamely. 'We were moving again and I was late. I'm sorry.'

'You've done remarkably well,' Blake said, looking first to Harding, who nodded to show he'd finished, and then invitingly to Claudine.

'Monsieur Rompuy,' she said at once. 'I have some different sorts of questions which might seem odd but bear with me. The woman was looking sideways across the car, with Mary still on the pavement? And then she leaned across the car to encourage Mary in?'

'Yes?'

'That would have tilted her off balance, unless she supported herself. How did she do that? Was she resting against the seat or was her arm visible, along the seat back where it joins the rear shelf?'

'Along the back of the seat, all the time.'

'Throughout the entire time the door was open, for Mary to get in, you could clearly see the woman's arm along the back of the seat?'

'Yes.'

Claudine saw Blake and Harding exchange glances, aware of their oversight.

'Was she wearing a bracelet?'

'Three gold bands that seemed joined together. I got the impression they matched the earrings.'

'What about rings on her fingers?'

'I didn't see any.'

'What about her arm? Did she just let it lie there, casually supporting herself? Or did she gesture for the child to get in?'

'She kept it along the back of the seat.'

148

'What about her free hand? Did you see any movement with that?'

'Not until she reached forward to take the girl's back-pack. The girl took that off before getting into the car.'

Claudine resisted the temptation to take the direction the answer offered. 'You were stuck behind their car. Were there any other vehicles held up behind you?'

'One. It was the car that cut in front of me when we started moving again.'

'That's our next positive witness,' intruded Poncellet, imagining he was helping.

Claudine ignored the interruption, wishing the Belgian commissioner hadn't broken the flow. 'Had that car sounded its horn?'

'Several times. It made the child look, which put her fully facing me. That's why I was able to recognize her from the newspaper and television pictures.'

'Knowing that they were causing a traffic jam – irritating other drivers – the woman still sat casually with her arm along the seat?'

'Yes.'

'And the driver didn't react, either?'

'Not that I saw.'

'Tell me about Mary. Did you see her walking along the pavement, before the car stopped?'

'I wasn't conscious of her until the car stopped.'

'Was she carrying her backpack then? Or wearing it?'

'Definitely wearing it. I remember her slipping out of the straps to take it off.'

'She did it herself, quite willingly?'

'Yes. Then she handed it into the back of the car, to the woman. She wouldn't have been able to have sat comfortably if she hadn't.'

'I understand,' said Claudine. 'Because she turned towards the car behind you could see Mary's face very clearly. What was Mary's expression? Was she frightened? Upset? Frowning? Laughing? Crying?'

Rompuy shook his head uncomfortably. 'She wasn't laughing or crying. It's difficult but I thought she looked annoyed.'

'At the driver behind you?'

'I'm not sure at whom.'

'What about being frightened?'

'That wasn't my impression.'

'She got quite willingly into the car?'

'Yes. As if she expected it. She simply handed her backpack through the open door and followed it into the car.'

'When Mary did that, the woman still had her arm along the back of the seat?'

'Yes.'

'I know the car behind you overtook, blocking your view. But that didn't happen immediately. In those first few seconds Mary was sitting in the seat along the back of which the woman had her arm outstretched?'

'Yes.'

'Could you see Mary?'

'Just the top of her head.'

'What about the woman? Did she bring her arm down, to put it round Mary?'

'I don't think so.'

'In those last few seconds, when you could still see the woman and Mary, how were they sitting?'

'Quite ordinarily. Side by side.'

Claudine stopped, satisfied at the improvement to her profile. She said: 'You've given us a great deal of your time and a great deal of help. For the moment we're almost through. Having seen the woman as you did, how old would you think she was?'

The two detectives exchanged looks again at another oversight.

'I'm not very good at guessing ages.'

'Give it your best try.'

'Fortyish. Early forties.'

'One final question. Could you work with a police artist to create a sketch of the woman you saw lure Mary into the car?'

'I could try,' agreed the man.

Claudine thought, uncritically, that by the end of Johan Rompuy's interview – which had begun so well – Blake and Harding had no longer been able to think with total objectivity, which in both their circumstances was totally understandable.

For a long time – she didn't know how long – Peter Blake had not been an investigator, needing to pick and prise the information from others. He had, in fact, been the infiltrated eye-witness assembling the evidence and facts for others to accept and assimilate: the giver, not the hopeful taker.

And an embassy posting, like Paul Harding's, was again different. In a foreign country it was scarcely operational. At best it was a liaison function with in-country law enforcement, with as much unadmitted but tacitly acknowledged intelligence-gathering as possible. It was too much to expect an instant adjustment from a man literally thrust back into the field, as Harding had been.

It was the most basic of all psychological mistakes, even from professionals, to imagine that because a person had been an eye-witness – had been there, watching everything, seeing everything – they would possess the unprompted gift of total recall. No one did. A hundred people, standing side by side, would give a hundred different accounts of something happening literally in front of them, depending upon their age, attitudes, feelings and personalities: it wasn't human nature – it wasn't humanly possible – for two people to see the same thing the same way.

The commonest failing was investing a situation with a logical progression. There was no such thing as a logic to human interaction. There was even a recognized psychological term, the phenomenon of closure. Nothing was logical – nothing should have happened in the way it appeared to have happened – in the disappearance of Mary Beth McBride. So it couldn't be investigated logically. The questioning by the two detectives had been copy-book, a building block attempt to perform their function. And Johan Rompuy had been a deceptive one-in-a-million witness: because he had been so good – so observant – he'd lulled them into carelessness. It was incredible, after learning so much, that neither had suggested Rompuy work with a police artist to create a visual impression of the woman: obvious by not being obvious.

Both men looked sheepishly at her as the second motorist came into the room and Harding said: 'Do you want to join in as we go along?'

'Let's stay as we are,' said Claudine, hoping they did not infer disapproval.

René Lunckner was an air traffic controller at Zaventem airport and like Rompuy had been late for his afternoon shift. He hadn't known at first why the cars in front had suddenly stopped and only just managed to avoid colliding with Rompuy's vehicle. He thought he'd sounded his horn three or four times before slightly reversing to swing round the car in front of him. It was then he'd seen Mary Beth McBride, seeming to look directly at him. The driver of the Mercedes had his window down and was gesturing for him to pass but oncoming traffic was too heavy for him to pull out as far as he needed: for a few moments he had, in fact, caused greater traffic congestion than already existed. The driver had signalled with his hand and his indicator that he was pulling away from the kerb. Lunckner was adamant the car into which Mary got was dark blue, top of the range – 'definitely larger than a 230' – and that it had a Brussels registration. 'I couldn't believe someone who knew the city would stop like that and block the traffic.'

'Stuck out in the road as you were, could you see the driver?' demanded Harding.

'Not very well. He was going bald and he wore spectacles; I think they had heavy black frames. And he had a beaked nose. That's the best I can do.'

'A thin man? Or fat?'

'Quite heavily built.'

'Did you see enough of him to help a police artist create a picture?' asked Blake, avoiding their earlier oversight.

The man shook his head. 'I really don't think so. I don't want to mislead.'

'We'd really like you to try,' urged Blake. 'We'll keep your reservations in mind.'

'All right.'

'How old would you say the man was?' said Harding, also avoiding the earlier omission.

'Again, I don't want to mislead. Late forties, early fifties. I can't get any closer than that.'

'What about the woman?' asked Blake.

'I hardly saw her at all: I was looking at the front of their car, trying to judge the distance to get by.'

'But you didn't get by,' reminded Harding. 'You had to pull in behind.'

'Blond. Hair very tightly pinned at the back. I didn't see her face at all. I wasn't really interested: it was a mother picking up her daughter, as far as I was concerned. All I wanted to do was get by and get to work.'

'Is that the impression you had?' asked Claudine

quickly, not wanting to miss the moment. 'That it was a mother picking up her child?'

'I drive along the road all the time. I know the school's there and I'm used to seeing the kids picked up. That usually causes jams, too. I try to beat them by coming along earlier but that day I didn't make it.'

'Was there anything other than your knowing there was a school that made you think it was mother and daughter? Anything unusual about the way the child was behaving?'

Lunckner shook his head. 'She was scowling, as if she was annoyed.'

'Annoyed?' persisted Claudine. 'Not frightened?'

'Annoyed,' insisted the man. 'I thought it was because her mother was late and had made her walk. Or that she was being told off.'

'When you were driving behind them did you see the woman drop her arm, to put it round the child, which would have been a natural thing to do if she'd been late and her daughter was upset?'

'It wouldn't have been comfortable,' the man pointed out. 'She was too small against the woman in the back seat. If she'd put her arm down it would have been round the child's neck, not round her shoulders or her back.'

'And the woman definitely didn't do that, reach down to hold Mary?'

'Not that I saw.'

'While they were in your view, did you get any impression that Mary didn't want to be there? Any indication of their arguing or Mary fighting: trying to get out?'

'Not at all.'

'How long were they in your view?'

'Only a few minutes. At the rue de Laeken they turned left and I turned right.'

'This is very important,' warned Claudine. 'You could see Mary's head, above the top of the seat.'

'Just.'

'The whole of her head, down to her neck? Or just the top: her hair?'

'Not much more than her hair.'

'How far up the woman's arm was the top of Mary's head?'

The man put the flat of his hand virtually at his shoulder. 'About there.'

Poncellet summoned an aide to take Lunckner to a police artist, waiting for the man to leave the room before saying: 'I think that was very good.' He spoke as if he were personally responsible for the success.

'I agree,' said Claudine. 'We've got a lot to work from.'

'I think so, too,' said Harding. 'Rompuy particularly: I prefer his recall to the other guy's. Rompuy's drawing will be important.'

'But will it really take us that much further forward?' asked Jean Smet, coming into the discussion for the first time.

'Very much,' predicted Claudine. 'I'm getting to know who it is I'm up against.'

'Well?' asked Norris impatiently. He was leaning forward intently over Paul Harding's desk in the embassy's FBI office.

'Nothing much so far,' apologized Duncan McCulloch uncomfortably. A towering, raw-boned man, he was a Texas descendant of a Scottish immigrant whose given name he disdained in favour of Duke. 'Quite a lot of newspaper cuttings about her involvement in some serial killings a few months back: Chinese gangs terrorizing illegal immigrants into prostitution and drugs. There was a failed hit on her. It was at a railway station. A knife

155

attack. She caught it in the arm but the Chinese went under a train.'

'What about personal stuff?' insisted Norris. That was where he'd find the lead to her association with the kidnappers.

Robert Ritchie said: 'She's described as a widow in some of the cuttings. Apparently she was Britain's lead profiler before she transferred here.'

'Anything between her and Blake?'

'It doesn't look like it,' said McCulloch.

'You lying down on this?' demanded Norris, abruptly accusing.

'For Christ's sake, John! We've only just started!' protested Ritchie.

'I don't like being sworn at. And I don't like being told there's nothing dirty when I know there is.'

'What is it?' demanded McCulloch. 'If you've got a lead give it to us to follow.'

'I'm talking instinct. I've given you the job of finding it. You fixed a wire?'

'Yes,' said McCulloch. 'Nothing.'

'We got her personal Europol file?'

Each man waited for the other to respond. Finally Ritchie said: 'We haven't got any assets inside Europol, which would be our only chance. Getting hold of a personal Europol file cold, from outside, would be as impossible as getting any of our stuff out of Pennsylvania Avenue. Which you know as well as I do can't be done.'

Norris patted the table at which he sat. 'You think Paul might have a contact inside?'

McCulloch shrugged. 'I've no idea. But I thought this was a sealed operation?'

'It was,' said Norris. 'Now maybe you guys need help.'

McCulloch managed to restrain himself until they reached the rue Guimard and the bar to which Harding had introduced the FBI's Washington contingent. 'Jesus

H Christ!' exploded the Texan. 'Where the fuck does the asshole think he's coming from!'

Ritchie, a laid-back survivor of California's flower power era, was as angry but better controlled. 'I don't think the sonofabitch knows where he's coming from. You ever hear of James Angleton?'

'The CIA's master spycatcher,' remembered McCulloch. 'Internal counter-intelligence. Only he never caught a single fucking traitor in the Agency – although they were there – broke every law there ever was and ended up a paranoid basket case.'

'I think we've got ourselves the son of Angleton.'

'The story is that Angleton destroyed as many people as Stalin if it just crossed his mind that they weren't on his side.'

'And Norris has just started to have doubts about us,' declared Ritchie.

CHAPTER ELEVEN

It would probably have occurred to each of them, at some stage, but it was Peter Blake who suggested it first so the credit went to him and in Claudine's opinion more than made up for any earlier oversight. It was admittedly prompted by the appearance of Kurt Volker in the main operational room just as Johan Rompuy and René Lunckner re-entered with the police artist, but it was still Blake's idea. Most encouragingly of all, Paul Harding at once acknowledged it as such.

They'd had to promise Poncellet and the Justice Ministry lawyer a full profile and copies of the artist's drawings by the end of the day before either of them accepted that Claudine and the detectives needed to work through the information, and even then the reluctant Jean Smet had tried to argue his right to remain.

'Videofit!' declared Blake.

It was Volker who responded, spurred by the word. 'Of what?'

'The man and the woman who snatched Mary,' announced Blake. He smiled, sure of his proposal and pleased with it. Quickly, almost too staccato, he recounted the physical description given by the two motorists and offered the sketches.

Volker said, casually: 'Easiest computer graphic in the world. I can draw the faces as they appeared to both witnesses and then enhance them three-dimensionally. It'll be counter-productive if either of them has any obvious facial disfigurement but gambling that they don't

I can make a right and a left profile and a full frontal.'
He smiled. 'We established our own web site with the
serial killing. We can post the images on our own home
page and then advertise, through the main providers.
Include a digitalized picture of Mary, too . . .' He hesitated, nodding back to his communications set-up. 'It'll
start a fresh avalanche. The first one's dwindled, incidentally, down to a trickle.'

'Do we want to start it up again?' wondered Harding.
'Both our witnesses think it's a Belgian car: Brussels
maybe. Here's where the concentration needs to be, not
worldwide.'

Claudine wished the Belgian motorists weren't hearing
a conversation they might later repeat. 'There won't be
any facial disfigurement: Mary wouldn't have got so
readily into the car if there had been. And we *need* to
emphasize it worldwide. It'll feed their power need but at
the same time it will be the beginning of the pressure I
want to impose.' To Volker she said: 'The graphics could
be shown on television, couldn't they?'

'Of course. In colour and actually moving, from profile
to full face.'

'That's how we'll guarantee the saturation here in
Brussels.'

According priority to the computer graphics Claudine
and the two detectives concentrated upon the physical
descriptions of the man and woman to accompany Volker's drawing, which the German began from the artist's
impressions and built up from the prompting of the two
motorists blocked by the kidnap Mercedes. Volker had
already created the three-dimensional portrait of the
woman by the time Claudine delivered her suggested
statistics with the undertaking for more, specifically the
estimated height of both.

It was Blake again who suggested a way of calculating
that from the known seat height of Mercedes up to and

including the 300 range and the rough approximation of where Mary's head came, against the woman's shoulder, from Mary's known height.

'We're learning what they look like,' said Blake. 'You getting to know what's in their minds?'

Claudine nodded. 'There's no doubt that it began as a classic paedophile snatch, with a woman to allay the child's fear. The woman's the key, possibly the ringleader. And she's recklessly arrogant, sitting casually, not hurrying, even when they'd caused a traffic block. The man was anxious, hurrying people by and even using his indicators when he pulled away, trying to minimize the inconvenience he'd caused by stopping as suddenly as he had at what I'd guess to be the woman's command when she saw Mary walking by herself. The woman's very quick, mentally. Mary's scowling was at having an adventure spoiled. She was expecting a car and must have said something the woman was able to pick up on. She got Mary into the car and was able – at first, at least – to control her verbally. The most obvious way would have been by pretending to be the back-up car taking her where she expected to go. Physically to have touched Mary would have frightened her so she's a practised child abuser. She's probably taken kids this way before so we've got to go carefully through those previous case histories Poncellet is assembling. There *is* money. The jewellery description sounds like a Cartier set: I know because I've got the same. It's called Constellation. So she likes expensive jewellery. That – coupled with the reckless arrogance – tells me she's vain, overly sure of herself. The way she dresses her hair supports that: everything in place, controlled. When Kurt and Rompuy are happy with the computer compilation we should blanket hairdressing and beauty salons with it.' She paused, searching for anything she needed to add. 'And I've very little doubt that it was the woman who created the Mary, Mary Quite Contrary message: arrogance again. If it was her, it confirms her as the person in charge.'

'A woman paedophile, targeting a girl?' queried Blake, frowning.

'It's an unusual pattern but not totally unknown,' said Claudine.

'The publicity will be intense when the computer pictures are released,' suggested Harding. 'Won't the physical risk to Mary increase – quite apart from the sexual danger – if they think we're getting too close?'

'Yes,' agreed Claudine flatly. 'But it's something we can't avoid.'

'Would there be an element of protection in the fact that a woman is involved?' wondered Blake.

Claudine shook her head positively. Even more flatly she said: 'The majority of case histories of women sex perverts show them more physically cruel and deviant than men.'

'Thanks for picking up on the things we missed,' said Harding.

Claudine saw the opening at once. She hadn't expected it to be so easy. 'It's a combined effort now, not a contest any more, isn't it?'

'It certainly is as far as I am concerned,' said the American guardedly. 'And I think today's gone pretty damned well.'

With an aggression that surprised Claudine, Blake said: 'You sure about that, Paul?'

'I don't think I understand that question,' protested the American.

'I thought we'd ironed out the working relationship,' said Blake.

'So did I.'

'It would be unfortunate if it got fouled up again.'

Claudine had imagined she would have to lead this

161

discussion and frowned curiously at her partner. Blake refused to meet the look.

'It won't on my part,' assured Harding.

'It didn't make sense, John walking out as he did,' said Claudine. It had to be confronted, not allowed to drift into innuendo and misunderstanding. 'I know re-interviewing the eye-witnesses was primarily an investigative procedure but I'd have expected someone as obsessional as John to insist on remaining.'

'I know,' said the American. 'I was as surprised as you.'

Claudine didn't think she could go as far as openly suggesting Norris was suffering a mental problem. 'So what are we going to do about it?'

'He's got a lot of respect, back in Washington,' said Harding. What the hell was he doing, talking disloyally of a colleague? But Norris was behaving like a horse's ass. Harding was more discomfited by the man's behaviour today than he had been when he received the initial Iceman cable alerting him to Norris's arrival.

'I thought McBride had clout, too,' said Blake.

'I don't have any reason – or the authority – to question John. If I tried my feet wouldn't touch the ground until I got to Washington, probably in protective custody.'

'Which would seem to sum up the problem,' said Claudine.

'Any move is going to have to come from your side,' Harding insisted.

'It would help if we knew when and where to make it,' said Blake.

Harding shook his head despairingly. 'I can't work against my own task force commander!'

'Don't work against us, either,' said Blake.

'I won't,' repeated the American. Shit, he thought: what a total fuck-up!

Blake was about to speak when the telephone sounded. Harding grabbed it, eager for the respite. It was a very brief conversation. To Claudine he said: 'It was Harrison, at the embassy. The ambassador has asked to see you.'

Claudine went alone to the Boulevard du Régent, leaving the two detectives watching Volker creating a startlingly life-like portrait of a narrow-faced, suntanned blond that both Rompuy and to a lesser extent Lunckner insisted was an amazing re-creation of the woman in the back of the Mercedes. It would, Volker assured them, be ready by the evening.

James McBride was more composed than Claudine had previously seen him. So was Hillary. Norris was facing them across the desk, legs outstretched in easy relaxation. The chief of mission remained standing.

'The ambassador—' started Harrison, but McBride broke in at once.

'—can talk for himself. I'm not sure this second television appearance is a good idea. John doesn't think so, either.'

Norris smiled and nodded. He looked beyond Claudine, clearly searching for Harding. The smile disappeared.

Claudine realized at once that the ambassador respected her opinion. So she'd impressed the man at their earlier encounter. She didn't think it would be difficult to do it again: inexplicably leaving, as he had, meant Norris was totally ignorant of what they'd achieved with the eye-witnesses. It wasn't going to help the man's mental condition but Claudine wasn't sure anything short of hospitalization would.

She repeated her conviction that the abductors had to be drawn into contact upon Europol's initiative ('the first, unwitting, erosion of their control') and that it should be achieved in the shortest possible time ('it's the fourth day now: Mary mustn't be allowed to think no one is trying to help her and start trusting those who are holding her'). Throughout Norris sat complacently, shaking his head in dismissal to every point.

McBride provided the opportunity for which Claudine was waiting. 'Won't it simply be a repetition of the appeal I've already made?'

'That would be sufficient by itself,' said Claudine easily. 'But we've got digitalized pictures of the man and woman who took Mary—'

'You know who they are!' Hillary interrupted.

'We think we've got a fairly accurate picture of what they look like,' qualified Claudine. 'They'll be ready by late afternoon, early evening. And their impact will be that much more if you appear, reiterating your appeal directly to them.'

'Why didn't you tell me this, John?' McBride demanded.

Norris was sitting primly upright now, his face fixed, knowing Claudine Carter was lying. She wouldn't allow anything like an accurate picture of her accomplices to appear publicly. 'I was waiting to hear from Paul,' he said inadequately. 'There's a danger of getting a lot of bad leads if the pictures aren't good.'

'The witnesses are happy with them,' Claudine assured him. To the ambassador she added: 'I don't want to expose you or your wife to any more distress than you've already suffered. But I really want these pictures to achieve the maximum impact. Your appearance would ensure that.'

'I made a fool of myself last time,' blurted McBride.

'Not for the first time,' said Hillary.

'You couldn't have done better if you'd been rehearsed,' insisted Claudine, pleased to contradict the other woman.

'You sure about that?' asked McBride doubtfully.

Norris was shaking his head vigorously.

'We've got to make the biggest possible impact, to get

164

them to come to us,' repeated Claudine. 'Don't stage a press conference, as such. Make it a television appeal, limited to yourselves and an interview . . .' She hesitated, remembering the need for diplomatic correctness. 'Include Poncellet, to talk about the importance of the computer graphics to the investigation.'

'We'll do it,' decided Hillary.

McBride nodded, in agreement. 'I'm to appeal—'

'Plead,' broke in Norris contemptuously.

'Yes!' said Claudine, eagerly again. 'That's what you've got to do. Plead. Do whatever it takes to bring them to us.'

McBride was silent for several moments before saying: 'Will you prep us?'

'Willingly,' said Claudine, relieved. 'We'll rehearse it word for word.'

Turning to Harrison, McBride said: 'Fix it through public affairs. And involve Poncellet.'

Norris stayed, listening disparagingly to Claudine's advice but offering none himself. He realized the woman was extremely clever. His mistake had been in underestimating her. It was possible he'd have to take some very direct action. Detain her and interrogate her. *Make* her talk.

Norris was waiting in Paul Harding's chair at Paul Harding's desk when the local FBI man arrived back at the embassy. He didn't make any effort to move.

'You should have called me about the computer graphics. The woman wrong-footed me.'

'I was still working!' protested Harding.

'You got print-outs of the pictures?'

Harding offered them across the desk.

'I'm not impressed,' Norris said dismissively. 'Could be anyone.'

'The two motorists who saw them are happy.'

'I think it's all very clever,' said Norris solemnly.

'Their German computer guy is a genius,' agreed Harding, misunderstanding.

Norris frowned. 'What do you know about her?'

Harding's misunderstanding remained. He looked at the digitalized image on the table between them and said: 'We don't have a name, John.'

'Dr Carter!'

Harding couldn't speak for several moments. At last he managed: 'You're losing me here.'

'I've got a bad feeling about her. I want her thoroughly checked out. I've assigned Ritchie and McCulloch but they're drawing blanks. I want you to do better.'

On the scale of bad feelings Paul Harding's score was eleven where the graph stopped at ten. What the fuck was he going to do! Remembering, he said: 'We checked the school again. The principal had an odd phone call from a woman wanting to know the curriculum languages. The phone number she left was wrong.'

'I'm interested in the Carter woman,' said Norris, dismissive still. 'Concentrate on her.'

Kurt Volker was waiting impatiently for Claudine when she re-entered their offices at the Belgian police HQ. 'I think there's something significant,' he announced.

'It's time to declare yourself,' said Lucien Bigot. He'd made the first approach, all those months ago.

'I know that,' agreed Sanglier.

'So what's it going to be?' demanded the politician.

'I'd like a final meeting.' He had to have the commitment, even if only verbally.

'We'd like that too.'

'For positive undertakings,' said Sanglier.

'That's what we all want,' said the other man.

CHAPTER TWELVE

Félicité recognized that she was right, as she usually was: there was a sexual excitement about danger. It was, perhaps, why she so much enjoyed cruising the streets, hunting. The pleasure had gone on now for more than half an hour, ever since Jean Smet had burst into the Anspach house babbling about pictures of her and Henri Cool to be shown on television.

'You'll be recognized! Identified!' The man was unable to keep still, striding about the room as he had at the beach house, his mind butterflying from anxiety to anxiety, his words jumbled. He'd tried to smoke, too, but Félicité had forbidden it. She detested the smell of stale tobacco in her home.

'Sit down!' she ordered sharply. 'How can they know about me?'

'Two motorists saw you pick her up.' Smet remained standing, shifting from foot to foot.

It was the first comprehensible sentence the man had uttered and Félicité felt another spurt of excitement. She rose and put both hands against Smet's shoulders to press him into a chair on her way to the drinks tray, where she poured brandy for both of them. As she handed his glass to him she said: 'From the beginning. Everything that was said, *how* it was said.'

Smet made a slurping sound with his first drink and the cognac caught his breath, making him cough. He tugged a tightly folded wad of paper from inside his jacket and said: 'Read it yourself. That's a copy of today's report to the Minister.'

Félicité took her time, sipping her drink as she read, acknowledging that this investigation appeared much more thorough than the previous one. Which was why it was that much more satisfying. When she finished the account she remained looking down at it, turning several sheets over before looking up. 'So where's the computer graphic?'

'I only heard there was going to be one in a telephone call from Poncellet on his way to the television studio! We're not getting a copy until tomorrow, in time for our cooperation meeting. And that's the problem I'm trying to make you understand. I don't know everything they're doing, not all the time! And not quickly enough.'

There was still ten minutes to go before the special newscast, Félicité saw. She waved the report. 'You read this?'

'Of course I've read it: I wrote most of it. And it's *you*, isn't it!'

'It's a very general description of a woman who is older than me and wears indeterminate blond hair in a chignon.' Félicité ran her fingers exaggeratedly through the lightly waved hair that fell almost to her shoulders. 'Which I never do except when I'm choosing someone new: precisely *because* it will be confusing, if I'm seen. My hair is more golden than blond. The estimate of how tall I am makes me almost into a giant. Cool too. It's ridiculous. They haven't even got the car right: it's dark green, not blue or black. And it's a 320.' She cupped her breast with her free hand. 'And I'm not at all flat-chested: I've got nice tits. You like them, don't you?'

Smet shook his head, although not in answer to her question. 'This isn't anything to joke about.'

'Nor is it anything to wet yourself about.' She had

imagined far more from the man's garbled rambling and her excitement was going. 'You told the others?'

'I wanted to speak to you first.'

Too frightened to do anything by himself, Félicité thought. Or even to be trusted. There could never be any question of Smet going to the authorities. He was too deeply involved, as legally culpable as the rest of them. Which he well knew. But the risk – not a danger by which she was sexually aroused – was in his making a stupid mistake. Unlikely, she reassured herself. Not that he wouldn't make a mistake – as nervous as he was Félicité didn't doubt he'd do something wrong – but that it would in any way direct attention towards them. But Smet was still a weak link, useful only because of the position he occupied. Not just weak. Boring, too. Boring like them all: as Marcel had complained, just before he died. Maybe she should abandon them, after this. There'd be nothing they could do about it and she had other connections, through Lascelles and Lebron. Moving on, finding new people, was definitely something to think about.

'It's time,' announced Smet, anxiously.

It wasn't but Félicité turned the television on anyway and was glad because the introduction had already begun, with a clip from the earlier conference at which the ambassador had openly wept. The main newscast anchorman talked over the old footage, announcing a different format. Tonight was not going to be a media event. It was to be a personal appeal, by McBride and his wife, following important new evidence that the Brussels police commissioner would disclose. On that cue the previous conference faded, to be replaced by a screen-filling photograph of Mary Beth McBride which held for at least thirty seconds before cutting to the studio.

McBride and his wife were seated at an oval table, with André Poncellet to their right. The three were facing the

169

anchor, an eagerly talking, dark-haired man who spoke in sound bites. To his prompting Poncellet described the eye-witness information as dramatic, sensational, vital, a breakthrough, only just stopping short of predicting an early arrest.

The camera focused tight on the ambassador's face for the man's appeal. There were no tears but McBride was grave-faced, Hillary visibly strained beside him. They held hands, although listlessly. McBride's plea was for private and immediate contact with Mary's captors.

'Come on! Come on,' said Félicité impatiently. 'Where am I?'

Smet broke away from the screen, frowning curiously at the woman.

'We want to negotiate,' McBride was insisting, keeping strictly to Claudine's instructions, even using the words she'd suggested. 'But that's not possible on the Internet. Find another way. Tell us and we'll follow it: we'll obey every instruction. Please let us know that Mary Beth is unharmed.'

The camera pulled back again to include the anchorman who used a renewed selection of sound bites to reintroduce Poncellet and the digitalized computer images of Félicité Galan and Henri Cool.

Félicité stretched towards the screen, feeling the sensation return. It was a reasonable impression, she conceded. But not good enough for a positive identification. She'd been made too thin-faced and her nose was too pronounced and elongated, as if it dominated her face, which in reality it didn't. And the graphic showed her hair pinned right to left, which was opposite to the way she wore it. Henri Cool was made to look much too heavy and again the nose was too pronounced. On the right hand side of each graphic the physical description was printed, making them both much too tall. Pedantically Poncellet recited every statistic.

'It's you!' whispered Smet breathily. 'It's definitely you and Henri!'

'No it's not,' snapped the woman brusquely. 'There's a resemblance, nothing more. Certainly insufficient to bring anyone knocking on my door. Henri's either. You're recognizing us because you *know* it's us. That's altogether different. And the printed description is too vague, as well.' Abruptly she felt deflated, disappointed. Trying to bring back the feeling she said: 'See the power we've got. How we're making them beg and plead?'

'What are we going to do now?'

'You mean what am *I* going to do now?'

'Yes,' mumbled the lawyer. 'You.'

'I'm in no hurry,' said Félicité. 'I like a worldwide stage. We'll change our approach when I feel like it, not because James McBride wants us to.'

'Let's get it over with,' the man implored.

Félicité ignored him. 'You can write the next message,' she decided. 'Make it better than Michel's: another rhyme, maybe.'

'I'm doing too much as it is,' Smet argued. 'Let someone else do it.'

'I want you to do it,' insisted Félicité, ending the protest. She paused. 'It was a pity there wasn't time to get to Antwerp and watch the broadcast with Mary: let her see how desperately dependent her big important papa is upon us . . .'

The telephone jarred into the room, interrupting her. Smet, his nerves stretched, noticeably jumped. Félicité said: 'It'll be one of the others, shitting himself like you.'

The expectant smile with which she answered the telephone faded almost at once. It was a very short conversation, with Félicité constantly interrupting. As she replaced the receiver she said vehemently: 'Damn Charles Mehre!'

171

'What is it?' demanded Smet, in fresh alarm.

'He's killed,' said Félicité shortly.

A television had been installed in the largest of their allocated rooms and they watched McBride's appeal in silence. When the programme finished Claudine said: 'I wish I'd had time to brief Poncellet: he exaggerated far too much. But McBride was better than I expected: caught exactly the right note. Even Hillary saying nothing but looking like she did fitted what I wanted, a couple totally at the mercy of those who've got their child. They even held hands as I asked them, which they didn't want to do.'

'Can you imagine what it's like!' said Volker sympathetically.

'Maybe it's not enough to reassure them – I might be interpreting it wrongly – but I think Mary's still alive,' announced Blake quietly.

Claudine and Volker looked at him, waiting.

'I thought I'd check the school again: see if anyone had remembered anything, after all the publicity,' said Blake. 'It probably wouldn't have meant anything to Madame Flahaur if it hadn't been the only call like it she's had, since Mary disappeared. A woman telephoned two days ago, asking about the curriculum, particularly about the languages that are taught. That's all she appeared interested in, according to Madame Flahaur. The prospectus she sent out was returned this morning: the address doesn't exist. Neither does the phone number the woman left: I checked both with Belgacom on my way back.'

'What language did the woman speak?' demanded Claudine, immediately understanding.

'French.'

'Mary learning it?'

Blake nodded. 'She started it late, behind all the other pupils. It's her second semester.'

'Comprehension?'

'Below average for her age, because of the late start.'

'It's got the arrogance of our blond in the Mercedes,' judged Claudine slowly. 'Arrogance coupled with clever caution. If you're right – and I think you might well be – we now know whoever have Mary are French-speaking. But don't want Mary to understand what they're saying in front of her.'

Volker nodded, also understanding now. 'It could be a crank call. A lot of the e-mail stuff so far has been, particularly after the press conference identification.'

'It's feasible,' agreed Claudine. 'I don't think it's sufficient to reassure the parents that Mary's still alive – and risk their agony if we're wrong – but I think it's something we can add to the profile as a possibility.'

'It was two day ago,' reminded Blake. 'She could be dead by now.'

'If they were going to kill her that quickly they wouldn't have bothered to call the school in the first place,' said Claudine. 'It could also indicate they haven't touched her sexually, either.'

John Norris was mortified by McBride's television appeal, practically unable to believe an ambassador of his great and wonderful country could have been reduced to begging like a bum on a street corner by the manipulation of just one woman. He'd even used some of the words and expressions that she'd suggested. They'd have laughed at that, all of them: known just how successful they were being, infiltrating the very investigation the way they had. Fooled everyone except him.

But he was getting his own profile together. It was still very disjointed, a lot of threads hanging loose and needing to be tied together, but the unanswered discrepancies were there, like he'd known they would be.

He still couldn't find the fit for the Carter woman. Just knew that she was part of it because that was his job, to see things other investigators didn't see and point the way for them to go. Which he would, when the other indicators slid into place. It wouldn't take long.

He'd already sent a priority demand for the full details upon which a Grand Jury arms embargo indictment had been issued against Italian arms dealer Luigi della Sialvo, in whose name two End User certificates had been issued for multi-million-dollar purchases from McBride's corporation, before the man came on to the political scene. And another 'what's happening' chase-up on all the possible disgruntled employees who'd been dismissed by Mrs McBride.

Norris was becoming suspicious of Harding's working relationship with the English detective: by not alerting him about the eye-witnesses to the kidnap ahead of the ambassador's preparation for that humiliating TV appeal Harding had exposed him to ridicule. The man couldn't be trusted. Neither could McCulloch or Ritchie. If anything was going to be done properly, he'd have to do it himself. And as quickly as possible.

God knows what that poor child was going through. And there was only him to save her.

Harding had his usual table at the rue Guimard bar and got the drinks in, as the in-country host. There was a lot of noise from other tables where other agents were determinedly enjoying the unexpected pleasure of an overseas assignment but Harding's table was quiet. He said: 'You want to know the truth? The truth is I'm scared shitless. I knew it was going to be bad, before I even heard he was involved. But I never imagined it could be like this. He's totally fucking paranoid.'

'I'm not arguing with that,' agreed McCulloch, propping his feet on the only unoccupied chair to prevent anyone's joining them. 'The question is: what are we going to do about it? It's our asses in a sling.'

The Texan actually wore cowboy boots, Harding saw. He said: 'The Europol guys know it, too. Virtually spelled it out.'

'There's nothing we can do,' said Ritchie. 'They're the only people who can stop him.'

'The sonofabitch is only getting a check run on the ambassador himself!' McCulloch disclosed.

CHAPTER THIRTEEN

Gaston Mehre had very roughly re-dressed the boy in trousers, although he hadn't zipped the fly or bothered with underpants. Otherwise the body was naked to the waist and without socks or shoes. The crumpled shirt nearby was flamboyantly ruched and the shoes were patent leather, with large silver buckles. There was a dried trickle of blood from the corner of his lipsticked mouth and after-death lividity, where the blood had pooled, darkened his face despite the make-up which also failed to hide completely an emerging beardline. The nipples were rouged. The eyes were bulging and the long black hair lankly matted by gel and sweat. The lingering cologne was still quite strong.

Charles Mehre's canopied bed was in chaotic disorder, the sheets balled up and in places torn, hanging from the bed in tendrils. Only one pillow remained on the bed, heavily indented and spotted with blood. There was also a splash of blood on a mirror set into the bedhead. Directly in front of the mirror was a pair of handcuffs and beside them a thin-thonged whip. On the floor nearby there was a black leather bag, on its side: a dildo and a set of nipple clamps were spilling out.

Félicité turned away from the body, uninterested, walking back into the main room of the rambling, two-floored apartment above Gaston's antique shop in Antwerp's Schoenmarkt. Smet and Henri Cool were by the window, overlooking the city's still bustling shopping district. Freed from Félicité's restraint, Smet was smoking defiantly. Both he and Cool held whisky glasses. Gaston was by the drinks tray, pouring for himself, when Félicité entered. She shook her head against the gestured invitation. Charles Mehre was isolated in a far corner, hunched on a very upright chair. His head was low on his chest, a child caught doing something wrong. He hadn't been given a drink. No one was talking.

Félicité said: 'Where did you get him?'

'On the Paardenstraat,' said Gaston, naming Amsterdam's homosexual centre.

'When?'

'Last night.'

'Anyone see you?'

Gaston shrugged. 'It was the busiest time.'

'Were you in your car?'

The antique dealer shook his head, gesturing towards his brother. 'He wanted to choose himself.'

'What was his name?'

'He called himself Stefan. Stefanie.'

Félicité frowned. 'What nationality?'

'Romanian, he said. A lot of them have come from the East. He had an accent.'

'What happened?'

'It was to calm Charles down: you told me I had to. It meant getting him someone,' said Gaston, defensively. 'We were all together, when we got back. He was very good. He had to stay, obviously. This morning Charles said he wanted Stefan for another day: that he liked him. We fixed a price. I left them up here this afternoon, while I was downstairs in the shop.'

'How?'

'Pushed his face down into the pillow from behind, until he suffocated. That's how I found him. Charles says he didn't know he was doing it: that he was excited.'

Félicité crossed to the corner. Charles hunched down, cowering, at her approach. 'Why!' she shouted.

177

The man tried to make himself smaller, not replying.

'Why!' she shouted again.

'Sorry,' he said, mouse-voiced.

'Tell me why.' Félicité's tone wasn't so strident. It wasn't as good as the feeling she got taking risks or partying with a group but it was close: there was a thrill making grown men cringe, nervously doing whatever she told them.

'Wanted to,' mumbled the man. 'Felt nice.'

It was an inconvenience, decided Félicité, allowing the anger: an intrusion for which she had to adjust when she'd thought she had everything worked out in its logical sequence. She leaned even closer to the man who still smelled of his victim's cologne. 'You're stupid!'

He looked up and as close as she was Félicité clearly saw the madness in his eyes and was momentarily unsure how much longer she could control him. Another reason for moving on from this inherited group, she thought, recalling her earlier uncertainty about Jean Smet.

'Not stupid,' snarled Charles.

It would be wrong to show any fear: wrong to betray it to the man in front of her, to whom she couldn't surrender control, and wrong, too, in front of the other men who had always and unquestioningly had to accept her as their leader. 'Stupid!' she repeated, her voice loud again. 'Admit to me you're stupid!'

'No!'

'Say it!'

'Stupid,' whispered the man.

'Louder!'

'Stupid.'

'Louder still!'

'Stupid!' Charles shouted. He began to cry.

'That's good,' said Félicité, soft again, encouraging. 'Now promise me you won't do anything like it again.'

'Promise.'

'Say I promise I won't hurt anyone again: won't kill anyone again.'

'I promise I won't hurt anyone again: won't kill anyone again.'

'That's very good, Charles. You won't forget that, will you?'

'No.'

Félicité turned to his brother. 'Your storage basement has a security door, right? And your own cell?'

'Yes?' queried Gaston.

To the head-bowed man in front of her Félicité said: 'I want you to take Stefan down into the basement. And all his clothes. Do you understand?'

'Yes.'

'Tell me what you've got to do.'

'Take him downstairs and put him in the cell.'

'With his clothes,' she prompted.

'With his clothes,' he agreed.

'No!' said Gaston, still close to where the drinks were. As Félicité turned again, she saw him pouring more whisky for the agitated Smet. Charles had been straightening but now he stopped, looking for guidance beyond Félicité to his protective brother. Gaston said: 'I'll get rid of the body, tonight. Cleanse it with a detergent, a spirit, before putting it naked into the river. It'll be all right.'

'No,' said Félicité. 'I want it kept, for the moment.'

'Why?' demanded the nervous Smet from the window.

'Because I say so,' insisted Félicité, who had no clear idea why she'd said what she had but didn't want to be seen immediately to change her mind. She moved away from Charles Mehre, returning to the others. 'Gin,' she ordered. 'Just ice.'

'I want to get rid of the body,' insisted Gaston stubbornly.

'There might be a use for it. He's a whore, probably entered Holland illegally in the first place. No one's going

179

to miss him. Whores disappear all the time.' She turned back to the hunched man in the corner. 'I said take him downstairs!'

Charles Mehre looked between Félicité and his brother, like a trapped animal.

Gaston capitulated. 'Take him downstairs.'

'That's better,' said Félicité. She was becoming irritated by the constant challenge, from too many people. She waited until Charles had stumped from the bedroom, the body heavy over his shoulder, and Gaston had fetched her drink before she said: 'I don't want him around Mary any more. Not until I say so. He's too dangerous.'

'Who's going to look after her?' demanded Cool.

'Has anyone been to the house today?' Félicité said, to Gaston.

'Charles was going tonight,' said the man.

'I'll go,' decided Félicité. This had to be the last time: the end. Everything was falling apart. She supposed she should talk about the television appeal: she'd left Smet telling them when she looked at the body. She felt suddenly tired of them, not wanting to be with them any more that night. Instead she was anxious to get to the beach house. To be by herself with Mary. Her Mary. She said: 'The pictures don't look anything like me. Nothing's changed.'

Mary didn't intend it to happen – didn't know why it did – but a tiny mewing sound escaped when she heard the key. She didn't care who it was, even if it was the woman. When it *was* the woman Mary was glad the heaviness of the door would have hidden the sound she'd made. She didn't know how she came to be there but she found herself close to the door, expectantly, when it swung open. She moved back slightly, but the woman didn't come into the cell. Instead she stepped back, smiling, gesturing Mary out into the larger room.

'Did you think I'd forgotten you?' Félicité's voice was quiet, friendly, with only a trace of huskiness.

'I don't know.' Mary shrugged. She felt better, being with someone. The woman didn't seem so threatening tonight.

'You should have known I wouldn't do that. I don't want to hurt you.'

'Let me go, then.'

'Soon. You must be hungry.'

Mary was. The last she'd had to eat were the two rolls the snuffling man had brought for breakfast the previous morning. 'Yes,' she admitted.

'I've got us both a meal,' said Félicité, pointing. There was a tray on one of the low tables, by the central dance floor. On it was laid out bread, cold meat, fruit and cheese. There was also a bottle of red wine and a bottle of water and two glasses.

'Do you eat with your mama and papa?' asked Félicité, leading the way.

'At the weekends, mostly. They're too busy during the week. There's a nanny. Joyce.' She decided against telling the woman that mom and dad squabbled all the time.

'I'm going to enjoy having supper with you.'

'Yes.' The food couldn't be poisoned if the woman was going to eat it as well. She was very hungry, her tummy growling. She was embarrassed, not wanting the woman to hear. Mom said it was rude when your stomach made noises. She liked the woman being kind to her, not shouting or hitting her.

Seeing Mary's hesitation and guessing the reason Félicité served meat on both plates, tasted hers immediately and said: 'It's very nice. Try it.'

Mary did, at first hungrily but then more slowly, not wanting to annoy the woman. The meat tasted wonderful, the first proper food she'd had for days. She'd forgotten how long: forgotten to keep checking the date on her watch. She didn't mind the way the woman was looking at her, smiling. It was good, just being next to someone: not being alone.

'How about some wine?' suggested Félicité, taking out the already withdrawn but lightly replaced cork.

'Mom doesn't let me.'

'Haven't you ever?'

Mary smiled, guiltily. 'Once or twice. Bits left over after meals at the weekends.'

Félicité poured into both goblets. 'I'll let you, because we're friends.'

She extended her glass and Mary clinked hers against it. She liked the taste of the wine: like fruit. She felt grown up.

'How is it?'

'Nice.'

'Would you like more meat?'

'Please.'

Félicité helped her to more and when Mary finished the second helping changed her plate for cheese and fruit. 'Drink up. There's a whole bottle for us to finish.'

'Maybe some water.'

'I didn't bring enough glasses.'

'Where's the man who usually comes?'

'I've come instead. Aren't you glad?'

'I don't want you to hit me.' She felt funny. Not ill or sick, as if she'd been poisoned, but dizzy, things going in circles inside her head.

'I promise I won't hit you.' Félicité offered her glass again and when Mary responded said: 'Cheers. This is nice, isn't it: just the two of us together?'

'I suppose.'

'More than suppose,' encouraged Félicité.

'It's nice. Is there going to be someone for me to play with?'

'I'm sorry. The girl couldn't come, after all.'

'You promised!' Mary's face felt numb.

'I'm sorry.' Félicité reached out and took Mary's hand.

It was too much trouble – felt too heavy – for Mary to move it. 'You broke a promise.'

'There'll be boys and girls soon.'

'When?'

'Very soon.' Félicité shared the remainder of the wine between them, pouring more for Mary than for herself.

'Have you spoken to my father?' Mary felt sleepy, as well as dizzy.

'We're making plans.'

'Honest?'

'Honest.'

'Please let me go.' It was very hard, not to cry.

'You haven't showered for two days.'

'No.'

'It was very hot today.'

'Not down here.'

'I should shower, too. Shall we shower together?'

'No.'

'We're both girls, aren't we?'

'You're grown up.'

'So are you, drinking wine.'

'I suppose.'

'Then it's all right, isn't it?'

'I don't know.'

'I've seen you with no clothes on.'

'I know.'

'You don't mind seeing me with no clothes on, do you?'

'I don't know.'

'Haven't you ever bathed with mama?'

'Not since I got big.'

'Why don't we try?'

'You won't hit me? Make me jump for the towel?'

'No, I promise,' said Félicité, her voice thicker now.

'You broke your other promise.'

'I won't break this one.'

'All right.'

'Let me help you,' offered Félicité.

Neither Henri Cool nor Gaston Mehre had seen the television appeal. Both had listened horrified, Cool open-mouthed, to Smet's repeated and much more detailed account after Félicité left.

'Was I recognizable?' demanded the schoolteacher.

'I think so,' said Smet. 'She said not: that it was because I knew it was the two of you.'

'What am I going to do!'

'Decide for yourself,' said Smet. 'They'll be shown tonight on the late news programmes. And in the papers tomorrow.'

'Oh, dear God!' moaned the man, hurrying to the drinks tray.

Charles Mehre came back into the room, standing uncertainly by the door. He said: 'He's downstairs. I covered him up.' The other men said nothing and Charles went back to the chair in which he had sat earlier.

'It's a mess,' complained Gaston. 'Everything's a total mess. And getting worse. And there's no way we can get out.'

Smet was still looking at Charles. He said: 'Félicité's right about the whore. There won't be a big investigation into his disappearance: even into his killing, when the body is found.'

Cool returned with a refilled whisky glass, his hand shaking. 'That's not our problem.'

'I know,' said Smet, coming back to the two men. 'It's the girl, and she's only a problem as long as she's alive. Dead – cleaned against any forensic examination and properly disposed of – there'd be nothing to link her to us.'

Neither Cool nor Gaston spoke immediately.

Cool said: 'You're right. It's what I wanted from the start.'

Gaston said: 'Who?'

Smet looked back to the man's hunched brother. 'Would he, if you told him to?'

'She'd be furious,' said the antique dealer.

'What's worse, our being caught or Félicité bloody Galan being angry over something it would be too late for her to do anything about?'

'We should talk about it with the others first,' said Gaston.

'Why?' asked Cool. 'Let's get the whole damned thing over and done with.'

'We're a group. We rely on each other: protect each other,' said Gaston. 'They should all agree.'

'You're trying to avoid it,' accused Cool.

'You do it yourself then!' demanded Gaston at once, seeing his escape. 'I agree we have to get rid of her! But don't use Charles. Or me, to make him do it. Kill her yourselves. Dispose of her yourselves, the way I've got to dispose of Stefan.'

There was another long silence. 'Let's talk to the others,' agreed Smet finally.

'They won't do it either,' Gaston said. 'Not themselves. It's always been Charles.'

'Someone's got to,' insisted Cool.

'What are you talking about?' asked Charles from his corner.

'Nothing,' said Gaston. 'Don't get upset: I'll look after you.'

For the first time since they'd arrived in Brussels Kurt Volker ate with them – at the Comme Chez Soi on the Place Rouppe, another first – and proved to be an unusual dinner companion. He dominated the conversation

185

with cyberspace through-the-keyhole anecdotes of peccadillos, foibles and downright carelessnesses of the rich and unrich, famous and infamous, ordinary and extraordinary. Mostly with the people he spoke about, it was extraordinary.

When Blake said so, actually using the word, Volker said: 'Who's to judge extraordinary?' and Claudine, impressed, said: 'He's right. Psychologically – mentally – there are no criteria for ordinary. So no one can be *extra*ordinary, can they?'

'What about the people we're investigating?' said Blake. 'Aren't they extraordinary?'

'The point is that paedophiles convince themselves – actually *believe* – that they are ordinary. That it's normal to have sex with children. And if I forget for a moment that we're hunting people who think their sexual preferences are perfectly natural, we're going to lose Mary.'

'What if you get to them?' demanded Blake urgently. 'What will you be feeling and thinking if you get to negotiate one to one, in some way?'

Claudine was surprised by the question, disconcerted by it. 'I'd suspend any personal judgement. Revulsion, contempt, would come through, and I can't afford that. More importantly, Mary can't afford that.'

'You've never negotiated a kidnap before: certainly not a paedophile kidnap,' Blake said solemnly. 'Can you do it?'

'I won't know until I try,' Claudine conceded, wishing she hadn't been confronted by such a direct question. Peter's attitude had, in fact, confused her from the very start of the evening. He'd appeared tense, unaccustomedly ill at ease, and for want of any other explanation she'd put it down to Volker's unexpected presence, although that could scarcely be considered an intrusion. Peter, she suddenly thought: she'd obviously called him that, from the beginning, but until now had distanced him in her mind by using his surname. It was an unimportant reflection, she decided: like thinking that Blake's attitude tonight was any different from what it had been on the previous nights.

Volker worked hard to restore some lightness with further stories of a marauding cyberspace Robin Hood ('to benefit the good and defeat the bad') and Claudine enjoyed the change from the Grande Place restaurant.

Volker turned out to have a low tolerance but great liking for alcohol and became heavy-eyed, thick-tongued when he retold two of his best stories. Blake had the restaurant order them a car, rather than hail a street taxi. Volker, between them in the back seat, fell almost immediately asleep. Blake sat supporting the man with his arm along the back seat exactly, Claudine realized, as the blond-haired woman had sat enticing Mary into the Mercedes. He stayed like that for most of the time, half facing Claudine. When, on two occasions, she looked pointedly across the car towards him, he turned away to stare through the rear window.

They both had to help the German to his feet on the Place de Brouckère. It brought Blake and Claudine close together and Blake said quietly: 'Let me in when I come to your room.'

'No!'

'Do it!'

They ascended without speaking in the open-grilled elevator, the half-asleep German leaning amiably between them. Claudine stared fixedly at Blake, who looked back expressionlessly. Volker's floor was below hers and as Blake helped the German out she again said: 'No!'

Blake ignored her.

Inside her room Claudine put the dead bolt across the door as well as double locking it. She was confused. Offended, too. She wouldn't let him in. What right did

187

he think he had – what right did any of the bastards at Europol have – to think every woman was going to roll over on her back and open her legs, grateful to be fucked! Disappointment joined her other feelings. Peter – Blake, she corrected herself at once – was attractive: considerate, attentive, fun to be with. In other circumstances – a lot of other circumstances, chief of which had to be the exclusion of Hugo – she might have been drawn to the man. But not like this: not with the slam-bam-thank-you-ma'am cowboy approach.

The knock was soft. She ignored it. The next time was louder and when she still didn't respond he said: 'Claudine, don't say anything. Just let me in.'

'I don't—' she started but he repeated: 'Don't say anything.'

The urgency wasn't sexual, she realized at once. She didn't know what it was – didn't know what was happening – but she was abruptly sure she'd misunderstood everything so far. She unbolted the door and tentatively opened it.

Blake was standing anxiously on the threshold. Loudly – too loudly – he said as he hurried in: 'I'm sorry. I had to put him to bed: he's completely gone,' and made exaggerated rolling motions with his hands to indicate that she should respond. He went straight past her, to the bottom of the bed, orientating himself to the room.

Bewildered but obeying, Claudine said: 'Will he be all right?'

'He'll probably feel like shit in the morning.' Blake revolved both hands again, telling her to keep talking, nodding as well.

Claudine nodded back, comprehending at last. An absurd charade unfolded in which Claudine remained by the door, discussing the evening – apologizing even for not having anything to drink – while Blake swept the room, keeping up the empty conversation with her as he did so. She'd never seen it done before and occasionally faltered in what she was saying, distracted by his obvious expertise. He came back to where she remained standing to unscrew the light switch just inside the door. From there he moved on to every light fitting and socket and every electrical plug and connection, using a handkerchief pad to remove hot bulbs.

The bedside telephone was clean but there was a listening device in the extension phone on a table, in front of the curtained window. It was so minute, little more than a pinhead fitting snugly into one of the tiny diaphragm holes, that she had difficulty seeing it when he pointed it out to her and wouldn't have suspected it even if she'd unscrewed the instrument herself.

Blake reassembled the telephone without removing the bug, moving some way away before saying: 'As you haven't got any booze here I guess we'll have to go back to the bar.'

'OK,' Claudine accepted at once.

At that moment the telephone rang.

'I left messages,' said Hugo Rosetti accusingly.

'It was too late to return them when I got back.'

'What about today? Tonight?'

'There are a lot of problems we didn't expect.' Go away! she thought, hating herself for thinking it.

'Like what?'

'I don't want to talk about them on the telephone.' She was being listened to. She didn't know by whom or why but everything they were saying – Hugo as well as herself – was being overheard. And Blake was in the room, as well, although he'd started searching again, disappearing into the bathroom.

'What's so mysterious?'

'It's far more difficult than we thought it was going to be: problems with the Americans.'

189

'I thought you allowed for that.'

'Not enough.'

'What are you going to do about it?'

Blake appeared at the bathroom door, pointing with a jabbing finger at what she guessed to be the switch just inside the door.

'I don't know yet.'

'The Americans send a negotiator?'

'He's the problem.'

Blake sat down on a chair by the door, stretching his legs in front of him.

'Can you handle it?'

'I'm going to have to.'

'I'm missing you,' said Rosetti.

'I'm missing you, too,' she made herself say, face burning. There was no reason for her to be embarrassed, not in front of Blake. This was awful: terrible.

'It hardly sounds like it.'

'I've got to go.'

'It's eleven o'clock at night!'

'Something's come up.'

From his chair Blake made warding-off gestures.

'What?'

'Something I've got to talk about with someone.'

'Blake?'

Oh God! 'Yes.'

'Is he a problem?'

'Of course not! That's a silly question.' Why had she said that!

'Sorry!' He stretched the word, to show he was offended.

'You're misunderstanding.'

'It's difficult not to.'

'I said I didn't want to talk on the telephone!'

'I love you,' said Rosetti.

'I'll call you back tomorrow. Say around seven.'

'I said I loved you.'

'I'll explain later.'

'What's the matter?'

'Nothing! I really do have to go.'

'I thought I'd come down this weekend.'

'Aren't you going to Rome?'

'Would it be inconvenient for me to come down? Apart from anything that might come up with the case, I mean.'

'Of course not. I'd like you to come down. Let's talk about it tomorrow. Goodnight.' Claudine hurriedly replaced the receiver but remained standing by it.

Blake grinned and said: 'How about that drink?'

Claudine's hands were shaking, from anger not fear, rippling the brandy in her glass, which she held in both hands. She'd sat where he directed, at a table some way from the bar and other late night drinkers. She at once recalled the bizarre conversation about carrying a gun when he identified the night he'd detected the surveillance at La Maison du Cygne and said: 'You thought it was on you!'

He nodded. 'Had it been we probably wouldn't have got back across the square, either of us. It was the fact that we did that made me doubt I was the target in the first place, even before I found my room was clean.'

He'd kept himself curiously apart from her, she remembered. 'Norris?'

'Obviously. It's not the people who'd like to find me and it'll hardly be the people holding Mary, will it? Norris will never admit responsibility, though. No one will.'

'The paranoid bastard!' she said, fresh anger surging through her. 'How long's it been there?'

He shrugged. 'Sometime during that day, I expect. That was when you positively faced him down.'

Claudine forced herself to be calm, frowning. 'I haven't

used the phone much: certainly haven't talked about anything the Americans don't know about.'

'They're open transmitters, in both the telephone and the bathroom light switch.'

'You mean they're live all the time: relaying everything that happens, not just the telephone calls?'

'Yes.'

'I don't want to stay in that room any more.'

He smiled again, trying to relax her. 'There's mine but I'm not going to risk the rebuff. You know you're being listened to now. Use it to our benefit.'

'You think Harding knows?'

'I'm not sure. He came a long way towards us with his concern about Norris. I think if he had, he might have said something.'

'It's so fucking stupid! So pointless!'

'What are you going to do?' he asked.

'I don't know, but I suppose it makes sense to pretend we're unaware.' She looked directly at him. 'There were a lot of times tonight when you could have told me what you thought there was in my room. Why all the drama?'

'I might have been wrong. Then I would have looked foolish.'

'You still made it into a drama. And you must have been sure.'

He grinned. 'I wanted to see if you'd let me in.'

'Bastard!'

'But not a paranoid one.'

Claudine put her glass down, relieved her hands had stopped shaking. 'Are there really people who'd like to kill you?'

'Not until they'd hurt me as much as they could.'

August Dehane's wife was completely unaware of his membership of Félicité Galan's group, which always made it difficult speaking to the man at home. The conversation was one-sided and led by Jean Smet. The lawyer impatiently dictated the message upon which Félicité insisted and said he did not, of course, expect it to be convenient for the telephone executive to meet the rest of them until the following evening. Dehane's hesitation was obvious when Smet gave his address off the rue de Flandres as the meeting place.

'Is Félicité going to be there?' he asked in a whisper.

'No. We're going to settle things. Remove the problem,' promised Smet.

'That's good,' agreed Dehane.

CHAPTER FOURTEEN

There are in Paris a very small number of restaurants, three the most notable, renowned as much for their discretion as for their highest *Guide Michelin* awards. That on the rue du Miel, the first of the notable three, was a place of dark wood, small-paned windows, subdued lighting and conveniently anonymous rooms. The most conveniently anonymous of all were two on the very top floor. The epitome of *belle époque* – as indeed the restaurant was – such *salons particuliers* were originally conceived as private rooms where the rich and famous could dine their mistresses in intimate mirrored luxury before moving to the only other furnishing, an opulent chaise-longue. Favours were expected to be returned for favours received. It was the practice for the courtesans to test the genuineness of their gifted diamond by inscribing their intitials round the mirrors' edges: those inscriptions – anonymous, of course – are now officially decreed to be national monuments.

The *salon particulier* that Sanglier entered, five minutes late, was, like all the others, a place where favours were still expected to be exchanged, although no longer cut into the ancient, still reflecting glass which his hosts were studying when he arrived. There were three of them. Guy Coty, the chairman of the party, was the oldest although he did not look eighty-five. He was a small, tightly plump, totally bald man who had spent his life as a pilot fish for sharks in murky French political waters. The diminutive but exalted ribbon of the *Légion d'honneur* was in the left lapel of his immaculate dove-grey suit. Roger Castille was half the other man's age, with the dark-haired, ivory-teethed, open-faced looks of a matinee idol disguising a ruthlessness inherited, along with Ff50,000,000, from a financier father. The third man, Lucien Bigot, was one of the few survivors of Castille's tread-on-anyone ascent to the party leadership. Bigot was a beetle-browed man who used his size to intimidate. His official position was party secretary: like Coty he preferred power-brokering in back rooms to his public parliamentary work. It was Bigot, already known to Sanglier from their six months of political flirtation, who performed the introductions.

There was pre-luncheon champagne but no pretence of toasts: as yet there was nothing to celebrate. As aware as he'd always been of the significance of the *Légion d'honneur* and the expectations of the recipients, Sanglier accorded Coty the necessary respect, conscious of how it was being properly shown by Castille and Bigot. And it wasn't stopping there, Sanglier realized. To a far lesser but still discernible degree the two politicians were acknowledging himself as the son of a man who had also gained France's highest honour.

'I knew your father,' said Coty, in a voice clouded by too many cigarettes. 'Not during the war, of course: I was in London, with de Gaulle, after I escaped the Gestapo. But afterwards, when the *sanglier*'s bravery became known. De Gaulle invited him to come into government but he declined.'

It seemed odd, hearing the name like that, properly used as the code designation by which his father had worked before officially adopting it as the family's legal surname after the war, like several other Resistance heroes. Coty was almost an exception for not having done so. It was the first time Sanglier had heard of the political invitation: another aspect of his father's life that had been secret. He said: 'He was a very modest man.'

'And now you've got the opportunity to take up the offer he refused,' said Castille, seizing the way to move on from reminiscence without offending the elder statesman.

Could he take the risk? Sanglier asked himself for the thousandth time. He didn't *know* that his father's exploits, re-routing Nazi labour-camp trains and execution orders, weren't totally true: there were, in fact, provable Gestapo records of the failed hunt for the mysterious *sanglier*. But there were so many gaps, verging on inconsistencies, in those and other records, omissions blamed on Claudine Carter's father who, as Interpol's chief archivist, had by almost unbelievable coincidence prepared Sanglier's wartime history for France's archive of heroes.

His emergence into political life would inevitably refocus attention upon his father's history: maybe, even, rekindle interest in a new biography by a new, more determined literary investigator than the authors of those that already existed, and who had unquestioningly accepted his uncooperative father's explanation that apparent discrepancies were unavoidable in the chaos of the war's end.

Cautiously, determined upon assurances that went far beyond his fear of the past, Sanglier said, with false diffidence: 'I'm very flattered to have received this approach, and I have had several months to consider it. But there are important matters for us to discuss before I can give you my reply.'

'Food first,' growled the husky-voiced Coty, pressing the waiter's bell just inside the door of the private room. He was smoking through a small malacca holder.

The others had already studied the menu, before occupying themselves with the initials of long-ago whores. Sanglier refused to hurry, keeping the attendant waiting while he carefully considered his meal. By the time his choice was made Castille was scuffing his chair impatiently.

As soon as the waiter left the room Castille said: 'There's no doubt the present government will fall within six months. No doubt, either, that we'll succeed them. And we'll remain in power for a very long time, after the scandals and failed policies of the last ten years—'

'But with a difference this time,' Coty broke in. 'Virtually every minor party making up the current coalition is associated with the disgrace and failures, either part of them or by association. We're not. We're clean: above it all. That's going to be our manifesto: how we're going to be seen by the electorate. It's going to give us an overwhelming, unassailable majority so that there'll be no need to rely on any of the smaller groupings.'

'We're going to be the clean party for a new Republic,' announced Castille, almost too obviously practising an election slogan.

This encounter was just as well rehearsed, decided Sanglier. 'I have been extremely fortunate in my profession,' he ventured, 'but until your approach I'd never considered a political career.'

'Consider it now!' urged Bigot. 'We'll guarantee you an electable constituency.'

'And I can also guarantee that I will never forget those who declare for me at this stage,' said Castille.

He needed an admission without portraying himself as naive, Sanglier knew. 'If I were to pursue this there would have to be complete truthfulness between us.'

'We wouldn't be sitting here if I didn't expect you to take everything that's said with total seriousness,' said Castille. 'And never for a moment will I be anything but completely truthful: I intend to practise among colleagues the central core of my manifesto.'

He *had* learned at the EU meetings in Brussels and Luxembourg and Strasbourg! 'Colleagues?' Sanglier demanded, shortly. 'More than simply members of the party in the Assembly?'

The arrival of the food covered what Sanglier guessed would have been a hesitation among the other men. His oysters were superb, the bone-dry Muscadet the perfect complement. Coty reluctantly extinguished his cigarette.

'I've already made it clear we do not see you simply as a parliamentary member,' said Bigot, with a hint of impatience.

Sanglier applied lemon in preference to onioned vinegar. It was the moment to wait, saying nothing.

Coty said: 'You went to Brussels after an extraordinarily successful period as police commissioner here, in Paris. And continued that success there.'

Time for absolute directness, judged Sanglier. 'What role would you see me fulfilling if I were to become part of your administration?'

'Justice Minister,' declared Castille.

'I would consider nothing less,' said Sanglier. 'I am well aware – and proud – of my achievements here in Paris . . .' He paused, determined never to be treated lightly or underestimated. 'Just as I am well aware – and perhaps even prouder – of the cachet that goes with my name.'

Coty smiled, a flinty expression, fitting another cigarette into its holder. 'The art of politics is assembling maximum resources to achieve optimum advantage—'

'—consistent with honesty,' Castille hurried in.

'I'm glad we're fully understanding each other,' said Sanglier, content with Coty's admission that like all politicians these men were observing the golden rule of expediency. He recognized that he did not have a positive guarantee – anything in writing – but acknowledged that to expect that *would* be naive. 'I have your promise?'

'My absolute word,' said Castille.

'Do we have yours?' demanded Coty.

Sanglier paused, at the very moment of commitment. 'Yes,' he said.

The venison Sanglier had chosen to follow the oysters was excellent, like the Margaux. With something to celebrate now, it was Coty who proposed the toast.

Castille said: 'I have given you my solemn undertaking.'

'Which I accept,' said Sanglier, curiously.

'Now I am seeking undertakings from you,' announced the man. 'I have no wish to cause offence. But there are questions I have to ask you. My platform, remember, is that of honesty, integrity and selflessness towards the people who will put us into office.'

'Yes?' If Sanglier hadn't felt the first stir of uncertainty the unctuous hypocrisy would have been amusing.

Castille turned invitingly to Coty. The *éminence grise* of the party said: 'Is there anything in your past that could emerge once we're in power – once you held a ministerial portfolio – that could cause the sort of scandal that has besmirched the present government?'

'No,' declared Sanglier. No going back, he realized.

'I repeat that I do not intend any offence,' said Castille. 'But neither do I intend to allow any risk to my election. Are you prepared for the party secretariat to investigate your past fully, to confirm that assurance independently?'

He had to take the risk about his father. What about Françoise? She was by far the greater danger, prowling too many public places like a bitch permanently on heat. Could he control her – persuade her to control herself – with the lure of being the wife of a government minister? Close to being an unrealistic question, he forced himself to admit. There'd been enough to lose – quite apart from the Sanglier reputation – when he was commissioner in Paris before the Europol appointment, and neither consideration had curbed her. It wasn't Françoise or his father that gave him pause. Rather it was his determination to speak and act in every circumstance as they would expect, to prevent any doubt. Despite Castille's caveat, they would expect him to be affronted. 'Your apparent need to do so hardly fits with undertakings of personal honesty that we've pledged between ourselves.'

'It fits with my intention to establish an administration above reproach,' said Castille, a prepared retort.

'*Do* you object?' said Bigot.

'Of course not,' said Sanglier. 'I'm prepared to cooperate in any way.'

'That's reassuring,' said Coty. 'It's going to give me great pleasure getting to know the son of a man I greatly admired.'

It was mid-afternoon before the meal ended. They parted with effusive handshakes and assurances of how much each was looking forward to working with the other.

Bigot was the first to speak after Sanglier left. 'It's a coup. And not just for the Sanglier name. His wife was a Dior model: spectacular woman. There'll be a lot of good publicity around the two of them. We could maybe build them up as the perfect couple.'

Kurt Volker tracked the third message.

He wasn't suffering any hangover from the previous night and was actually early at his embassy-linked terminals when the e-mail was delivered. Because he'd established a program of as many connections to Mary Beth McBride as possible the sender address instantly registered, which gave him at least forty seconds to follow backwards the stepping stones between sender and embassy before the disconnection.

Claudine and Blake arrived at their police headquarter offices as it was happening, unaware of the potential breakthrough until being beckoned urgently into the computer room by one of the early shift Belgian operators ploughing through the renewed incoming deluge prompted by the previous night's TV appearance.

Several other operators had abandoned their stations, crowding round the German, but even their excitement was subdued. Volker himself appeared quite relaxed, although his hands were darting with astonishing coordination between the keyboards of three terminals in a semicircle in front of him. Claudine was once more reminded, as she had been on their first assignment together, of a theatre act to which she had been taken as a child to watch a man perform simultaneously upon three pianos. Completing the impression, Volker was humming, at first tunelessly but then something vaguely Wagnerian. No one else was making any sound.

Claudine had no idea what she was watching: didn't try, even, to read the words and the instructions that kept appearing, becoming fainter each time, upon the main screen in front of the German. At one stage, like the theatre pianist, Volker operated his central keyboard with his left hand and with his other punched keys on the board to his right, conjuring e-mail addresses on to the connected screen.

'Bah!' he exclaimed, in final frustration, when the screen directly in front of him remained blank after the message faded. 'Lost him!'

He spun the swivel chair, scattering the other operators, to face Claudine and Blake. 'They'd buried themselves in at least four different systems, moving just as I thought in source-covering sequence from one to the other . . .' He stabbed a finger at the last address on the side screen. 'That's where I lost them . . . at least I think I did. There's an outside chance – a very outside chance – it could be where they're operating from.'

'Where is it, for Christ's sake!' demanded Blake urgently.

Volker turned another revolution, accessed INEX, and

typed in the address. At once the screen filled with a blank home page of a computer café in Menen, on the Belgian–French border. 'It would certainly be easy,' said Volker, still looking at his screen. 'You can be quite anonymous in places like this. You just go in, get allocated a terminal to surf wherever you want and simply walk away after you've paid.'

'Get me the rest,' demanded Blake, hurrying from the room.

Claudine followed, accepting that apart from analysing the latest message she was largely superfluous. And she didn't hurry with the message.

Needing the operation-initiating authority of the Belgian Justice Ministry Blake first telephoned Jean Smet and asked for total surveillance to be placed upon the Menen café. Before disconnecting he cancelled that morning's scheduled conference with the promise to reconvene at the already arranged afternoon time unless a new development intervened. He gave the same undertaking – and account – to André Poncellet and Paul Harding, in that order.

Finally Blake tried to reach Sanglier. Told the commissioner was unavailable, he sent a full account to the man's secretariat, with a request for Sanglier to contact him as soon as possible.

By the time Blake finished, Volker had located the Internet-linked computers through which Mary Beth's abductors had ridden Sinbad-like to reach the US embassy home page. From the specialized Menen café the message had travelled unseen and unsuspected to the Foreign Ministry system in Bonn. From there it had been sent to a Trojan Horse unknowingly installed in the mainframe computer of the American Express office at the foot of the Spanish Steps, in Rome. From there it had been automatically routed to the flagship of the Kempinski hotel chain on Berlin's Kurfürstendamm. The last stage from there had been to the school on the rue du Canal from which Mary Beth McBride had disappeared, six days earlier, whose e-mail address Volker had put on to his search program.

Claudine realized her own need to talk to Sanglier had become secondary in the light of the morning's developments, but remained determined to insist he use his authority to stop the nonsense degenerating any further. She wasn't interested in playing silly games and using her knowledge of the tap to their own advantage. They had to recover a child and to achieve that a paranoid man had to be removed before he caused God knew how much damage.

By midday Blake's flurry of activity had eased. Smet telephoned that the computer outlet was under intense observation and Volker had independently accessed the café's system and attached tracers programmed to react to the embassy's e-mail address.

Blake was at Claudine's shoulder when she at last spread the print-out of the latest communication between them. It was written in two lines and read: WE DETERMINE HOW AND WHEN. YOU WAIT AND OBEY.

'We're not going to get much from that, are we?' he said.

'Enough,' said Claudine gravely. 'Maybe more than enough.'

'What?'

'I need to think more about it,' Claudine said. 'Make sure I've got all there is to get.'

Nothing occurred to alter the scheduled afternoon session and by the time they assembled disappointment had begun to erode the initial excitement of the cyberspace chase. Volker explained, stage by stage, stopping short only of his newly installed monitor of the café's inward and outward traffic. As if on cue Smet said the Justice

Ministry had asked Belgacom to suggest any electronic check that might be possible on the Menen outlet, completing the irony by pointing out that to attach an eavesdropping facility would be illegal, although they were seeking a ruling from a High Court judge. The physical surveillance was absolute, insisted the lawyer. Computer literate plainclothes officers had been drafted in to use the facility during the day, taking the observation actually inside the café to identify regular users, and there were rotating squads watching from outside. A separate team had been assigned to investigate the registered owners and all their known associates. If it was established the café's use was innocent the owners and all its regular users would be specifically questioned about the computerized pictures. The café was on the outskirts of a pedestrian and shopping precinct and all security camera film was being collected, again for comparison with Volker's digital images.

André Poncellet picked up as soon as Smet finished, describing as 'overwhelming' the response within Brussels to the previous night's television and that day's newspaper publication of the kidnap computer graphics. It was going to take several days – maybe even longer – to investigate every one.

Claudine always regarded what she did as a contribution to an investigation, not its most important element, and was content for the practical discussions to dominate the meeting. It was, she acknowledged, the first time this supposed overall planning group had been given the opportunity to operate in anything like a proper, practical way. Consciously Claudine let the discussion swirl about her, always aware of it, listening to it, but at the same time instinctively lapsing as well into people-watching.

From their earlier encounters she hadn't expected quite such a forceful emergence from Jean Smet, although she accepted Blake's direct approach that morning had lifted the Justice Ministry lawyer's participation beyond its original liaison remit. André Poncellet was showing no surprise at the other Belgian's occupying centre stage: seemed prepared, even, to surrender a leading role to the man.

Claudine's greatest concentration was upon John Norris. When she'd first entered the room in which Norris was already waiting she'd been briefly gripped by the fury she'd felt finding herself tiptoeing around her hotel room, actually taking care to avoid cupboard-closing or clothes-rustling noises. She was completely controlled now, still angry but able to find an excuse for what had happened in the man's illness. She hoped it wouldn't be too much longer before she was able to reach Sanglier: certainly before the day was out. His not being available was a nuisance.

Norris appeared as attentive as everyone else, but there was an artificial studiousness about the way he was avoiding her gaze: several times it seemed difficult for the man to stop himself smiling in a situation in which there was no reason to smile. And he was making no contribution to the discussion.

She was frightened, Norris decided: guessing how close he was although there was no way she could know how he'd got there. She'd have to wait to learn that: wait for the confrontation. He'd look directly enough at her then. Face her down: force an admission. He had enough on tape from the hotel recording. Words that could only have one meaning: words that told him she was involved in the kidnapping and how scared she was at being caught out.

The Americans send a negotiator?

He's the problem.

She didn't know the half of it. She'd even conceded that, too. *There are a lot of problems we didn't expect.*

Other parts of the conversation presented themselves in his mind, each as damning as the other.

Can you handle it?

I'm going to have to.

She wasn't going to be able to, though. Not after that morning's computer chase that they were all so excited about: that he was excited about, because it had given him the positive tie-in. From Bonn to Rome: to Rome and the convenient money-managing expertise of an American Express office. Which fitted perfectly with another part of last night's taped exchange.

Aren't you going to Rome?

'What about the message itself?' Norris was suddenly conscious that Poncellet was directing the question not to him but to the woman.

Claudine did not bother with the pretence of including Norris, consciously subjugating her still lingering medical distaste. 'It worries me,' she admitted bluntly.

'Why?' demanded Smet.

'It hasn't taken us any further forward,' said Claudine. 'The ambassador and his wife performed brilliantly last night. Psychologically it should have got a different response.'

'Perhaps your advice was wrong,' said Norris at once. McBride was a separate issue but Norris was sure he had something there, too. The indictments against Luigi della Sialvo were all for illegal arms dealing with Baghdad during the Gulf War, obtaining weaponry from a corporation that at the time had been McBride's chief rival and was now the subject of four separate and enjoined indictments. Norris found it difficult to believe that whoever in the Bureau had checked out McBride before the ambassadorial appointment hadn't taken the inquiry further, comparing the computer-recorded volume of material leaving McBride's company against End User certificates for the Far East – della Sialvo's favoured route – during

Operation Desert Storm. He'd put an 'Utmost Priority' tag on his request, after studying the indictments, so he expected to hear within twenty-four hours. It didn't matter whether McBride was a close personal friend of the President or a major campaign contributor. If he'd broken the law he had to answer to it.

'My advice wasn't wrong,' insisted Claudine, confronting the American verbally as well as physically. 'This isn't a response to the broadcast. This is an angry message.'

'What's there to be angry about?' queried Harding. 'McBride pleaded: virtually said he'd pay anything.'

'I don't think the anger is directed at us,' said Claudine. 'I think there's some disagreement among the people who've got Mary: irritation that subconsciously came through in the message.'

Oh, this was clever, thought Norris: trying to confuse them all with psychological double-talk no one could recognize except him.

'Couldn't it be reasserting the control you say is so important to them?' suggested Smet.

The lawyer now very clearly considered himself an active player in the group, decided Claudine. Why not? He *was* a lawyer and all his questions and comments so far had been valid. She said: 'There's an aggression that wasn't in the earlier contacts. And this one, incidentally, was written by yet another person, so we know there are at least three.'

'What could the disagreement be about?' wondered Blake.

'The most obvious reason is that they're not unanimous over how to continue the situation,' said Claudine.

'What situation?' protested Harding. 'They've hardly started yet!'

'That's another thing that worries me,' conceded Claudine quietly.

'You think the danger's sexual? Or worse even than that?' asked Poncellet.

'I don't know,' said Claudine, unhappy at a further admission. 'But I think there's more now to the arrogance that I talked about in the beginning.'

'Like what?' demanded Smet.

Claudine paused, briefly unsure whether to express the fear. 'They've snatched a child: not just a child, the daughter of an American ambassador. They should be frightened: apprehensive at least. But they're not: not enough. So they've done it before: snatched a child and not been caught.'

'We're still working through investigations over the past three years, re-interviewing child sex suspects against whom no charges were brought as well as convicted paedophiles,' said Poncellet. 'Everyone will be compared to the computer graphic, obviously.'

'Any women involved?' demanded Blake.

Poncellet looked uncomfortable. 'Not that I'm aware of: I'll make a specific check.'

'Could the sort of disagreement you think this message shows be making them careless?' asked Harding, smiling apologetically to the German in advance. 'Kurt wasn't able to follow a trail before.'

'They had to risk it this time,' said Claudine quickly, seeing Volker's offended frown. 'They had to let us pick up the school address: that's the proof the message is genuine, not a crank response from last night's broadcast. They had to leave it on the screen long enough for it to be recognized: Kurt's genius was in having created a program that identified it in seconds – far more quickly than they probably expected – and then being able to follow it back as far as he did.'

'Thank you,' said Volker, the frown replaced by an even-toothed smile.

She was extremely convincing, thought Norris, in

reluctant admiration. But that was hardly difficult for her, knowing it all from the inside as she did. This was going to be one of his most successful investigations – spectacular even – exposing her for what she was.

'But the fact that they used the school for proof could be another cause for concern,' Claudine continued. 'The first two messages had identification that could have only come from Mary herself. Why didn't the third, to maintain the pattern?'

'You think she's dead?' demanded Harding.

Was she trying to soften them up, prepare them for something that had happened? wondered Norris. That couldn't be right: he couldn't save Mary – prove to everyone that he'd been right – if she was already dead. So it couldn't be true. It didn't fit. 'No! She can't be.'

Blake and Harding regarded the American psychologist in surprise, as if they'd forgotten he was in the room. Seemingly abruptly aware of their attention, Norris said: 'I don't read the message as Dr Carter does. In my opinion Mary Beth's still alive.'

There were discomfited looks between Blake and Harding. Poncellet openly shook his head. Only Smet gave no reaction.

Forcefully Claudine said: 'The lack of anything that must have come from the child herself is the strongest indicator so far that Mary's dead. It could even be the reason for the anger that I believe is there.'

'How much more difficult will it be to find them if she is dead? If the body is buried or disposed of?' queried Smet.

Harding looked sideways, inviting Norris to respond. When he didn't the local FBI man said: 'I think it would make Washington doubly determined to catch them. The investigation would increase rather than decrease.'

'If this morning's message hasn't carried any nego-tiation forward what do we do?' asked Poncellet.

Claudine was positive. 'Now's the time to wait.'

'What if they don't come back to us?' said Blake.

'She'll definitely be dead,' declared Claudine. 'And we'll have failed.'

'*You'll* have failed,' said Norris.

Jean Smet kept his house as the venue but individually warned the others that Félicité would be attending too. She had to know – they all had to know – everything that had happened. It didn't change the need to get rid of the child – it made it all the more necessary, despite Harding's bravado – and when she heard how close the investigation was getting Félicité would have to agree. That way they'd all be in it together, without any falling out. Which he wanted as much as the rest of them.

He expected Félicité to arrive last, which she did, but wasn't prepared for the triumphal entrance, a diva commanding the stage. 'Well?' she demanded.

It was Henri Cool, the one most worried about identification, who first realized Félicité actually had her hair in a chignon, although crossed in the way she always wore it, not as it had been shown in the computer picture. 'You're mad! Totally mad!'

She laughed at the schoolteacher. 'I walked here by the longest route I could find. I started in the Grande Place and actually obliged two tourists by taking their pictures in front of the *Manneken Pis*, imagining what fun we could have had with a chubby little chap with a prick like that.' She smiled towards Smet. 'Just for you I wandered by the Palais de Justice – it really is the ugliest building in Europe, isn't it? – and went through the park to the royal palace before making my way here.' She paused again, surveying them all. 'And even with my hair like this no one looked at me a second time.' She snapped her fingers. 'So *that* for the pictures you were all shitting yourselves about.' She slumped into a chair, shaking her clamped hair free of its pins. 'I'm totally exhausted.' She looked at Henri Cool. 'Anything happen to you?'

'I called in sick. Stayed home.'

'That was very clever!' sneered Félicité. 'That wouldn't cause any curiosity in anyone who might have seen a resemblance, would it, you bloody fool!' She made a languid gesture towards Smet and said: 'I'll have champagne.'

Smet had two bottles already cooling in their buckets. He gestured for Michel Blott to serve, wanting to concentrate entirely upon the woman. 'Today was incredible. It's gone a long way beyond computer pictures.'

'What is it now?' she sighed wearily.

It was not something he would have admitted to the rest – he was reluctant to admit it to himself – but Smet had actually come close to enjoying that afternoon. Of course he had been frightened, weighing everything he said and heard, but the fear had even added to the sensation. He found it difficult to define precisely – a combination of power, at perhaps being able to influence the very people hunting him; and mockery, at being able to laugh at their stupid ignorance; and the tingling fear itself, at actually being there, so close to them, talking to them, being accepted by them – but supposed it was akin to what Félicité felt. The difference between himself and her was that he didn't constantly need the experience, like an addict permanently in search of a better and bigger high. There was even something like a physical satisfaction – another manifestation of power, he supposed – at the varying, horrified reactions from everyone except Félicité. He'd anticipated that, too.

'There was only one more cut-out, after Menen,' disclosed Dehane, hollow-voiced. 'If he'd got through that he would have been back to me! Oh my God!'

'It was stupid, using the school,' said Félicité.

'What else did I have? You didn't give me anything to identify her with!' retorted Smet. '*That* was stupid.'

Félicité didn't like being so openly opposed, certainly not in front of the rest. Nor did she like having to admit, if only to herself, that the man was right: she had been stupid. To Dehane she said: 'You've got a relay bug in the café system?'

'Yes.'

'Could you get it out?'

Dehane shook his head doubtfully. 'They would expect me to do it. Be waiting for an unauthorized entry.'

'Would it lead to you, if they found it?'

'No. It's a one-way system: I've got to access it.'

'So there's no danger, even if they find it?'

'Not really. And it would take a very long time, no matter how good this man Volker is.'

'So we can use what they think is a breakthrough to our advantage again,' said Félicité. 'We simply leave dozens of policemen wasting their time in a part of the country we're never going to go near again.'

The insane bitch still didn't intend changing her plans, Smet realized. The others had to hear her say it, to convince them later what was necessary. 'We mustn't go on with it.'

'It doesn't alter anything,' chanted Félicité, like a mantra.

'We've got to get rid of her.'

'There's nothing to discuss. I've told all of you what's going to happen. And it will. Exactly as I say.'

'You can't be serious!' protested the other lawyer. 'This doesn't make any sense at all.'

Félicité was extremely serious, although still outwardly showing the sangfroid with which she'd arrived an hour earlier. The investigation – everything – was very different from the last time. *Nothing* was like what had happened then: not so technical nor as determined nor with such an inexhaustible supply of police and specialists to be called upon at a moment's notice.

So it would be madness to prolong it much further: madness to try to recapture the exquisite, first-time pleasure of last night, being with Mary but ultimately holding back from touching her. Ecstasy from abstinence: priestly fulfilment.

She couldn't – wouldn't! – give the slightest indication that they'd been right, of course. *They* hadn't been right. It was the investigators who had been better: investigators she still had to confront to prove who, ultimately, was best.

'We'll further confuse them, beyond Menen,' she announced. 'Now they've got so much manpower invested in e-mail, we'll change our approach.' She turned to Dehane. 'How many Belgacom mobile telephones get stolen every day, not just here in Belgium but throughout Europe?'

Dehane snorted in disbelief. 'Thousands. Tens of thousands.'

'And all the losses – and the numbers – get recorded, to prevent their unauthorized use, don't they?'

The telephone executive shifted uneasily. 'Eventually.'

'Exactly!' smiled Félicité. 'I want you to programme newly reported stolen numbers into unprogrammed telephones for me. We'll only use a number once, before switching to another. Even if a number is scanned and the holder identified, it won't lead to us. All it will do is compound the confusion we started at Menen.' Her smiled widened. 'Now isn't that the cleverest thing!'

No one replied immediately.

Smet said: 'Who's going to make the telephone contact?'

'Me, of course! Unless any of you want to volunteer.'

The silence this time was longer.

'That's settled then,' said Félicité, hurrying now as she came to another decision: it would be easy enough to bring forward that night's dinner with Pieter Lascelles. Everyone ate unnaturally early in Holland anyway. 'And I'll go to the house again tonight to look after Mary.'

'What about tomorrow?' asked Cool.

Félicité extended a wavering finger, moving it back and forth between the assembled men before coming back to the schoolteacher. 'You!' she decided. 'Unless, that is, I change my mind.'

'We were all agreed, even before what happened today,' reminded Smet. 'So there's nothing more to discuss, is there?'

'Except who's going to do it,' said Gaston Mehre.

'He likes it,' said Smet, looking at the man's brother. Gaston was holding Charles's hand comfortingly. Charles appeared to have retreated into his private world, unaware of the discussion around him.

'We're all part of it, whoever actually kills her,' said the other lawyer.

'When?' asked Gaston Mehre.

'Tomorrow,' said Smet. 'We don't know how long Félicité will stay at the house tonight.'

'You've got to get rid of the body,' insisted Gaston. 'Charles can kill her but the rest of you must get rid of the body.'

'Of course,' said Blott, too eagerly.

'I could have come to Antwerp,' offered Lascelles. He was extremely thin as well as being tall and he held himself forward, so his body appeared concave. He had a soft, cajoling voice.

'It won't take me long to drive back.' Their table was in a cubicle shielding them from the rest of the diners.

She passed the brochure of the Namur château across to him. 'This is it.'

Lascelles studied the illustrations and said: 'It looks magnificent. Have you shown Lebron?'

'Two days ago. He was impressed. He's probably bringing as many as ten of his people.'

'I'll probably have around the same. Maybe more. They're looking forward to it.'

'When will you make your snatch?'

'Not until you give me a definite date.'

'Certainly the weekend after next. Maybe sooner.'

'You've caused a sensation.'

Félicité smiled. 'It's exciting.'

'You will be careful, won't you?'

'Don't you lose your nerve, like the others.'

It was still only nine o'clock when Félicité reached the Antwerp house overlooking the Schelde river. She smiled at the child waiting anxiously just inside the heavy door.

'Hello, darling,' said the woman. 'Are you pleased to see me?'

'Very glad,' said Mary. She liked the woman being kind to her: kinder than her mother and father, who didn't seem to care what was happening to her.

In Brussels Blake finally got a call from Henri Sanglier, who said that after picking up the message from his secretariat he'd decided to go to Menen personally to ensure the surveillance was properly in place. He rang off before Blake could transfer the call to Claudine.

At the city's Zaventem airport the American embassy's diplomatic bag arrived from Washington carrying the information John Norris had requested about McBride's armaments corporation.

At the café on the rue Guimard that the FBI had made their own Duncan McCulloch said: 'If you won't talk to Blake tomorrow I will. It's fucking ridiculous.'

'I'll do it,' undertook Harding, finally overcoming his reluctance. He was damned if he did and damned if he didn't, he decided. And just three years before he would have been out of it all.

CHAPTER FIFTEEN

The depression was tangible at the first gathering of the day, people talking because they had to but knowing they weren't offering anything to keep alive the brief hope of the previous day. The clandestine surveillance had produced nothing. Henri Sanglier had agreed with the Belgian squad at Menen that the café proprietor was uninvolved and approved direct questioning with the computer-drawn images of the wanted man and woman. The proprietor, a retired Customs officer, recognized neither. Nor did any of his regular users, whose names he'd offered before being asked. None of them resembled the couple or recognized them.

Poncellet said the Belgian police record search had been extended to cover the entire country, not just Brussels. There was no computer graphic match with any arrest photograph in police archives. Nor was there on any Europol or Interpol register. Making up for his previous day's ignorance the police commissioner said there were only two women with child sex convictions – both with boys, not girls – and neither bore any resemblance to the computer pictures. Both had witness-supported alibis for the day and time Mary Beth McBride had been snatched: one had been in Ghent, visiting a sick mother, the other at a hairdressing salon where she was well known. Both had nevertheless been detained for an identification parade that afternoon that both Johan Rompuy and René Lunckner had agreed to attend.

There was nothing for Claudine to contribute.

Although John Norris was saying nothing, either, there was more animation about the man: having so studiously ignored her the previous day he now appeared almost anxious to catch her eye, twice openly smiling. It was, Claudine decided, typical of the mood swings recorded against the severe obsessional condition from which she suspected Norris to be suffering. Claudine was anxious for Sanglier's promised arrival that afternoon. She'd been circumspect on the police headquarters telephone but she'd ensured Sanglier understood the importance of coming direct from Menen to Brussels instead of returning to The Hague. By tonight, after the scheduled five o'clock embassy meeting with McBride, the problem with John Norris should be all over. It had been an unnecessary distraction but it had not interfered with what they were there to achieve. Claudine was dissatisfied. She'd drawn every conclusion she could from what evidence there was, which could practically be fitted on to a pinhead with room to spare for a football match with spectators. Until there was further contact there was absolutely nothing more she could think of doing. And if that contact was still by e-mail she was not certain there would be anything to add to the profile she'd already created. Their continued hope would have to be that Volker's pursuit would be more successful the next time.

In rare and unsettling self-doubt Claudine wondered if she had been right to guide the ambassador's public responses as she had. She was sure the messages conveyed disagreement among those holding the child, from which it logically followed one faction dominated the other. And if domination of any sort was a factor, which was a psychologically accepted characteristic of any kidnap, whether sexually initiated or not, then it was right initially to accede to it. But she'd always resisted obedience to supposedly rigid rules in something as inexact as psychology, which as a medical science remained as unexplored as life in outer space.

One eroding doubt created another. Could she be so sure that no contact within twenty-four hours – not twenty-four any longer, little more than twelve – almost certainly meant that Mary Beth was dead? Claudine still thought so. She didn't want to – it was, she accepted, the subconscious reason for her self-questioning – but after so long without a positive ransom demand, it had to be the strongest possibility. And if Mary Beth was dead, Claudine acknowledged that she'd failed. Others might not think it – Hillary certainly wouldn't – but Claudine knew it would be so. Which brought her (know thyself! know thyself!) to the very nub of her problem: her reason for reflecting as she now did.

As she'd stood in numbed horror in the doorway of their London home, looking at Warwick's lifeless body slowly turning from his suicide rope, Claudine had determined never again to fail in a mental analysis, as she'd failed to realize until it was too late her work-stressed husband's condition. Now she faced failure again but fought against accepting it, as she had before. Things hadn't fallen out as she'd expected. To allow herself to think as she was thinking at that moment was to panic without cause. A fault she would be the first to criticize in anyone else: a fault that would endanger the child she had to save, if saving her was any longer possible.

Throughout the self-examination Claudine had, as always, remained aware of the justifying discussion continuing all around and was not caught out when it settled upon her. Her surprise, in fact, was that of all people the question came from Jean Smet, further establishing himself as the unelected but so far unquestioned coordinator of their daily, largely unproductive information-sharing. She saw no reason to question it either: someone had to coordinate.

'Anything you'd like to add?' asked the Belgian. He was getting the same satisfaction as on the previous day, enjoying himself.

'I think we should now start to consider bringing them to us,' announced Claudine, her mind filled with her most recent thoughts.

The concentration upon her was immediate. Smet said: 'Yesterday you said we should wait.'

'Not indefinitely,' qualified Claudine, wishing she'd earlier expressed herself more fully: wishing she'd thought about it more fully, earlier. 'If there's nothing by the end of the day, we should change our attitude.'

'To what?' demanded Smet.

'To challenging,' said Claudine.

'I thought it was wrong to be confrontational?' frowned Blake.

'Initially,' explained Claudine. 'We've gone past that time now. We've got to face down the arrogance: tilt the balance away from them, towards us.'

'*After* today?' pressed Harding.

'Yes,' agreed Claudine, guessing from the emphasis it was only half the question. She was conscious of Norris openly smiling, his head going back and forth between her and those questioning her.

'By which time it's more than likely she'll be dead?' the American finished.

Claudine said: 'We've got to accept that as the strongest possibility. But obviously we've got to go on acting in the belief that she's still alive.'

'She is,' asserted John Norris suddenly. And by the end of the day he knew he was going to prove it. He was going to get her back, as well as discovering from James McBride what his corporation's documented business dealings had been with the indicted Luigi della Sialvo three months before Saddam Hussein's incursion into Kuwait.

'I hope you're right,' said Smet. There had to be a secret agenda to which this man was working. That was the only possible reason for the American's inexplicable but obvious uninterest – practically non-participation – in these sessions, empty though most of them were. Another uncertainty he wouldn't have to worry about after tonight. He wanted Mary Beth dumped as far away as possible and believed he knew how that could be done, too. Gaston Mehre had demanded that others in the group dispose of her, but there was still the body of the Romanian rent boy in the cellar of his antique shop. Which was very much the brothers' problem, no one else's. Definitely not his. In their eagerness to avoid becoming physically involved the others would back his insistence that Charles and Gaston get rid of the girl as well as the boy at the same time and in the same place.

'Something else I may be able to judge from whatever response I can generate,' said Claudine. Now she was speaking in the first person, ignoring Norris, she realized.

'You're surely not thinking of the ambassador again?' said Burt Harrison, coming into the discussion.

'Not directly,' said Claudine. 'He – they – are just the route. From now on I want them to focus on me.'

She had arranged to meet Henri Sanglier at the Metropole hotel to show him the two listening devices before he went to James McBride, and Claudine had expected Blake to return there with her. But as they broke up Blake said that although it would almost certainly be unproductive he thought he should attend the identification parade including the two convicted women sex offenders.

'And Harding says there's something he wants to talk to me about.'

John Norris was tight with excitement, his overriding feeling oddly one of relief that he was at last going to achieve so much in such a short time. He didn't have the slightest doubt that it would all fall into place precisely as he'd planned it would. That was all it needed, precise and detailed planning, and Norris had all that in order: all the sessions spaced out according to their priority, all the evidence assembled, memorized and ready to be presented. The ambassador first, then the Carter woman. The Iceman myth was going to be well and truly established after today.

During the drive back to the embassy Norris waited, testingly, for the chief of mission to refer to his impending appointment with the ambassador but Burt Harrison said nothing, which Norris regarded as important. McBride obviously hadn't mentioned it, anxious to contain things between the two of them. A further indicator, Norris decided, to go with the familiar uncertainty he'd detected in McBride's voice when the ambassador had agreed to see him, that hesitant intonation of nervous guilt he'd heard a thousand times and never once been wrong about.

There was still time to spare when they got back to the embassy and Norris went first to the FBI office, determined everything should be ready there. He carelessly cleared Harding's desk, with only one exception, opening and filling drawers at random until all that remained on its top was an unmarked blotter, a multi-lined telephone and the overnight Washington dossier he intended carrying intimidatingly into his confrontation with the ambassador. The exception was the top right-hand drawer of Harding's desk, which Norris withdrew and closed several times to ensure its smoothness before installing its unaccustomed contents, the tape recorder uppermost. His final act, before leaving the room, was to position a single chair directly opposite the one he would occupy on the far side of the desk.

James McBride was alone, stiffly upright and blank-faced behind his overpowering desk, which by comparison with the one Norris had just left was cluttered with papers and files and documents. Norris at once identified the ploy, the workplace of a busy man with little time to spare. It was all so predictable, like a soap opera script.

'What is it you want me to do?' demanded McBride briskly.

Clever, conceded Norris: predictable again but still clever. 'I'd like you to help me about certain things.' Abruptly there was the briefest sweep of dizziness, gone as quickly as it had come.

'Harrison's just told me there were no real developments this morning?'

'It's not about your daughter.' This was what he'd always liked best, the thrust and parry of interrogation. He had it all marshalled in his mind, dates and times ready for any challenge or evasion. He felt very hot: probably the reason for the dizziness.

'Mr Norris,' said McBride, with threatening condescension. 'As well as being a very busy man I'm also a very worried one. There is, in fact, only one concern on my mind at the moment and only one thing I want to talk to you about. And that's Mary Beth: our only necessary point of contact. I'll give you all the time you want if it's to do with her. But if it isn't I'm going to have to ask you to let me get on with being an ambassador.'

Time to kick the struts away, to bring everything crashing down. 'Can you tell me about Luigi della Sialvo?'

The question was like a physical blow, low in the stomach: McBride actually came close to feeling breathless. 'Who?'

'Don't you know a Luigi della Sialvo?'

He'd already said he was too busy to discuss anything but Mary Beth, so he could demand the man leave. But if he did that he wouldn't learn just how much Norris –

or the FBI back home – knew. 'I don't recognize the name. Who is he? What's this about?'

That wasn't right: not the reaction it should have been. McBride should have been more unsteady when the name was thrown at him. It was important to keep up the pressure. He went to speak but then didn't, his mind suddenly thick, as if it was filled with mush. Forcing himself, he said: 'Illegal arms dealing.'

McBride told himself not to panic; not to betray any awareness. Not yet. He had to wait for the accusation: demand the proof. Even then he could deny knowing the man, pleading the passage of time. 'What the hell are you talking about?'

'Luigi della Sialvo is currently under Grand Jury indictment on five counts of illegal arms dealing with the regime of Saddam Hussein during the Gulf War. A fugitive, in fact.' That was better. Clear-headed again. Everything assembled in his mind.

Fugitive! McBride seized on the word. Not under arrest, likely to horse-trade or plea-bargain, spilling his guts for a lenient sentence. The sensation of breathlessness began to recede. 'All my stock is in a blind trust escrow account, but I would have been informed of any investigation into my former corporation . . .'

Norris had wanted a definite sign by now: the twitching shiftiness that always came just before a collapse. 'Your own records show your corporation actively traded with Luigi della Sialvo five months prior to the Iraqi invasion of Kuwait.' Was it five or seven? The dates he'd wanted to be so pedantic about, showing he knew everything, wouldn't come. 'Two deals worth about . . .' Norris's mind blanked again, stranding him '. . . worth many millions of dollars.'

It was right that he should show total shock, decided McBride: appear to be momentarily unable to respond. When he did speak it was loudly, in furious indignation.

'Are *you* accusing *me* – executives in my corporation – of illegal arms dealings? Telling me my companies are under investigation?'

The response came half formed in Norris's mind, then slipped away again. 'No accusation . . . just asking about a man currently under indictment. There isn't an investigation yet.'

Yet, thought McBride. It was a fishing expedition: the bastard was looking for a confession! 'On whose authority or instructions did you request this meeting?'

'I am ranked as a senior field executive of the Federal Bureau of Investigation, a deputy division director. I have sufficient personal authority.' That was better: thinking properly again. He wished the muzziness would stop coming and going: that it wasn't so hot in the room.

The man had left himself wide open, thought McBride. So which course should he take? Outraged, ambassadorial-level dismissal, or the astonished disbelief of an innocent man at a horrifying possibility of embarrassment? He'd learn more playing the innocent. 'Which company is named in the indictments against this man?'

Norris couldn't remember! One moment he had the name, the next it had gone, his head thick. Not mush; as if it was filled with cotton waste. 'Lextop,' he finally managed.

'Lestrop,' corrected McBride, curious at the mistake. It was a passing thought, replaced in a moment. So this was the unspecified rumour that was causing the Lestrop stock to slide: where della Sialvo had gone after he'd told the Italian to go fuck himself! It still didn't help McBride gauge the danger he faced.

'That's it, Lestrop,' accepted Norris gratefully. This wasn't going at all as it should have done: how he'd planned it. By now McBride should have broken, made a mistake he could have picked up and used to trap the man into making more. It was so difficult, keeping things

225

straight and in the order he intended. He didn't want at this late stage actually to consult the Washington dossier but he couldn't afford another mistake. At once came the contradiction. The file was intimidatingly thick. Consulting it now might convince McBride it contained more about him than it really did. He dropped one of the indictments taking them out of the folder and had to grope awkwardly under his chair to retrieve it. 'There's an international arrest warrant out against della Sialvo. He's thought to be somewhere here, in Europe.'

Where he'd be relatively safe and able to operate, McBride knew: international arrest warrants were notoriously difficult to enforce, particularly in countries with different legal systems. He would have known of an active investigation: it would have been inevitable. 'How did Washington discover the trading with my company?'

Norris realized the ambassador was questioning him, not the other way round as it should have been. Had to get the order reversed: get everything back on track. It was difficult to keep the loose papers from sliding off his lap, the facts from slipping out of his mind. 'I asked for an in-depth examination, checking for enemies you might have made. I mentioned the possibility, remember?'

So it wasn't yet properly official, a Washington operation. There never had been any secret about the two deals he'd done with della Sialvo. They were totally legal, a matter of public record, apart from the Zürich bank commission payments and that was a problem for Sialvo's native Italy, not the United States. And the Italian was free and likely to remain so. McBride was glad he'd played the innocent. It made the rest of the meeting easy. He said: 'This is potentially very worrying.'

Here it comes, thought Norris triumphantly: it had taken longer than he'd expected – he'd begun to feel uneasy, which was ridiculous – but the first trickle had just seeped through the breach in the dam. It would come in a tidal wave now. It always did. 'The more you can tell me the better it will be.'

'Quite so.' MrBride's mind veered sideways, off on a sharp tangent. Thank God there'd been the confrontation at the beginning, taking the negotiations for Mary Beth's freedom away from this bumbling, almost incoherent idiot! When it was all over – when Mary was safely back – he'd have the FBI Director's ass for sending someone like Norris.

'I always think it's best . . . what I prefer . . . what I'd like us to do would be to set it out chronologically, from the very beginning,' said Norris.

'The Gulf War was a long time ago. Seven, eight years.'

'There's no hurry. Your own time.' He'd won, beaten an ambassador friend of the President!

There wasn't any purpose in prolonging this charade: it was almost cruel, like a cat taunting a captured mouse. 'I don't have any official position in the corporation any more but obviously in the circumstances the board will do as I ask. I'll send them a very full explanation, immediately. Ask them to cooperate in every way with the Bureau. And advise your Director, of course: send both sides copies of what I've told the other. And tell State and the President.'

Norris sat staring at the other man, his mind wiped clean once more. 'No,' he said dully.

'No what?' McBride frowned.

'I want you, now . . . to tell me, now. It's my case.'

'There's nothing to tell you. After so long I can't remember anyone named Luigi della Sialvo but if he's an indicted criminal . . . a fugitive from American justice . . . then quite obviously my former colleagues have to cooperate in every way they can . . . as I will if it turns out that I dealt with him personally . . .' McBride rose, ending the encounter. 'You're to be congratulated for digging deep enough to find this, Mr Norris.'

Norris rose, without any positive intention of doing so, and papers cascaded on to the floor. He had to kneel to pick them up. Still kneeling he said to the other man: 'Please. Tell me!'

'I've told you, there's nothing I can help you with at the moment,' McBride said. 'It's too long ago. But your people in Washington will get every help: I guarantee it.' He came round the monstrous desk to put his hand on Norris's shoulder, physically urging the man from the study.

In her room at the Metropole, Claudine was disconcerted when the telephone rang. She stared at it for several moments, unwilling to pick it up. It wouldn't be Hugo. She'd spoken to him much earlier, from the security of the Belgian police headquarters, explaining how – and why – it had been difficult for her the previous night. It was far more likely to be Peter Blake.

'Something important has come up,' said Norris, when she finally lifted the receiver. 'Can you come down here to the embassy?'

'What is it?'

'I don't want to talk about it on the phone.'

Claudine hesitated. Henri Sanglier still hadn't arrived and the American embassy was where they were going anyway: she could leave a message for Peter to show Sanglier the devices. 'I'll be there in half an hour.'

The embassy's *rezidentura* – the quarters of the CIA and the FBI – was far away both in distance and appearance from the lavish ambassadorial officialdom Claudine had seen on her first visit, a series of identical, box-like rectangles, four of which now formed part of the emergency communications centre. Those of Rampling and Harding were at the very rear of the complex, slightly larger than the rest to designate their local status of controller, but each restricted by only one door and no windows to outside light. Rampling saw Claudine as she was escorted past and waved but she didn't see him. To Robert Ritchie, who was with him, Rampling said: 'You know something I don't?'

'I don't know nothing,' said Ritchie. 'It's called staying alive.'

Norris checked his watch as she entered Harding's clear-desked room and Claudine at once registered both signs. Excessive cleanliness and rigid conformity, particularly to time, were both features of severe obsession: she had, in fact, made the journey within the promised thirty minutes but she should have avoided the self-imposed stipulation. She was aware of the brief frown when the indicated chair scraped slightly sideways as she sat. There was a sheen of sweat on the man's sallow face and unusually his jacket was open.

The chair movement wasn't sufficient to cause a problem, Norris decided. The microphone he'd fed round the desk, taping out of sight beneath its rim the lead to the recorder in the right-hand drawer, was sensitive enough to pick up everything she said.

'So,' began Claudine enthusiastically. 'What's the big mystery you couldn't tell me on the phone?' She'd had misgivings on the way there: not so much misgivings as belated curiosity. The arrangement was for Jean Smet to bring them together if there was a development: Norris, in fact, was the last person who should have done it. But in the man's mental state there could be a dozen explanations: she hoped at least one of them was useful.

Norris declared: 'Technically this embassy is American property.' He was quite sure of the technique to use with her: hit her hard, without giving her any room for manoeuvre.

She'd made a mistake, Claudine knew at once. She

229

said: 'I know, John. We went through the question of jurisdiction at the beginning, didn't we?'

'So you're in America.' She had to realize how trapped she was.

'Listen to me,' urged Claudine gently. 'You telephoned me at the hotel. Asked me to come here because you had something to tell me. What was it you wanted to tell me?'

'That!' insisted the man irritably. 'That you're subject to American law because you're in America.' Why was she being so stupid!

She could walk out, Claudine supposed: leave the embassy and get back to the hotel before Sanglier and Blake. She felt a sweep of embarrassment. No one would be able to understand her coming here like this: *she* couldn't understand it now. He was a sick man, she reminded herself: a sick man who was going to be confronted very soon with the demand that he be removed from the investigation. She wouldn't walk away from a sick man. She said: 'There isn't anything, is there? Nothing you needed to tell me about the case?'

'I know,' Norris announced. He had to maintain the pressure, constantly keep her on edge.

'What do you know, John? Tell me. Let's talk about it.' This wasn't any sort of treatment – it couldn't be – but there would be an element of paranoia, his confused mind overcrowded with disjointed delusions, and if she could coax some of them out she might, temporarily, ease his burden.

'Why don't *you* tell *me*?' He wasn't going to lose control, as he'd lost control with the ambassador: find himself answering questions instead of asking them. Couldn't understand how that had happened. A trick. Wouldn't do McBride any good.

'What do you want me to tell you?'

She was giving up! Far easier – far quicker – than he'd

expected. But it happened sometimes. You could never tell. 'All of it. How you managed to get in, on the inside. Where she is, so I can get her out. Everything.'

Claudine felt the first pop of unease, deep in the pit of her stomach. The moment of collapse at the highest point of tension, she thought. 'We've got to work together, John. Help each other. I want to help you and I know you'll help me.'

'Just do as I ask. Tell me where Mary Beth is. She's been missing for too long. I've got to get her back.' Why couldn't she understand!

Claudine knew she had to establish a central thread, something he could recognize and hold on to. 'We're trying to find Mary Beth together.'

She was trying to trick him! The muzziness, the cotton waste feeling, was coming back. And it was hot again. It was the artificial light that had to be on all the time. There should be air conditioning somewhere. Too late to look for it now. 'You know where she is . . . who they are . . .'

'I don't.'

'You do!' Norris grabbed sideways, for the other item he'd carefully installed in the top right-hand drawer alongside the tape recorder: not the new-issue 9mm that a lot in the Bureau carried because of its stopping power but the Smith and Wesson he'd always preferred. He saw the fear in her eyes when he brought it out and laid it on the table between them, keeping his hand on the butt. 'If you don't tell me you'll be obstructing a federal officer in pursuit of his duties and I am legally authorized, in the United States of America in which at this moment we both technically are, to use whatever force is necessary to make you comply with my requests.' He brought the weapon up, pointing it directly at her. 'So, answer my question.' He had thought he wasn't going to get through the formal warning – twice he'd almost lost it – but he had. The warmth was satisfaction now, a feeling of complete power. He was legally authoritzed to shoot to kill if she tried to escape. He'd only wound her: put a round in her arm, to break it. Prove he wasn't making empty threats. He wanted very much to fire the gun: feel the kick and hear the explosion. 'I'm waiting . . .'

Five streets away Robert Ritchie shouldered his way into the familiarly crowded bar on the rue Guimard, checking himself at the unexpected sight of the Englishman at the same table as Harding and McCulloch. He realized at once that they'd seen him so he had to continue, saying 'Hi' and glad-handing as he made his way through the crush.

Ritchie didn't say anything when he reached their table. McCulloch said: 'He'd already found the wire: both of them. And made you, the first night. I always said you were shit at surveillance. Their commissioner's coming in this afternoon to stop the whole fucking nonsense.'

'She's with Norris at the embassy now,' disclosed Ritchie. 'I checked the transcript. He called her room, just over an hour ago: said something had come up that was too important to tell her over the phone.'

'Nothing has come up,' said Blake.

She had to bring him back from the edge, give him the thread. Her life hung upon her being able to open whatever door there might be to what remained of his rational, reasoning mind. If nothing did remain, then it was almost inevitable he would shoot her. From a metre away, he couldn't miss. 'We were supposed to work as a team, you and I.'

'Inveigled yourself in, so they'd know everything we were doing, right?'

It would be a mistake to pander to the delusion, letting

it grow. 'I'm not involved with those who've got Mary Beth. I couldn't be.'

'No one saw it but me.'

He was closed off against her. 'What did you see?'

'You getting inside. Knowing everything we were doing.'

'It made you angry, didn't it, my replacing you?'

Trying to change the order, making him answer questions again. 'Didn't replace me. Thought you did but you didn't. I'm still in charge.'

Why wasn't she frightened when a gun was being held unwaveringly on her from point blank range? There were feelings – anger at being tricked, frustration at not being able to reach him mentally – but no actual gut-dropping fear. She isolated the pride – the boastfulness – in the man's remark, wondering if it might be the chink she was seeking. There was the sudden flurry of movement behind her, obviously from the only door. She didn't turn.

'John!' said a voice she recognized as Harding's. 'What's the problem here, John?'

'No problem: sorting everything out,' said Norris, his eyes flicking over Claudine's shoulder. 'No need for you here: no need for any of you. Get out!' The gun came up towards her.

'We don't need the gun, John. Let's put the gun down, OK?'

'Get out!'

'Do as he says,' insisted Claudine, still not turning.

'John, I tell you what I'm going to do,' said Harding. 'I'm going to come on in here. Help things along a little.' There was a nervous laugh. 'It's my office, for Christ's sake! Guy's gotta be able to get into his own office.'

'Don't need help!' shouted Norris, his voice cracking. 'My case. I'll bring it in.' The gun abruptly shook, in his fury.

'OK! OK!' said Harding urgently. 'Everything's down to you.'

There was renewed sound from behind and Claudine guessed more people had arrived. She heard McBride say: 'Norris! John! This is the ambassador. You hearing me?'

'Of course I'm hearing you.' He wasn't looking away from Claudine now.

'What's going on here?'

'Getting your daughter back, sir. That's what I was sent here to do.' The gun wavered up and down, gesturing to Claudine. 'She knows where Mary is. She's going to tell me.'

'Good man,' said McBride. 'Well done. I want you to put the gun down and we'll take Dr Carter back to my office and she can tell me herself. Then I'm going to cable your Director just how damned well you did on this.'

'She's got to tell me, no one else!' Norris's thumb moved, visibly, flicking off the safety catch.

At the doorway McBride whispered to Harding: 'Could you hit him from here? Disable him?'

'He's half hidden by her. He'd know what I was trying to do – see my gun – if I moved along the inside wall for a full shot,' replied Harding, soft-voiced. 'Oh shit!'

'I could hit him,' offered Blake. 'But his reflex would be to pull his own trigger. He couldn't miss her.'

Claudine, unaware of the import of the hushed conversation, said loudly; 'Please be quiet, everyone. Let us alone.'

'Yes,' said Norris distantly. 'That's what I want, everyone to be quiet. Everyone except her.' He was confused by so many people. He was pleased that McBride, all of them, were going to witness how good he was: be taught how to interrogate a felon properly. But he'd lost his concentration. Couldn't think how to pick up the ques-

234

tioning. The gun felt suddenly heavy. He couldn't remember why he'd pulled the weapon. Had she pulled hers, to challenge him? Couldn't see it. To frighten her, he remembered. That was it, to frightened her!

Claudine could detect the rustle of movement behind her but no one was speaking. It was important that they didn't. She didn't want any more anger: didn't want him to lose what little self-control, if any, was left. He was fixated on her involvement, so she couldn't positively confront him; that would make him angry, too. And he'd defied the ambassador, the ultimate authority: the sort of authority to which he'd always deferred in the past. So there was an absolute refusal any longer to acknowledge anyone as his superior, either officially or professionally. It made his paranoia, his delusion, absolute, and him a totally dangerous man, clinically a psychopath: a psychopath sitting a metre away pointing at her a gun with the safety catch off. What was her entry to someone who believed himself above all others? *She's got to tell me, no one else,* she remembered: not the ambassador, or his Director in Washington. Only John Norris, God-like among the little people. So he was the entry. The only way to get through to John Norris was through John Norris, the one person he'd listen to: the only person whose opinion made any sense to him. Extremely careful to infuse admiration and to make it a statement, not a question, she said: 'You must feel very satisfied, holding me here like this.'

'I haven't got her back yet.'

No, thought Claudine, anxiously: Mary Beth mustn't come into the conversation. 'I feel very inadequate.'

'You were. Are.' Norris shook his head, against the thickness. The gun rattled against the desk top. Everyone stiffened.

There was no way of guessing how long it would be before Norris completely collapsed. It wouldn't be long.

235

Stressing the admiration even more, she said: 'And you're the master.'

She was helpless: admitting it. And those at the door were quiet now, attentive like his audiences at Quantico: attentive and respectful. 'You were careless, taking calls at the hotel about Rome and saying how worried you were about me.'

There was an opening! She risked a question at last. 'Is that the way, trusting no one?'

He smiled, first to Claudine and then to the men behind her: lecturing was always satisfying. 'I always know a lie. Can find guilt.'

Claudine hadn't wanted to put another question until she was surer but she didn't have a choice. 'How can you decide who to trust?' Norris had been responding with reasonable coherence, not taking too long to reply, but now he hesitated, frowning, and Claudine thought, Dear God, don't let him slip away: don't let me lose him. She didn't think she'd get him back even to this uncertain rationality if he drifted away.

'We check everything, don't we?' he said, his face clearing, his voice even.

She was there! She'd got past the mental barriers to what was left of his reasoning mind. She couldn't guess how long it would last, but for the moment she was through.

'So you had me checked out?'

He looked at the gun he still loosely held, then at the unseen people behind her, and Claudine decided the frowning was not his mental confusion but his inability to understand what everyone was doing there: most of all what he was doing there.

'So you had me checked out?' she repeated.

'I'm sorry. I . . .'

'It was a First I got at the Sorbonne, wasn't it?'

'Yes,' he said doubtfully.

It had to start coming from him: it had to be his realization. 'What about London?'

'First choice criminal psychologist at the Home Office.' He was knuckling his eyes with his free hand, looking again at the people behind her, and Claudine wondered if McBride was still there.

How much more time did she have? 'Your Bureau helped set up our Behavioural Division at Europol.'

'I know. Guy called Scott Burrows was seconded . . . What's this all about . . .? I don't understand?'

Claudine snatched at the long sleeve of her dress, baring her left arm and holding it towards the man. The scar from the attempted assassination was still livid and wide, not because of bad surgery but because it had been a professional attempt and the knife had been smeared with excreta to infect the wound, which it had. 'You know how I got this!'

The man actually started back, as if he were frightened of the ugliness. 'A hit. A previous case.'

She couldn't risk going any further. Norris had held out far longer and far better than she could have hoped. 'You know all that to be true, don't you, John?'

'Of course I do.'

'Who do I work for?'

A wariness flicked across his face.

'Who do I work for?' persisted Claudine. For God's sake don't let there be any intervention from behind.

Norris said: 'Europol . . . I think . . .'

'John, concentrate!' demanded Claudine. 'I work for Europol, don't I?'

'Yes.'

'I couldn't have inveigled my way into this investigation, could I?'

The eyes began to glaze, the grip on the gun tightening. 'Don't trick—'

'It's not a trick, John! Hold on! Concentrate! You've

made a mistake, because you're not well. You've become ill but we're all going to help you get better.'

'Gotta get the kid back . . .'

'We're going to do that. You've got to get better. Go back to America and get some treatment.'

There was a sudden burst of redness to Norris's face and his body tensed and Claudine guessed he was making a superhuman attempt to stop his mind clouding once more. Through clamped-together lips he managed: 'What?'

'Obsession,' said Claudine. 'That's what I think it is, severe obsession. Developed into a psychosis. But it's treatable: you know it's treatable.'

'What have I done?' The words groaned out of him. He was staring down at the gun.

'Nothing! There were some misunderstandings, that's all. No harm.'

'I was sent personally by the Director. The President knows . . . The investigation . . .'

'You didn't affect the investigation.'

Norris looked up at her with quick, bright-eyed clarity, the stiffness easing from his body. 'I don't want to be psychopathic.'

'You know it can be treated.'

'I'll have to leave the Bureau.'

'You won't,' lied Claudine.

'I'm sorry . . . for whatever . . .' It was becoming difficult for him to understand: one minute clear, one minute fog. 'You were part . . . no, sorry . . . disgraced the Bureau . . .'

Claudine detected the movement before the man actually began it, guessing it was safe to move herself. She said: 'Let me have the gun, John,' and started forward across the desk and then became properly aware of what he was doing and yelled: 'NO! DON'T!' but the barrel was already in his mouth.

238

She wasn't actually aware of the sound although there must have been one. In front of her Norris's face and head disintegrated in an enormous, gushing burst of red and because she was so close, her hand actually but too late upon his wrist, Claudine was engulfed in the gore.

'By myself?'

'Yes,' said Gaston Mehre.

'Félicité said I wasn't to go there,' said Charles.

'It's changed.'

'Does Félicité know?'

'Yes.'

'I won't hurt her.'

'You can.'

'But I won't this time. Félicité was angry with me. Shouted.'

'She's changed her mind. She wants you to do what I tell you.'

'Why?'

'That's what Félicité wants.'

'What do you want?'

'The same. It's what we all want.'

'You're very good to me,' said Charles. 'You all are.'

'You've got to go on doing what we tell you, though,' warned Gaston. 'You know that, don't you?'

'Yes.'

'And you know what we want you to do now?'

'Yes.'

'You sure?'

'Yes. And thank you.'

'Go and do it then.'

CHAPTER SIXTEEN

Claudine vomited, uncontrollably, over the desk and the headless, tendril-necked body that remained grotesquely upright in its chair, and over Blake who grabbed her and turned her away from the horror. She continued retching, huddled in his arms, long after she couldn't be sick any more, the empty, stomach-wrenching convulsions turning into constant, violent shaking, uncontrollable again, as the trauma gripped her. She was vaguely aware of Blake and Harding hurrying her from the room, both talking, but she was still deafened by the shot and shook her head uncomprehendingly, unaware that she was crying until Blake started wiping her face. When she saw the contents of the handkerchief she realized, distantly, that it wasn't tears or even blood he was wiping away but bone and brain debris. She whimpered and the shuddering worsened.

Others crowded around her in the corridor, a man and two women, taking over, and she went unprotestingly into an elevator which took her downwards. She was striving for control by the time it stopped, tensing her arms tightly by her side to stop the twitching, concentrating upon her surroundings – looking for an outside focus – to bring herself back to reality. She still couldn't hear what the unknown man was saying and brought her hands up to her ears, to tell him it was deafness, not shock.

It was the embassy's basement gymnasium. She was bustled straight through, past two bewildered men lifting weights, into the women's changing rooms. At the showers one of the women started to undress her, stripping off the blood- and fragment-covered clothes, but Claudine gestured her away.

She began to recover in the shower, forcing herself to look at the blood-streaked water streaming off her, turning the spray to its hardest adjustment and holding her breath to stand directly under it. It was several minutes before she could make herself actually wash her hair, not wanting to touch what might still be in it. There was nothing. When she squeezed her eyes shut she saw an immediate mental picture of a crimson explosion and a head disappearing and quickly opened them again. Twice there was loud rapping against the glass door. Only when she shouted for the second time that she was all right did Claudine become aware that her ears were clearing.

She stepped away from the water at last but didn't immediately try to leave the stall, partially extending her arms and looking down at herself. The tremor was still there but not as bad. Her ribs and stomach ached from the vomiting. Consciously she closed her eyes again, tightly. There was no head-bursting image.

One of the women was waiting directly outside, offering an enveloping white towelling robe. It had a hood attached but the second nurse handed her a separate towel for her hair.

The attentive man said: 'Kenyon, Bill Kenyon. I'm the embassy physician. Can you hear me?'

Claudine nodded: there was still a vague echoing sensation but his words were quite audible. She said: 'I'm fine.'

'You're a doctor. You know you're not,' the man said. 'We've got a small emergency infirmary here but I think you should go to hospital.'

Kenyon had blond, almost white, hair and rimless glasses. Claudine saw that the nurse who'd put her arm round her had blood on the side of her uniform. She said: 'I *am* a doctor – a psychologist – and I know about post-traumatic stress. I'm not going to your infirmary or to an outside hospital.'

'You can't shrug off what's just happened to you,' the physician protested.

'I'm not trying to shrug it off: the very opposite. I'm fully acknowledging it – think I know, even, why it happened – and I believe I can go on.'

'You're making a mistake,' he insisted.

'If I am then I'll recognize that, too. I'll be all right.'

Kenyon shook his head, unconvinced. 'I could let you have some chlordiazepoxide.'

It could be a useful precaution to have a tranquilizer available, Claudine conceded. 'That would be very kind.'

By the time Kenyon returned from his dispensary the nurses – the blonde was named Anne, the brunette Betty – had located an embassy-issue track suit in Claudine's size, still in its wrapping, and training pants for underwear. Claudine said she wanted everything she'd been wearing incinerated. Both nurses tried to persuade her to rest at least for a few hours in the embassy sick bay. She ignored them. As well as the tranquilizer Kenyon gave her his card, with his home as well as his direct embassy number. 'Call me. I mean it. I'm here. Promise?'

'I promise.'

'I don't believe you.'

'I want to go back upstairs.' Claudine was pleased she could remember in which direction the lift had brought her. She still felt suspended between reality and disbelief. The disorienting echo was intermittent in her ears.

'You're wrong, you know,' said Kenyon.

'No, I do know,' insisted Claudine. But did she *really* know how strong she was?

'I'll arrange a car to take you back to your hotel,' offered Betty.

'I want to find everyone else,' Claudine said positively. 'I didn't take much notice of the route on my way down here. That's all the help I need.'

'Let's hope you're right,' said Kenyon cynically.

'I might not be. And if I'm not, I've got your numbers.' She conjured the contact card between her fingers.

Claudine's arrival in the ambassador's suite was met with astonishment.

'I didn't . . . I thought . . .' groped McBride, standing awkwardly but bringing everyone else to their feet with him.

'I just want to be here,' said Claudine awkwardly. 'I'm all right.' She saw Peter Blake was the only person in the room without a jacket and remembered his pulling her into him, swamped in Norris's gore and her own vomit. Then she saw him crossing towards her.

'You sure this is a good idea?' he said, too quietly for anyone else to hear.

'No,' Claudine admitted. The shaking had gone, but despite the comforting thickness of the track suit she felt suddenly cold.

'Why then?'

'Because I want to.'

Claudine was pressing her eyes tightly together again (no blood-red explosion!) when Sanglier arrived close behind Blake. Until that moment she hadn't been aware of his being in the room.

'You don't need to be here,' insisted the Frenchman.

'I want to be,' she repeated. Now she was there, she wasn't sure that was true.

From behind his protective desk McBride, still standing, said: 'Dr Carter, I want to say . . .' but Claudine, faint-voiced, stopped him.

'There's no need to say anything. It's over.'

★

Claudine had never known the sensation before: never wanted to know it again. It was as if she were suspended above them all, in an out-of-body experience in which she could hear and see them but they were unaware of her presence. Her uncertain ears even made their words echo, ghost-like, and she had to hold very tightly on to her ebbing and flowing concentration: several times, when it ebbed, her vision actually blurred, merging people together with distant voices.

Claudine clung, like a drowning person to a fragile handhold, to her decision to be there. It was right that she should be. Not to contribute: she wasn't able to contribute to anything at that precise moment. But she could listen, difficult though that might physically be.

Claudine sat apart from the closely arranged group round the ambassador, welcoming the distance although becoming aware that, mostly unconsciously, the discussion was directed towards her, not for approval but from courtesy. McBride did most of the talking.

For Claudine irony piled upon irony when the ambassador insisted that American sovereignty in US embassies overseas made John Norris's suicide a matter entirely removed from Belgian jurisdiction or public awareness. Without mentioning Claudine or even looking in her direction McBride said there had been sufficient witnesses to the incident for an internal inquest, to be held that evening, prior to the body's being returned to America. It had been the climax of a series of extremely unfortunate incidents – here at last he looked at Claudine – for which he apologized but in no way did he expect it to affect the principal reason – the *only* reason – for their all being there. No replacement negotiator, either FBI or CIA, was being sent from Washington. Paul Harding was to assume overall command of the combined agencies' commitment, with the assurance at presidential level that it was seconded to Europol.

McBride was about to launch into a formal speech of congratulation to Claudine when he was interrupted by the sound of the telephone. He stared at Harrison, who said: 'I held all calls! Except . . .'

McBride snatched up the phone, not immediately speaking. Holding the receiver away from him, as if it were hot against his ear, he said to Claudine: 'It's a woman. She says Mary got a B for the geography paper that was in her backpack.'

'Check that!' Claudine told Blake, as she moved towards the telephone.

'I want McBride.'

English but accented. French possibly. Claudine said: 'I'm speaking on his behalf.'

'The wife?'

'No.' The only lies she could risk were those she couldn't be caught out on. Damn her hearing! The voice kept rising and falling.

'Ah, the clever little mind-reader!'

'We want to negotiate.' This was probably the most difficult part, establishing the rapport from which to manipulate the woman without her being aware it was happening.

'Of course you do.'

'Tell me about Mary.'

'Demanding!'

Blake and Harding hurried back into the room together. The note Blake slipped in front of her said: 'School confirm B grade.' Harding made a rolling-over motion with his hands, encouraging her to extend the conversation as much as possible.

The woman's reaction was exactly what Claudine wanted. 'We have to know she's all right.' The sound abruptly dipped and Claudine said urgently: 'Hello!

Hello!' She saw Rampling re-enter the room, shaking his head to Blake and Harding.

There was a jeering laugh. 'You haven't lost me! You won't find me, either.'

'My name is Claudine. Claudine Carter.'

'So?'

'I wanted you to know.' Was she moving too quickly?

The laugh came again. 'What name would you like me to have?'

'Your choice.'

'How about Mercedes? That's appropriate, isn't it?'

Claudine felt a stir of satisfaction. The woman was responding, nibbling the unsuspected bait! 'Is it appropriate?'

There was a silence. She'd never get it, Claudine guessed: would the woman actually admit it?

'You tell me.'

Good enough. 'In its original Spanish it's a name that means compassionate or merciful. Are you compassionate and merciful?'

'You have to tell me that, too. And isn't name comparison invidious?'

Claudine didn't want her too angry: she had the child to take the irritation out on. 'I don't follow,' she admitted.

'In Latin, the name Claudine means the lame one.'

Anxious to show her cleverness: that was good. 'Let's hope you're Mercedes the merciful.'

The pause this time had nothing to do with the uneven sound. In apparent awareness the woman said: 'You *are* the mind-reader, aren't you?'

She had to avoid responding to questions as much as possible, always making the woman come to her. 'We need to know that Mary is all right,' Claudine repeated.

'She is.'

'How is she?'

'Learning.'

Claudine was chilled by the word. A challenge? Or a taunt? She couldn't avoid it. 'Learning what?'

'What do you think?'

'I don't know.'

'Not a clever negotiating lady like you!'

'What's Mary learning?'

The line abruptly became clear enough for a brief sound of background noise. 'How to be a good girl.'

'Let's talk about getting Mary back.'

'I'm not sure I want to give her back yet. I've become attached to her.'

This was wrong: dangerous! 'I said we wanted to negotiate.'

'There is nothing to negotiate really, is there?'

'Tell me what you want.'

'I want to speak to the ambassador.'

'He wants me to talk to you on his behalf.'

'You're not understanding, silly woman. You all do what I tell you, otherwise Mary isn't going to be a happy little girl. When I call tomorrow I want to speak to McBride, not you. And by tomorrow you'll know what will happen if you don't do precisely what I tell you.'

'There's something I want to say,' blurted Claudine, trying to hold the woman.

'I don't want to hear anything you've got to say. I want the ambassador waiting this time tomorrow. And I know he will be.'

'I want—' started Claudine but stopped as the line went dead. The receiver was suddenly heavy in her hand. She became aware she was shaking again and dropped rather than replaced the telephone on its rest. She looked up to see everyone staring at her.

Something was wrong. Didn't fit. Or jarred, maybe. There was something in the recording that they'd just sat

247

through that was out of context, but she couldn't isolate it. There'd been too much in too short a time, she told herself. Objectively, she shouldn't have even taken the call, although she was glad she had. Claudine believed, despite the discrepancy, whatever it was, that it had been useful and that there was a lot to learn from it. But later. Not now. Now she was stretched to breaking point, about to snap. Overwhelmed. The shaking came in spasms, starting, stopping, starting again.

'Are we going to get Mary back?'

Claudine only just avoided wincing at the desperation in McBride's voice. And at the wide-eyed strain on the face of Hillary, who Claudine had not realized was present until she'd replaced the telephone. Claudine felt crushed, as if the room – no, not the room: a force she couldn't see – was closing in to compress her into something very small, too small for them to hear or take notice of. Fumbling the Librium from her track suit pocket she said: 'Can I have some water, please?'

Blake poured it for her, once more using the closeness to say: 'You want the doctor again?'

Claudine shook her head. 'I need some time. To listen to the recording again, compare it to the written transcript . . .'

'You must have some impressions!' insisted Smet. 'It was the woman in the car, wasn't it?'

'Of course it was,' said Claudine irritably.

'On a mobile telephone,' said Rampling. 'That's why the sound level kept rising and falling: interference from bridges and highly built-up areas. That's why we couldn't get any sort of fix: tomorrow we'll use scanners.'

'Are we going to get Mary back?' Hillary McBride repeated her husband's question, even-voiced, rigidly in command of herself. She added: 'Back alive?' and Claudine wished she hadn't.

'I think so,' said Claudine reluctantly.

'That's not good enough,' protested McBride.

'It's the best I can offer,' said Claudine.

'You're supposed to know!'

'I don't know,' admitted Claudine. 'Not yet. I will but not yet.'

'I don't think we should press Dr Carter any more,' said Sanglier.

'The inquiry . . . inquest . . . ?' groped Claudine.

'It's a formality: we won't need you,' said Harrison.

'I'd like to go back to the hotel,' Claudine admitted.

'What if she calls again?' demanded Hillary McBride.

People seemed to be advancing towards her, retreating and advancing again and Claudine regretted taking the tranquillizer. With a monumental effort she said: 'She won't call again: not until the same time tomorrow. Maybe not even then.'

'So you *have* worked something out?' demanded Smet.

'I want to go home,' said Claudine.

She was unaware of the drive back to the Metropole or of Blake's being with her until focusing jerkily upon him helping her through the foyer. She began to wonder how he'd got the key to her room but couldn't hold the thought and then found hreself in it. He was there too, but moving around: momentarily she didn't know where he was. He emerged from the bathroom, tossing something up and down in his hand, and as he crossed to the bureau telephone Claudine remember the bugs.

'All clear,' he announced, holding out the tiny pin-heads in the palm of his hand.

'I don't want to be by myself,' said Claudine.

'No,' agreed Blake.

It hadn't gone at all as she'd intended and Félicité was angry: frustrated. Claudine fucking Carter wasn't frightened enough. None of them were, if they were prepared to let the woman take the call which they should all have been pleading to receive. They had to be taught a lesson.

She coasted the Mercedes into the limited parking zone outside the railway station and on her way to the public telephones thrust deeply into a refuse bin the mobile August Dehane had programmed with the number of one that had been stolen a week earlier in Bruges.

Lascelles came on the line as soon as Félicité had identified herself to his receptionist. 'A scalpel?'

'I'll explain when we meet.'

'I'm looking forward to seeing her,' said the doctor.

'She's beautiful,' promised Félicité.

CHAPTER SEVENTEEN

'H̲ello.'
'Where's the lady?' Mary had been waiting eagerly, on her feet just inside the door when she heard the key grate. Now there was a plunge of disappointment.

'She couldn't come,' said Charles Mehre.

'She promised!' She'd become her friend. Been kind to her. It wasn't fair.

'I don't know.'

'Is she coming later?'

'No. Just me.'

'She promised!' Mary repeated.

Charles Mehre shrugged.

'I want to come outside,' insisted Mary.

The man hesitated, blocking the entrance to the cell. 'All right.'

He hardly moved. To pass she would have to brush against him. Mary stayed where she was. 'I can't get by.'

He giggled, still not moving. 'You can if you squeeze.'

'I don't want to squeeze.' He was very much like Victor, the garden boy back home. She became aware of something, surprised, but decided against referring to it yet. She was very uncertain about what was happening.

He finally shifted, although still not very much. But she was able to pass without touching him. He smelled stale. Mary went to the bench seat in front of the table at which she'd eaten on previous evenings with the woman.

'We're going to play games,' he announced.

'I don't want to play games.' The woman hadn't told

her about this: about anyone coming but her. It was the two of them, she'd said: special friends. Better friends than she was with dad and mom. She'd started to believe her.

'You must!'

His voice was suddenly loud, harsh, and Mary didn't like it. Why hadn't the woman come, like she'd promised? 'Where's my food?'

'No food.'

'Why not? I always have food now.'

'Not tonight.'

'Why not?' Mary said again. That wasn't fair either. She *did* always have food now. Why was this man being mean?

'Because.'

'I'm hungry.'

'No food.'

'You're bad!' said Mary, talking to him as she talked to Victor at home.

'Not bad!' The voice was loud again but this time in protest.

'She'll be mad at you.'

'No!' The tone changed again, sulkily.

'You don't like her being angry at you, do you?'

'Won't be. Gaston said.'

Gaston, thought Mary. 'She will be, if you don't give me something to eat.'

'Dance for me.'

'No.' She didn't like this.

'I want you to dance for me.' The harshness was back.

'I'm too hungry.'

'Will you dance for me if I get you something to eat?'

'Maybe.'

'Properly, like I want you to dance?'

'I want to eat something.'

He remained uncertainly between her cell and where

she sat, shifting from foot to foot. 'All right.' He started across the room, towards the stairwell door, but stopped halfway, frowning back suspiciously as if there was something he didn't understand. His lips moved but Mary didn't hear what he said. She made herself sit back against the cushions, as if she were settled. He continued on and Mary tensed with his every step, moving the moment the door closed behind him.

The carpet deadened the faintest noise of her running across the room. She listened, against the door. All she could hear was her own heartbeat, bump-bumping in her ears. She pushed the door towards its frame before pressing the handle down, actually holding her breath. The door moved, swinging soundlessly inwards. She stood at the opening, staring upwards, able to see an oval of light at the top. A black and white checkered floor, she remembered. A heavy door, heavier than the one she'd just opened so easily, leading outside. She wouldn't be able to run, if it was blowing as hard as it had been when they'd brought her here. Didn't matter. She could hide, once she got outside. That's all she had to do, get outside. She went up the first two steps, then stopped. She was frightened. She knew downstairs: her room with the sliding peephole in the door and the bathroom and the strange room with a big screen and the round dance floor in the middle. Felt safe there: safe with the woman although not with this man. The man who wanted her to dance. That was silly, a man wanting her to dance. It wasn't like dad wanting her to dance. That would have been different. All right. She'd never danced for dad, though. It looked a long way up, to the oval of light. She had to get there. Get away. Get outside. She went up two more steps. Stopped again. She wished the woman was there. Someone she felt all right with. Mom or dad. Why hadn't they paid? The woman said they didn't care. Didn't want her. She hadn't believed it at first but they hadn't done anything to get her back. And she seemed to be the reason they had a lot of their fights. But she'd seen dad cry, on television. Heard him say he loved her and did want her. It was the woman who was kind to her now: showered and dried her. Last night they'd gone through her backpack and looked at her schoolwork and the woman had even given her a lesson, but as a game, not the proper geography for which she'd got the B. The questions had been easy but she'd really tried and the woman had been pleased with her: called her a clever girl. She'd been proud to be called clever. Now she was confused: confused and frightened, although she didn't know what she was frightened about. Just not knowing. Being alone. She didn't want to go outside: didn't know what was out there. Perhaps they were all up there, all the men in stupid masks who'd looked at her through the hatch. She wished there were more of them, not just this man who smelled bad and laughed in a silly way, as if he knew a joke that nobody else did.

There was the noise of a door, opening, closing. Footsteps across the hall. Mary scurried back, closing the downstairs door behind her and running to where she had been sitting. She was there, against the cushions, when he entered, a tray balanced across one arm.

There was bread and cheese from the previous day. The milk only half filled the glass and had lumps in it and was sour when she tasted it. The bread was stale but she made herself eat it, as slowly as she could. She pared off the cheese in small slivers.

'You've got to shower. Take your clothes off.'

'I don't want to.'

'You must.'

'Why?'

He frowned. 'She says.'

'She changed her mind. She told me yesterday she doesn't want me to do that, not any more.'

'Not true.'

'Why aren't you wearing your mask?' she asked finally.

When he smiled Mary saw his teeth were very uneven, as if there were too many crowded into his mouth: she hadn't worn her brace for days now.

He said: 'Don't have to, not any more.'

'Why not?'

'Doesn't matter any more.'

'Why not?' she repeated.

'Secret,' he snickered. He reached out, to touch her hair, but Mary pulled back. He sniggered again.

She'd eaten too much cheese, practically all of it, to prolong the meal and now she felt sick. She wished she'd gone up the stairs. She didn't feel safe down here any more.

'You're pretty.'

Mary couldn't think of anything to say.

'I like you. Like your hair.'

'I don't like you touching it,' said Mary, pulling away again.

'Nice hair.'

'Leave me alone!'

'Haven't got to.'

Mary didn't think the sickness she felt had anything to do with what she'd eaten: it wasn't like a tummy upset pain. 'Did she say that?'

'Yes.'

'She told me you did. Told me herself that you didn't have to touch me.'

'She didn't.' He'd been sitting next to her on the bench, close enough to reach out towards her. Now he got up and crossed to the tape deck and CD equipment against the wall beside the large screen. He stood there, staring at it in total bewilderment, awkwardly touching switches and knobs. 'No music,' he complained.

'We don't want any music,' Mary said nervously.

255

'To dance,' said the man. 'We need music to dance.'

'I don't want to dance.'

'Yes!' The harsh loudness was back. He wasn't sniggering or laughing any more. 'Have a shower and then dance: play like you did with her, for the towel. Play with me.'

'I didn't like that,' said the child. 'I don't want to do it again.'

'I'll slap you. I want to slap you.'

Victor! She had to treat him like Victor. 'That would be bad.'

He shook his head. 'No one knows.'

'It's not right, to hit people.'

'Nice. Good.'

'No! No, it's not good. It's wrong.'

'He said I could.'

'Who?' She didn't know what to do! Dad! Please, dad! There was no one to tell her what to do. I won't be naughty again, God. I promise. Help me and I'll be very good. Please, God.

'Gaston.'

'Gaston doesn't want you to hurt me.'

'He does. Said I could.'

Mary started to tremble. There was a lock on the inside of the bathroom door. Could she pretend to do what he wanted: get inside before he could follow her and lock him out! She might be able to, if she was quick: quicker than she'd been when she tried to run away from the woman the other time. She could pretend to dance a little first, make him sit down to watch to give herself the chance. What if he got to her before she locked it, like the woman had done? She'd be even more trapped then. Have to do what he wanted. Or he'd hit her. He'd said he would hit her: *wanted* to. 'I want to go back into my room now.'

He shook his head. 'Not any more.'

256

'You mustn't hurt me. Do anything bad to me.'

'I can.'

'If you do you'll go where bad people go.'

He frowned at her, head to one side. 'What?'

It had been the ultimate threat against Victor, when she'd wanted to make him cry. How much longer could she go on talking, keeping him away? She still felt sick and now her throat was beginning to get sore. I won't make Victor cry ever again, God. I promise. 'You know where bad people go?'

'Jail.'

'That's it, you'll go to jail.' Mary seized on the word. 'Go to jail for a very long time. For ever.'

'No one knows.'

'They'll find out.'

'Can't.'

'My father can. He's a very important man. Lots of special people work for him.'

'Doesn't matter.'

'If you go away – leave me alone – I'll tell my father you were kind to me,' promised Mary. 'Then they won't send you where the bad people go.' She wanted to make pee pee: already felt wet. Do the other thing: very much wanted to do the other thing. Her stomach was rumbling, making rude noises. She tried to keep her bottom tight together.

'ME NOW!'

The words roared from him, furiously. He'd shown no sign of losing his temper and Mary screamed out in shocked surprise at the unexpected noise. He was coming towards her, arms outstretched, hands cupped, and she cringed back against the seat, trying to slide sideways round the tiny table so that she could run. Run where? She didn't know. Just run. Around the room. Anywhere. Run to the bathroom. He snatched out, grabbing her arm as she darted to her right, pulling her towards him and Mary brought her other hand up, trying to push him off. His smell was much worse, not just his body but the breath from his ugly mouth. He was grunting, squeezing her.

'STOP IT! STOP IT! STOP IT!'

Mary was scarcely aware of the words at first, not until the woman reached them, beating at the man with open-handed slaps. The woman got between them, slapping the man again and again. He roared, not a word, just a sound, and slapped the woman back and she screeched, clawing at him so that Mary saw blood burst out on his face. Mary fell back against the table, hearing it split as it tilted, spilling her back on to the bench.

The man wasn't fighting back any more. He was standing with his arms cupped about his head, trying to protect himself but mostly just standing there, letting himself be beaten. And the woman was beating him, aiming her blows, kicking him, and shouting in French. The man began to retreat towards the door under the onslaught and she kept up the attack, driving him from the room and disappearing through the door, still clamouring at him in French.

It was only then that Mary saw there was someone else, a man she hadn't seen before, standing just inside the entrance. He was very tall and oddly thin, his stomach curved in instead of out, the strangeness made more obvious by the way his shoulders humped, bringing him forward. His mask was frightening, black leather cut with spaces for just his eyes and his mouth but very tight, like a skin over his head and face. He carried the sort of bag that doctors used.

In bad English he said: 'Poor little one. Poor, poor little one.'

'Don't hurt me,' pleaded Mary, her voice catching in a sob. 'Please don't hurt me.'

'I won't,' said Pieter Lascelles. 'I promise I won't hurt you.'

Mary was sick and she'd wet herself and there were tiny blood spots inside her knickers that frightened her but the woman said she wasn't ill but that it was growing up, becoming a woman, and she wasn't to worry. Until they dried, after she'd washed them, she didn't have to worry about u.p.'s.

The woman had showered her and afterwards cuddled her on the cushioned bench. Mary lay with her legs curled up, wanting to be held, wishing the man with the skin mask wasn't in the room with them, spoiling it. Mary didn't want anybody else with them: she liked it with just her and the woman.

It took some time for the catch to go out of Mary's voice as she told the woman what had happened and all the time the woman held her and smoothed her hair and several times Mary felt the woman press her lips to her head, kissing her. Over and over she kept repeating 'poor baby' and 'my poor darling' and 'poor love'.

'He wanted to hurt me,' sobbed Mary. 'Said Gaston said it would be all right. Wanted me to dance. Shower and dance.'

'It's all right. All over now. He won't come here ever again.'

'I want you.'

'I know you do, my darling. I'll take care of you now: I'll always take care of you.'

'Please don't leave me alone.'

'I've got to: there are things I have to do. But you'll be safe.' She pulled away from the child. 'I want your backpack: the one we looked through last night.'

'Why?'

'I want to use it for something.'

'All right.' Mary felt important being able to lend the woman something she wanted.

On their way into Antwerp Lascelles said: 'She's very pretty.'

'And she's mine!' declared Félicité.

The gaunt man looked across the car towards her. 'Would he have killed her?' There was no emotion in his voice.

'I think so.'

'He's a liability: all your people are. Can you stop him coming back again?'

'Yes,' said Félicité shortly.

'I think we should get it over with soon.'

'When I'm ready, not before.'

'She's not just pretty,' mused the doctor. 'Remarkably brave considering what she went through back there.'

Félicité was at the Mehre gallery, confronting the brothers. Charles sat even more huddled than before in the upright chair, crying. Gaston stood defensively by the window, as if he saw it as a way of escape. There was no pretence of drink-offering hospitality.

'I didn't know he'd gone. I sent him to collect a bureau in Ghent.'

'Liar!' accused Félicité. 'You sent him to kill her!'

'No.'

'Yes.'

Gaston stopped protesting.

'Who of the others knows?' Félicité demanded.

'All of them.'

'Bastards!'

'What are you going to do?'

Félicité didn't know. That realization made her even angrier. They weren't obeying her any more. 'Wait,' she said inadequately. 'You can wait – all of you – to find out.'

'Gaston said I could,' mumbled Charles from his isolated seat.

Claudine lay with her head into Blake's naked shoulder, liking the way his arm felt holding him to her: liking the whole feel of his body along the length of hers. It had been wonderful. She couldn't remember how long it had been – couldn't remember sex – but she didn't think it had ever been like this. He'd been incredible. Always thinking of her before himself, her pleasure before his, but at the same time there'd been a frenzy, an urgency more than passion the first time and then he'd taken her again, twice, and each time she'd come. She'd forgotten that, too. Now she felt wonderful. Relaxed, from the sex and the Librium, but with no tiredness. Instead her mind was pin-sharp and her skin burned, tingling against his.

'You OK?'

'Wonderful.' There had to be another word! 'You?'

'You wouldn't know.'

It seemed an odd thing to say. It didn't matter. 'Now we've joined the Europol club. I guess it's like the mile high club.'

'No!' he said.

Despite the darkness she was conscious of his seriousness. 'I don't think we need to analyse it,' she said. Which for her would be a change.

'Perhaps we do.'

'It happened, Peter. Because of a lot of outside things, but it happened and it was . . .' she stopped, refusing to use the word yet again '. . . and it was sensational but I don't expect you to propose marriage. If you did I'd refuse.'

'I used you,' he said.

'I don't remember complaining. Or fighting,' she said, trying to lighten his mood. He was spoiling things.

'I want to tell you something . . . need to tell you something . . . but I'm frightened.'

'What of?'

'What you'd think of me.'

'Does it matter what I think of you?'

'I think so.'

'Your choice,' she said.

Blake didn't speak for a long time. When he did it was with difficulty, the words uneven, disjointed. 'There were two of us. I didn't know that. I wasn't told. Neither was she. That's the system, you see. If one gets blown there's still another one in place, but you can't bring him down because you don't know . . .' He lapsed into another long silence.

Lying as she was Claudine was conscious of his breathing becoming shorter. 'What was her name?' she prompted, knowing his need.

'Anne. Her family were from Kildare . . .' He grunted, bitterly. 'I suppose that's how it started with her and me. Like you, tonight. Frightened, not wanting to be alone after seeing someone killed. We had to take part in operations, of course. Prove ourselves. Our initiation was a bombing in Enniskillen. A British soldier died. We both saw it happen: saw him blown to pieces . . .'

'But it became more than fear and sex?' Claudine prompted again, when he didn't continue after several minutes. It all had to come out, brutally if necessary. *Blown to pieces* echoed in her head: briefly she had a mental image of a crimson explosion and a body without a head.

'We still didn't know about each other: not properly, I mean. We used to have long conversations about how we'd get married when it was all over – when the cause had been won and there was just one Ireland, I mean – and all the time I knew it would never be possible because of who I really was and she would have been thinking the same because of who she really was, neither of us knowing that we could have got together when we were withdrawn . . .'

'What went wrong?' said Claudine.

'There was to be another operation on the mainland. The strategy of bombing the City of London, hitting the country's financial centre, was judged a success so it was decided to keep it up: force a lot of foreign banks to relocate in Frankfurt. My contact was a barman at the Europa Hotel, in Belfast. We used to drink there, Anne and I. She knew him by sight. The Semtex movement into Britain was decided at the last minute: more than a ton. The devastation would have been greater than either Canary Wharf or the Baltic Exchange. I hadn't used the emergency system before – actually met him away from the hotel – but I had to, for the van carrying the explosive to be identified and followed from its arrival at Holyhead. I made the call from her flat: I went there ahead of her from the planning meeting and decided I couldn't wait or risk a public kiosk, that Anne's phone was safer. She must have come in sooner than I thought and heard me, although I didn't think she had. I didn't think she was in the house. She must have followed me – can you imagine it, doing her proper job! – and I saw her, just after I passed the details . . .'

His breathing became even more difficult and Claudine guessed he was crying and was glad for his sake they were in darkness. 'Don't stop, not now.'

'He must have had an English watcher, too: someone compartmented like we all were who saw her and thought he was blown. I never knew. But he was withdrawn: took the information with him. We made a big thing about it in England. Followed the van to London, swept up the entire cell that was going to plant the bombs. The head of the anti-terrorist unit gave a press conference. And the stupid bastard talked about inside information: actually used the word infiltration. There were only ten people who could have known, Anne and I two of them. They had a source inside the Belfast telephone exchange I didn't know about. They traced the call from Anne's flat to the Europa bar: the bar from which my man had been withdrawn . . .'

Claudine waited.

'I don't want to go on.'

'Yes,' she insisted.

'They got her.'

'That's not it, is it?'

'That's enough.'

'Not for you it isn't.'

Blake's voice was flat, as if he was reading words that had been written down. 'There was what they called a trial: Anne in front of every one of us who'd known about the Semtex shipment. She denied it, of course. Said she didn't know about a hotel barman, which was true. Never once looked at me . . . They took her away, after finding her guilty. They decided to torture her, to find out if there were any others . . . we were all to gang rape her, then she was to be tortured.'

'You didn't let them get to her, did you?'

'She was already naked when I went into the room, spread-eagled on the bed. I went mad. Intentionally. Screamed and shouted that she was a whore and a slut: made myself uncontrollable, which wasn't difficult, although not for the reasons they all thought. She never said a word to betray me. Only looked directly at me at the very last minute. I shot her dead, before they realized what I was doing.' Blake moved slightly away from Claudine, who for the first time became aware how wet her cheek was, from his tears. 'I killed her twice. Once by being careless and then by pulling the trigger. She let it happen, to save me . . . And they all said what a good and loyal soldier I was: forgave me for spoiling their fun before they could find out if there was any other infiltrator.'

For once in her over-confident life Claudine didn't know what to say. 'The proper English trial at which you appeared?' she groped. 'They were the men?'

'Six of them. They all got life. But they'll be released, of course.'

'If you and Anne made up two who knew and there were six properly tried, that leaves two missing.'

'We were to put a bomb in Belfast city centre: our reprisal for the interception of the Semtex and the arrest of the cell in London. We were going to use the sewers: crawl in and crawl out. Devastate the place and kill God knows how many above. It was to be an hour fuse. I shortened it to two minutes. They went into the sewer ahead of me and I shouted down that there was a patrol and I had to close the manhole. It made a crater twenty metres deep and forty metres across.'

'You were believed, by other people?' queried Claudine.

'I didn't run: knew I couldn't if it was to be accepted as the sort of mistake they often made. The explosion broke my left leg and right ankle . . .'

'Were you trying to die?'

'The other six hadn't been sentenced then.'

'What if they had been?'

He didn't reply.

'Peter?'

'I'd have gone into the tunnel with them.'

'I'm glad you didn't. And I'm glad you told me. It's better . . .'

'I haven't finished. Since then I haven't been able to do this. Not until tonight.'

Oh God! thought Claudine. They weren't talking love – love didn't come into it – but there could be a dependency here.

'That's what I meant by using you. Are you angry?'

'No,' she said cautiously. 'But let's not think about what happened as anything more than it was.'

'I won't,' he said.

He would, she knew.

The first of the early morning cleaners found Mary Beth's rucksack just inside the school entrance and imagined it had been left there by a pupil the previous day, although it was rare for things to be left lying about. Madame Flahaur recognized it immediately for what it was and fortunately told her secretary to call the police before opening it. The school principal collapsed immediately with severe heart palpitations at the sight of its sole content, a child's severed toe.

CHAPTER EIGHTEEN

She had been desperately trying to prevent herself from getting shot, and she wasn't in any case capable of treating the man, but Claudine denied herself any excuse, hollowed by the guilt of failing sufficiently to identify John Norris's mental deterioration. The remorse was inevitable – tangible almost – and close to that she'd known after not recognizing Warwick's problems. Less easy to quantify was the psychological effect of seeing a man blow his head off right in front of her. She was sure, however, that neither remorse nor effect prevented her from functioning to the fullest of an ability it unsettled her to question.

There were a lot of other contributing uncertainties. Last night, for instance. Nothing that had happened affected how she felt about Hugo. To imagine it had, to think of it as anything more than a one night stand, would be ridiculous. Things like that happened a million times every day. It would be important, though, not to let it happen again. She didn't want it to happen again. Know thyself. She did want it to happen again but she wouldn't let it. It wouldn't be fair. Not to Peter, which was the chief consideration, nor to Hugo, peculiar though their situation was. She had to put it behind her. Not forget that it had happened – she certainly didn't want to forget – but not invest it with meaning and significance it didn't have. And anyway, Hugo would be in Brussels by midday to examine the grisly discovery in Mary Beth's backpack.

Which brought Claudine's thoughts back to yesterday's telephone conversation. She remained convinced that somewhere in the events of the preceding twenty-four hours she'd missed something of importance.

She'd left Henri Sanglier's breakfast review ahead of everyone else to arrive early at their police headquarters incident room to examine chronologically all the previous day's material, forcing herself through the tape of her conversation with John Norris and then her recorded exchanges with the woman. There *was* something! She couldn't decide what it was but neither could she lose the impression that it was there, waiting to be found.

She was still surrounded by dossiers, painstakingly going through them word by word to ensure she hadn't made the psychological mistake of closure – wrongly completing a picture by automatically inserting an expected fact or conclusion that wasn't there – when the rest of the control group arrived, virtually together. She abandoned the search, joining the others in the larger conference room.

'Anything?' asked Sanglier quietly, as he took a chair beside her. He'd listened to the Norris tape and heard the shot and was close to incredulous not just at her bravery but at her apparent recovery. It had been his decision that the Europol pathologist assigned to the investigation should be Hugo Rosetti, knowing as he did from his absurd mistake of exposing Claudine to Françoise at a dinner party at his Delft house that there was a relationship of sorts between her and the Italian.

Claudine shook her head without replying. She'd talked at breakfast of her lingering belief that something had been overlooked, and suspected they thought it imagination, a traumatized reaction to the suicide.

Jean Smet felt himself at a disadvantage in the presence of Henri Sanglier, nervous of trying to exercise the virtual chairmanship none of the others in the group had opposed. He didn't know exactly what had happened the previous night at the American embassy, only that John Norris was dead but there was going to be no public announcement or any Belgian involvement whatsoever. It had all been arranged, without his knowledge, in late night meetings between the Europol commissioner, McBride, Belgian Foreign Minister Hans van Dijk and Miet Ulieff, the Justice Minister who was supposed to be so reliant upon him. Smet was still furious – incredulous – at Ulieff's dismissal that it had been a matter to be decided at an upper government level, with no connection to the investigation and therefore nothing that he needed to know. An unexplained, officially concealed death of someone introduced into the investigation as its star negotiator – quite irrespective of all the doubts that he'd personally had about the strange man – had to have some bearing on the case, a bearing he had to discover if he and the others were to remain safe. His problem was finding out without drawing undue attention to himself. Equally worrying was not knowing what was going to happen when he obeyed Félicité's telephone-screamed insistence to meet after this conference.

Sanglier began the meeting by announcing that a Europol pathologist was arriving to examine the school find. The Americans at once followed the lead. Burt Harrison described the ambassador as devastated and disclosed that at that stage Mrs McBride hadn't been told. For that reason he was asking for the complete media black-out imposed upon the personal contact to be maintained and extended. Harding added that foot and hand prints were automatically taken at every birth in America and that Mary Beth's footprints were being wired for comparison, hopefully within hours.

'You had the conversation with the woman,' said Harrison, to Claudine. 'Do you really think they would have mutilated the child like that?'

Claudine hesitated, aware that all of them round the table were trying to push reality away with self-deception, clinging to the hope the toe did not belong to Mary, as they had tried to avoid admitting any sexual element in her original disappearance.

'Yes,' she said shortly, wanting positively to shatter any false hope. 'In addition to all the other opinions I've formed about her – and there's no doubt, of course, that the person on the telephone is the woman seen by the eye-witnesses to pick Mary up – I think there's a dangerous clinical psychosis that makes her capable of extreme violence.' She allowed another pause. 'And this morning's find answers your question anyway. It isn't an adult's toe. If it isn't Mary's it belongs to another youngster, one we don't yet know about, who's been maimed by the same people who've got Mary. If they're prepared to maim, they're prepared to kill.' She focused on Burt Harrison. 'Which puts our chances of getting Mary Beth back alive, even if we comply with every demand, at less than fifty per cent.'

Horrified silence enveloped the room: even the three clerks behind Smet came up from their notebooks and recording machines to look at her, shocked. Why, wondered Claudine, was it so difficult for everyone – most of them supposedly trained criminologists – to accept the likeliest outcome of this investigation!

'I don't think the ambassador should be told this,' said the American diplomat, his voice wavering.

'Neither do I,' agreed Claudine.

'Severing the toe was to force the ambassador to talk to her,' Sanglier reminded them. 'Can he? Is he up to it?'

'He says he is,' replied the US head of mission doubtfully. Again looking directly at Claudine, he added: 'Should he, in view of what you've just said?'

'Without any question!' answered Claudine at once.

'His not doing so would put Mary in enormous danger. There'd certainly be another body part.'

'What can your involvement be now?'

'A conference call, with me on an extension alongside McBride,' replied Claudine. 'Hopefully I can guide everything he says: avoid the wrong response. Mary's safety could depend upon something as small as that: one wrong word, one wrong reaction.'

'Jesus!' said Harding.

Smet was as staggered as everyone else by the assessment, although for totally different reasons. The psychologist was so close – actually appeared to *know* – their thoughts.

'Are you up to it, Dr Carter?' demanded Harrison pointedly.

'If I didn't believe that I was I would have withdrawn,' responded Claudine at once, conscious of both Poncellet and Jean Smet frowning between her and the American. 'To have done anything else would have risked Mary's safe recovery.'

Harrison blinked at the rebuke. Trying to recover, he said in sudden exasperation: 'All we want to do is pay the money and get her back!'

'They haven't specifically asked for money,' she reminded him. 'And don't forget that in my opinion money wasn't what they took Mary for in the first place.'

'Can we talk about yesterday's conversation?' intruded Smet, anxious to fill the gaps in what he knew. He patted the dossier in front of him. 'We've got a transcript but no interpretation.'

There was a hesitation between Claudine and Harding, who had had a brief telephone conversation that morning to discuss connected aspects of the tape. At Claudine's gestured invitation Harding said: 'In the original recording, before our people enhanced it, there was a lot of distortion we didn't understand. Now we do. She used a

271

mobile phone and drove around all the time: the sound dips and interferences are caused by her going under bridges or through highly built up bad reception areas. Enhanced, it's easy to detect the noise of traffic in the background.'

'It lasted a long time: you couldn't trace it?' demanded Poncellet.

'Not yesterday,' admitted Harding uncomfortably. 'The equipment we had was to locate a landline approach. Overnight we've installed scanners, for both analog and digitalized systems. Our people are hoping it'll be analog: they're easier. Unfortunately, most new systems are digital.'

'Can your technicians guarantee a location?' asked Smet at once.

'I'm told it'll be practically impossible if she keeps moving,' further conceded Harding. 'The hope is to get a number, which will be difficult if she's routing through any of the Iridium or Globalstar satellites.' To Poncellet he said: 'Before she's due to call tonight we have to set up number-trace arrangements through Belgacom and the major mobile phone companies and satellite servers. And have a lot of people on instant-response readiness if we get a fix. Now that the contact method has changed we're scaling down our e-mail monitor at the embassy, to have most of our Washington people on standby.' It had been Harding's first command decision. He'd talked with Claudine before issuing it, and was still uneasy despite her assurance that it was probably safe.

Peter Blake said: 'A copy of the tape went to Europol's forensic laboratories last night for positive voice analyses. At the moment Dr Carter is guessing that the woman is a French speaker, not Flemish. The backpack has gone for all the forensic tests, too. I'm not hopeful of anything being found, from people as organized as these.'

'What about the actual contents of the tape, Dr Carter?' asked the Belgian lawyer hopefully.

'More than enough confirmation of the arrogance I'd already suggested,' said Claudine. 'The entire tone – virtually every word – is taunting. Take identifying herself as Mercedes, for instance. And there's very clear reference to sex, in all the remarks about what Mary is learning. The most worrying phrase, particularly after this morning's backpack find, is when she gloats that she's not sure she wants to give the child back.'

'What's the overall picture?' queried a subdued André Poncellet.

Claudine considered the question for some moments. 'The woman we're looking for is suffering an extreme psychosis. She is accustomed to achieving absolute and total control over everyone around her but is, in fact, on the very edge of losing it over herself. And she is, as I've already said, capable of extreme violence.'

It was, thought Smet, a superb characterization of Félicité Galan. He said: 'Would you say she was insane?'

'Without any doubt very seriously mentally ill,' agreed Claudine. 'What a layman would definitely call mad.'

Hugo Rosetti collected Claudine at police headquarters and on the brief journey to the mortuary he said: 'It's been difficult to get in touch.'

'I've been very busy.'

'So you said when you finally called. You sure you're all right?'

'A lot's happened. I'll tell you about it later.'

'Happened personally or happened professionally?' he pressed.

'Professionally, of course! What else?' Almost too stridently defensive, she thought.

'I've missed you.'

'I've missed you, too. How's Flavia?' Why the hell had she said that? It was pointless.

He took some time to answer. 'The same as always. How's it worked out with Blake?'

'He's very professional.'

'No personal problems?'

'None.'

The main autopsy room was obviously unnecessary for such a small article. Instead they used one of the small side laboratories in which immediate tests were carried out during full crime-victim post-mortems and didn't completely robe up, just putting on protective aprons and gloves.

Claudine had watched the Italian work before – there'd been eight dismembered corpses in the serial killing investigation – and was impressed again by the finesse, even with a body part like this.

Rosetti had a series of pictures taken, a selection against measuring graphs and others under magnification, by a waiting photographer before studying the toe under even greater magnification. He scraped on to separate slides from beneath and on top of the nail before slicing a selection of surface skin on other slides. On to yet more he smeared the invisible result of several swabs. Only after completing all his surface examinations did Rosetti take prints for later comparison with those due to arrive from America later that day. He carefully cleaned away every vestige of dye before finally making a deeper incision for tissue samples within the toe itself. Claudine was conscious of although not offended by the smell.

'Anything you want me to do?' he asked without looking at her. On their earlier case she'd sometimes asked for tests beyond his, to help her profile.

'No,' said Claudine.

'Do you have a precise time of what was obviously the threat to do something like this, in the telephone call?'

'Five sixteen in the evening,' replied Claudine at once.

'And the time this was found?'

'Seven this morning.'

'How old, exactly, is Mary Beth?'

'Ten years and four months.'

'Build?'

'Small for her age.'

'The tests will take me a while.'

'I'll wait.' Claudine stripped off the protective clothing and perched on a stool just inside the door, watching him work. He was completely absorbed, seemingly unaware of her presence, muttering the verbatim record of what he was doing into the recorder strung around his neck and pinned out of the way against his chest.

Had last night – the entire time she'd spent with Peter on the inquiry – affected her feelings for Hugo? There was a newness, an excitement, about Peter. And what he'd done in Ireland – and its appalling cost – was incredible. But there surely had to be more than exciting novelty, fuelled by awed admiration? Remaining strictly objective, Claudine didn't think her feelings went beyond that. Which wasn't, of course, saying they wouldn't.

She didn't want to search now for the answer to a question she didn't know, Claudine decided. It was too soon. But it wasn't sex: if she'd wanted sex she could have got it from any one of the dozens who regarded Europol as a harem. She was lonely, Claudine acknowledged, with know-thyself honesty. Lonely and too often sad: fed up not living a proper life, using work as a substitute to subjugate everything else. That was what John Norris had done.

She didn't want a man to think for her or decide for her or protect her: she could do all of those things by herself. She wanted . . . she didn't actually know what she wanted, not fully. All she knew was that she needed a personal life very different from what it was at the moment, because at the moment it was non-existent. Outside work *she* was non-existent. Last night she hadn't been.

She became aware of Rosetti crossing the small room towards her, unpinning his microphone as he walked.

'There's one thing that I'm sure about,' announced the man. 'It was a professional amputation, not hacked off by an amateur. So one of those you're looking for is a doctor or surgeon . . .'

'. . . which could narrow down the records search.'

Rosetti nodded. 'We'll need the confirmation of the footprint, obviously, but I don't think the toe belongs to Mary. In dimension and length I think it belongs to someone older: certainly not a child just gone ten who is small for her age. According to your time frame, if it came from Mary the amputation occurred within the last fifteen hours. There's far more than fifteen hours' decomposition in the toe I've just examined: there was a noticeable smell of putrefaction, even before I put a tissue sample under the slide. I'd estimate death four or five days ago.'

'Mary could have been dead that long,' Claudine pointed out.

'I know,' said Rosetti. 'That's why we need the print confirmation. But there's another guide we can get from the parents. The nail was carefully manicured and kept: there was no scrape residue at all from beneath it. But I got a lot from on *top*: traces of ethyl acetate and glycols copolymer. Both are constituents of nail varnish: in this case extremely pale pink. The parents can obviously tell us if they had Mary's feet manicured.'

'She was a pampered kid but I don't think she would have been that pampered,' said Claudine.

'It won't be necessary if the prints don't compare but I've naturally got sufficient skin samples for a DNA match with anything we can recover from Mary's bed or clothing – hair, for instance – and we could also make a comparison with the parents' DNA.'

'Did the toe come from a dead body or from someone who was still alive?' asked Claudine.

'Dead, unquestionably.'

'So we've got a separate murder, quite apart from what's happened to Mary?'

'I could be wrong, although I don't think I am,' said Rosetti.

He wasn't. There was no match at all with the print that arrived two hours later from Washington.

Félicité Galan had insisted that Jean Smet and August Dehane meet her that lunchtime at the Comme Chez Soi on the Place Rouppe, which they'd both initially welcomed because it was a public restaurant in which she could not openly berate them, but they were immediately terrified when she arrived. Félicité again had her hair in the tight chignon of the day of the abduction and was wearing the same jacket that had been described in the wanted posters and appeals. She strode from the entrance, exaggerating her walk like a model's catwalk parade, and didn't immediately take the waiter's offered chair, smirking down at the lawyer and the telephone company executive.

'Why not hide beneath the table?' she said.

'Sit down, for God's sake!' Smet spoke in a fierce whisper.

'Please!' added Dehane.

Smet waited for the waiter to leave. 'You're mad. She said you're mad and you are. Totally insane.'

'And you disobeyed me. Both of you. All of you. You sent Charles to kill her, didn't you?'

'No,' Smet said, keeping to the rehearsed story they'd agreed with Gaston to follow. 'You know what Charles is like. And he's getting worse. Has been for months.'

'How could we have known what he was going to do?' protested Dehane unconvincingly.

'You're a liar. You're all liars. None of you are to go near her any more.'

'I don't want to go near her at all,' said Smet.

Dehane said nothing.

'I'm not sure that I'll let any of you, even when we have the party.' She wished there was a greater penalty she could impose. Hurt them, disgrace them in some way that wouldn't involve her.

'Claudine knows all about you,' declared the Justice Ministry lawyer. 'Knows what sort of person you are. It's frightening, how accurately she's described you.'

'Did she really say I was mad?'

'Yes,' said Smet petulantly. 'And she's right: you are.'

'Tell me everything,' ordered Félicité.

'They've excluded me,' announced Smet dramatically. 'The bastard Poncellet!'

'How?'

'They're staging a big operation at the embassy for your call. To trap you. The others would have accepted my being there as a matter of course but Poncellet made a fuss about its having nothing to do with liaison: said I'd get a transcript later for the Ministry. I'd have drawn too much attention to myself if I'd argued against it.'

'To trap me!' echoed Félicité, looking to Dehane. 'I hope you've got the phone ready!'

'Don't do it!' pleaded the man. 'I've no idea what sort of tracking equipment they'll have but it's bound to be state of the art.'

Félicité's hand was already outstretched. She snapped her fingers and said: 'Give it to me.'

Reluctantly Dehane passed over the instrument.

'Whose number is it?' she asked.

'A director of a restaurant group. His phone was stolen from his car two nights ago. It hasn't been recovered yet.'

'Excellent,' said Félicité, dropping the mobile into her satchel handbag. 'Now I need to know everything that's happened . . .' She paused. 'But most of all I want to hear her opinion of me.'

CHAPTER NINETEEN

Only Claudine saw a twisted contradiction in her
guiding James McBride in the rudiments of negotiation so soon after what she considered her disastrous
attempt to talk John Norris into compliant surrender.
She tried to drive the thought from her mind: to drive
everything from her mind except preventing the man
from making any mistake in the telephone confrontation
that was to come.

Her first concern was that it should not be a public
spectacle, as it had been with her the previous day. Her
attempted insistence that only she and McBride be in the
room was met with shouted objections from Hillary, to
whom Claudine had to concede. Everyone else was
relegated to the communication centre and its audible,
two-way reception.

Claudine briefed the ambassador in the sealed office,
too, wanting him to become accustomed to the circumstances in which he had to conduct the conversation. It
was ludicrous to expect the man to be relaxed but
Claudine strived to achieve something as close to it as
possible. It didn't help having Hillary there. Nor did the
woman's sneer that if McBride became incapable she
would take over.

There was no way Claudine could know that
McBride's initially intrusive euphoria had almost as
much to do with the death of his personal embarrassment
along with John Norris as it did with his learning the
severed toe was not his daughter's, although the disclo-

sure led to another brief dispute with Hillary, who complained that she hadn't been told that a toe had been found and demanded that in future she be informed of everything. 'Everything! You understand?'

The over-excitement made McBride dangerously confident. It was essential to bring him down to a manageable level of self-assurance without swinging the pendulum too far in the other direction and making him realize the real danger the amputation still represented to his daughter.

'If the woman keeps to her timing – which I think she will because it's all part of her control syndrome – in two hours' time you'll be speaking to the monster who snatched your child,' said Claudine. She used the word intentionally.

'Yes?' said McBride.

Claudine was pleased at the body language, the way McBride's lips tightened and he straightened in his chair. 'A possible sex monster,' she said, using the word again.

'Yes?' The voice was quieter.

'Someone who's maimed your child.'

'But . . .'

'We've avoided your first mistake,' declared Claudine. 'I don't want her to know we've discovered the toe isn't Mary's. It's part of her control: it mustn't be taken away from her yet.'

'OK,' said McBride doubtfully.

'You hate her,' said Claudine. 'You'd like to kill her, wouldn't you?'

McBride blinked. 'Yes.'

'And if she were in the room with you, instead of on the other end of a telephone, you'd probably try.'

'I would,' said the man. 'And I'd do it. I want her dead.' He'd loosened his tie and taken his jacket off.

'Good,' said Claudine, pleased with the admission. 'Make yourself think hate.'

'I don't have to make myself.'

'You can't kill her, though.'

'I will, if I ever get to her.'

'But you can't, not today.'

'No,' he conceded.

'So what can you do to her today?'

McBride looked at Claudine uncertainly. 'What you tell me, I suppose.'

He'd come down as far as she wanted. 'Use your hate to beat her,' she said.

'How?'

'You negotiated a lot, in business?'

'Yes?' McBride thought uneasily of his recent fear of Norris.

'How often did you lose a negotiation?'

'A few times.'

'Did you ever hate the people you negotiated with?'

'Of course not. It was business.'

'What about those who beat you?'

'No.'

'Ever lose your temper?'

'That's the way to lose negotiations.'

Claudine smiled. 'Exactly! You're going to be talking to the woman who's got your child, a woman you think of as a monster who's prepared to disfigure her and whom you hate. But if for one single moment you allow that hate to come through, lose your temper, then you're going to lose Mary Beth. Show emotion – plead, cry, beg – but don't genuinely lose your temper and threaten to kill her like you did just now. She's got Mary Beth to hurt you with. You've got nothing, except the words you use and the money you're prepared to pay. And at the moment it comes down to words.'

McBride nodded, in what Claudine read as determination, not despair. For once Hillary was listening too, not trying instinctively to compete.

'What do I do?'

'Follow her lead. Let her be in control all the time. Only argue or oppose her when I tell you. I'm going to be right here, directly beside you. If you're unsure let it show that you're unsure, stumble to give me time to guide you.'

'Will she settle it today? Demand a ransom and say how it's to be delivered?' demanded Hillary.

'There's no way I can answer that,' replied Claudine, who didn't expect things to move that fast.

'If I can talk long enough we might get a positional fix: be able to get her back?' suggested McBride.

Claudine was worried the confidence was sinking below the optimum level. 'You're the key. You. And what you say and how you say it.'

McBride stared at her, swallowing, all thoughts of his escape by John Norris's death wiped from his mind. Ignoring Hillary's presence, he said: 'I've never been so frightened in my life.'

'It doesn't matter at all if she realizes that,' Claudine assured him. 'Now we're going to do something you'll probably think is ridiculous but isn't, believe me.'

'What?'

'I'm going to be the woman who's got Mary. Negotiate with me to get her back.'

The embassy communications room was the focal point of the operation and Claudine went to it an hour before the expected kidnap call, needing to know what the back-up was going to be.

One wall was dominated by a hugely magnified map of central Brussels, with linked adjoining charts spreading out into the city's major suburbs. On each were marked the outwardly radiating waiting positions of thirty unmarked radio-controlled cars and fifteen anonymous motorcycles ready to be dispatched in a pincer movement at the first indication of a route being established by the woman's call: when Claudine got to the crowded room the cars and motorcycles were testing in turn for sound levels and interference, each separately identified by a flashing light against its numbered designation on the central control panel in front of which sat three technicians, all American.

One was slightly apart from the other two, connected at a divided section of the control board not to the road vehicles but to two helicopters at that moment preparing to lift off from the NATO military complex close to Zaventem airport to be in a spotting formation directly over the city at the time of the anticipated call: two replacements were being held at the base in case a contact delay encroached into the fuel reserves of the airborne machines.

There were two separate mobile telephone scanners, both linked to roof-mounted satellite dishes installed that day and each again operated by a three-man crew. There was so much apparatus to record every spoken word and command if an operation were initiated that it had needed to be assembled in two banks, one behind the other, one man responsible for every two machines.

After a guided tour of the communication and tracking systems Sanglier led a retreat out into the less congested corridor.

'How's McBride?' he said.

'All right, I think. I've rehearsed him as much as I believe I safely can. Once he lost his self-consciousness he did quite well. His wife being there is a nuisance.'

'I'll go to see if there's anything he wants,' announced Harrison.

'No,' said Claudine. 'He needs to be left alone.'

'And we don't have to be told what he wants,' said Harding heavily. 'What either of them wants.'

★

Claudine went back to McBride's office fifteen minutes before the expected call. McBride was at the open cocktail cabinet, the Jack Daniel's bottle already in his hand. He turned and said: 'You want anything?'

'No,' said Claudine. 'And I don't think you should.' Damn! Something else she'd overlooked.

'Listen to her if you won't listen to me,' said Hillary.

'I can handle one.'

'I don't think you need it.' When he stayed with the bottle she said: 'She'd be winning, before you even started to talk.'

McBride shrugged, replacing the whiskey and closing the doors. 'I'm OK.'

'I know you are.'

'I wish I knew it as well,' said the other woman.

'You're not helping, Mrs McBride,' said Claudine. 'In fact, you're making things more difficult.'

'Who the hell do you think you're talking to?'

'Let's think about helping Mary, shall we?' said Claudine, refusing the argument.

'What if she doesn't call?'

'She will.' The woman was too unpredictable for such a guarantee and Claudine accepted she'd lose credibility if there was no contact, but McBride couldn't be allowed any doubt. She didn't like the nervousness obvious from his pacing round the study but said nothing. Hillary lounged contemptuously in a chair. As he walked McBride constantly checked his watch. To calm him, Claudine sat easily in her already arranged chair, positioned the special, large-faced clock with the sweep second hand where they would both be able to time the call and then toyed reflectively with the prepared jotting pad before beginning to write a series of quick, torn-off notes.

'What are you doing?' demanded the ambassador.

To her relief he stopped moving. 'There are things I can anticipate. Prepare for.'

'What?'

'Things she would expect you to say.'

'I thought we'd been through all that.'

'Reminders,' said Claudine.

'It's time!'

'She'll make us wait.'

'How long?'

'As long as she likes. But she'll call.'

He started walking aimlessly again. Claudine said: 'It'll be better if you sit down. You've got to be ready.'

McBride completed a circle and came back to lower himself into his chair. It was so large his feet only just touched the ground. His hands were shaking and his forehead was sheened with perspiration. There were three concealed call buttons, on the left of the knee recess. She wondered what they were for. The clock was registering four minutes after the time of yesterday's call.

McBride had got as far as 'She's not—' when the phone rang. All three jumped, McBride more than the women. Claudine knew the transfer from the main switchboard would have already been delayed for a few seconds, for the scan to begin. McBride stared at the instrument, transfixed.

'Pick it up,' said Claudine calmly.

McBride did so, hesitantly, but remembered to look sideways to her so that both receivers came off their cradles together. 'Hello?'

'McBride?' The voice was faint.

'Yes.'

'How do I know?'

Claudine mouthed 'You must tell me' and the American repeated the words aloud.

'What's Granny McBride's birthday?' asked the caller.

'August second,' replied the ambassador at once.

286

'And grandpa's?'

'Grandpa's dead.'

'When did he die?'

'Two years ago. November.'

There was a laugh, overlaid at the end by outside traffic noise. 'Hello, Mr Ambassador!'

Quickly Claudine slipped across the first of her notes. It read: 'Horror. She's maimed your child.'

McBride said: 'You've hurt Mary! Badly. Please give her back, so I can get her treated: get her to hospital!'

There was a pause at the other end. Claudine nodded approvingly to the man beside her. The line had been open for almost two minutes.

'She's been properly treated.'

'Who by?' mouthed Claudine.

'By a doctor?'

'How?'

'She's not in any pain.'

Claudine's second note read: Anger but not hatred. Frustration.

'Bastard,' said McBride. 'Why? I want to pay to get her back: pay anything.' He was performing far better than Claudine could have hoped.

'I wanted you to know you've got to do everything I demand . . .'

The line faded into silence and McBride said urgently: 'I didn't hear! The line's gone . . .'

'. . . demand or something worse will happen to her,' echoed down the line as the volume returned.

'No!' protested McBride, unprompted. 'There's no need to hurt her any more. Just tell me what you want and I'll do it: let's just end this.'

'We want two hundred and fifty thousand dollars,' announced the woman.

Claudine had been making profile notes throughout. She pressed down at the ransom figure so heavily the pencil point broke. She switched to another, angry at her over-reaction, important though the demand was. Hurriedly she passed another note.

Responding to it McBride said: 'You can have it now! Tonight! Tell me how to deliver it and you can have it tonight . . . so I can get Mary back tonight . . .'

Four minutes, Claudine saw. Surely with the sort of technical equipment at the other side of the embassy they would have got a fix by now!

'All in good time: I can't have us walking into a trap.'

'I promise . . .'

Before Claudine's headshake registered with McBride the woman cut him off. 'I know that won't be true, so don't lie. You don't want Mary coming to any more harm, do you?'

The man opened his mouth to speak but Claudine held up a stopping hand, mouthing her instruction.

'I'm sorry . . . I didn't mean . . . I'm so desperate to get Mary back,' stumbled McBride obediently.

The volume collapsed into static. Almost six minutes, noted Claudine. The words were indistinct when the sound came back. Then the voice said: 'Guess you didn't hear that: I lost you too. And how's the clever lady today? I know you're there, Claudine!'

The remark reverberated through Claudine's head like a pistol shot. She'd been right in thinking she'd missed something but she wasn't missing it any more and the recognition was so astonishing that momentarily Claudine's mind blocked. She was conscious of McBride's startled expression and of his intention to speak and urgently shook her head. She said: 'I'm very well, Mercedes. Trying to be a clever lady yourself?'

The laugh was uneven. 'It was obvious you'd listen in. Just as it's obvious they'll be trying to trace this call. That's why I won't be talking to you much longer.'

Could she do it! She had to, Claudine told herself.

There was a risk but she'd already made up her mind about the chances of getting Mary Beth back alive. Abandoning everything she'd rehearsed with the ambassador, she embarked on an approach she'd considered at the very beginning. 'We're having the toe scientifically examined, to establish if it's from Mary.' She held her free hand up against any interruption from McBride.

'Your idea?'

'Yes,' said Claudine. 'And I've got a lot more.' Bite! she thought desperately.

'The clever psychologist, imagining you know my mind!'

Claudine felt another sweep of disbelief. 'Oh, I know your mind very well, Mercedes: probably better than you know it yourself.' There was so much to think about: considerations to weigh. But later. Not now. Now her entire concentration had to be upon every nuance and word of this conversation.

'You're a conceited fool!'

Claudine was pleased at the irritated edge in the woman's voice. 'One of us is, Mercedes.' She hoped the woman discerned the contempt she was trying to infuse into her voice every time she uttered the ridiculous assumed name.

'Didn't you hear the warning I gave McBride about what would happen to Mary if he annoyed me?'

Once more Claudine shook her head against any interruption from the ambassador. The door on the opposite side of the office opened softly but urgently. Without coming any further into the room Blake gave exaggerated nods to indicate a location followed by one of the familiar rolling gestures with his hands for the woman to be kept on the line. Trying to make the sneer in her voice as obvious as she could, Claudine said: 'You didn't actually say annoyed, Mercedes, but then I guess you're confused—'

'I'm not at all confused!' broke in the woman.

Dare she go on? If she were right – and Claudine didn't doubt that she was – there was another way, a much more effective way, for her to achieve what she wanted. McBride, beside her, was damp with sweat, smelling of it. 'It's a common belief . . .' Claudine said, letting her voice trail. At the same time she slid another prompt sheet to the man.

McBride said: 'Let me speak to Mary. Talk to her to know she's all right.'

'Where's Claudine? I want Claudine!'

Claudine allowed the briefest of pauses, aware of the satisfaction surging through her: so much, so quickly. Dismissively, she demanded: 'What?'

'What's a common belief? What are you talking about?'

Quite irrespective of anything else, they'd kept the woman talking for a further three minutes: she had to be surrounded now, on the point of arrest. 'The ambassador wants to talk to Mary.'

'You haven't answered my question!'

'The only thing we need to talk about is the arrangement for getting Mary back.'

'I'll—' began the woman loudly, but then stopped. There was a sound as if the instrument had been hurriedly dropped, and distant talking, in French too indistinct to decipher, but no police sirens or the shouts and yells Claudine would have expected at a moment of arrest.

'What . . .?' started McBride, but Claudine gestured him down.

For precisely four more minutes, timed by the clock in front of them, the indistinct talking continued. Claudine thought she detected a child's voice and from the disbelieving look on his face she knew McBride had heard it too. Then there were sirens, a screaming cacophony, and the expected shouting began: there was definitely at least one child's voice among the screaming before all the noise was drowned by the whuck-whuck of descending helicopters.

'They've got her!' said McBride, his voice trembling. 'They've got the woman and they've got Mary back.'

'Come on!' shouted Claudine, already running towards the door.

Way was made for McBride and his wife to squeeze into the communications room, alongside Sanglier against the wall at the very rear. The only sound, the volume adjusted to be properly audible, not deafening, was relayed over an open channel that all could hear. It was in French. There was definitely a child's cry. Demands, clearly from the arresting officers, for the adults not to move and to keep their hands and arms visible. One voice kept repeating a threat to shoot. Claudine's first dip of uncertainty came with the sound of a man's voice, close to hysteria, demanding to know what was happening and pleading that no one shoot. And of a child screaming, hysterical too.

Blake was beside her. She leaned towards him and whispered: 'It's gone wrong.' He frowned back at her, not replying.

She looked intently at Poncellet, on the other side of the blond-haired man. It surely couldn't be the police chief? She hadn't thought whom she could continue to trust, until that moment: hadn't thought about anything, except her conviction. Now she did. She thought about how they could use what she'd learned and how she could keep Mary alive and wondered how much easier or more difficult it made everything. And she wondered who it was. There was only a small possible number. Through all the confusion and conflicting impressions Claudine abruptly felt very confident. She couldn't risk telling anyone – her biggest and most immediate problem was deciding whom she could tell about anything – but for the first time almost since the investigation started she believed there was a chance of getting Mary back alive. Just as she decided, suddenly, that Mary *was* still alive. If she'd been dead, it would have been Mary's toe in the backpack, not someone else's.

Claudine was briefly thrown off balance, for just seconds, by the implications of that awareness, sickening but at the same time hopeful though it was. *I'm not sure I want to give her back yet. I've become attached to her.* There could be another interpretation of that remark, as obscene but not as life-threatening as her first. Bizarre though it might be to a rational mind – which she already knew the woman didn't possess – but totally in keeping with the sexual deviancy of paedophilia, Claudine thought it more than likely that the unknown woman had fallen in love with Mary Beth McBride. Which, while posing a terrible sexual danger, meant that she wouldn't, for the moment at least, be subjected to any other physical danger. Rather, bizarre upon the bizarre, that she would be protected from it.

Poncellet leaned from Claudine's other side and said: 'This doesn't sound right.'

'It isn't,' said Claudine. 'She's beaten us.'

The family was brought to the US embassy because that was where the investigation was concentrated, but long before their arrival there was an explanation of crushing disappointment.

There was no reason whatsoever for embarrassment or recrimination, because the location operation had worked perfectly. But there was a squabble of accusations between the Belgian, American and Europol squads, particularly among those who'd first arrived at the supermarket car park in the Ganshoren suburb of the city.

Paradoxically, Hortense, the daughter of Horst and

Sonia Eindicks, was the same age as Mary Beth McBride to within a day. The family always did their major supermarket shopping on the last Friday of every month, when Horst got paid. Neither parent could remember the Mercedes parked next to them when they'd emerged to unpack their trolleys, but Hortense said she was sure the nice lady who'd taken one of their trolleys instead of getting one for herself and given her the deposit money had yellow hair. Certainly none of them had seen her drop the telephone, still connected to the embassy, among the plastic bags in the back of the family Ford.

'And while we all went one way she went the other,' said Poncellet bitterly.

Harding paid double for the trolley coin to be sent for forensic analysis, along with the abandoned telephone. The Eindicks family, awed by the sensation in which they had become so innocently involved, accepted apologies for earlier being terrorized.

It was not until the family was being escorted from the embassy that Claudine had the opportunity to draw Sanglier aside.

'We've got to have a meeting but without Poncellet,' she said urgently.

'What about?'

'The person who knows who's got Mary,' said Claudine simply.

CHAPTER TWENTY

It didn't take long to organize, after the departure of André Poncellet, but there was a lot of questioning impatience from everyone, particularly Sanglier, after Claudine's dramatic announcement. Sanglier demanded a preliminary explanation, which Claudine avoided by insisting that they needed complete transcripts as well as the tapes of both her conversations with the woman to understand her discovery.

Unable to gauge how serious the leak was and with the bugging of her hotel room very much in mind she asked to remain at the embassy instead of returning to their police headquarters accommodation, claiming it might no longer be safe. That assertion heightened the drama and increased the demands.

The delay of transcribing and then copying the second tape gave time for Rosetti and Volker to arrive from the hotel. Both men made contributions to an investigation far beyond their individual disciplines, but observing her know thyself dictum Claudine acknowledged a determination to present something that would turn the entire investigation on its head to both Hugo Rosetti and Peter Blake. She at once confronted the self-examination. It wasn't immaturity, although maybe there was a small, disturbing element. It was, instead, the far deeper need after John Norris's suicide to prove herself not just to two men to whom she felt emotionally attracted but to everyone else as well. Including herself. She wanted to stage a performance, almost literally, in front of them all.

Gain their plaudits. She didn't like the awareness. It was good – cathartic – that she'd diagnosed it but she had to rid herself of it.

They used the CIA quarters, which meant Lance Rampling had to be included. Because of the possible political consequences Claudine had considered including the ambassador as well, and there was no doubt his larger office would have been far more comfortable. However, she decided it was unnecessary as well as wrong to cause McBride and his wife any more distress. Hopefully Burt Harrison could assess the political repercussions far more dispassionately.

Belatedly trying to minimize the stage-like appearance, Claudine did not actually sit behind Rampling's desk but perched casually on its side edge. Even so, as Rosetti and Volker finally entered, Sanglier said testily: 'I hope you can justify all this mystery: we're supposed to be working with the Belgians, not against them.'

Claudine decided she could not have sought a better cue. 'As they're supposed to be working with us. But someone isn't.'

'What?' That was Harrison.

'The people who've got Mary are aware of every word we've spoken and every move we've considered making against them, virtually from the start of this investigation.'

The stunned, disbelieving reaction came from Harding. 'How in the name of Christ can you know that?'

Instead of replying Claudine depressed the play button on the machine beside her. Into the room echoed her previous day's exchange.

I want McBride. The woman.

I'm speaking on his behalf. Claudine.

The wife?

No.

Ah, the clever little mind-reader!

295

Claudine stopped the tape, looked expectantly – hopefully – towards the men ranged in front of her. Rosetti had his head to one side, frowning in what she thought was half-awareness. Blake's face was blank. So were those of Sanglier and Harding. Harrison was looking to them for guidance. Rampling was still hunched over the transcript from which he'd followed the replay. There was a half-smile on the face of the always laterally thinking Volker.

Claudine minimally rewound the tape for just one sentence.

Ah, the clever little mind-reader!

'It's wrong!' declared Claudine urgently. 'She doesn't get McBride, whom she expects. Mrs McBride is an outside possibility, whom she doesn't get either. And when I deny it's Mrs McBride there's an immediate recognition: *Ah, the clever little mind-reader!* Not "Who are you?" Not "Put me on to McBride, he's the only one I want to talk to." No threats. No arguments, until much too late. She was waiting for me . . .' Claudine started the tape again.

We want to negotiate.

Of course you do.

Tell me about Mary.

Demanding!

'But she doesn't demand in return,' insisted Claudine. 'She should have done – had every reason to do so – but she doesn't because she *knows* who I am! There'd been no public announcement of my being here: whether I was male or female. There's no way she could have known unless someone at the very highest level – at *our* level – told her.' She started the tape again, continuing the conversation. 'She accepts me, without question! Plays word games about names, needing to show me how clever she is: wanting to be cleverer than me. Having to regain control.'

'There *is* an acceptance, from the beginning,' said Volker.

'I'm not so sure,' disputed Blake.

Claudine rejected the first tape, fumbling in her eagerness to replace it with the second. She began it at the wrong section, fast forwarded to where she wanted to be.

The clever psychologist, imagining you know my mind! echoed into the room. Claudine said: 'There's been no public reference anywhere to a psychologist being part of the investigation. And I said exactly that at one of our meetings: that I was getting to know her mind.'

'"And how's the clever lady today? I know you're there, Claudine,"' challenged Rampling, reading from the transcript. He looked up. 'It was obvious you'd listen in. Just as it's obvious there'd have been a trained negotiator from the beginning. Hostage or kidnap negotiators are invariably psychologists. It's all intelligent reasoning.'

'It's *not* intelligent reasoning that the negotiator would be female,' persisted Claudine. 'The more likely reasoning, from a woman, would be that a negotiator would be male.'

'I don't think that's logical,' said Rosetti.

'How many other women are there in this room?' demanded Claudine. Going to Sanglier, then Harding, and finally Rampling, she said: 'How many female psychologists are there in Europol? Or the FBI? Or the CIA?' Why wasn't it as obvious to them as it was to her?

'You're being sexist, we aren't,' said Sanglier inadequately. He didn't want her to be right: didn't want to become embroiled in the alternative that she was suggesting. It was too fraught with personal difficulties.

'Listen to today's conversation, in full!' pleaded Claudine 'Really *listen*!'

Total silence enclosed the room and Claudine didn't

speak for several moments after the tape had finished. Finally she said: 'What's wrong?'

'You're antagonizing her,' Harrison suggested fatuously.

Claudine refused the bait. 'She challenged *me*, at the very beginning: announced that she knew I'd be listening in. But hear how she loses control – the last thing she wanted to do: total anathema to her – when I tell her I know her mind better than she does.'

'What's the significance of that?' queried Sanglier. She couldn't be right. It wasn't possible. Yet . . .

'At this morning's conference I said she was mad, in layman's terms,' Claudine reminded him. 'Someone suffering from her psychopathy will never accept that they are mentally deranged: everyone else is mad, not them. Today's call wasn't to taunt the ambassador or announce a ransom. It was to argue with me: prove to me that she wasn't mad.'

'Yes, I can see that,' said Volker.

'Me too,' agreed Rampling.

'But for someone in the group to be involved would be . . .' Blake began.

'. . . inconceivable,' finished Claudine. 'But why? Paedophiles – perhaps more than any other criminal category – come from across the widest spectrum of society. More often than not they're from the professional class. Look how clever they've been, with e-mail and now mobile phones . . . that points to an executive expertise.'

'They abandoned their e-mail approach, switched to telephones, the moment I traced their route to Menen. Which only our group knew I'd done,' Volker pointed out. Heavily he added: 'And they haven't used it since.'

'How many in the control group could be involved?' demanded Rampling.

'Eight,' replied Harding at once. 'Poncellet and Smet. Or any one of the six clerks who've been keeping records on a rotational basis.'

'Three are women, two of them blond,' remembered Blake.

'Neither answers the description or looks anything like the videofit picture,' cautioned Volker.

'The source could also be anyone at police headquarters with a duplicate key to the incident room and all its records and transcripts,' suggested Blake.

'The transcript of this morning's meeting, when I called her mad, won't be in the incident room records yet,' Claudine pointed out. 'It can only be one of the eight.'

'If Dr Carter's interpretation is wrong the fall-out will be incalculable,' said Sanglier. How could a future Justice Minister answer for wrongly suspecting another Justice Ministry! It was precisely the sort of embarrassment he'd been warned about in Paris. On the other hand, if her suspicions were right . . . Why did things become so difficult just when he imagined they were becoming simpler!

'My function is to interpret words and behaviour,' Claudine said slowly. 'There are some interpretations of today's conversation that I've still got to suggest to you. But the most important is my total conviction that there is an informer, among us.' She was reluctant to challenge Sanglier openly, after the apparent relaxation of their earlier uneven relationship, but she couldn't avoid it. 'We surely can't risk the other incalculable: what's going to happen to Mary Beth if my interpretation is correct?'

He couldn't argue against her and he didn't want to go along with her, Sanglier thought desperately. Why had he stayed! Why hadn't he gone back to The Hague immediately after resolving the problem of the suicide? He would have been safe there, able to claim that operational details had been kept from him if there was a disaster.

'What are the other interpretations you mentioned?' asked Harrison.

'Principally a further confirmation of what I've feared and warned against: probably the biggest,' said Claudine. 'She's seen McBride openly cry, on television. Knows his desperation. She knows, too, how rich he is. That he'll pay anything. Yet all she asks for is two hundred and fifty thousand dollars. Which is derisory.'

'No intention of giving Mary back?' Blake realized.

'There never has been,' insisted Claudine. 'Now, for the first time, we've got a real chance to prevent that happening. Our first real chance, in fact, to get her back. But from now on our proper decision-making has got to be carried out like this: just by us, in this room. Our sessions at police headquarters have to be conducted solely to manipulate the woman and the people with her, through whoever their source is.'

'We need to do more than that,' insisted Harding, presented at last with an operational opportunity. 'There're only eight people to check out, for Christ's sake!'

'And we've got an army looking for work,' endorsed Rampling, equally enthusiastic.

'An American operation, you mean?' Sanglier said, trying to keep any eagerness from being obvious.

'We've been through the problem of legality,' Harding pointed out. 'I don't think the circumstances are the same any more.'

'We're straying into dangerous water,' protested Harrison, as diplomatically uneasy as Sanglier. 'In effect – in fact! – we'd be spying upon and investigating justice officials of a sovereign state actually in their own country.'

'That's exactly what we'll be doing,' said the aggressive Rampling, intentionally changing tense. 'And need to do.'

'Can you do it?' demanded Harrison of Claudine. 'Manipulate a response we'd recognize, I mean?'

'Very easily,' she assured him.

'And with Poncellet, Smet and at least three of the clerks at your meeting in the morning we know where more than half our suspects will be, don't we?' smiled Rampling.

'I don't think any positive action should be taken until we've fully assessed Dr Carter's success at the morning conference,' said Harrison.

'Neither do I,' said Sanglier, anxious to support the reluctant diplomat.

'I totally agree,' said Harding, not caring if the lie was obvious. What was even more obvious was what he had to do, as the operational commander. By this time tomorrow – sooner if possible – he wasn't just going to know the favourite breakfast cereal of eight near strangers, he'd be able to say in which hand they held the spoon.

By the end of the meal Claudine accepted she had been the only person with any real problem but believed she had lost it early enough for neither of them to have been aware of it. Blake appeared very much at ease and Rosetti, usually a reserved man, matched his friendliness. She'd wished Hugo hadn't been so territorially obvious, cupping her arm and holding out chairs and unfolding dinner napkins: twice she'd caught the curiosity on Blake's face. They ate at the hotel at the request of Claudine, who pleaded exhaustion at the end of such a crowded day, which was only part of the reason. It would, she decided, make it easier to leave both men at the end of the evening.

There was only the vaguest of tensions, each man competing to admire the profiling and analysis that had led to the breakthrough, which neither doubted. The more cynical Blake was genuinely funny parodying the desperation of Harrison and Sanglier, who'd gone off alone to eat together, to avoid any personal responsibility for whatever Harding and Rampling did.

'Let's just hope they do it well,' said Claudine, quickly cutting off the laughter.

Blake didn't look at her when he pleaded tiredness to excuse himself as soon as the meal ended, leaving her with Rosetti. Claudine felt a sudden warmth and hoped she hadn't coloured. That would have been ridiculous.

'Kurt told me about the American,' said Rosetti.

'I'm all right.'

'You sure?'

'I should have prevented it.'

'So you're not all right,' said the man.

'I'll be OK.'

'It would be wrong to blame yourself.'

'Easy to say.'

'But true. He wasn't your responsibility – or your patient.'

'I said I'll be OK: I can function. I don't want to analyse it any more.' She regretted the sharpness.

'Peter's a nice guy.'

'Yes.'

'You obviously get on well.'

'I told you we did.' She felt a sudden sweep of anger.

'I remember.'

'I'm very tired. I'm going to bed.'

'Of course.'

She expected it to be Blake when her phone rang. 'You didn't tell me about you and Hugo.'

'There's nothing to tell.'

'It didn't look like that tonight.'

'We see each other. But we're not sleeping together.' Why was she defending herself: telling him that!

'Oh.'

'I really am tired.'

'How about lonely?'

'Yes,' she said. 'But no.'

'You sure?'

'Quite sure.' She hoped she hadn't created an unnecessary problem for herself.

Rosetti and Volker were at the bar and both drunk when Henri Sanglier got back to the Metropole. The German, emboldened by whisky, invited him to join them but Sanglier said he had calls to make.

'Things could really start to move tomorrow,' forecast Volker, carefully enunciating each word.

'I hope you're right,' said the Frenchman.

'We've done our best,' Volker assured him enigmatically.

'I don't want to know!'

In his suite Sanglier remained undecided for several moments before picking up the telephone to dial Françoise, to whom he hadn't spoken since Paris and hardly expected to reach now. He was actually surprised when she answered almost immediately. She appeared as surprised to hear from him. There was noise – music and people – in the background.

Instead of talking about Paris, which he'd intended, he said: 'What's going on?'

'Friends. A party.'

Sanglier felt his throat block. She was very bright, excited, chattering grown-up birdsong. It wasn't alcohol. He didn't want to think what it was. 'I said never the house.'

'You say lots of things.'

'Get them out, Françoise.'

'They're my friends.'

'How long has it been going on?'

303

'Days. Who knows? Great fun.'

'I'm coming home,' lied Sanglier. 'I want everyone out before I get there.'

'Don't be such a pompous shit! Why doesn't everybody stay so you can join us when you get back?'

Sanglier put the phone down but remained sitting on the side of his bed, eyes tightly shut in despair. What was he going to do? Dear God, what was he going to do?

CHAPTER TWENTY-ONE

The effectiveness of Kurt Volker's computer marauding enabled the enlarged FBI and CIA surveillance
operation to be in place by 6 a.m.

Through Europol's temporary incident room Volker
was officially part of the police headquarters system,
knowing its password, so it wasn't even necessary to hack
in from the US embassy to access its personnel files,
which had no protecting firewall against unauthorized
intrusion.

The full print-out of Police Commissioner André Poncellet included two photographs clearly taken some years
previously but still sufficient for identification – a prime
requirement – so Volker digitalized both. There were two
listed addresses, one within the city on the rue des
Commerçants and what was clearly a summer house by
the lake at Auderghem. From their dates of birth one
daughter was twenty-one, the other twenty-four, making
it unlikely either still lived at home. Information about
how many people were likely to occupy a property was
another essential requirement.

Volker switched from police headquarter records to its
computer directory, guessing the access code to the
Justice Ministry would be registered, which it was. So he
didn't have to hack an entry there, either. As with police
personnel, every ministry file held two subject photographs, full face and profile. Again he digitalized those of
the six clerks, as well as those of Jean Smet.

The rue de Flandres was the only listed house for

Smet, who was described as a bachelor with no dependants. Two of the Europol-assigned female clerks were married. So were two of the men. Each of the four had school-age children. Only the unmarried man lived outside the city, close to the Astrid park in Anderlecht.

To each of the eight targets Paul Harding assigned a six-man squad, with two 'floating' operatives for any unforeseen development or emergency. The necessary forty additional agents – twenty from the FBI, twenty from the CIA – had been embarked at Washington's Andrews Air Force base before Volker completed his computer searches. With them they brought the Bibles and literature to support the textbook CIA cover of overseas Jehovah's Witnesses or Mormon missionaries if they mistakenly approached a still occupied foreign household.

The 6 a.m. deployment of each team was designed to avoid that risk – which it did in every case – by recording each departure against the likely remaining occupancy of premises to be burgled and searched after the target left for work. At that exit, the watching team split, three detaching to maintain the physical surveillance, three remaining to enter the house or apartment after determining it was empty. Each of the forty-eight officers, fifteen of them women, were equipped with Volker's computer-hijacked personnel print-outs with their essential recognitive photographs.

All the clerks left their homes roughly within fifteen minutes of each other, for their 9 a.m. ministry start. Three dropped their children off at school. The wife of the fourth male clerk left separately, in her own car, with their two children.

The apparently unoccupied houses of the bachelor male clerk who lived at Anderlecht and the unmarried female whose rented home was on the rue Pieremans were the first to be entered. Both were telephoned first, to ensure they were empty. The others were burgled as their occupants left during the course of the day, the last not until 2 p.m. All the burglaries were to an established pattern, two agents entering while the third, the spot man, remained outside to warn of any unexpected return.

Jean Smet's house was broken into at 10 a.m., fifteen minutes after he left for the ministry and that morning's meeting of the control group. The team assigned to André Poncellet had to wait until 1.30 p.m., an hour after his wife left for her luncheon club meeting; they had to wait an extra half an hour for the departure of the non-resident housekeeper whose earlier arrival they'd noted.

The police commissioner's home was the only one equipped with a burglar alarm, although it was not set. No house had any dogs, although there were cats in three, one with a litter. There was only one hurried exit at an unexpected return, that of the wife of a clerk living on rue Brogniez. It was achieved without panic or discovery, through an already opened rear door and along an already reconnoitred side path.

The establishment of an escape route was always the first step in the strictly regimented and well-rehearsed entry routine. The sweep was conducted from the very top – the loft, if there was one – and descended to the basement. Before the search of any room began it was photographed from four different angles by Polaroid with one operator checking the other at the completion of the examination to ensure every article, piece of furniture, picture, drawer, ornament, vase, book, magazine or newspaper was replaced precisely in the position in which it had been before they started. Any letter or document they thought might have the slightest relevance was photographed with a more sophisticated camera fitted with a proxile copying lens. So were all bank and financial records and every address book. All pictures, photographs, bureaux and furniture that might have concealed

307

hiding places were moved, particularly in lofts and basements. Listening devices were installed in every telephone and in the light fittings and skirting boards of every room. The primary objective was obviously anything sexual, of any nature whatsoever. All videos were run for their first five minutes on the available television screens. There were two soft porn videos at the home of one of the married male clerks and three, more hard core, at the Anderlecht house of the unmarried man. There were also twelve sex magazines. All the videos and the magazines portrayed heterosexual sex. In every case the 'floating' agent on standby outside each house ferried the videos back to the US embassy and waited while Kurt Volker made instant copies.

The unmarried female clerk had two vibrators, one black, in her bedside cabinet and a selection of soft porn male magazines.

Duncan McCulloch and Robert Ritchie carried out the search of Jean Smet's house. It was immaculately kept, every shirt folded in its drawer, every shoe on its tree, no dust or fallen flower petal anywhere. They took particular care with their Polaroid record and with the loaded Hochner pistol they briefly removed from the bedside table.

So cleverly was it concealed that McCulloch almost missed the safe, only at the last minute lifting the corner of the bedroom carpet that had been extended to cover the bottom of the wardrobe to see its edge, sunk into the floor. He shouted the find to Ritchie, who continued his search while McCulloch hunched over the safe, stethoscope microphone against the combination box. It was hardly necessary. Like nine out of ten people Smet had used the date, month and year of his birth – all of which McCulloch had from Volker's print-out – for his security. The safe was empty apart from a selection of pornographic photographs, all featuring children – predominantly boys – and two videos. One of the videos was the acquisition from Amsterdam that Smet had shown Félicité three days earlier. It was only after he'd hurried it off to the rue du Régent that McCulloch located his partner in the basement.

'I got two paedophile films and a lot of stills,' announced McCulloch.

Ritchie didn't turn, too intent on the photographs he was taking. 'And this original coal cellar has been converted into a cell with a metal-grilled door . . .' He turned. 'But Mary Beth isn't in it.'

That morning's gathering was the last at which the identity of the informer remained unknown. There had been a brief, preliminary meeting at the American embassy at which Claudine had argued that neither Poncellet nor Smet – and certainly none of that day's clerks – would know she was twisting her assessment of the previous evening's telephone conversation. The others also agreed not to question the unexpected result of the overnight forensic and number check on the mobile telephone unless Poncellet drew attention to it.

At police headquarters, Smet again asked for the actual conversation to be played, following it from the prepared transcript, coming up to Claudine enquiringly the moment it finished.

'She's panicking,' responded Claudine easily. 'Dumping the telephone as she did clearly indicates that. And she's frightened of me, personally. The whole conversation is directed against me, not the ambassador. And she hasn't got a clue how to arrange a ransom.'

'I didn't think you believed there was ever any serious intention of getting a ransom?' pressed Smet.

'What I doubted was her intention of giving Mary back,' corrected Claudine. 'To have got away, undetected, with a ransom would have been her ultimate victory. She won't get that now. She'll abandon the ransom idea.'

'If she doesn't go ahead with the ransom there's no reason to maintain contact, is there?' said Poncellet.

Claudine wished the policeman hadn't asked the question, although there was an opening to continue the goading. 'It was always the most worrying possibility. I never imagined she would collapse so quickly or so easily.'

'You don't know that she has,' persisted Poncellet.

'I do,' said Claudine. She was uncomfortable, offering wrong assessments. More immaturity, she recognized. It wasn't a wrong assessment. It was an absolutely correct procedure to achieve a very necessary objective. The doubt was whether she would succeed in doing so.

'Was there anything in the scientific examination of the telephone?' asked Smet.

Blake said: 'Nothing. It was stolen in Ghent seven days ago.'

'A blank there, then?' said Poncellet.

For a further five hours that single remark focused the suspicion upon the police chief, in front of whom were set out the findings – including the one obvious but seemingly unnoticed inconsistency – of the mobile telephone company, who had cooperated fully from the first moment of their being contacted, once the number had been identified.

'Nothing that I can see to help us along,' said Harding, setting a fresh snare for the policeman who immediately appeared to fall into it by saying nothing.

'So everything revolves around another telephone call?' said Smet.

'Which she'll be too frightened to make,' declared Claudine.

There was nothing from the surveillance when they got back to the embassy. Although the hope of a possible discovery within six hours had been unrealistic, the disappointment was nevertheless intense.

'I've changed the entire strategy,' Claudine explained to the doubtful Burt Harrison. 'Directly challenged her with being scared: behaving like someone mentally unstable. She won't be able to stop herself from responding.'

'I couldn't do your job,' said the diplomat.

I know you couldn't, thought Claudine. Aloud she said: 'Most times I don't enjoy doing it myself.' Had that morning been another confidence-building public performance? She certainly hadn't thought so until now. And with no professional reason for him to attend, Hugo Rosetti hadn't been there to witness it. He hadn't come down for breakfast before she'd left the hotel, either.

It was four thirty before the courier hurried in with Jean Smet's two tapes and a selection of the stills to be copied. Both were hard core paedophilia pornography.

Harrison became visibly distressed halfway through the first film and openly protested at the need to watch the second in its entirety. 'Why?' he demanded.

'To see if Mary Beth is featured,' said Blake bluntly.

The man objected again when Volker rewound both to replay them simultaneously. The German ignored him, exclaiming in satisfied triumph when he freeze-framed both at the meaningless strip of letters and figures that preceded both performances.

'What?' demanded Claudine expectantly.

'They're identical.' Volker traced his finger along each matching set of symbols. 'It's cryptography: encoding data against unauthorized entry. In this case it'll be the details of the distributors. It's the newest and safest way for paedophiles to hide: the current anti-hacking firewall.'

'Where's this going to take us?' asked Harding.

'To who they are and where they operate from. To all

311

the pornography they've got on offer, to see if Mary is among those already featured . . .' Volker hesitated, nodding in renewed satisfaction. 'And hopefully to their subscriber list to see who else in Belgium, particularly in Brussels, is on it as well as Jean Smet.'

The illegal burglaries had been totally justified, decided Henri Sanglier. And all except that of Smet's house could remain undisclosed. So he was in no career-obstructing personal danger. In fact, as the acknowledged head of the investigating force, there would at the end of the case be a great deal of public recognition. He said: 'We've done extremely well. I'm very pleased.'

Briskly, actually moving towards the door, Harrison said: 'We could have Mary back by tonight! I'll tell the ambassador.'

'You won't!' snapped Blake. 'This is the beginning, not the end. And that could still be a long way off.'

CHAPTER TWENTY-TWO

At first, when they left the house, Félicité held tightly to Mary's hand, but it was difficult for the girl to throw the bread to the screeching gulls hovering against the warm wind so Félicité let her go. The gulls swarmed very close and Mary screamed and laughed, although nervously, finally hurling the remainder of the broken-up loaf in one shower, to send the birds from her. The sun was silvering the water and after so long in the basement Mary still had her eyes screwed up against the brightness: already there was some faint colour coming back to her cheeks.

'Isn't this nice?' said Félicité. She was completely recovered, quite calm: content even. Certainly much better than she had been after talking to Smet. Then she'd been so furious she hadn't even been able to think properly, her mind jumping from one half-thought to another, nothing in its proper order. It was now; as it always was. Everything worked out, all the uncertainties resolved. There was a lot to do, despite all that she'd already done since the previous day, but there was no longer any hurry.

'Can I collect shells and things?' asked Mary, as the disappointed gulls at last left them alone.

'Don't go too far ahead.' There was nowhere Mary could go but Félicité was watchful. Two barges were passing each other in the centre channel of the Schelde but Félicité wasn't worried. Both were too far away to see any crew so she and Mary would be just as distant: tiny unrecognizable figures.

'I like my new things. And the u.p.'s,' said Mary. She was glad she could throw the old, stained pair away. And that the pain in her tummy had gone and there weren't any more blood spots. She wasn't sure the woman was telling the truth about her becoming a big girl. The woman told lies.

'You look beautiful.' The clothes had been the last things Félicité had bought before leaving Brussels. The red sweater, roll-necked with reindeer in a blue line across the front, fitted perfectly but she'd had to take the jeans up by one turn.

'Why didn't you let me come out here before?' Mary was scurrying by the waterline, turning over debris with a stick. She wondered if there was a road beyond the rising bank to her right. She couldn't hear any traffic.

'There was never time.' Félicité could only just pick out the closest house, nothing more than a dark shape on the horizon far ahead. There was even less danger from that than from the barges, but they'd still turn back soon. She didn't want to tire Mary. And she was tired herself: it had been late by the time she'd got to Luxembourg the previous night and she'd had to drive hard to get back to Brussels and do everything necessary there before coming to Antwerp. But it was all going to be worth it.

'Why is there time now?'

'I'm going to stay with you: not leave you alone any more. Would you like that?' How wonderful – magical – to be with her for ever. To travel, just the two of them. A fantasy, Félicité knew. But one she could indulge in, during the next few days. A fantasy that would become her personal Greek tragedy.

Mary frowned up from her beachcoming. 'How long's that going to be?'

'I'm not sure, not yet. A while.' She couldn't conceive

what it would be like, when it had to end: refused to think about it. All she wanted was for them to be together. Something beautiful. She wouldn't let there be any pain. She'd have Lascelles do it. Just a pin prick.

Mary suddenly swooped, crying out, coming up triumphantly with her hand above her head. 'A stone with a hole in it! That's lucky.'

'Is it?'

'Back home.' Solemnly the child held out her hand. The stone was white, water-bleached. 'A present, for you. Your own lucky stone.'

Félicité swallowed heavily. 'Thank you, my darling. I'll treasure it.' She would. For ever. Mary was so beautiful: so utterly, adorably beautiful.

'Can I go to see what's on the other side of the bank?'

'There's nothing. Just marsh.'

'Can I go and look anyway?'

'There are mosquitoes.'

'I don't care.'

'Stay down here.'

Mary detected the change in the woman's voice, knowing she had to stop. 'It *is* nice, being able to come outside.'

'I knew you'd like it.'

'Can we go somewhere else?' Mary could see a house, a long way off. It looked dark, shuttered. The sun should have been shining off the windows but it wasn't.

'What?'

'As well as here, by the river. Go somewhere else for a walk?'

'We'll see.'

'I'd like to.'

'We'll see,' repeated Félicité. 'I think we should go back now. We've walked a long way.'

'I'm not tired.'

'We'll still go back.'

'Just a little further?'

'No!'

There was that sound in her voice again. 'I don't want to look for shells or stones any more.'

'We're going back,' insisted Félicité.

Mary reached out for the woman's hand. 'When will I go home?'

'Don't you like me?' Mary's hand was velvet soft, pudgy fingers searching for hers.

'Yes, now that you don't hit me.'

'I won't ever hit you again. I promise.'

She broke her promises when she felt like it, remembered Mary. 'Why did you before?'

'I made a mistake. I'm sorry.'

Mary liked making her feel sorry. There definitely wasn't any car noise from the other side of the bank so perhaps it was just marsh. 'So when will I go home?'

Félicité walked for several moments without talking. 'Would you like to talk to your papa?' It was a new idea. The bitch who thought she knew so much wouldn't expect that: wouldn't expect a lot of what was going to happen. She was a piss-poor psychologist, believing she was frightened of her. Soon prove that was ridiculous.

'Can I! Can I!' said Mary urgently.

'What would you say about me?'

Now Mary remained silent, although not for as long as Félicité. 'I don't know. Nothing. Can I speak to him? Please!'

'Why don't you want to stay with me?'

Mary flinched at the sudden harshness. 'I can't stay with you for ever. You know I can't.'

'Would you, if you could?' said Félicité, allowing the fantasy.

Mary knew the answer was important. 'Yes, if I didn't already have a mom and dad.'

The simplistic logic blunted Félicité's irritation. She

wouldn't be giving in, letting Mary speak to her father: she'd be increasing the pressure. An additional idea began to form. 'They might try to stop you.'

'Who?'

'People who are with your papa. A woman. Her name's Claudine. That's why it's taken so long: sometimes when I call she won't let me talk to him.'

'Why not?'

'She won't believe it's about you. A lot of people are playing jokes on your papa: calling and pretending to be you.'

'We're not pretending!'

'I know.'

'Tell her she must let me!'

'I'll try. If I do, will you promise to tell her something for me?'

'What?' asked Mary doubtfully.

'Something that might sound silly but she'll understand.'

'All right.'

They were close to the house now. Hopeful gulls swooped and called overhead. A ship so laden with containers it seemed to have a city skyline was making its way slowly from the port towards the open sea. It was still too far away for anyone to be visible but Mary waved.

'Did you see anyone?' demanded Félicité sharply.

'No.'

'Why did you wave?'

Mary shrugged. 'Because.' She stood in the middle of the pattern-floored entrance hall, watching Félicité carefully lock, bolt and test the huge front door. 'Are any of the others coming?'

'No.'

'When will they?'

'Never.' Félicité smiled. Of all the decisions she'd

made in the last twenty-four hours, the one to abandon Smet and all the others satisfied her the most.

'I don't want to go back downstairs,' announced Mary, risking the defiance.

The telephone conversations would be in French: there was no way the child would be able to understand. Félicité said: 'If you stay upstairs you've got to be a good girl.'

'I will be.'

'You know what I mean by being a good girl, don't you?'

'Yes.'

'What?'

'Not try to get away.' She was glad she hadn't run to the top of the bank. She'd intended to, at first.

'If you do try I'll bring back the man I stopped hurting you to look after you again. And I'll leave.' Félicité felt almost physical pain at the fear that registered at once on Mary's face. 'So you will be good, won't you?' she added hurriedly.

'Yes,' said the child quietly. She tensed when Félicité put her arm round her to take her into the huge room with the panoramic windows. Inside Mary curled up in a large chair, staring out over the river with her back to the room and Félicité.

Hans Doorn said he was glad she'd called to rearrange the postponed booking. It was fortunate the house was still available. He'd arrange for it to be prepared before the arrival of her and her party and understood they'd be bringing their own staff. If there was a change of plan he could fix local cooking and cleaning people. Félicité said there wouldn't be any change.

The Luxembourg lawyer whom she'd continued to use after Marcel's death and had briefed that morning said he'd already started the chain in Andorra and Liechtenstein and hoped to complete with the confirmation in Switzerland within three days. He remained unsure whether the expense was justified but accepted it was her money and she could do what she wanted with it. In the meantime, now that she'd confirmed the rental, he'd release the money transfer she'd authorized and hoped she'd have a good vacation. Félicité said she was sure she would.

Pieter Lascelles admitted being surprised by her moving into the Antwerp house but didn't question it, more immediately interested in the arrangements for what was going to happen.

'What do you think about the identification?'

He smiled quizzically. 'What is it?'

'An English nursery rhyme I learned at school.'

'Very appropriate.'

'You still bringing the same number of people?'

'Yes. You?'

'Just me.'

The surgeon didn't speak for several moments. 'What's wrong?'

'I'm simply not including anyone.'

'Your decision,' Lascelles conceded.

'I'll probably be seeing a lot more of you in the future,' said Félicité.

'I'll look forward to that.'

In Lille Georges Lebron responded as excitedly as Lascelles. 'I was becoming impatient,' he complained.

'How many of you will there be?'

'Ten, as arranged,' said the man. 'And a special guest, of course.'

Throughout the conversations Mary hadn't turned from the window. Félicité said: 'I've got hamburgers.'

'I'm not hungry,' said the child sullenly, her back to the woman.

'Hamburgers and then we'll telephone papa,' said Félicité.

Mary turned, finally. 'All right.'

★

319

The outraged head of mission insisted upon summoning the young embassy lawyer, Elliot Smith, and that McBride be told, so they'd all transferred yet again to the ambassador's study, taking McCulloch and Ritchie with them. McBride's reaction was mixed. Like Harrison he showed incredulous disbelief, but he was quicker to recognize the restrictions of the discovery. 'The bastard!'

'He's got to be arrested! Made to talk,' exclaimed Hillary.

The reluctant Elliot Smith was once more thrust into the forefront, as he had been during the original jurisdictional problem and again when Norris had committed suicide. It seemed, he thought, as if events had come full circle. Nervously – apologetically – he said: 'In my opinion there is no official action that can be brought against Smet. There's probably a Belgian law against possessing pornography featuring children: there is in most EU countries. But that information was gained illegally. It can't form the basis for any formal investigation. He's a lawyer. He'd know that.'

'What about the basement cell, for Christ's sake!' demanded McBride.

'It's a coal bunker, with a strengthened door,' said Blake. 'It could be for burglar prevention from the street outside.'

'You absolutely sure he's in contact with who's got Mary?' demanded Hillary.

'Yes. But I can't prove it,' said Claudine.

Ignoring her qualification McBride said: 'You telling me we couldn't sweat it out of the bastard?'

'That's exactly what we're telling you,' said Claudine pityingly. 'He'd have to be arrested to be interrogated. We've got no legally obtained evidence for his arrest. And he'd know more than that: he'd know the only way he could face prosecution would be by admitting knowledge of Mary's captors. So there's no way he'd do that. At this moment we've got a way through to them, whoever and wherever they are. We'd lose all that even if we could persuade the Belgians to pick him up.'

McBride thrust up from his desk, stomping to the window overlooking the formal grounds and the avenue beyond. No one spoke. After several minutes, without turning back into the room, he said: 'My kid's out there somewhere with a bunch of perverts who could be doing God knows what to her. We know who one of them is. And we can't do a goddamned thing about it?'

'I just don't believe it!' said Hillary, in rare agreement with her husband.

No one wanted to reply. Claudine looked to Sanglier. Uncomfortably the Europol commissioner said: 'I know it sounds absurd. But we can't do anything. Not if we want to save her. It *is* absurd. But that's precisely what the situation is.'

McBride turned back into the room, but he did not go immediately behind his desk. Instead he came to Claudine. 'Which brings it all back to you, Dr Carter. To how well you can mislead him into showing her a direction and how well you can manoeuvre the woman without her realizing it's being done.'

'Not totally,' said Harding. 'Every telephone and every room in Smet's house is wired. He can't make or receive a call, talk to anyone who comes there, without our hearing every word. And we know there's more than just Smet and the woman. He's bound to speak to the others. When he does he'll take us with him.'

'What's come from the house since the devices were installed?' challenged McBride.

Rampling shook his head. 'Not even an incoming call.' Bitterly he added: 'Obviously a guy with a very limited circle of particular friends.'

'There's a point about that,' said McCulloch, nodding sideways to his partner. 'We combed that house. Gave it

321

a second shake after we'd found the pictures and the cell. I'm sure we didn't miss anything. There wasn't an address book. Not one he left lying around in the house, anyway. Nor any personal letter. Just business stuff.'

'He'll carry it with him,' guessed Harding. 'There's a damned great briefcase in all this morning's surveillance pictures.'

'The entire ring – the woman herself – are most likely in it,' said Ritchie. 'So how do we get it?'

'Not easily,' said Rampling.

'But we've got to,' said Blake.

The American looked sourly at him. 'That so?'

McBride had gone back behind his desk and was listening intently, gaunt-faced, to the operational discussion. For once Hillary was silent.

'And there's his office,' added Blake, unembarrassed. 'We don't have any wires there.'

'The Justice Ministry is an official government building!' protested Harrison. 'You're not suggesting—'

'You know damned well what he's suggesting and it sounds good to me,' snapped McBride impatiently. 'If anyone wants superior authority, I've just given it. And if that's not enough I'll get it from the fucking President. You got any problem with that?'

'No, sir,' said Harrison.

For the record Sanglier supposed he should voice an official caution but this was a meeting where records were not being taken. He'd have to be very careful of the Americans when he took up office in Paris. But then, he reflected, he'd been careful about everything and everyone ever since he could remember. It would be a relief, just once, to be able to relax: a relief but impossible. He said: 'What are we going to tell Poncellet?'

'Nothing,' said Harding shortly, totally confident now as the overall American supervisor. 'I don't imagine he'd have a problem but he *is* the police commissioner and we are acting illegally. We can't take the risk he wouldn't try to intervene in some way: screw everything.'

'His house is bugged!' reminded Sanglier.

'We won't listen,' said Harding.

Still with two hours to go before the earliest the woman might call, even if she kept to her roughly established schedule, Sanglier remained with McBride and the chastened Harrison when everyone else left.

With time to kill, the rest moved without any positive decision back to the room made available to the Europol group now that the embassy had become the focal point for the investigation. The accommodation was actually a rarely used briefing room for both the CIA and the FBI and slightly bigger although less comfortable than Rampling's suite, which they'd used previously. It was also, considerably, at the furthest end of the corridor from where Norris had killed himself: the area remained behind canvas screens but cleaners, workmen and decorators had moved in.

'I guess we've just been given the carte blanche to stage a second Watergate,' said McCulloch.

'Let's hope we do it better this time,' said Harding. 'Anyone got any ideas?'

'We haven't talked about the mobile telephone,' suggested Claudine, who didn't like moving on to new problems with others unsolved.

'What about it?' asked McCulloch, a newcomer to the inner circle.

'The number belonged to the mobile of an accountant in Ghent. It was stolen six days ago: the stop had only just gone through.'

'So?' queried Ritchie.

'It wasn't the same telephone dumped in the back of the Ford,' said Harding. 'It's a mass-produced, medium-priced instrument. Used by Belgacom as well as a couple of independent mobile companies.'

'Why bother to transfer the number to another phone?' questioned McCulloch. 'It doesn't make sense.'

'It must do, to someone,' said Rampling. 'But who? And why?'

There was a flurry of movement at the doorway as a beaming Volker hurried in from the adjoining computer room. 'I've accessed the cryptograph entry code on the two paedophile videos,' he announced. 'The company is trading out of Amsterdam, offering a whole range of pornographic specialities. Even animals.'

'Can we get the paedophilia?' asked Rampling.

'Already ordered,' Volker assured him. 'We thought there was a sex element in the serial killings: there was, but not what we thought. But we established a home page, supposedly of a subscriber in Copenhagen, through several illegal bulletin boards specializing in sex. Used it to close down quite a few outlets since. I've ordered through there. Asked for anything new in the past fortnight.'

'They wouldn't have made anything featuring Mary as quickly as this,' said Blake.

'One of the videos found in Smet's safe was issued seven days ago,' said Volker. 'It's dated.'

'Normally I don't have a problem with dirty movies but I guess this time I will,' said Ritchie. He became abruptly aware of Claudine and blushed.

'We all will if Mary's featured,' said Rampling.

All the car, motorcycle and helicopter intercepts were re-established according to the previous day's pattern. Claudine left the systems check just after it started, less than an hour before the time of the previous day's call, and made her way to McBride's study. The ambassador was in shirt sleeves, his tie loosened, away from his desk.

Hillary had changed from what she'd been wearing earlier, into a tailored safari suit. Action Woman, thought Claudine.

McBride's impatient shifting around the room was now stoked as much – if not more so – by the frustration of not being able to move against Jean Smet as by the obvious nervousness. At least he was ignoring the cocktail cabinet and the Jack Daniel's bottle.

Claudine sat at once as she had before, trying to quieten the man by her own calmness. Which she didn't have to force. It had to be frustrating for McBride: double torture. But it couldn't be much longer now. Disaster was still only one misplaced word away but Claudine didn't think there was a risk of her uttering it. The pendulum swung abruptly, worryingly. She wouldn't say the wrong thing but McBride had sat in on a lot – too much – of their operational discussion. And he knew about Jean Smet. It was possible – likely even – that unconsciously he'd blurt something.

Hurriedly she said: 'Please remember what I said yesterday. No hate, no aggression. And don't respond to any challenge. As soon as you can, switch the conversation to me. I'm the person she wants to confront.'

'Are we talking about Mary? Or some private fight between you and the fucking woman?' demanded Hillary.

'A private fight between me and the fucking woman,' responded Claudine. 'I've got to be the person her anger's directed against all the time: who she's trying to humiliate. Not Mary.'

McBride stood forlornly before her, gripping and ungripping his hands. 'I feel so . . .' he began.

'. . . helpless,' she finished. 'I know. But we're not, not any longer.'

'Tell me you're going to get her back!'

She shouldn't lie: couldn't lie if she was going to retain her integrity. 'I'm going to get her back.'

'I'll destroy you, if you don't.'

'You won't have to. I will have destroyed myself. And threats don't achieve anything, ambassador.'

He didn't apologize. 'It's time.'

'She'll definitely make us wait today.'

'Why?'

'To prove all the things she needs to prove to herself: maintain her imagined control.'

'Why late? Why not early? That would have the same effect of disorientating us,' said Hillary.

Claudine shook her head. 'That would make her seem too anxious. She can't ever let herself appear to be that.'

'Nothing touches you,' protested McBride abruptly.

If only you knew, thought Claudine. She wasn't surprised at his wanting to hit out at someone: find a focus for the impotent anger. She said: 'I couldn't do my job if I allowed myself to become personally involved. None of us could. The investigators, I mean.'

'You ever doubt yourself?' said Hillary.

Stop it! Claudine thought. 'I can't allow that, either.'

McBride looked at the large, second-sweep clock re-established on his desk. 'She's almost thirty minutes past schedule.'

'She has her own design, not a schedule.'

'I'm not sure how much longer I can go on.'

'You can go on as long as it takes to save your daughter!' insisted Claudine forcefully.

'If you can't I will,' challenged Hillary.

'Nothing's happening!'

'This is reality. Not a movie with people and cars going round in circles.' That hardly made sense, Claudine conceded: that was precisely what they'd done yesterday. But others, not McBride. He just had to sit and wait.

'I'm sorry,' said McBride.

'What for?'

'Saying I'd destroy you. I didn't mean it.'

'I know.' She welcomed his uncertain smile. He'd stopped moving around the room: been able, for the briefest moment, to put out of his mind what was happening. What they were waiting for.

'She's an hour late.'

'She's making us suffer. She has to.'

'How much is she making Mary suffer?' said Hillary.

Fuck, thought Claudine, angry at her carelessness. 'We're going to get her back.'

'In what sort of physical condition?'

She couldn't allow the self-pity to go any further. 'Alive!'

It halted him. He began stop-starting around the room again, stretching his fingers as if they were cramped. 'You haven't written out any prompts.'

'I can do it quickly enough when she calls.'

'I forgot to ask you if you were all right now,' said McBride, belatedly solicitous.

'I'm fine.'

'It was terrible.'

He wanted to transfer his anguish on to her. 'Yes.'

'Did you think you were going to die?'

'I knew it was possible,' she said cautiously.

'What do you think about – feel like – imagining you're going to die?'

The wrong direction, Claudine quickly recognized. 'Children as young as Mary don't think they're going to die. Death is beyond their imagination.'

'I can't begin to think what she's suffering.'

'Don't try,' urged Claudine. 'She's strong.'

'You don't know what she is by now. None of us do. We can't.' McBride's wanderings had fortunately brought him close to the desk when the telephone sounded. Again the three of them jumped. Claudine held up a slowing hand as the man darted round the desk. He snatched his receiver up slightly ahead of her.

327

There was momentary blankness. Then: 'Dad?'

McBride retched. 'Honey!' he managed, coughing.

Claudine kept moving her hand, trying to slow him down.

'It's me.'

'Let me speak to her!' demanded Hillary.

'I know . . .! Oh, honey . . .' said McBride.

'I want to come home, dad.'

The effort to get hold of himself shivered through the man. 'I want that too, honey.'

The volume was uneven and a blankness came after every exchange, Claudine noted. Two minutes had passed, according to the clock.

'Why haven't you fixed it, then?' The petulance was immediate, angry. 'Are you and mom fighting?'

Hillary was in front of her husband, beckoning demands.

'No, honey. We're not fighting.'

Claudine gestured the woman back. To McBride she mouthed 'Let her tell me how' and when the man repeated it, word for word, Mary said: 'You must do everything she says.'

Perspiration was streaming down McBride's face now, soaking his shirt. 'I will! I promise I will! How are you, honey? Tell me how you are.'

'All right.' A brief blankness. Then: 'Is Claudine there?'

Hillary actually tried to snatch McBride's phone. He physically slapped her away.

'Hello, Mary,' said Claudine.

'I don't like you!'

'Why not?'

'Not letting me speak to dad.'

'He's here. You can speak to him now.' Four minutes, she saw. What Mary had said was important.

'Not today. Before.'

Satisfaction surged through Claudine. 'Do you want to speak to mummy? She's here too.'

'I've got to tell you something. It's . . .'

To the still demanding Hillary Claudine shook her head and mouthed 'No'.

Aloud she said: 'I think you're being a very brave girl.'

'I . . .' Silence. 'Tiny fingers come after tiny toes,' the child blurted.

McBride squeezed his eyes shut in despair.

Claudine felt perspiration prick out on her face. 'You're very pretty. I've seen lots of pictures of you.'

'Thank you,' said Mary and for the first time Claudine guessed the reply had been unprompted. There was a gap before Mary said: 'I've got to go!'

Claudine gestured against the frantic protest she saw McBride about to make. Anxious for a response she could identify from her hopeful manipulation of Smet, Claudine made the sigh, like the contempt, as obvious as she could in her voice. 'So she isn't going to talk herself: just through you? I'm not surprised.'

'Oh yes I am going to talk!' came the woman's voice harshly. 'Why shouldn't I want to talk?'

McBride surrendered the phone but Hillary didn't speak.

'I can think of a lot of reasons.'

'You think *I'm* afraid of *you*!'

Confirmation of the Smet conduit! thought Claudine, triumphantly. 'Aren't you?'

'You know what you've just done? You've just cost McBride another two hundred and fifty thousand. That's my new price. Half a million. And you'll never guess the good use it's going to be put to. Not much of a negotiator, are you?'

'How do you want it paid?' said Claudine evenly, refusing any reaction.

'Arrangements are being made.'

'I'm sure,' said Claudine disbelievingly.

'Seven hundred and fifty thousand!' declared the woman. 'You'd better watch your mouth. Every time you say something I don't like I'm going to fine you.'

'How much longer?' said Claudine, with another sigh. Psychologically she had to press the woman as far as she could. And she was as confident as she could be that the woman had developed a bizarre love for Mary.

'I'll tell you when I'm ready.'

'It's taking a long time.' Like this conversation, Claudine thought: ten minutes without any indication from outside that the scanners had traced the signal.

'The newspapers say McBride's a friend of the President but I don't believe it.'

Claudine frowned, unsure of a response. Go with it, she decided. 'Why not?'

'They'd have sent someone better than you if he was really important.'

The almost juvenile desperation was unsettling. 'Maybe it's you who aren't sufficiently important,' she said.

'You really do have to watch your mouth. We're up to a million now.'

'Why not collect it?'

'You haven't suffered enough yet. Maybe Mary hasn't, either.'

'Mary Beth!' broke in Hillary at last but there was no response from the other end. Just before it went dead she and Claudine heard Mary's distant, muffled shout. 'Please, dad . . . please . . .!'

McBride looked at Claudine, his face purple with rage. 'You stupid bitch! You made her hang up!'

'I hope it was because of me and not the sudden interruption from someone she didn't expect!' said Claudine. Furiously confronting the woman, she said: 'Mrs McBride, you could have just killed your daughter.'

CHAPTER TWENTY-THREE

Jean Smet was the way to bring the woman back. Only if she failed to respond would Hillary McBride have caused a catastrophe by confronting her with something for which she hadn't been prepared, and Claudine regretted her outburst against the ambassador's wife.

Hillary and McBride were literally eyeball to eyeball after Claudine's accusation, screaming abuse at each other. Claudine shouted: 'Shut up! Shut up and start thinking properly about Mary Beth!'

The fresh outburst silenced both of them. Claudine said: 'It's recoverable. The important thing is that I've become the person she hates: the person towards whom all her hostility is directed now. And today I was coming very close to gaining control without her knowing it: making her do what I want. Which is seriously to attempt a ransom. I've challenged her: doubted that she's capable.'

'If today's call didn't start out to fix a ransom what was it for?' demanded Hillary, wanting to recover from her mistake.

'She wants Mary to hate me as much as she does. You heard what Mary said, about not liking me. And her reply when I asked her why.' With perfect recall, Claudine quoted: '"Not letting me speak to dad . . . Not today. Before." She's transferring the blame in her own mind and trying to do the same in Mary's for what's happened to Mary. She's trying to bond the child to her.'

'Make Mary like her, you mean?' asked McBride incredulously. 'How the hell can she do that!'

'I didn't say she could do it. I said that's what she's *trying* to do.' Paradoxical though it seemed it was psychologically possible, particularly with someone impressionable, for a victim to become emotionally dependent upon a captor.

'What about the fingers and toes remark?' persisted the father.

'That's to alienate you from me: continue the attack upon me,' Claudine assured him. 'She won't maim someone she wants to like her.'

'Why is she doing that? I don't understand!' protested Hillary.

She'd spare them by not talking about love. 'It's the way her mind works.'

Claudine was momentarily surprised to see Hugo Rosetti with everyone else in the briefing room when she re-entered. He smiled, fleetingly, and just as quickly she smiled back. Blake, expressionless, watched the interchange.

'What happened to the scanners?' demanded Claudine at once.

'The transmission was too far away: that's why the volume fluctuated so much,' said Volker. 'They couldn't get any sort of fix, although they don't think she was moving around, the way she did yesterday.'

For Poncellet's benefit Claudine summarized to its minimum but still accurately the complete profile she'd given to McBride. To get rid of the police chief, she said she needed to assess the woman's mental state before they held another planning meeting, and the moment Poncellet left the embassy Peter Blake gave them his explanation for the mobile telephone number.

'They didn't *have* the telephone,' he said. 'Only the

332

number, knowing it was stolen. So they had to get an instrument to programme it into.'

'Jesus!' said Harding.

'The simplest answer is always the best,' said Rampling, in immediate agreement. 'It was too obvious for us to see!'

'So who'd have access to stolen numbers?' asked Harrison, anxious to contribute.

'Too many people,' said Blake. 'Belgacom, the Brussels manual exchange, the mobile phone company . . .'

'That's not the way to find them,' said Claudine. 'We can make whoever it is come to us through Smet. All he's got to believe is that we've got a lead to him. His own fear will do the rest.'

'How?' demanded Harrison.

'We give Smet the same reason we gave Poncellet for not meeting again today, but add that there's an even more important development with the phone, as well. He'll immediately warn whoever it is.'

'He's waiting in his office,' said Rampling. 'He'll do it from there and we don't have it tapped.'

'We force him home,' said Blake at once. 'When we speak to him in his office we say that there's something important about the phone but that we're not sure what it is: forensic haven't yet spelled it out. And promise to call him at home tonight, if it's really important. Which we'll do—'

'Smet's telephones,' interrupted Volker. 'Do they have dials? Or are they push button?'

'Push button,' said McCulloch.

Volker gave a satisfied nod. 'It's not possible to trace the number of an incoming call on a bugged telephone. But it is when a number is rung out. Each number on a push button phone has a different electronic signal: that's how the system works, tonally. And Smet will dial out to speak to whoever it is, won't he?'

'As soon as he does we'll have him!' Rampling said.

'And it'll be someone in Belgacom, not the mobile company,' added the German. 'A technical expert, with access and ability far beyond phones. That's who set up the e-mail exchange in the beginning.'

'This is coming together!' enthused Rampling.

'Who's going to make the bastard dance?' asked Harding.

Rampling looked at Sanglier. 'You're the task force head, the senior investigatory officer.'

'He couldn't argue against my decision to cancel,' agreed Sanglier, alert to a safe advantage. He was already committed, as far as the illegality was concerned, so he'd hardly be enmeshing himself further. And later, when that illegality became acceptable, he would have done something positive, definitely involved himself, in the investigation. A lot of worthwhile publicity could be worked up for his political emergence. He'd be the only Justice Minister in the world personally to have headed the investigation into a famous crime. And the fame would be his, not inherited from his father.

Jean Smet responded at the first ring, the respectful tone discernible as soon as Sanglier identified himself. Sanglier spoke autocratically, a police commander complying with a liaison agreement but not inviting a protracted discussion. It had been his decision not to have another meeting. Dr Carter thought there was a lot to be gained from that afternoon's exchange. And they'd just been warned by forensic officers of something potentially vital – he actually used the word breakthrough – about the telephone that had been abandoned the previous day.

'Something that could lead to an arrest?' asked Smet.

'They haven't been specific. We won't know until later tonight: maybe not even then. We hope to have something definite by tomorrow.' Sanglier was enjoying himself, knowing from the expression on the faces around him that he was doing well.

'If it's really important the minister would want to know immediately. Tonight.'

Sanglier's pause, for apparent consideration, was perfect. 'If it's as vital as they think it is, I could have someone call you at home.' He allowed another hesitation. 'Do we have your home number?'

Harding and Rampling smiled, nodding in open approval as the lawyer hurriedly dictated it, repeated it, and then asked Sanglier if he was sure he'd noted it correctly.

'The minister really will be most anxious to hear at once,' emphasized Smet.

'I'll see you're called, if there's anything,' said Sanglier dismissively, replacing the telephone ahead of the other man's gabbled thanks.

'Now what?' said Harrison.

'We wait,' said Blake.

They didn't have to for very long.

'Anything?' A man's voice, strained, without any identifying greeting.

'Nothing.'

Harding made a thumbs-up gesture to the other smiling American. It was only fifteen minutes after the first sounds of the homecoming Jean Smet. The front door had slammed, two more opened without being closed. There'd been the scuff of his moving from room to room, the tinkle of a decanter against a glass. A lot of coughing and throat clearing.

'Maybe they called while you were on your way from the office. Call them back!'

'I don't even know where they'll be.'

'The hotel! Try the hotel!'

'I can't! I've got to wait for them!'

'What in the name of God can it be!' It was practically a whimper.

There was no movement in the communications room, almost everyone physically leaning towards the speaker. Claudine sat directly in front, cramped against the operator, making notes.

'I don't know.'

'What can I do?'

'There's nothing: nothing either of us can do.'

'It's her fault. Everything's her fault. We should have disposed of the kid the day she picked her up.'

'You're blocking the line if they're trying to get through,' Smet said.

'Don't call me.'

'Why not?'

'Antoinette's here. It's difficult.'

'Then how can I . . .?'

'I'll keep calling you, when it's convenient here.'

'Damn!' said Blake quietly. Rampling shook his head in frustration.

'You heard from the others?' asked Smet.

'No. You?'

'She called as usual after this morning's conference. Said they hadn't got a clue what they were doing. She wasn't at home when I telephoned her later, about this.'

There was a snort of derision. Then: 'I've got to go. Antoinette's coming!'

No one spoke for several moments after the line went dead. Through the speaker came the noise of decanter against glass again. Claudine revolved her swivel chair, to face the half-circle of men.

Rampling said: 'It's so close I feel I could reach out and touch it!'

More practically, Blake said: 'It could be the driver.'

'Whoever the man is he's not the one who's holding Mary,' said Claudine. 'He's got a wife or a partner –

Antoinette – who doesn't know what's going on. And they *have* fallen out: it's something to concentrate on.'

'We've got to get a wire in that bloody office,' said Harding.

'How long would it take?' asked Claudine. 'Minimum, maximum?'

McCulloch shrugged. 'Seconds to stick a microphone with an adhesive base where he hopefully wouldn't find it. Five minutes, tops, to put something inside the phone like we've done at his house.'

'We'd put pressure on her if we broke the routine of his always being available in his office when she calls,' said Claudine reflectively. From behind her there were short bursts of noise as Smet clicked his way through television channels, and then the crackle of static as he roamed radio frequencies in an equally unsuccessful search for a news programme.

'That's tomorrow. What about tonight?' demanded Sanglier.

'You did warn there might not be anything until tomorrow,' Harrison reminded him.

'They'd be frantic by then,' said Rampling.

'Smet tried to call her from the office,' Claudine pointed out. 'He's almost bound to try again as soon as he hears from us.'

'We shouldn't wait,' decided Sanglier.

Blake made the call. Smet actually dropped the receiver in his anxiety to pick it up, repeating 'Yes?' every few seconds to urge the explanation on.

'You think you can trace who it is?' he demanded.

'It'll be time-consuming but we've got the manpower,' Blake said. 'It's our first direct and positive line. We're going to get him. And through him everyone else.'

'The minister will want to know how soon,' Smet pressed.

Blake said: 'We could have it all wrapped up in days. By this time tomorrow we could be well on our way.'

Claudine made cutting-off gestures and Blake said: 'We're setting things up now. Speak to you tomorrow.'

They waited tensely, silently. At once Smet's telephone was lifted. A digit – within minutes isolated as 2, the first number of the Brussels code – was punched before the handset was replaced. It was lifted within seconds and 2 pressed again before once more being put down.

'Come on! Come on!' hissed Rampling. 'Make the fucking call!'

Everyone jumped when Smet's telephone rang, the over-amplified sound echoing into the room.

'Shit!' exclaimed Blake.

'Anything?' The same voice as before.

'They've worked it out.'

'What?' shouted the man, his voice breaking.

Smet even used some of Blake's exaggerated words and phrases. The other man never once interrupted. Not until the end did he say: 'That's it? All of it?'

'Blake said it was a simple process of elimination.'

'I've got access to the numbers, sure. But I'm much too senior ever to bother to look at them. There are dozens – hundreds – more likely than me. And the phones aren't traceable to me, either.'

'You think you're safe?'

The laugh was genuine, unforced. 'I am now that I know what to expect.'

Smet gave a loud sigh. 'Thank God for that.'

'You told Félicité?'

'I was going to. I decided to talk to you first. Don't you think I should bother?'

'I'd like to frighten the bitch but this wouldn't. She had me explain everything when I gave her the phones. She knows the only danger is being picked up by a scanner. And she's only going to use a number once.'

'How many has she got?'

'Six.' The man cleared his throat. 'Gaston called.'

'You tell him?'

'I said I'd call him back, if it was serious.'

'What did he want?'

'He said he doesn't give a shit what Félicité says. He's going to get rid of the other thing. It's beginning to stink.'

'Let's talk tomorrow.'

'I'll call you.'

'That didn't work out at all as it should have done,' said Harrison, as the call disconnected.

'I would have liked more,' agreed Claudine. 'But we have her name now: Félicité. And the number Smet began to ring puts her within the city, not outside. We've got two more given names, Antoinette and Gaston. We know we're looking for someone at the top – a senior executive – at Belgacom. That hugely narrows down our search there. And if Félicité is only using a stolen number once, she's got three left. That gives me a time frame for the dialogue.'

'And he'll call out,' Volker said. 'It's just bad luck that he hasn't already. He still might.'

They made arrangements to be immediately alerted if he did, and returned to the Metropole. At dinner Sanglier, anxious at the lack of convenience and freedom to keep in touch with Paris, announced that he intended returning to Europol headquarters the following day and Hugo Rosetti wondered, looking very directly at Claudine, if there was any practical reason for his remaining, either.

'I've got an idea how to get a listening device into Smet's office but we'll need your help to achieve it,' Claudine told the commissioner. To the pathologist she said: 'The stinking "other thing" that Gaston is going to get rid of will be missing a toe. There might be a lot to learn from that body.'

339

CHAPTER TWENTY-FOUR

Claudine proposed the office bugging idea but didn't take part in its implementation, not wanting the slightest suspicion from Smet at her unnecessary presence. Equally objective, although with less enthusiasm than on the previous evening, Henri Sanglier accepted he had to head the delegation as well as impose his authority upon Jean Smet to gain the personal meeting with the Justice Minister immediately after that morning's planning session, hopefully using the approach to unsettle the lawyer further by refusing to give a reason for the request. Burt Harrison was the obvious US diplomatic counterpart, just as Paul Harding balanced the inclusion of Peter Blake. Duncan McCulloch, with more recent home-based training, went through the basic practicalities with the FBI chief. Harding insisted they weren't to worry, it would be a piece of cake, and McCulloch wondered by how many years the expression dated the older man.

Claudine did, obviously, attend the regular morning review and exaggerated the analysis of the previous afternoon's conversation with Félicité, insisting it showed the woman terrified of the confrontation – 'she's running away from me' – and clearly at a loss how to conceive a ransom exchange. André Poncellet reacted with the anticipated eagerness to Harding's suggestion that the available and unemployed FBI and CIA personnel should supplement the mobile phone inquiry within Belgacom.

Smet maintained the reserve of the previous day during the meeting but forcefully bustled into the car with

Sanglier and Blake for the trip to the ministry, making Poncellet take the second vehicle with Harding. Before the lead car cleared the forecourt Smet asked openly if there was a reason of which he was unaware for the unexpected request to meet Miet Ulieff ('I need to know, in case he wants some legal advice') and when Sanglier remained non-committal made more than one convoluted attempt to get an indication from Blake. Throughout the short trip the lawyer sat with his sagging briefcase clamped between his legs, the way, Blake noted for the first time, that he'd held it at the earlier briefing.

They were swept up to Ulieff's ornate, rococo-style suite where the greying, urbane man waited surrounded by a retinue of officials, only some of whom – his immediate deputy and the chief public prosecutor – were introduced. Again Smet ingratiated himself into the lead group. He put the briefcase less obviously beside the chair in which he sat, only one place away from Ulieff.

This was, Sanglier supposed, the sort of event to which he had in the near future to become accustomed, a totally pointless charade of high political officials making the pretence of personally contributing to affairs of great importance which underlings were resolving. There was an obligatory photocall of Sanglier and Ulieff shaking hands for the cameras in apparent serious-faced discussion. Before the media were excluded Sanglier responded impromptu to a shouted question that the meeting was to discuss important developments which at that stage couldn't be publicly disclosed.

As soon as the media left Sanglier announced that he'd wanted to meet Ulieff – and welcomed the inclusion of so many unexpected officials – formally to express on behalf of Europol their gratitude for the total Belgian cooperation at every level in the investigation. Knowing Smet would not yet have had time to brief Ulieff on the mobile telephone discovery he used that to explain his important development remark to the journalist. It was, Sanglier added, the first of what he confidently expected to be many more.

Sanglier listened to himself mouthing the empty words, actually impressed with how he sounded: while he probably needed to become accustomed to such occasions he hardly needed to be any more adept. Following the unwritten script, the moment Sanglier finished the Belgian officials asked their prepared questions – usually one apiece, although Ulieff allowed himself three – to which the answers either had just been given by Sanglier or were already available to them on the daily records. When the questioning concluded Burt Harrison echoed Sanglier's official thanks on behalf of the United States of America and Ulieff suggested they all adjourn to a larger, adjoining chamber for a reception.

Smet followed, for the first time made too awkward by the briefcase to remain close to where the minister, his deputy and Sanglier were grouped. The man did his best, standing by the very end of the table upon which the drinks were stacked. He took mineral water.

Blake and Harding joined him together. Both chose whisky.

'Little point at all in that!' complained the lawyer.

There hadn't been. The hope had been to get into Smet's office in advance of the formal gathering and somehow separate the man from his briefcase as well as plant a device within the telephone. It left them with only one final option.

'Bullshit protocol,' agreed the disappointed Harding. 'Greases the wheels of government.'

'I warned you it would be a waste of time,' Blake said. Close up he saw Smet was sweating.

'I don't see that we're making much progress at all,' invited Smet encouragingly.

Blake accepted two more whiskies, handing one to the American. To Smet he said: 'How about you?'

'I don't drink during working hours,' replied the Belgian, holding up his water glass. 'I said I don't see that we're making much progress.'

'I know more about the woman than I do my own mother,' said Harding. 'And Claudine knows ten times more than me: she's really inside the bitch's mind. Claudine will get her. I'll put my pension on it.' He hadn't thought much about his pension lately. He certainly wasn't worried about it any more.

'If I was part of her group I'd be shitting myself,' said Blake, maintaining the pressure.

'Me and you both,' agreed Harding.

There was movement from further along the table as the reception began to break up. Sanglier gestured that he was leaving with Ulieff and Poncellet. The detective and the FBI man moved when Smet did, crowding into the same elevator.

'See you this afternoon,' said Smet, getting off at the minister's secretariat level on the second floor.

The two men continued to the ground floor, unspeaking, pressed the ascend button the moment everyone else got off and were back at the second floor in less than a minute. There was a central secretarial pool directly ahead of them, with personal assistants and secretaries separated by a low, wood-slatted barrier. Beyond them were the offices of Ulieff's immediate staff, their names inscribed on each door. Smet's was facing them.

They strode briskly forward, smiling and calling greetings to the outer circle clerks who took their conference records and reached the gated barrier before anyone began to wonder at their presence. A woman started to stand protectively as they went through. Harding smiled and gestured and said: 'Changed our mind about Jean,' to convey an impression they were expected and physically blocked her way so that Blake could knock on Smet's door and enter at the same time.

Smet was behind his desk, about to sit. There was no sign of the briefcase. He looked visibly frightened at their entry and said: 'What the . . .!' before fully recognizing them.

'Hi!' said Harding cheerfully. 'We've had a great idea!'

'All we've done is meet round a conference table,' added Blake. 'Let's lunch.'

Smet seemed to need the chair. He lowered himself swallowing heavily, giving a dismissive gesture to the hapless secretary in the doorway. He forced a smile. 'I can't possibly. The minister expects a report on this morning's meeting.'

'He just got it from Sanglier,' said the American, leaning forward invitingly over the man's desk. 'Take a break. We deserve it.'

'Maybe another time. I've got other things to keep up to date with, as well as the kidnap.'

'You sure you can't make it?' pressed Harding. 'We've got pagers: they could get us at once if anything breaks.'

Smet had recovered. 'No. Thank you, but no.'

'Our guests,' insisted Harding.

'No.'

'OK then,' said Harding. 'Another time.'

'Until this afternoon,' said Blake, at the door.

In the car Harding said: 'There's a great little restaurant on the Avenue Adolphe Buyl.'

'Sounds good,' said Blake. 'Pity the whole thing didn't work out. The briefcase particularly.'

'We've got something into his office. It's better than nothing.'

'Where did you put it?'

'Under the desk edge when I leaned forward the first time. As near as I could to the telephones.'

344

'There was what looked like an individual private line, next to the multi-extension bank.'

'That's the one I got closest to.'

It had been premature to celebrate installing a bug in Jean Smet's office. They learned from the two relevant calls among a lot of extraneous inter-office communication not to expect contact that day from Félicité, and while that allayed the apprehension there would otherwise have been Claudine thought that only to be able to hear Smet's side of a conversation was almost worse than not being able to listen to anything at all.

Félicité's was the first and obviously complaining call, Smet apologizing at once for being kept from his office by Ulieff's reception when she'd first called. There was a comprehensive account of that morning's briefing, an apparent agreement that the investigation was stalled and a lot of subservient grunts from the lawyer. Several times he asked the woman to explain whatever it was she'd told him and at the end a long period of silence before the line closed down.

From Smet's responses Claudine at once identified the second caller as the Belgacom executive. She guessed the man to be more concerned than he'd ended up the previous night from Smet's saying it had not been one of that morning's decisions that the Belgacom investigation should start at senior management level.

It was only at the very end that Smet's remarks became unambiguously clear. The lawyer declared outright: 'She's not calling them today,' and when the man obviously asked why said: 'She wants to make them sweat for a day. Says she wants to teach them a lesson.'

There was initially more lost bewilderment than anger from the ambassador and his wife. After having the appropriate remark replayed twice McBride said dully: 'Nothing until tomorrow?'

'No,' said Claudine. 'But it's an attack on me, not Mary.'

'What the fuck reassurance is that! You're safe, here! Mary's with a monster. Mary isn't safe.'

She didn't have an adequate reply. 'It's not just to make us sweat. She will attempt a ransom.'

'A day!' insisted the man, irrational anger taking over. 'If she doesn't make a definite demand – set out how she wants it paid – in twenty-four hours I'm going to insist Smet is picked up, by our people if necessary. I don't give a penny fuck about legality. I'll make him talk myself if I have to. I want it over. I want my baby back.'

There wasn't any point in arguing, Claudine knew. 'Twenty-four hours,' she agreed.

Mary was squatting cross-legged in front of the television on the other side of the river-view room, a tub of popcorn in her lap, engrossed in the satellite cartoon channel.

Félicité, who had already delayed the call twice, finally picked up the house phone. As usual, Lascelles answered at once.

'Everything is going to be in place for tomorrow.'

'Wonderful!' said the doctor. 'We've got our special guests. The boy is named Robert. The girl is Yvette.'

'How are they being taken down?'

'Separately, of course.'

'Either by you?'

'No.'

'I need to get the key from the agents in Namur. And someone to drive me. By myself Mary might try to get away.'

'You want me to pick you up?'

'I'll call McBride at three.'

'She'll see my face.'

'That's not going to matter, is it?'

'I suppose not.'

346

'I don't want it to hurt. Is there something? An injection?'

'Of course. Pills, too: a choice of pills.'

'There mustn't be any pain.'

'There won't be.'

'She wouldn't know?'

'She'd just go to sleep. Feel nothing.'

'That's what I want.'

'You must have grown very fond of her?'

'I love her,' said Félicité.

Although there was a specific understanding between them that Françoise never brought her friends to the house, Sanglier warned her of his return after an hour-long conversation from his Europol office with Lucien Bigot in Paris. He was immediately alarmed by the unknown, Paris-registered Citroën parked at the head of the drive, his first thought was that it might be someone carrying out the background investigation that Castille had talked about, although he would have expected Bigot to have mentioned it and Françoise had said nothing about a visitor.

They met him in the hallway, Françoise with her arm round the shoulders of a startlingly attractive dark-haired girl. She wore jeans and a shirt that was too tight, so that her nipples protruded. Françoise wore trousers, too, part of a black silk evening suit.

'I wanted you to meet Maria,' announced Françoise. 'I told you about her.'

Sanglier said nothing.

'Hello,' the girl smiled.

Still Sanglier said nothing, waiting.

'Aren't you going to say hello?' demanded Françoise.

'I want you to go. Immediately,' Sanglier told the girl.

'She was just leaving anyway.' Françoise kissed Maria

347

lightly on the cheek and said: 'I told you he was a bore, didn't I?'

That night the naked body of a boy was found on the edge of a forest near Dilbeek, on the outskirts of Brussels. The big toe was missing from the left foot.

CHAPTER TWENTY-FIVE

There were too many people. In Claudine's view there always were at crime scenes and their arrival – the FBI forensic team with Harding, Rosetti and Blake with Claudine – added to the congestion. Poncellet had come on ahead, after alerting them, and established some order but Claudine wished there had been more. A protective evidence tent had been erected over the body and a generator manhandled alongside for floodlights that not only illuminated the body within the tent but lit an area of about three square metres outside.

The body was ten metres along a rutted, dry stone-and-dirt track running into the forest from a minor metalled road. What tyre imprints there might have been in the dirt had been trampled underfoot by the bald-headed man who'd discovered the body while walking his dog and now stood trembling beside the police car that had answered his call so urgently the further obliterating skid marks still stretched from where it had come to a halt. As they approached, the dog, a mongrel, was completing the damage by scratching dirt over its urine puddle.

They'd all been approaching in a single, minimally destructive line along the edge of the track. Over his shoulder the leading forensic officer said: 'Why the fuck are we bothering?'

The forensic team were already suited. Harding and Blake stood back for Rosetti and Claudine to put on their coveralls and plastic galoshes. Poncellet was standing ashen-faced away from the tent, a handkerchief against his mouth and nose. 'He's been dead a long time.'

Claudine said: 'We know.'

The sickly sweet smell of decomposing flesh engulfed them as they went into the tent. Already inside were a Belgian pathologist and a police photographer. There were greetings in French but no handshakes: the Belgians were already contaminated. They wore nose clamps and their upper lips were smeared with camphor unguent. Rosetti and Claudine both applied cream and clips beneath their totally encompassing masks.

The boy was face down and partially on his left side. The left shoulder was humped and the left arm and hand hidden beneath it. The body was grotesquely ballooned by decomposition gases, the skin split in places and the major lesions moving with maggots. It was on the edge of a sheet of hessian, glued to it in places by congealed body fluid. The anal entry was greatly distended and on both shoulders and the neck were bite marks difficult at first to identify because of the bloated flesh. The eye sockets were wide open and writhed with maggots that had already destroyed the eyes themselves. There was no visible cause of death. The two pathologists stood side by side to heave the body over on to its back. As they did so the stomach split, spilling choking fluid and gas. Rosetti used a magnifying glass to examine what was left of the penis and had photographs taken of it. Maggots had attacked the stump of the missing toe, making it imposs- ible to recognize a professional amputation.

'Anything extra you want?' asked Rosetti, his voice muffled and adenoidal.

Claudine shook her head, holding her hand up against any approach from either Harding or Blake as she and Rosetti emerged. Both men had been driven back by the smell from inside the tent.

They took off their masks and nose clips and Rosetti said: 'We're badly contaminated. Infectious.'

The Belgian pathologist and photographer had already stripped off their forensic suits, head coverings and shoes and piled them in the middle of the path. Claudine and Rosetti added to the pyre and stood back for the mortuary attendant to soak the bundle in petrol. It exploded into flame at the thrown match, melting plastic adding a new smell.

'You want to go into the tent?' Rosetti asked Harding and Blake. Both investigators remained some way away.

Harding said: 'We'll take your word for it.'

'You going to do the autopsy straight away or wait until it's properly morning?' called Blake. 'It's still only four thirty.'

'I'll do it as soon as we get back to Brussels,' said Rosetti.

'You want to attend?' invited Claudine. 'I'm going to.' She went towards the two men, away from the stink. Rosetti followed.

'We'll leave that to you, too,' said Blake. 'And we've seen all we want here.' He shook his head ruefully. 'Or rather not enough. There's not a tyre tread to be seen and a herd of elephants couldn't have trodden the side track and undergrowth any flatter.'

'And the guy who found the body heard nothing, saw nothing and knows nothing,' added Harding. 'It was the dog, obviously, who found it: smelled it.'

'Maybe there'll be something from the autopsy,' said the disappointed Poncellet.

The mortuary attendants emerged from the tent with the remains sealed inside a body bag, leaving it on the ambulance gunney while they added their overalls to the dying bonfire.

Claudine and Rosetti, both long inured to the horror of violent death, returned to the city separately from the

351

others, their bodies cramped together in the front of the ambulance, each aware of the closeness of the other but not acknowledging it. It was, thought Claudine, a bizarre surrounding in which to come physically closer to the man than she ever had before.

There were changing facilities at the mortuary and Claudine stripped and showered with strongly disinfected emulsion before re-suiting and re-masking herself, sprinkling the inside of the protective clothing with disinfecting powder. She only bothered with bra and pants beneath.

The body was already on the metal dissecting table when she entered the examination room, Rosetti, the Belgian pathologist and the photographer about to start. Three of the American forensic scientists were in the side laboratory in which Claudine and Rosetti had earlier examined the amputated toe. One was already working on the hessian. The other two were waiting to test samples from the body.

Rosetti led the dissection but in consultation with the other surgeon. Their masks, as well as Claudine's, were electronically linked, enabling them to communicate with each other. Everything said was automatically recorded. Rosetti dictated quietly, in French, and formally, according to the accepted medical format. He identified himself, the Belgian and the mortuary and stipulated the date and the time. He also named Claudine as an official observer.

He worked quickly but methodically, removing facial skin scrapings, body fluid, head and pubic hair and finger and toenail samples for the waiting forensic experts. He had to break the jaw to carry out the dental examination. When he sawed into the chest cavity – carrying the opening up to the humped left shoulder – they were all covered in a fine spray of bone and body fluid and had to stop to sponge clean each other's visors. At Rosetti's urging, as soon as the chest had been opened, the Belgian pathologist sectioned several lung samples for the side laboratory, first having each photographed. Rosetti also had several pictures taken of the anal distension before carrying out an internal examination. To do so he had to turn the collapsing body on to its front. Having done so he shaved the back of the head up to the crown, pointing out to the other man the patterned discoloration that became visible.

Until that moment Rosetti had completed ignored Claudine. Now he turned, although keeping strictly to medical protocol, declaring for the recording that he was interrupting the autopsy for preliminary discussion. And gave the time – 5.45 a.m. – of the break.

It was, literally, like an alarm clock awakening Claudine. Her first impulse was to excuse herself and leave at once but just as quickly she realized she had more than enough time to listen to what Rosetti had stopped to tell her. There was just the possibility there would be something she could use in what he said, although for what she wanted to achieve she doubted it.

Rosetti did not come to her immediately. From the side laboratory he collected the clipboard log, flicking through the several attached notes as he approached.

'A professional male prostitute,' declared Rosetti. There was a metallic playback to his voice through the headset. 'Very active. I wouldn't put him older than seventeen but I found tunnelling during the internal anal examination. The epithelium is thick, too, indicating constant intercourse . . .' Rosetti went to the clipboard. 'There were traces of make-up on the facial skin.' He paused. 'Also of a glue that quite heavily impregnated the hessian in which the body was wrapped . . .'

The clock on the autopsy wall registered 6.05 a.m. Claudine saw, impatiently. Why hadn't she thought of it before! Why! Why! Why!

353

'There was also the same varnish on the nails that we found on the severed toe,' continued Rosetti.

'How long has he been dead?' asked Claudine, forcing the calmness. Six eight.

'Sometime during the last fortnight,' said Rosetti. 'I can't be more definite than that. There is still some residual rigor: that's why the shoulder snapped when the body was thrown down. It was just picked up, obviously from a vehicle, and tossed aside, landing on the shoulder. That's why it had rolled almost completely free of the hessian. As you saw there was no attempt to conceal it.'

'What the caller told Smet Gaston was going to do, just get rid of it,' remembered Claudine. 'Anything special about the hessian? It looked comparatively new.'

'It was, although he'd been wrapped in it for a long time.' He looked quickly at his clipboard. 'Forensic say it's high-quality sacking: the sort of stuff used for wrapping things of value.'

'How did he die?'

Rosetti led her to the dissecting table. Claudine followed, unworried by the closeness to a partially dissected carcase. He pointed to the opened anus, then to the blackened pattern on the back of the shaven head.

'They're finger bruising; could be either ante or post death. Hands being pressed either side of the head. I think it was during anal intercourse, not necrophilia. There's no rectal lesion or tearing, which there would have been if entry was forced after death. The lungs are bubble-enlarged, definitely showing suffocation. During the act of buggery his face was forced into something soft, most likely a pillow, until he died. The anus is distended because muscles don't contract after death.' He indicated another pattern, wounds this time. 'Bite marks. Which could give us a jaw formation impression of the killer. I think the penis was bitten, too.'

Momentarily Claudine lost her impatience to leave the

room. Almost to herself she said: 'And that was done by one of the people who've got the ten-year-old child we're trying to get back unharmed.'

'Yes,' said Rosetti. 'I don't think I've ever examined a worse manic sex attack. It's totally animal.'

'I've got to go. Now!'

'But . . .'

'Later.' It was six fifteen.

Claudine ran clumsily from the room, hampered by the encumbering suit. Remembering the victim's homosexuality and the spray of the body fluids she forced herself to slow, stripping off the protective clothing, and was even more careful against outside contact while thrusting it down the incinerator chute.

It was six twenty-three when she emerged from the shower, six twenty-eight when she burst into the corridor, searching wildly for a telephone. And physically collided with Peter Blake.

'I've been stupid,' she gabbled. 'If we tell Smet this early he'll call . . .'

'I already did,' Blake said, holding her at arm's length, smiling. 'And he called, too. Twice. And we got the numbers. Félicité is Félicité Galan. She lives at the Boulevard Anspach. Gaston's name is Mehre. He's an antique dealer in Antwerp.' The smile expanded. 'We're well up to speed, so you don't have to run.'

With the image of the distorted and sexually mutilated body horrifically vivid in her mind throughout the remainder of the long day, Claudine couldn't dispel the feeling that to run was exactly what she – all of them – had to do. To run as fast as they could in every newly pointed direction and break any law to get to Mary Beth.

It was irrational and unprofessional, she accepted, and totally opposite from what they actually had to do. Which was to proceed step by step with the utmost care. Make

355

no unpremeditated move until they'd located Félicité Galan and established the child was with her, and only then risk a strike to prevent Mary Beth being the next disfigured body on the mortuary slab.

By the time Claudine reached the embassy the surveillance had already been organized and in Brussels was in place. Sure of their target and knowing from Smet's panicked telephone call that Gaston Mehre was at home over his gallery in Antwerp's Schoenmarkt, Harding assigned a thirty-man squad to put the antique dealer under total observation.

The lawyer's call to Félicité Galan, while identifying her from the number, had rung out unanswered. It was again McCulloch and Ritchie who led the operation in Boulevard Anspach. Watchers were positioned outside as before, to warn of the woman's unexpected return, separate from the evidence-collecting 'floaters'. In addition there were four CIA agents, all women, two with paramedic qualifications, if Mary Beth were found to be imprisoned in the house.

She wasn't.

It was the first and immediate disappointment after McCulloch and Ritchie immobilized the rear-mounted, out-of-date alarm box with instant setting foam and picked the rear door lock.

The two men varied their routine in their immediate search for the child, both looking initially for basement cells before quickly working upwards, room by room. At the same time as McCulloch reported failure on his mobile phone he said that from the disarray and cast-aside clothes in Félicité's bedroom and en suite dressing room – as well as an open-doored cupboard in which suitcases were stored – she'd obviously packed and left in a hurry. He and Ritchie were reverting to routine: some proxile copied material, including bank statements, was

356

already being ferried back. Again they hadn't found an address book.

Kurt Volker deputed himself, without argument, to collate what came from the house.

Rosetti got to the embassy by mid-morning. For the benefit of the entire group he repeated what he'd earlier told Claudine, adding that around the anal area and stuck by body fluid to the hessian he'd found four red-pigmented pubic hairs, obviously not those of the auburn-haired victim, from which the killer could be identified by DNA comparison. The body was too decomposed for any semen trace to have remained. There was no dental work from which the victim could be identified from orthodontic or dental records and although quite a substantial amount of the face was intact he thought a model reconstruction from skull and facial bone formation would be necessary if they wanted to issue a picture appeal. A mouth impression of the killer was possible from at least two of the bite marks. No effort had been made to clean the body and there were a lot of forensic tests still to be carried out. No one commented on the quickly developed photographs of the boy that Rosetti circulated.

Harding was actually remarking that antique dealers used hessian to wrap sale items – and specialized glue for repairs – when the first contact came from Antwerp. None of the combined FBI and CIA team had yet entered the premises as purchasing American tourists – the prepared cover – but from external observation there appeared to be two men working there. Both had red hair and from their facial similarity were clearly related.

'The hessian will match that in the shop, as well as the hair,' predicted Harding. 'So we've got ourselves a couple of murderers. One at least.'

The still unknown executive at Belgacom was the first caller, just after eleven, to be picked up on the agonizingly limited microphone in Smet's office. The lawyer did most of the talking, as he did on the three subsequent and connected calls, and a murmur of anticipation went round the listening group at the repetition in every one.

'My house tonight. Seven.' To the man they now knew to be Gaston Mehre, he added: 'It's desperate. Terrible.'

Harding had already phoned the controller of the Antwerp squad, giving the time when the shop would be empty that night. By then the search of Boulevard Anspach had been completed, listening devices installed in every room and telephone and all documentation McCulloch and Ritchie considered relevant copied and returned to where they had been found. There were thirty CIA and FBI agents dispersed around the house and along every road feeding into it.

Smet didn't dominate the conversation when Félicité Galan called. He told her about the discovery of the body and in reply to her obvious question said: 'I don't know if we're going to meet this afternoon! The bastard wouldn't say what was so important about what they'd found! Just that it was good. Important. I'm going to try Poncellet if they go on saying they're too busy.'

There was a long period of silence, interspersed with grunts and single-word agreement. Towards the end Smet complained: 'I know they're stupid. It's too late now: too late for anything.' To her unheard response to that, he said: 'Kill myself.'

His final words were: 'Please, I'm begging you . . . I can't help it . . . do it now. . .? When . . .? Now, it's got to be now . . .'

They were careful to keep the sequence in the proper order. Blake told Poncellet there appeared to be a useful amount of forensic clues connected with the body find that wouldn't be analysed in time for any meeting that afternoon. Further contact from the woman in any case had priority. He said exactly the same to Smet, promising to call him again at the office or even at home that evening if there was any development. They all listened to Poncellet accurately recount his conversation with Blake to the other Belgian when Smet reached him.

'It looks as if things are moving at last,' said Poncellet.

'They haven't told you what it is?'

'No.'

Félicité did call McBride. Her attitude – her tone of voice even – was totally different from what it had been on any previous occasion. Claudine tried to involve herself – although not goading, alert to the change and careful to avoid antagonizing her – but the woman told her, without anger, to get off the line. Claudine did. After her earlier debacle, Hillary didn't attempt to grab the telephone.

'It's a million.'

'I know,' said McBride.

'It's ready?'

'Yes.'

'Cash?'

'Yes.'

'Deposit it at a branch of Crédit Lyonnais. You choose which. Tomorrow, precisely at 11 a.m., I'll give you a bank and an account number into which it's to be transferred. If it's not in the account I designate by 11.30 a.m. Mary Beth will be killed. Understood?'

'No, wait . . .'

'Shut up! You there, Claudine?'

'Yes.'

'Pay attention and you'll learn how a ransom exchange can be made to work.'

The line went dead. The scanner failed to isolate the source of the call. It was, the technicians later insisted again, because it had been long distance, nowhere within the city limits.

In his study McBride looked sideways to Claudine and said: 'She didn't sound the same.'

'No,' agreed Claudine. It wasn't right: not right at all.

'Am I going home?' asked the child, urgently, as Lascelles entered the beach house.

'Yes. But you've got to be very good,' said Félicité.

'I will be. Honest I will be.' She smiled up at Lascelles and said: 'Hello.'

'Hello.'

'Are you going to take me home?'

'Both of us,' said the man.

'Can I wear my new clothes?'

'Yes,' said Félicité. 'But hurry.'

'Why are you crying?'

'I'm not crying. The wind flicked my hair into my eyes.' She'd actually been hoping the Luxembourg lawyer would tell her that the bank chain hadn't been established.

As they got into Lascelles' car Félicité said, in French: 'You're quite sure it won't hurt?'

'Positive. Pills will be best. For all of them.'

'Mary Beth first,' insisted Félicité. 'I want to be the one to do it. It's got to be me.'

CHAPTER TWENTY-SIX

James McBride chose the nearest convenient bank, on the rue de Louvain, and Claudine used the absence of both the ambassador and the accompanying Harrison to issue the warning. Only Rosetti wasn't there to hear it, back at the mortuary to conclude his finding with the Belgian pathologist. She replayed that afternoon's brief tape and Blake said: 'Yes. She sounds very different.'

'It's resignation,' identified Claudine. 'Practically from the time she snatched Mary Beth she's been living a fantasy, her own private idyll. She's fallen in love with the child, convinced herself she's protecting her from everyone else – it will have been the rest of the group at first, now it's probably me as well – but today some reality has come back. There's still more fantasy than anything else but she's accepting, although she probably doesn't want to, that it's coming to an end.'

'How bad?' queried Harding.

'As bad as it could be.'

'You want to spell that out a little clearer?' asked Rampling.

'I hoped the ransom would be enough. That making her hate me and then letting her have the money – beating me – would be sufficient . . .' Claudine hesitated, the admission thick in her throat. 'I don't think that any longer.'

'So the ransom's not important any more?' frowned Rampling.

'Yes it is! She still has to beat me with that. But when the money's handed over, she's won.'

'So by paying it we kill Mary Beth?'

'We were always going to,' reminded Claudine. 'That's why I argued against it from the beginning: turned it instead into a way of delaying things until we found her. She's beaten us by getting out of her house.'

'But you say she loves Mary!' protested Rampling. 'You don't kill people you love!'

'You do, if that love is absolute, to prevent them falling into the hands of the enemy. I'm the enemy.'

'That's fan—' started Harding, stopping halfway through the protest.

'Biblical, romantic fantasy,' agreed Claudine. 'I know. I wish I wasn't so convinced I'm right.'

'We don't wait any longer,' declared Harding. 'We've got her house as tight as a drum, although she's calling from some place outside the city. And we know where a bunch of them are going to be tonight. If Félicité isn't back by then we hit Smet's place. They'll know where she's got the kid. And we've got enough proof of murder to interrogate the shit out of them. They'll tell us. And then we hit her.'

'Tonight,' agreed Rampling. 'And we know Mary Beth's safe until eleven thirty tomorrow morning. Everything's going to work like clockwork.'

'Let's hope,' said Claudine. It was five o'clock. It was going to be a long two hours.

Smet arrived home at 5.30 p.m. There was the familiar sound of decanter against glass. The television was switched on, in anticipation of the main evening newscast.

By then McBride had returned from depositing the $1,000,000 ransom to endorse ('about goddamned time!') the decision to raid the rue de Flandre and insist on being present at the rescue of his daughter. Hillary announced she would be there too. Claudine, concerned at the easy assumption that Mary Beth's recovery was a foregone conclusion, didn't explain her reasoning for recommending the assault and McBride didn't ask. Instead he announced that he was going to speak to both State and the President by telephone. That guarantee of Washington support failed to reassure Elliot Smith, who remained uncertain of legal jurisdiction despite the assurance from Peter Blake that Europol, which he represented and from which, additionally, Commissioner Sanglier would shortly be arriving, had power of arrest in an EU country in which a serious crime had been committed and that the murder of the rent boy provided the justification.

'After we get Mary Beth back the courts can argue about legality for as long as they like,' dismissed McBride. 'Do it!'

To provide his promised legal authority Blake went with Harding physically to take part in the entry. That wasn't to be until Rampling, who remained as liaison at the embassy, was satisfied from what he overheard that everyone whom Smet expected had arrived. A speaker was installed in the ambassador's suite to relay from the communications room every sound picked up from the bugged house. Smet's listening to the six o'clock news, upon which that day's press release predicting major developments within the next twenty-four hours in the kidnap of Mary Beth McBride was the lead item, provided the sound test. It was perfect.

Claudine attended each hurriedly convened discussion and contributed when asked – doubting there would be any physical resistance, although not ruling out a panicked suicide attempt – but fully accepted her subsidiary part in what was an operational field situation. She wasn't, either, as affected as everyone else increasingly became by a tense, almost nervous, expectation. It wasn't any real danger here, at the embassy, but on the ground mistakes were more likely in a nervous atmosphere.

Still with almost an hour to go before the gathering at Smet's home, Claudine decided to combine the background Kurt Volker had compiled from what had been taken from Félicité Galan's house with what she had suggested before the woman had been identified. Practically all of it dovetailed. Even the video-fit pictures created from the descriptions of the two kidnap witnesses were reasonable representations of the four actual photographs that had been copied.

Félicité's passport put her at thirty-nine, to within three years of Claudine's estimate. The town house, the itemized jewellery, the money in copied deposit and current bank accounts – in total the Belgian franc equivalent of almost $200,000 – as well as the dark green Mercedes attested to substantial wealth, which Claudine had also guessed. She had been prepared for Marcel still to be alive and one of the paedophile group but she wasn't surprised to read in one of the several preserved obituary notices that Félicité's late husband had been a leading Brussels stockbroker, the head of his own firm and a trading member of the city's *bourse*. The several retained newspaper and magazine references to Félicité's interest in and support for local charities didn't surprise her, either. Nor that two of them involved the protection of children.

Volker entered the briefing room as she was finishing comparing the computer reproductions with Félicité's photographs.

'I thought that was disappointing,' said the German. 'Those witnesses' descriptions were remarkably good. And she's reasonably well known, from the newspaper cuttings. Yet we didn't get a single recognition.'

'That's human nature,' said Claudine. 'No one

thought it could be Félicité because she's far too respectable. They were frightened of making fools of themselves.'

'Although it doesn't show paedophilia there's someone remarkably similar in one of the pornographic films that arrived yesterday through the Amsterdam outlet,' said Volker. 'Come and see what you think.'

Only five operators remained in the computer room, now that the e-mail flood had dried to a trickle. They had been concentrated at the far end of the room, separated by a line of dead screens from Volker's three-machine command post. There were two television sets immediately adjacent, a cassette still in the gate of one VCR.

It was a lesbian orgy. Most of the participants were totally naked, several with dildoes strapped to their crotch as penises, others with manual vibrators. Without exception all the women wore grotesquely ornate animal or occult half-masks that left their mouths free. In almost every shot there were scenes of cunnilingus.

'There!' said Volker, freezing the frame to point to a heavily busted woman in a satyr's headpiece. She was one of the performers wearing a dildo.

Claudine made herself look away from another participant, studying the figure that had attracted Volker's attention. 'I don't think so,' she said. 'Look: there's dark hair – brunette – showing beneath the mask at the forehead and at the nape of the neck. And the pubis is black.'

'You're right,' agreed the German. 'I thought that was a shadow.' He restarted the film. 'Looks like quite a party.'

'Yes,' said Claudine, looking back to the other participant.

Henri Sanglier made a noisy entry and said: 'I've been looking for everyone. What are you doing?'

'I thought we had a connection but I was wrong,' admitted Volker, as Claudine snapped the film off.

'No need to waste time on it,' Claudine said, leading the commissioner back out of the room.

The devil's mask had done nothing to hide Sanglier's wife from Claudine, quite apart from the setting of the film. She at once recognized Françoise from the languid model's grace with which the woman moved and from the extraordinarily long-fingered hands that had tried so hard to explore her. She hadn't known about Françoise's tiny bird tattoo, which matched that on the thigh of the woman upon whom Françoise was using a vibrator. But then she'd never allowed herself to get into a situation in which Françoise was naked, despite the woman's persistent efforts.

In addition to all of which it was the location of the film that was the easiest to identify. From the still unexplained dinner party to which Henri Sanglier had invited her and Rosetti, Claudine knew the panelled hallway and opulent, antique-crowded room beyond actually to be Sanglier's *manoir*, on the road between The Hague and Delft. And so would anyone else who had been to the man's home.

The first to arrive, together, were greeted as Gaston and Charles.

'It's the antique dealer and his relative,' confirmed Harding, over his mobile link. 'Our guys followed them from Antwerp. They're on their way back to you.'

McBride, who'd made a help-yourself gesture towards the cocktail cabinet but been the only one to take a drink, Jack Daniel's, sat hunched towards the huge speaker. Hillary was wearing her green safari suit.

Smet said: 'Everyone's coming.'

'Félicité?' queried a voice.

'Everyone except Félicité.'

'What's happening?' It was Gaston.

'Let's wait for the others,' said Smet.

'It's a fat guy,' warned Harding, before the sound of the doorbell.

Smet said: 'You and I might have a lot of legal matters to talk about, Michel.'

'A new name,' Rampling told the watching FBI head. 'Michel.'

'We've got the car registration, for the full name,' Harding assured him. Then: 'Here's another one!'

'August,' said Smet, at the door.

'It's the Belgacom executive,' said Rampling, into his telephone.

'From the back of the guy coming in now there's a resemblance to the video-fit of the driver of the kidnap car,' said Harding, as the sound of a bell echoed through the speaker. Smet opened and closed the door, without speaking. There was the sound of carpet-muffled footsteps.

'It's good that you all came,' said Smet. 'We're at the very edge of disaster.'

'They're all there!' declared Rampling.

'Go!' ordered Harding, not speaking to those listening in the ambassador's study.

They didn't need the hydraulic rams to smash the door off its hinges. Blake rang the bell and Harding shouted, through a bullhorn and in remarkably good French: 'Let us in, Smet. We're ready to take the door down.'

From the lounge window Dehane, his voice chipped by hysteria, said: 'They're everywhere! Swarming in!'

Smet said: 'Don't say anything. There's nothing to connect us with the girl,' and then there was the sound of a lot of people all moving at once.

Michel Blott was the first to flee through the rear door, outside which McCulloch and Ritchie were waiting with a squad. McCulloch said: 'Thanks for opening the door,' and pushed past the fat lawyer.

Henri Cool was cowering inside the rear hallway. When he saw the entering Americans he said: 'Don't hurt me! Please don't hurt me!' and began to cry.

The Mehre brothers were standing in the middle of the main room, with Dehane. Gaston was holding the hand of the trembling Charles. Dehane kept repeating: 'Oh my God, oh my God.'

Smet was taking the pistol from his mouth when McCulloch entered the bedroom. McCulloch said: 'We distorted the pin. It won't fire. I'll help you jam it down your throat if you like.'

By the time they were all brought back together in the lounge the still weeping Henri Cool had wet himself. So had Charles Mehre. He was also crying.

In the ambassador's study they heard Harding say: 'OK. Which one of you is going to tell me where Félicité is, with Mary Beth?'

'No!' moaned Claudine.

None of the men spoke.

CHAPTER TWENTY-SEVEN

Henri Sanglier accepted at once that it would mean sacrificing a lot of potential personal benefit: he could no longer, for instance, claim to have masterminded the entire operation, which had been an early intention. But speed, at last with official knowledge and authority, was the only consideration now: how quickly they could recover the child. Which made the inevitable Belgian outrage an irritating delay and Claudine's suggestion how best to overcome it a godsend. It also made McBride an urgent accomplice.

It was the ambassador who pressed the Justice Minister ('there is an absolutely essential political need that can't be put off until tomorrow') to meet them at the central police headquarters. Only when they arrived, within minutes of each other and ahead of anyone from the rue de Flandres, did Sanglier call Poncellet. The police commissioner said he could be there in ten minutes. Sanglier hoped that would be sufficient intervening time. He wished there'd been a justifiable reason to have Claudine remain part of the discussion.

In Poncellet's pristinely neat office the Justice Minister listened stone-faced, seemingly reluctant to accept copies of everything that had been recorded from Smet's home telephone and the incomplete transcripts from the lawyer's office line. He waved the bundle like a flag of surrender and said, his voice jagged: 'This is inconceivable. Horrifying. I can't believe it.'

'They're on their way here now, all except the woman. And they know where the child is,' said Sanglier.

There was too much for Ulieff to absorb: too much to think about. It was appalling. A total disaster. Smet was a member of his staff. Someone he personally knew. Someone who'd inveigled himself into an unquestioned position of trust, actually as a liaison in the investigation. Just as, Ulieff reminded himself in further horror, the man had made himself part of a previous investigation into a child sex murder, one that had never been solved. How could he, Ulieff, escape personal responsibility? Distance himself. All he could do. Distance himself by as much as possible. He made another gesture with the transcripts. 'Does he know you've got this?'

Instead of answering Sanglier said: 'It was necessary to behave as we did. We didn't know, in the beginning, who among us was the informer.'

Doubtful awareness registered upon the face of the no longer urbane man. So occupied was he by personal concern that it never occurred to him to be affronted by what Europol and the Americans had done. 'Are they admissible?'

'It's arguable. And we don't have time to argue. We need to know now, this moment, where Mary Beth is.'

'Of course.' Getting the child back was the most important factor: it always had been. The quicker they managed that, the better able he would be to confront the scandal: manoeuvre his way out. He'd have to lead, Ulieff decided. Announce the fullest inquiry the moment they recovered the child: recovered her alive, not dead. He wouldn't be able to survive if she was found dead and one of his own staff was part of whatever had happened to her. He'd have to resign. No choice. No alternative. Destroyed. The bastard! The insinuating, evil, perverted bastard!

McBride said: 'I spoke to Washington before coming

here tonight. Personally to the Secretary of State. He hoped there wouldn't be any difficulty in our continued cooperation.'

Ulieff frowned, realizing he was being told something other than the obvious but not easily able to understand what it was. It sounded like an apology but what did they have to apologize for! 'I hope that too. I don't see why there should be.'

Sanglier looked obviously disappointed. 'We don't want Smet hiding behind legal barriers.'

Ulieff saw a faraway light. 'I won't allow that to happen.'

'With so many being the potential informer, having access as they did to every early planning discussion, it would have been difficult obtaining a judge's order authorizing a wire tap without their knowing it,' persisted Sanglier. He let a silence grow. 'You could privately have approved it, in consultation with myself and the ambassador.' It begged the question of why they hadn't and Sanglier had an explainable apology if Ulieff challenged him.

The man didn't. Instead his face cleared. 'If it removes an obstacle . . .'

'Smet is a criminal lawyer. One of the others seems somehow connected with the law from a remark that was made when he arrived at Smet's house tonight.'

To McBride the minister said: 'Is this what your Secretary meant by cooperation?'

'We did not speak in specifics, only generalities,' said McBride, easing the Belgian's way. 'This conversation is between the three of us. As it will always remain.'

At that moment André Poncellet bustled into the room, stopping uncertainly at finding the other three men obviously well settled ahead of him. Ulieff said: 'Commissioner Sanglier has something to explain to you.'

Poncellet remained standing – he had little choice

while Ulieff expansively occupied his desk – his face tightening as the minister's had initially done for different reasons, although Sanglier said nothing about the man's own house being entered and bugged.

'You actually thought I could have been one of them!' protested Poncellet, aghast.

'We couldn't trust anyone,' said Ulieff, taking up the role he had been offered. 'It was my decision it should be this way.'

Welcome to the club, thought Sanglier, waiting for the obvious demand about his own home to come from the still incensed policeman. It didn't. Quickly Sanglier said: 'Your credibility – your authority – has not publicly been questioned or impugned. Nor will it ever be: there is no reason why it should be. You were personally present much earlier today at the discovery of a murder victim. The men being brought to this building tonight are unquestionably involved. They are also part of the kidnap of the ambassador's daughter that has yet to be resolved. When it is, again tonight, you'll be there as the represent-ative of Belgian authority: of the Belgian police.'

'I greatly resent being doubted; being suspected.' The protest wasn't as stiff as it should have been.

'Until we had positive proof I couldn't make any exception,' said Ulieff. 'I would like now personally to apologize. Which I do, unreservedly.' The police com-missioner would leak the apology to restore his credibil-ity, guessed Ulieff. And by so doing confirm his knowledge as minister from the beginning of the trap. Everything had settled perfectly.

Poncellet accepted the regret with a short head jerk. As he did so the intercom on his desk announced the arrival of the first arrests from the rue de Flandres. Ulieff said: 'Let's get the child back. End the whole unfortunate business.'

As the lift descended Sanglier decided that diplomacy

was like a child's early comprehension exercise. All you had to do was fit the pieces into their correct shapes to make a smooth, unbroken picture.

Everyone had been brought in by the time they reached the ground floor. The vestibule was in chaos. There had been no advance warning of any arrests on any charge and once again there were too many people milling about, virtually all with no idea what to do. Poncellet at once took officious charge, loudly declaring the detentions were connected with that morning's murder and without prompting ordered that each man should be detained in an individual cell.

Charles Mehre screamed, loud enough to startle, when he realized he was being parted from Gaston, who instinctively reached out a comforting hand. Charles's escort hesitated, looking to Poncellet for guidance. Claudine had anticipated the moment, manoeuvring herself next to the commissioner. Quietly she insisted: 'By himself. Solitary.'

Charles immediately began to fight, violently, scattering everyone around him. He head-butted his escort, bursting the man's nose, and split the eye of one of the three policemen it finally took to subdue him. Claudine was among those thrown back by the outburst, close to where Rosetti had remained, against the wall.

'Well?' she said.

'Both of them have got red hair and misshapen teeth,' the pathologist pointed out. 'The orthodontic cast should be conclusive but one of them's the most likely candidate.'

'Something easy at last,' remarked Claudine.

Little else proved to be.

Smet's cosseted briefcase did contain an address book. There was also a diary. The book carried the names and addresses of the five men seized with him in the rue de Flandres house, as well as that of Félicité Galan. Only the house they'd already entered and found empty was listed against the woman's name. The diary appeared strictly limited to business appointments but Claudine quickly isolated the simplistic code, red-inked stars dotted alongside various dates, the majority at weekends. One star, however, was against the mid-week date of Mary Beth's disappearance.

The only other contents of the briefcase, apart from every record of their planning meetings, were three separate and undesignated keyrings. One ring, gold-coloured, held a single key.

The ideal psychology – indeed virtually a universal practice among police interrogators seeking incriminating confessions from a gang – would have been to leave them separated overnight, for each man to be eroded by his fear of what the others might admit or accuse him of. That night, with everyone's eyes constantly drawn to the ever-moving police station clocks, it was difficult for Claudine to argue restraint for longer than an hour. Sanglier agreed to her sharing Rampling's questioning of Jean Smet.

Claudine guessed at once that the psychology was totally skewed. A gap of twenty-four hours would probably have broken the lawyer. Leaving him alone for just one had given the man the opportunity to recover and prepare himself. It was clearly forced but when they entered the interview cell there was even an unworried languidness about the way Smet was sitting, right arm lolled over the back of his chair.

The room was bare, except for the table at which Smet already sat and upon which the apparatus was assembled to record the interview. Alongside was a second tape machine that had been installed in each interview room in the intervening hour. Claudine saw, uncomfortably, that they faced the clock. She made much of putting a folder on the table in front of her, which Smet made just as much effort to ignore.

Rampling started the machine and identified everyone in the room before at once listing dates and times that tapes he intended to produce had been made. And then pressed the second play button.

Smet was visibly shaken by the greatly amplified sound of his own voice echoing into the interview room, involuntarily pulling his arm from the chair back to come forward over the table. He half opened his mouth but didn't speak.

'You know what a voice print is?' demanded the American briskly, trying to indicate the encounter was a formality.

Claudine admired the quick ploy to get a voice comparison at the very beginning but it wasn't successful. Smet remained silent.

Rampling said: 'It's as accurate as a fingerprint or DNA. Scientifically we can prove that's you, talking to someone we now know to be August Dehane, about the kidnap of Mary Beth McBride.'

Smet stared tight-lipped across the table.

'Now what have we got?' Rampling pressed on. 'We've got you talking to Dehane about killing the child. We've got Félicité mentioned and the mobile phones. In fact, Jean, I think we've got you pretty tightly parcelled up and tied in ribbon. What do you think?'

Claudine liked the mocking technique.

'My home has clearly been illegally entered,' said the man at last. 'I don't know what any of this is about but it was blatantly illegally obtained. I demand a lawyer, at once.'

'What do red stars in your diary signify?' asked Claudine. 'Particularly on the day Mary Beth vanished. Are the red-star days those when you all got together? The days you abused children you snatched or rented?' She tried to infuse as much contempt as possible into her voice.

Smet just stared.

'Why'd you put a gun in your mouth and try to blow your head off?' demanded Rampling. 'You want to tell us about that?'

'I demand a lawyer.' Smet was controlled again – polite – not showing the hysteria of the bugged telephone exchanges. Or, even, the anxiety of their planning meetings.

'Félicité is going to kill the child, isn't she?' said Claudine.

'I don't know anyone called Félicité.'

'Who's Félicité Galan, listed in your address book?'

'Going into my briefcase was an illegal search. Please get me a lawyer.'

'It was Charles Mehre who killed the rent boy, wasn't it: smothered him during the act of buggery.'

Smet didn't reply.

Claudine took the photographs of the anal distension from her folder, pushed them across the table. 'That's what he looked like after Mehre finished with him. That's what the jury are going to see when you're arraigned with Charles Mehre, accused of complicity to murder.'

Smet gave no facial reaction. 'I know nothing about this.'

It was nine thirty, Claudine saw.

'Charles Mehre was arrested in your house,' said Rampling. 'It's on suspicion of murder that you're all being held.'

The tapes of the intercepted conversation were as always marked at relevant passages. Claudine made her selection, starting the playback. Into the room came Smet's voice. '. . . *Gaston called . . . He said he doesn't give a shit what Félicité says. He's going to get rid of the other thing. It's beginning to stink . . .*' Claudine said: 'That's timed and dated before the body was found. You knew about it in advance.'

'You've got to find some way of helping yourself,' urged Rampling. 'You're a lawyer, for Christ's sake. You can judge how bad things are for you.'

'Were my house and office burgled with the approval of a judge?'

Formally Claudine said: 'Miet Ulieff, the Justice Minister – your superior – authorized both.'

'He doesn't have the legal authority.'

'He does for anything that's done within the ministry he heads, involving a ministry official suspected of serious crime. Which you are.' Elliot Smith, the American embassy lawyer, hadn't been that adamant. At most he had conceded it was possible, but a brief flicker of uncertainty showed on Smet's face.

'I have nothing to say apart from repeating my demand for a lawyer.'

The mocking clock showed nine forty-five. Why wouldn't Smet break! thought Claudine desperately. Because his position *was* so hopeless, she decided, answering her own frustrated question.

There was the sound of a door opening behind them. At once Rampling recorded Blake's entry. The man bent to Claudine's ear and whispered: 'Not one of the bastards is saying anything: Charles Mehre has had to be sedated. Smile, like I've just told you something you've been waiting to hear.'

Blake straightened, isolating the three sets of keys from the diary and the address book that had been in Smet's briefcase. 'Charles was the weak link. Had to be. He said you know all about it and that you've got the key.'

The lawyer hesitated, swallowing. Then he said: 'Dear Jesus . . .!' He began to shake. 'It was Félicité. She made us do it. Always her ideas . . . I didn't have anything to do with the murder.' And finally he pushed across the single key on its gold ring.

Blake picked it up, dangling it in front of the man. 'That's the way. Now tell us where the house is.'

Smet stared at the fair-haired detective. 'That was a trick . . . it isn't . . .'

Blake looked directly towards the recorders. 'Let the record show that Jean Smet isolated from a choice of several the key that fits the house in which Mary Beth McBride is being held.' He smiled broadly. 'You just forgot your own advice and convicted yourself.'

She'd forgotten the kamikaze legacy of Ireland, Claudine thought, following Blake from the interview room. In the corridor directly outside she said furiously: 'What if it hadn't worked!'

'I'd have tried something similar on all the rest until it did,' admitted Blake easily. 'Now we haven't got to waste any more time.' He grinned. 'You didn't smile when I told you to.'

The helicopters were utilized at last, to fly the advance group to Antwerp. The party included Miet Ulieff as well as the tense ambassador and his safari-suited wife. Sanglier had wanted to be the most senior judicial figure at the child's recovery but the Justice Minister's presence guaranteed that every local need was instantly provided.

By the time the American back-up arrived by road the entire Antwerp detective division had been mobilized and there were three of the city's river police boats on the Schelde opposite the house with their engines muted, just holding them against the current, and far enough away for them not to be obvious. Officials in the planning, land registry and rating departments of Antwerp City Council had been located and returned to their offices. The original architects' drawings for the house's construction, incorporating the wartime Nazi bunker, had

378

been located for their inspection and Pieter Lascelles, an Eindhoven surgeon, identified as its owner.

Lance Rampling accompanied Peter Blake in the three-car cavalcade that went to Eindhoven. From a radio car Sanglier alerted the Eindhoven police to their impending arrival – until which no approach was to be made to the doctor's home – and gave a fuller explanation to the awakened Dutch Justice Minister after Ulieff ended his conversation with the man. Into their car as Rampling and Blake drove towards Holland was radioed the message that a ten-year-old boy named Robert Flet and a girl of eleven, Yvette Piquette, had vanished in Eindhoven the previous day.

It was eleven thirty-five when Harding and McCulloch led the assault upon the riverside house, which was in total darkness. Claudine remained at the head of the drive, drawn against a clump of trees with Sanglier, Ulieff and the ambassador and his wife. There was remarkably little noise from so many men spreading out through the grounds. Only occasionally was she able to pick out the shape of someone becoming part of the encirclement.

Lights suddenly blazed on ahead of them. Abruptly there was a scurried rush of men pouring into the house. Lights pricked out as room after room was entered. McBride began to run and immediately Hillary sprinted after him, literally racing. Everyone followed at a run. Claudine was directly behind the ambassador when he went into the house. A grave-faced Harding was waiting in the hallway, the basement door open behind him.

'Down there,' he said.

McBride got to the basement just ahead of Hillary. Claudine followed. Men already in the bunker basement shifted away from an open door, as if embarrassed.

Mary Beth's school hat was on top of the neatly made bed. Her brace was on the sill of the sink. On a bathroom stool some shells and water-bleached stones were laid out in a pattern. On the wall, by the bed, were drawn two stick figures. 'Dad' was in uneven print beneath the bigger, 'mom' beneath the smaller. Their arms were raised against each other.

It was five minutes to midnight.

CHAPTER TWENTY-EIGHT

By 3 a.m. – with just eight and a half hours to go before her deadline – they had it all except for what they wanted most, a location for where Félicité Galan held Mary Beth McBride.

The search of Pieter Lascelles' Eindhoven home, authorized by the Dutch Justice Minister on suspicion of serious crime, produced a substantial amount of paedophile pornography but no clue to Félicité's whereabouts. Or his. Her dark green Mercedes was discovered garaged at the riverside house but Lascelles' Jaguar was missing from his home. The registration-linked Dutch national police computer provided the number as well as the make, which was circulated with stop-and-detain orders to all road traffic units in Holland and Belgium.

Confronted in Brussels with the proof that Mary Beth had been in the Antwerp house, Félicité Galan's paedophile group collapsed into recriminating accusations against her, with the exception of the still deeply sedated Charles Mehre, and any confession he might have made became unnecessary, so full were the frantic admissions of the other five desperate to shift guilt and blame away from themselves.

So desperate were they – Jean Smet seemingly most of all – that Claudine became convinced within an hour of the interrogations' resuming at the Belgian police headquarters that one if not all would have disclosed an address if they'd known one. Which meant that the lead had to come from them subconsciously. And that she had to recognize it when it did.

It was the once devoted Gaston Mehre who rushed to name his retarded brother as the killer of the Dilbeek victim as well as the previous rent boy, even before being faced with the preliminary forensic comparison matching of what had been found on the decomposing body and the hessian: glue, specialized antique polish and dirt recovered from the basement storeroom of his Schoenmarkt antique gallery in which, additionally, had been found blood from which a DNA comparison was already being made.

Jean Smet eagerly volunteered his misdirecting part as the Justice Ministry liaison during that earlier murder investigation, which surprised Claudine until she accepted that he was virtually setting out his defence to foreseeable criminal charges, acknowledging paedophilia in a country of minimal child-sex sentencing but denying any part in murder. 'I certainly obstructed justice. But I had nothing to do with that killing. Nor this one. Neither was I in any way involved with the kidnap of the ambassador's daughter. It was Félicité. Félicité and Henri Cool. From the first day I argued for her to be safely returned.'

Before they'd left Antwerp, Sanglier had drafted a new Europol squad into Eindhoven and Rampling was only thirty minutes behind Claudine returning to Brussels, enabling them to resume their questioning of the ministry lawyer together.

They were briefly hopeful – despite his insistence that Félicité and the child wouldn't be there – when Smet explained how the groups had protected themselves by not owning secondary property in their country of residence and revealed Félicité's ownership of a country villa in Goirle. It was locked and shuttered when Europol and Eindhoven police raided it minutes after being alerted.

'*How* did you know she wouldn't be there?' demanded Rampling.

'She's planning a special party. Bigger than anything she's ever organized before. Goirle is too small.'

'Is that what Mary Beth was snatched for, a special party?' asked Claudine. Her concentration was absolute, searching for the smallest tell-tale sign.

Smet nodded, not replying.

'Is that where she's gone with Lascelles, to wherever it's being held?' asked the American.

'I'd expect so.'

'Don't you know?' said the disbelieving Rampling.

'No.'

'You're part of her group. Why aren't you and the others included?'

'I don't know about the others. I told her I wasn't interested. Like I said, I'm not involved.'

A defensive lie, judged Claudine: the disagreement between them had been as serious as she'd guessed. Could that help her? Maybe, if she knew the proper questions. But she didn't. 'Who is going?'

The lean-faced man shrugged. 'Lascelles' group, I suppose. I don't know how many. And some French, I think.'

'Who are the French group?' pounced Rampling.

'I don't know.'

'Why not?'

'That's the way the system worked. Only the people who organize the gatherings know each other. It's safer, in case anyone gets arrested. They can't talk about people they don't know.'

'How come you know about Lascelles?' persisted the American.

'Because of the Antwerp house. I held the spare key.'

'Is it Lascelles' group who snatched two children in

383

Eindhoven yesterday?' There must be something, some-where!

'I don't know anything about what happened in Eindhoven.'

'Who are the people in Lascelles' group?'

'I don't know any of them.'

'You've had "parties" with them before, haven't you?'

'We don't use names. Usually we wear masks.'

It wasn't coming, thought Claudine: nothing was coming that she could follow. 'So you film what happens?'

Smet shifted uncomfortably. 'Sometimes.'

'Will this special party be filmed?'

'I told you I don't know anything about this special party.'

'What happens to the films?'

'They're kept.'

'Have you got any, apart from the two in your safe?'

'How do you know what I've got in my safe?'

'We opened it,' said Rampling impatiently. 'Answer the question.'

'No, I haven't got any.'

'Do you know anyone who has?'

'No.'

'Who takes the films?'

'Someone who has a camera. I never did.'

'How far in advance are these parties planned?' said Claudine. If something didn't become obvious soon she'd check the transcripts of the other resumed interviews, seeking her lead there. She tried to push away the frustration, aware it could cloud her judgement.

'This one took a long time. Months. She wanted it to be better than any before it.'

In a sharp, outside-herself moment Claudine was dis-tracted by the awareness that they were talking in ordi-nary, low-voiced conversational tones – no one visibly angry, no one visibly offended, no one visibly judgemental – about other adults conspiring sexually, perhaps in other ways too, to abuse children sometimes young enough to need comfort blankets and imagine their favourite bunny rabbit or teddy bear could hear what was said to it. What, she wondered, happened to that imagination when people like Jean Smet and Félicité Galan and all the other stunted freaks finished with them, even if they allowed them to live? Wrong: allowing personal emotion to intrude. If she stood any chance whatsoever – and with the taunting clock inexorably counting off every minute of every hour she was beginning to doubt that she did stand any chance – allowing that sort of intrusion actually put Mary Beth at risk.

'The host?'

'Absolutely,' agreed Smet. 'She was determined to control the others as she controlled us. She liked disciples.'

Claudine frowned at the biblical analogy, disliking it. Instead she thought of another, unsure in her absence of religion of the accuracy of her recall. It was something about suffer the little children. Reluctant to concede defeat, Claudine said: 'Tell me about Félicité Galan as a person.'

Smet weighed the question. 'Arrogant. Needing constantly to be the object of all attention: to be admired, never opposed. Sophisticated. Used to every good thing in life, after being married to Marcel. A hedonist willing – anxious – for every new experience.'

Claudine had been prepared for the man to attempt every possible personal benefit rather than give a truly accurate opinion but decided that he hadn't. Instead, surprisingly, he'd answered honestly. Curiously she said: 'You admired her, didn't you? Maybe you were even physically attracted to her!'

'She terrifies me,' confessed the man. 'I could never

lose the feeling that one day she'd destroy me: suck from me every ounce of blood and leave me to rot in her web.' He gave a bitter snort of a laugh. 'And she has, hasn't she?'

Claudine said: 'Charles would have killed Mary Beth, wouldn't he?'

Smet gazed steadily at her across the table. 'To kill someone would be an experience Félicité hasn't had before. I think she'll want to do it.'

Mary Beth hadn't been able to sleep again after waking up to make pee pee, although she pretended to, trying to breathe how people breathed when they were asleep, in and out and making funny gurgling noises.

The woman had startled her, being right there in the chair when she'd put the light on, jerking awake at the sudden glare and coming to the bathroom with her. And she hadn't liked it afterwards, when the woman had taken off most of her clothes and got on the bed, not beneath the covers but on top, so that the bedclothes were tight, trapping her, like the woman's arm was trapping her, heavy over her shoulders and along her arm.

She hadn't liked either the way the tall, bony man had held her too tightly to carry her into the house when she could easily have walked. Or the noises the house itself made, creaking and groaning, like an old man who couldn't move properly any more.

But most of all she didn't like – hated – the pink fairy costume the woman said she had to wear for the party before going home tomorrow. The material had been stiff and scratchy when they'd made her try it on and she knew she hadn't looked lovely, as they'd said she did. It was too tight around her tummy and the straps cut into her shoulders, hurting her.

'You're not asleep, are you, darling?'

'Almost.'

'I'm going to miss you.'

Mary Beth said nothing.

'Would you miss me, if you didn't have me any more?'

It was another one of those silly conversations. 'I suppose. I don't like the fairy dress.'

'It's a fancy dress party. All of us are going to dress up.'

'Why? It sounds silly.' She wished the woman's arm wasn't so tight around her. She shrugged, trying to ease it off.

'Don't you want me to cuddle you?'

'You're too heavy.'

'Will you wear the fairy costume, just for me?'

'I'm going home, after the party, aren't I?'

'Yes.'

'Promise?'

'I promise.'

'But I want to change first. Back into my new clothes.'

'All right.'

'I'll wear it then. Will there be a cake?'

'And candy. Very special candy.'

The soaring expectation and plunging despair increased everyone's exhaustion. Only Blake and Harding were still determinedly interviewing Michel Blott. Everyone else slumped listlessly around, beaten. Harrison said he'd persuaded the ambassador and his wife there was no sense in their staying, promising to call if there was any development. Henri Sanglier had left with them. Miet Ulieff had gone with Poncellet. Claudine was vaguely aware of Volker, hunched before his three-screen computer assembly in the adjoining communications room, more surprised at finding Rosetti still there.

Seeing the look on Claudine's face the pathologist said: 'I didn't have anywhere else to go after McCulloch had me explain to Gaston Mehre all the forensic and medical evidence. And I wanted to see it through anyway.'

'We've lost Félicité,' said Claudine. 'And by the time we find her it's going to be too late.'

'No idea at all?'

'None,' she admitted. There was still none two hours later, with the new day lightening up outside, when she finished listening to all the interviews. Volker was with the patient Rosetti when the Italian carried in the third cup of coffee. Peter Blake followed almost at once. Volker offered Claudine the papers he was carrying and said: 'Eindhoven police wired the specification of Félicité's Goirle house. Our people are still going through it. So far there's nothing.'

'And won't be,' said Claudine dully.

'You can't find what isn't there,' sympathized Rosetti.

'And it isn't,' said Blake. 'The ransom instructions are our only chance. This time we've got to get a fix. She won't kill the child immediately. With helicopters we'd have time to get to her before anything happened.'

The coffee was stewed and disgusting and Claudine put it aside, undrunk. 'There *has* to be a way!' she insisted stubbornly. 'We've got so much, know so much – about Félicité Galan in particular – that there has to be a direction to follow. We're just not seeing it!'

'There isn't!' Blake was equally insistent. 'We've been through it all each and every way.'

Claudine stared down unseeingly at the villa details, forcing every iota of her profile through her tired mind. 'As well as suffering a psychosis Félicité Galan is arrogant, opinionated and rich,' she recited to herself. 'She's the link between her own and at least one other paedophile ring and she's determined to impress them with the best child-sex orgy she can organize. She's going to be the host . . .' Claudine stopped, blinking, finally focusing upon the papers in front of her. 'Spread them,' she told

Blake, hurrying away from the table. He had done so by the time she returned with the architects' drawings of the Antwerp river house they'd obtained earlier from the city's planning department.

She used the remaining half-filled coffee cups to weigh down the edges to make a side-by-side comparison.

'What?' demanded Blake.

'Antwerp's got the huge basement room we all saw tonight,' said Claudine, tracing the drawing with her finger. 'As well as that huge room overlooking the river. And six bedrooms.' She switched to the other set of specifications. 'Goirle's got an even bigger main room. And five bedrooms.' She looked up, stretching, trying to ease the ache from her back and neck. 'Félicité's the host. That's what Smet said. So they're all coming to *her*. It's her party so it's going to be somewhere of her choice. But these two houses aren't big enough. And we know it's not at the Boulevard Anspach here in Brussels. If you're throwing a party – a very special party like this – and your own house isn't big enough for all the guests, what do you do?'

'You rent something,' said the ever-anticipating Volker.

It took him less than an hour. Knowing the name and branch of Félicité Galan's Brussels bank from the statements taken from her Boulevard Anspach house, he hacked into its mainframe computer and accessed her personal financial records. They listed two legally held accounts opened in Luxembourg ten years earlier, at first held jointly in the names of both herself and Marcel Galan. They had reverted to Félicité within a month of her husband's death. One was an investment account, serviced by five different share portfolios. From the investment holding there was an automatic quarterly transfer of $10,000 into a working current account. From that account, two days earlier, $2,500 had been paid to

Bildeek and Doorn, which was listed in the Namur telephone directory as an estate and house rental agency.

'I should have found the Luxembourg accounts within an hour of getting the Brussels bank statement,' said Volker apologetically.

'We've still got it in time,' Claudine reassured him.

'I know how she planned to get the money, too,' offered Volker. 'From Luxembourg in the last week accounts have been opened in Andorra, Liechtenstein and Switzerland. It's classic money laundering. She'll have McBride's money transferred into one of them and move it on immediately from bank to bank and country to country, until it gets back to the "mother" account in Luxembourg. And each time it moves, the account will be electronically closed. We wouldn't be able to trace it after the first transfer.'

'But how long will the whole process take until she knows it's finally got to Luxembourg?' demanded Blake. 'It'll surely give us an extension on her eleven thirty deadline!'

Volker smiled at the naivety of the question. 'As long as it takes to press a computer button. Say two or three seconds. Félicité Galan's $1,000,000 could go from whichever bank she nominates through two more countries and be in Luxembourg in less than five minutes. That's the joy of electronic money transfer.'

'It's one that she isn't going to know,' promised Rampling.

CHAPTER TWENTY-NINE

Having predictably started, the irritating dispute between James McBride and his wife continued longer than it should have done but it didn't delay the practical effort to find their daughter.

Miet Ulieff decreed the operation be centralized from the Namur police building and that the local police chief and the mayor, having mobilized their gendarmerie, meet him there. He added the warning that he would hold both personally responsible for the slightest public leak. Henri Sanglier, dismayed at having to share the potential glory for Mary Beth's rescue but unable to argue against Ulieff's presence, despatched almost half the task force by road, together with radio and telephone vans, before organizing the second helicopter airlift in less than twelve hours to ferry the remainder – and themselves – south. Also by helicopter went the mobile forensic and photographic facilities, as well as specialized cameras.

And through it all James and Hillary McBride fought over their child as a spoil of their own very personal war and yet again Claudine was unwillingly caught in the crossfire.

'I must be there!' insisted McBride. 'She'd expect me to be.'

Hillary said nothing, having already heard most of the argument and Claudine's reaction to it.

'You can't be,' Claudine said. 'We don't know what we're going to find in Namur. Mary Beth might not be there yet. Not be there at all. You've got to be in Brussels

– just as I have – if things go wrong and Félicité Galan calls the embassy at the time she's given. We could – literally – still be Mary Beth's lifeline.'

'And there really is no need for you to be there,' said the perfectly prepared Hillary, who'd returned from the residency in another freshly pressed Action Woman safari outfit, jungle green like the first. 'I'll be there when Mary Beth is brought out.'

Having suffered what, wondered Claudine: the woman was talking like a Hollywood movie.

McBride said: 'My authority might be needed on the ground. You stay and take the call.' His attempts were getting weaker.

'It's you the Galan woman's negotiated with up till now. Not me,' Hillary pointed out. 'You insisted on talking to her all the time, remember.'

It wasn't until people began leaving the building for the NATO base and the waiting helicopters that McBride finally capitulated, personally demanding from both Harding and Rampling that the radio and telephone link from the mobile communications centre that Kurt Volker was going to monitor at the embassy remain permanently open for him to get a minute-by-minute account.

'I'll give Mary Beth your love,' Hillary threw over her shoulder to her husband as she left.

'Bitch!' said McBride to the empty doorway, and for the first time Claudine thought that if Mary Beth existed in anything like this level of tension between her parents it would not have been difficult for Félicité Galan to insinuate herself into the child's feelings.

Hans Doorn was a prematurely balding, complacently fat man of thirty who had inherited Namur's most prestigious estate agency, along with its chairmanship, upon the death of his father and in whose comfortably settled, uneventful life nothing disturbing had ever occurred. The totally unannounced 7 a.m. doorstep arrival of the Belgian Justice Minister, a Europol commissioner and an assortment of field investigators was so unbelievable that it took Ulieff several minutes – and Rampling's and Harding's CIA and FBI shields – to convince the man he wasn't the victim of an elaborate practical joke. It took him even longer to recognize the photograph of the sharp-featured, elegant woman that was thrust at him as Félicité Galan, who'd rented for the weekend one of their most imposing country properties – a château, no less – just outside the city near St Marc. She was, suggested Doorn, the sort of cultured and sophisticated person with whom his agency most liked to do business. Miet Ulieff's terse explanation of why they were there caused the night-shirted Doorn the biggest shock of all.

By seven twenty, dressed and no longer complacent, he was in their discreet convoy on his way into the city to provide photographs, floor plans and every other known detail of the château to a demanding Paul Harding.

Even while he was doing that the helicopters that had carried those in charge of the investigation and the ambassador's wife from the Belgian capital made a high, reconnaissance pass over the identified mansion, which was set in expansive woodland almost two kilometres from the only public thoroughfare, a minor country road. From the air there was no sign of movement around the house, which was hardly surprising so early, nor of Pieter Lascelles' Jaguar – or any other vehicle – which was less easily understandable, although the house plans showed extensive stabling converted into garages. They only risked one over-flight but managed to expose forty frames of high speed, high density film.

Ulieff commandeered the office of the local police chief, a nervous man who stuttered and didn't bathe often enough, as autocratically as he had taken over Poncellet's in Brussels, but sensibly deferred to local knowledge. Both the policeman and the mayor, who'd dressed in formal black, doubted that any surprise day-light assault could be made upon the château, an opinion quickly confirmed by the arrival of the aerial photographs which showed the outer boundaries thickly wooded but the area between the coppices and the turreted building totally open, in places for more than a hectare.

'Helicopters would give us an element of surprise,' suggested Blake, drawing upon his Northern Ireland experience.

Harding shook his head. 'Doorn's room plans are to describe the house to potential renters or buyers. The place was built over three hundred years ago and is honeycombed with escape passages and underground tunnels. When he first showed it to Félicité, five months ago, she asked particularly to see them: said she was interested in medieval architecture and the precautions people took for their safety all those years ago.' He looked uncomfortably to the ambassador's wife. 'There are also some original dungeons and *oublier* wells. For the unfam-iliar *oublier* means forget: *oublier* wells or holes were pits, sometimes bottomless, in which people who weren't wanted any more were dropped and never seen again. Renters think crap like that is cute, apparently. Félicité spent a lot of time looking at it all, as part of her historical tour.'

'He's right,' said Rampling, who'd shared the interview with the realtor. He indicated the photographs. 'There's a gatehouse that isn't visible through the trees in any of these photographs and according to Doorn can't be seen from the outside road either. It's around the first bend in the drive. There'll obviously be someone there, checking arrivals. We wouldn't even clear the trees before they were warned, inside. OK, so we go in a different way. There isn't one that isn't wide open, for hundreds of yards. All they'd have to do is see us coming – which they will – to lock and bar the doors. Which according to Doorn are about a foot thick. By the time we got past them there wouldn't be a person in the place.'

'Surely all you've got to do is guard the tunnel and passage exits?' protested Hillary McBride.

'We could if we knew where they all were,' agreed Harding. 'Doorn told me of three and we've already got them covered but he thinks there're more. He says there're no reliable maps and that he doesn't know of the existence of any.'

'This is ridiculous!' said Hillary. She was ignored.

'The local legend is that some of the escape routes lead into the cave systems,' offered the local police chief. 'And that there are a lot of ancient skeletons at the bottom of the *oublier* wells. It's supposed to be haunted, of course.'

'If we know the entrances to three passages why can't we go in along them?' persisted the woman.

'We're trying that,' sighed Harding. 'The people who built the château thought of it, too. According to Doorn the doors are iron-ribbed on the inside and secured by iron crossbars, as well as by locks. The idea is to get out but not to get in.'

'There are no cars. Not even Lascelles' Jaguar,' said Blake. 'The party obviously hasn't started but maybe Félicité hasn't arrived with Mary Beth yet, either.'

'Telephone!' demanded Hillary. 'If someone answers say it was a wrong number. At least we'd know someone was inside.'

This time Blake didn't ignore the woman. Instead he looked at her, head to one side, and said: 'We couldn't get away with a wrong number excuse: she's been told for days by Smet we're getting closer and closer. That's been her buzz. But a genuine call could work . . .'

'Doorn's office is five minutes away,' anticipated Harding. 'I left Ritchie with him.'

The FBI man brought the estate agent running in four,

although the man arrived breathless. He kept breathing heavily as Harding talked, long after he should have recovered.

'I don't think I can do it!' he pleaded.

'You will,' insisted Harding. 'You're the best realtor in town. She knows that. You take trouble over your clients. She knows that, too. She told you she didn't want any of the staff which are normally available. You're doing your job. You're calling to see if she's changed her mind about that: there are people you could send in at an hour's notice. You want to know if everything's all right or if there are any problems that need sorting out. If there's a drain or a john that's blocked or a fuse that's blown anywhere, we're in.'

'And if there's no reply, I'm going to become your assistant,' announced Blake. 'You've got the right to get past anyone at the gatehouse. She wouldn't panic if it was you, with someone else from the agency. She'd open the door. Which is all I'd need.'

'Why bother with the phone at all?' demanded Ulieff. 'Why don't one of you go up with Doorn?'

'She was adamant she wanted privacy,' said Doorn anxiously. 'Repeated over and over again that she didn't want any staff. I promised to leave her entirely alone.'

'By yourself it could be explained away: the diligent realtor,' Harding reluctantly conceded. 'A stranger would make her suspicious.'

'I think it's worth a chance,' said Rampling carelessly.

'Isn't chance what we're trying to avoid?' said Sanglier.

'We can't just sit here, doing nothing!' said Hillary.

Blake said: 'I think I should go up with Doorn. I could wear a wire: you'd know the minute I was through the door. Be right behind me.'

'The place has got twenty bedrooms alone!' pointed out Harding. 'There are ten rooms on the ground floor and that's not counting the kitchen and servant accommodation. Or whatever the hell's below ground apart from the storerooms and dungeons and holes that people disappear in which aren't even on the plans we've got here!'

'Somebody make a decision!' demanded Hillary and everyone looked at Henri Sanglier.

No! thought Sanglier, although not in answer to the choice. Whatever decision he made could ruin his grand exit triumph from Europol. Couldn't do that. It was going to be his electoral launch. Why wasn't Claudine Carter here! He couldn't call her: show his indecision.

'It's an operational judgement,' prompted Ulieff.

Bastard! thought Sanglier. Still almost three hours before the woman's deadline expired. Something – anything – could happen in three hours. There'd be a reason to speak to Claudine Carter before then. Sanglier said: 'We phone.'

Félicité answered.

Even Claudine was affected by the sense of isolation. It was physical within the embassy – with only McBride, Harrison and Rosetti with her in the ambassador's study, Volker moving between there and the radio room – and actual over their link with the mobile communication centre. Duncan McCulloch was maintaining voice contact from a tree-shielded track off the Namur to Gembloux road close enough to the St Marc turn-off to monitor the passage of cars with French and Dutch registrations, with the number of Lascelles' Jaguar the highest priority. As irrationally as everyone else, Claudine had expected the verbatim two-way exchange of Smet's bugged telephone. What they were getting was McCulloch's overall commentary on what was happening, comprehensive in itself but devoid of any back-and-forth discussion essential for the special pictures Claudine had to draw.

Without the closely defined maps of the area from which they were working at Namur there was no way for the five of them in the embassy to follow the dispersal of Belgians, Europol officers and Americans around the château, although Claudine visualized the same encirclement they'd imposed around the very centre of Brussels trying to scan Félicité's phone calls. They even had to imagine the impossibility of approaching unseen the towered château and it was only when Claudine impatiently spoke herself to McCulloch that she realized he was in turn relaying decisions being reached not on the ground, which she'd imagined, but in Namur, twenty-five kilometres away.

While they were speaking McCulloch hurriedly broke away for a muffled conversation with Namur, returning to her just as quickly. 'Félicité's inside! They had the agent call the château and she answered . . .' He broke away again for another mumbled conversation before coming back to her. 'A car with French licence plates has just turned off on the St Marc road. I'm sure it had a kid in it . . . and there's another just behind, Dutch car with two guys inside . . . They're starting to arrive.'

'When are we going in?' demanded Claudine.

'They haven't decided how.'

'Tell Namur I'm calling them.'

'Will there be other children?'

'Yes, darling.'

'Dressed like this?'

'Yes.'

'It's silly.'

'It's a fairy castle, isn't it?'

'Were the other children taken like me?'

'Yes.'

'Are they going back home?'

398

'Yes. That's what the party's for. Because you're all going home. But we're going to play games first.'

'What sort of games?'

'You'll see.'

'Are you dressing up?'

'Probably.'

'In those funny masks?'

'Yes.'

'You're not going to hurt me, are you?'

'No.'

'Do anything bad to me?'

'No.'

'I won't love you, if you do.'

'Don't say that: not that you don't love me.'

'Then don't hurt me.'

Claudine listened, astonished, to Peter Blake, cutting him off before he finished. 'Peter! They don't know each other! That's what Smet said: how they protect each other! If a lot of strangers are going in, your only problem is the gatehouse.'

And by then that had been minimized.

CHAPTER THIRTY

At last they moved from Namur to where the communication centre had been established, along the Gembloux road. Although the cars were obviously unmarked they still staged their arrival to avoid the appearance of a convoy to any participant on his way to the château.

Blake, Harding and Rampling were in the lead car, anxious to reach the electronics expert whose scanner had picked up the mobile conversation from the gatehouse to the château at the first arrival, the Citroën with the French registration.

It was an American technician, a fat, bearded man named Marion Burr who wore a check shirt and cowboy boots and emerged from the vehicle smoking a small cigar. A Europol technician flown in that morning from The Hague took over the scanner inside the truck. Another FBI man replaced McCulloch.

Burr's accent was strongly Southern. 'It's a man, speaking French. Good job I come from good old Louisiana. We've counted fifteen through so far. He says different things at different times, with no reason why as far as I can see. Sometimes it's "How does your garden grow?" Other times it's "With silver bells and cockle shells." And then there's "pretty maids all in a row", whatever the hell that all means.'

'The rest of Félicité's original nursery rhyme,' identified Blake at once.

'Jesus, what a sick, screwed-up bitch!' said Harding.

Blake disagreed. 'No. It means something. It's us who're screwed unless we work out what it is.'

'Who responds to the man in the gatehouse, male or female?'

'A man,' said Burr. 'Always a man.'

'The same man?' pressed the CIA chief.

Burr hesitated. 'Yes.'

'You're sure? It's important.'

'Always the same man,' insisted Burr.

'And we got the first call, so it has to be Lascelles,' said Harding. 'Sneaky bastard hid his car away in a garage.'

'Why are the phrases different?' wondered Blake.

Burr shrugged. 'No idea.'

'What's the response from the château?' asked Blake. Behind him other cars began arriving. He moved to the side of the road to allow them to pass out of sight further along the tree-canopied track. Hillary McBride was in the last vehicle, with Ulieff and Sanglier.

'Not much. "Thank you", mostly. Sometimes just "I understand" or "That's good".'

Ulieff, Sanglier and Hillary came up to join them.

'What's happening?' demanded Sanglier. Things were moving of their own volition and he knew he'd made the right decision about telephoning the château from Namur. It was important to go on giving the impression of still being in operational charge.

'We don't know,' replied Rampling, honestly but unhelpfully. At once he said: 'It's some sort of identification. It's got to be.'

'You're not making sense,' said Sanglier.

Rampling shouldered his way past the man, towards the communications van close to which Burr and McCulloch stood. Inside, at McBride's demand, McCulloch's replacement increased the volume for the discussion to be relayed to Brussels.

'Fifteen cars?' he demanded.

'Fifteen that made uncertain turns towards St Marc, as if they were strangers to the area looking for an unfamiliar address, and fifteen telephone intercepts,' answered McCulloch, ahead of the other man with whom he'd shared the communication vehicle.

Blake smiled doubtfully. 'And each time you logged the registration, French or Dutch?'

'To trace the identity of the owners,' agreed the Texan.

'And additionally those you think carried children?'

'Yes,' replied the man, curiously. 'Three, to my count.'

Blake switched to the scanner technician. 'And you recorded each line of the nursery rhyme against each arrival?'

'Yes.'

'Let me see the sheets,' demanded Blake. Around him everyone was quiet, no one understanding except Rampling. Blake didn't have to go further than the first comparison. 'The first car was a French-registered Citroën, possibly with a child.' He looked at McCulloch. 'There *was* a child.' He went to Burr. 'You didn't tell us that sometimes there were two lines recited to the mansion. There's two on that first message, but they're not consecutive: between "How does your garden grow?" there's a line missing before "And pretty maids all in a row".'

'What the hell are you talking about?' demanded Hillary.

Blake continued comparing the two record sheets for several minutes before looking up. '"How does your garden grow?" identifies the French group. "With silver bells and cockle shells" is the Dutch identification. "Pretty maids all in a row" designates cars carrying a child.' He offered the papers generally. 'It's all there. Félicité knows she hasn't got anyone coming. Lascelles

402

has a count of his people. So has whoever's organized the French. If the count doesn't tally, they've got trouble.'

'Brussels wants to talk to you,' called the liaison man from inside the van.

Blake put on the headphones to hear Claudine say: 'You're right! That's how I read it!'

'I know I'm right,' said Blake.

'Be careful. No kamikaze stuff.'

'Speak to you later.'

He emerged to hear Harding, forgetting Hillary's presence, say: 'So how the fuck do we get past that barrier?'

Blake went back to the scanner record. '"Not much longer,"' he read aloud.

'That was the last reply from the château,' said Burr.

'They haven't all arrived!' declared Blake. He jerked hurriedly round to Ulieff and the local police chief. 'We want cars, with French plates. They must be French because if Lascelles is talking to the gatehouse he'll know how many of his own people to expect: they might all have already arrived. And Félicité hasn't included any of hers.' He gestured towards the main road. 'Stop anyone. Persuade them, pay them, arrest them, whatever. Just get cars.' He included Sanglier. 'We can't see the gatehouse from the road, which means the gatehouse can't see the road. Any vehicle on that road from now on gets stopped and the occupants arrested. The party's over for them.'

At Ulieff's shooing gesture the local police chief moved off towards the main road, beckoning Namur officers to follow.

'It'll work,' agreed Rampling. 'There's a lot of people ahead of us so there'll be a lot of movement inside the house. And let's not forget as we did in Namur that we're all strangers. Once we're out of the car the Dutch will think we're French and the French will think we're Dutch and Félicité will think we're one or the other. It still won't give us much time but we'll be inside.'

Harding looked at McCulloch. 'You're aboard because you're the biggest bastard we've got. You don't move away from the front door once we're through it. You've got to keep it open for everyone who's going to come behind us . . .' The American came to a halt, belatedly remembering jurisdiction. To Sanglier he said: 'That would be my suggestion, of course. I understand the planning has to be yours.'

Another easy decision, thought Sanglier. 'You, Blake and Rampling in charge, in the lead car. Choose your own people to follow.'

'We'll be wired,' said Blake. 'Our getting inside the house is the signal to put everyone in, from every direction.'

'We don't worry about the perverted fuckers: Félicité Galan even,' suggested Harding. 'We just get the kids: find them and get them out. Including Mary Beth there's four. There could be more, so we go on looking even after four. Leave everything else to back-up.' It had become a discussion between themselves, the rest excluded. 'Anything else we need to talk about?'

'I don't think so,' said Rampling.

'Let's go,' said the FBI chief.

For the first time it had been possible to hear most of the briefing verbatim in the Brussels embassy. At Harding's final remark McBride said to Harrison: 'You got a helicopter ready?'

'Waiting,' said the other man.

As the ambassador rose, Claudine said: 'We don't leave until we hear Mary Beth – all of them, I hope – are safe.'

'Who the hell do you think you are, talking to me like that?' demanded McBride.

Looking steadily at the ambassador, Claudine said: 'I'm the person, if anything goes wrong, who's going to tell the world that scoring points off each other was more important to you and your wife than getting your daughter back.'

McBride sat down again. It was nine forty-five.

Thirty minutes later no French-registered car had gone in either direction along the Namur to Gembloux road and the local police chief had radioed Namur for any French car to be seized there.

At ten thirty a Dutch-licensed Ford was stopped on the narrow feeder road to the château. The Amsterdam tanker pilot angrily maintained that he was a lost tourist until a Namur constable found a bag containing a devil's costume, complete with mask and whip, and two child sex videos in the boot.

Ten minutes later the message came from Namur that two French cars, both Citroëns, were on their way and Rampling said: 'We're going to miss Félicité's deadline.'

'They've still got to have their party,' said Blake.

'Maybe they've already started,' said Harding.

'She won't have done, not until she's spoken to McBride,' said Blake.

At five past eleven the cars arrived. Neither police driver turned his engine off when he got out. There were two plainclothes Namur detectives in the four-man backup car.

The man at the gatehouse was small and hunched, with a profusion of dark hair worn long and falling over his face, a curtain through which he watched them drive up. He said: 'You're late.'

'Traffic,' said Harding.

'It's going to be a good party.'

'I'm looking forward to it.'

Félicité's call came precisely on time.

'Have you done what I told you to do?'

405

'Yes,' said McBride.

'You got a pen?'

'Yes.'

'I want the money wired to account number 0392845 at the Crédit Suisse bank on Zürich's Bahnhofstrasse. You got that?'

'Yes.'

'Read it back to me.'

While he was doing so Claudine pushed a prompt note sideways to McBride. 'What about Mary Beth? How am I going to get her back?'

'You'll be told when the bank transfer goes through. Not before.'

'But you —' McBride started to protest but Félicité cut him off.

'When I know the money has been sent! Is Claudine there?'

'Yes.'

'Put her on.'

'What do you want?' said Claudine.

'Well?'

'Well what?'

'Who won!'

'You did,' said Claudine.

'Say it!'

'You won. But we need to know how . . .' But Claudine was talking into a dead phone.

'You've got to send the money,' insisted Claudine. 'It's the kidnap evidence. And she'll probably check.'

'We'll do it on the way to the NATO base,' said McBride, hurrying up from his desk.

'There's nothing for me to do here,' Rosetti said, to Claudine. 'I'll go on back.'

'To Brussels? Or Rome?'

'Rome.'

★

406

Félicité had telephoned from the upstairs bedroom directly opposite that in which she'd locked Mary Beth. She remained there for several minutes, undecided whether to have the Luxembourg lawyer check the Swiss deposit before tossing the mobile telephone on to the bed beside a still closed cardboard box. They'd have made the deposit: been too frightened not to. It didn't matter any more. She was still standing there, arms tight by her sides, hands clenched, when Lascelles came into the room.

'You all right?'

'Yes.'

'Here.' There were three pills in the palm of his offered hand.

'She won't feel anything?'

'Nothing. Almost everyone's arrived. I'm going down.'

'Yes.'

There was only one small sob after he left. Quickly Félicité regained control, breathing in deeply and squaring her shoulders before picking up the box.

Mary Beth looked up at her entry. 'Are we going now?'

'When I've dressed.'

'What are you going as?'

'You're the fairy, I'm the fairy godmother.'

Mary Beth sniggered.

'What are you laughing at?'

It was the hard voice Mary Beth didn't like. 'Nothing.'

Briefly Félicité stood naked in front of the child before putting on the dress. 'Zip me up, darling.'

Mary Beth did, awkwardly.

'Do you think I'm pretty?'

'Yes.'

'Tell me.'

'You're very pretty.'

Félicité put the pills in a tiny handbag, hesitating. 'Look!' she said, taking something from it. 'The lucky stone you gave me by the river. I said I'd always keep it, didn't I?'

'Can we go to the party now?'

'Yes,' said Félicité.

'You haven't put any u.p.'s on.'

'I'm not going to.'

The last message Harding got from the communications vehicle before disconnecting his earpiece outside the château was that the scanner had monitored the conversation between McBride and Félicité.

They carried overnight grips and bags that could have held masks or fantasy clothing and once away from the cars didn't stay together. Instead they straggled towards the huge entrance, heads lowered, strangers about to meet strangers. The door opened to Harding's knock and at once he pushed through, Blake and Rampling now tightly behind him.

The man just inside was small and thin, blinking behind thick-lensed spectacles. In French he said: 'Who are you with?'

Harding continued walking, bringing the man further into the huge hallway guarded by two pedestalled sets of armour and frowned down upon by the mounted heads of stags and boar and antelope. Behind, those in the second car, including the two Belgian detectives, followed smoothly but didn't come deeply into the hall. Instead they went immediately sideways, in both directions. Harding said: 'I didn't think we spoke of who we were with. You heard from the gatehouse, didn't you?'

Blake said: 'I'd like to change. Where can I do that?' and before the man could answer Rampling said: 'Yes. Where can we go?'

Both started moving away, in opposite directions. There was a lot of noise and music coming from a room at the end of the hall and two men, one dressed as a clown, the other as a harlequin and both masked by their make-up, turned from the bottom of the stairs towards the sound.

'I took the call,' said a voice.

Harding turned, guessing the figure to be Lascelles from the physical description they'd got at Eindhoven, although the man was wearing a tight, face-fitting mask.

'And that's why I was at the door,' said Georges Lebron.

Harding started back towards the small man but saw a fairy-dressed Mary Beth descending the stairs, holding Félicité's hand. The child immediately recognized him. She smiled and said: 'Hello! Have you come to take me home?'

'Yes,' said Harding. He surged forward, spread-eagling Lebron as he pushed the French priest aside. Harding felt Lascelles' groping hands on his back but jerked free, continuing on.

'POLICE!' screamed Lebron, still on the floor, and pandemonium erupted.

Blake and Rampling ran towards the noise further along the corridor. Shouts and screams burst from other rooms and from upstairs there was a gunshot. From outside came the sound of over-revved cars slewing across the gravelled forecourt to block in already parked vehicles. And then helicopters, deafening, thunderous helicopters descending so close to the house the gravel and grass and plants were hurled against the windows in a man-made hurricane. Men and women flooded into the house.

Throughout those first few moments Félicité Galan remained frozen, disbelieving, as the chaos exploded around her in what seemed a slow-motion tableau. Harding was already climbing the stairs before Félicité grabbed out, enveloping Mary Beth. 'NO!' came out as a screaming wail. So tightly was the woman clinging to the child, holding her against her own body, that Harding couldn't immediately get his arms between the two, to pull Mary Beth away. He drove first his right then his left hand into them, careless of hurting either, at last dragging Mary Beth partially free.

The child was screaming, in pain from being pulled between two adults and fear at all the noise and people. As she began to lose her grip on Mary Beth, Félicité freed her right hand and clawed out, hysterically shouting: 'Mine! She's mine!' She missed gouging Harding's eyes by a fraction too difficult for surgeons later to calculate, but still marked him for life, so deeply did she rake her nails down the American's face from cheek to chin. The agony drove Harding back, making him loosen his hold, but only by one hand. Which he smashed, as hard as he could, into Félicité's face only inches away, feeling and hearing the sharply defined nose crush under his fist. The woman gurgled, falling backwards, finally releasing Mary Beth.

A green-masked man wearing a matching green tunic that ended at his waist, below which he was naked, ran towards the main door yelling: 'It's a trap! It's a trap!'

McCulloch said: 'I know. I'm part of it,' and doubled the man up with just one forearm side-swipe.

'Let me out!' wheezed the man.

'I will if you tell me where all the children are,' said McCulloch.

'In the party room,' groaned the man. 'Two upstairs, in the first bedroom.'

'I tell lies,' said McCulloch, hitting him again although not intending to break the man's jaw, which he did. He fractured two of his own knuckles as well. With no need any longer to keep the door open the Texan took the stairs two at a time, leaping over the moaning Félicité, and found a boy and a girl dressed as wood nymphs cowering in the first bedroom. 'We're going home,' he

410

said, scooping them up. Both began to fight him. The girl wet herself.

McCulloch held one child under each arm as he plunged back down the stairs. The groaning Félicité made what could have been a gesture to trip him but McCulloch kicked past.

Only when he got out into the forecourt was it established that the children he had rescued were Robert Flet and Yvette Piquette, the two snatched in Eindhoven. Blake had found a boy, later identified as Jacques Blom, a nine-year-old who had disappeared the previous day in Lille, in the party room. He, like the other two, was dressed as a wood nymph. All three were immediately handed over to a combined Belgian/American medical team.

Hillary McBride was refusing to surrender Mary Beth. She knelt in the very centre of the forecourt, crying and repeating: 'Oh, my darling! My own darling!'

What else she said was drowned by the arrival of another helicopter, although it landed further away from the château than the others had done. McBride ran from it, arms in the air. He threw himself down to the kneeling woman and child, embracing Mary Beth as best he could without including Hillary. 'I got you back, darling! I got you back.'

From between her parents Mary Beth said: 'I want to go back inside and take this silly costume off. It's got her blood on it. I've got some new clothes. I like them.'

Claudine was at the entrance to the château when the swollen-faced, bloodied woman was led out. She said: 'You didn't win after all, Félicité. You were never going to. I was never going to let you.'

Félicité took away the surgical dressing she had pressed to her face and spat, bloodily, but it missed.

'Christ, you're ugly,' said Claudine.

A total of thirty-three men, including the man at the gatehouse, were arrested at the château and three more at the outside road block. Félicité Galan was the only woman. Among them were two tax inspectors, unknown to each other, another priest and a police inspector, from Lille. The gunshot had been an attempt by an airline pilot to kill himself. He failed but the bullet lodged in his brain, destroying the left lobe and his mentality.

The finding of the medical team, later confirmed at Namur hospital, was that none of the children had been sexually abused, although all of them, apart from Mary Beth McBride, were severely traumatized.

'Makes you believe in miracles, doesn't it?' said Blake.

'Only just,' said Claudine. 'They'll still need a lot of counselling.'

'Bastards!' said the man. 'At least we got them.'

'There're still too many left,' said Claudine.

CHAPTER THIRTY-ONE

A disgruntled Henri Sanglier had to share the platform and the limelight with McBride and his wife, Miet Ulieff and the police chiefs of Brussels and Namur for the following day's press conference. McBride described the operation as a brilliant example of international police co-operation and Ulieff said it proved the worth of an organization like Europol. A very dangerous, cross-border crime conspiracy preying upon children had been irrevocably smashed. Proceedings against those detained would take months, maybe even years. Hillary McBride said that although her daughter had been recovered completely unharmed she intended taking the child back to America to recuperate from what had been a horrifying experience, and thanked the media for the restraint she knew she could expect them to show towards the child.

Claudine didn't attempt to contact Rosetti until after the weekend. When she failed to get a response from his apartment and found his answering machine turned off she called the medical division and was told that he'd taken leave for personal reasons, with no indication of a return date.

She was mildly unsettled by Blake's dinner invitation but saw no reason to refuse. By coincidence he chose the restaurant by the lake to which Rosetti had taken her the first time they had gone out together.

'It all got a bit hectic towards the end,' he said. 'How's Hugo?'

'He's away, in Rome. His wife's ill.' Why was she offering explanations again?

'Seriously?'

'She won't get better.'

'Poor guy.'

'Yes.'

'You told me in Brussels you were lonely.'

'Yes,' she said again.

'No reason why we shouldn't be friends, is there?'

'No.'

'Enjoy ourselves, without any serious commitment?'

'No.'

'Unless we wanted a serious commitment, that is.'

Why not? Claudine asked herself. The situation with Hugo was never going to resolve itself. And she'd decided she wasn't going to wait for ever. 'Why don't we, just for a change, stop trying to analyse it and do just that. Enjoy ourselves?'

It was the third week of Rosetti's absence – and Claudine's affair with Blake – that the rumour began. Claudine heard it first from Kurt Volker, whose predilection for surfing into other people's secret places made him a natural gossip. She was curious that he hadn't already tiptoed down some darkened electronic alley to confirm it.

The Europol Commission did that at the beginning of the fourth week, in a formal announcement of Henri Sanglier's resignation. It was timed to coincide with the Paris press conference at which Sanglier appeared flanked by Roger Castille and Guy Coty. Françoise, looking the epitome of French chic, was with him. There was a hugely enlarged photograph of Sanglier's father being decorated by de Gaulle as a backdrop to remind television viewers of the family honour and Sanglier made an impressive vow to maintain that honour in a political career that had been declined by his father but he had decided to pursue. It was the cue for Castille to denounce the corruption of the present government that he would sweep aside in the coming election. Henri Sanglier, his intended Justice Minister, would be in the vanguard of every fight against crime, as he had been as the most famous of Europol's governing commissioners.

It was only at the end of the televised conference that Claudine was reminded, annoyed that she hadn't remembered it earlier. She actually considered telephoning Volker that night but decided there was no urgency. She did, however, call him as soon as she got into the Europol building the following morning.

'I'm just tidying up my final report on the Mary Beth kidnap,' she said.

'I've already filed mine,' said the German.

'I was wondering about all that pornography you got in?' she said, recalling the miniature bird tattoo on the thigh of a masked Françoise parading in Sanglier's house.

'What about it?' asked Volker.

'I know it's hardly necessary to remind you, but the regulations are that it's got to be destroyed. With all the chaos at the end I thought you might have overlooked it.'

'No,' said the German, unoffended. 'I intended to.'

'Intended?'

'Sanglier asked for it all. When he said pornography was going to be his next priority I thought he meant here, in Europol. He meant when he becomes the French Justice Minister, obviously.'

'Obviously,' agreed Claudine.

Rosetti returned at the end of that week. He'd called from Rome, to warn her, and they met that night. It was virtually the only one she hadn't spent with Blake.

'Flavia died,' he announced bluntly. 'We actually thought there was going to be a recovery. Her eyes

415

opened and there was some movement but it came down to muscle reflexes: even the squeezing of my hand.'

'I'm sorry. So very sorry.'

'The priest said it was for the best. So did the doctors. And they're right.'

'Yes.'

'So now there's us.'

Claudine didn't reply.

'I love you. I want to wait, obviously. Out of respect. But I'm asking you to marry me.'

'Yes,' said Claudine. 'You should wait.' Her period was already more than a week late. Now she didn't think she should put off the pregnancy test any longer. That was the easy decision. The more difficult one was whether she still wanted to marry Hugo Rosetti.